POLDARK

The Complete Scripts
Series 1

POLDARK

The Complete Scripts

Series 1

DEBBIE HORSFIELD

MACMILLAN

First published 2016 by Macmillan
an imprint of Pan Macmillan
20 New Wharf Road, London N1 9RR
Associated companies throughout the world
www.panmacmillan.com

ISBN 978-1-5098-1465-7

1 3 5 7 9 8 6 4 2

A CIP catalogue record for this book is available from the British Library.

Typeset by Ellipsis Digital Limited, Glasgow
Printed and bound by CPI Group (UK) Ltd, Croydon, CR0 4YY

Introduction

As a teenager, I avidly read all the Poldark novels and fell completely in love with the unforgettable characters, the compelling stories, and Cornwall itself. The books were given to me by my mother, who had read them when she was younger and had similarly adored them.

When we decided we wanted to adapt Poldark into a television drama, Damien Timmer and I first sought approval from the estate and then set out to find a screenwriter. Despite the fact that Debbie Horsfield had never adapted a book for television, or indeed written period drama before, she was top of our wish list, for a number of reasons. Firstly, she is a wonderful writer who has been consistently writing top level dramas for many years – everyone at Mammoth Screen was totally in awe of her work! Also, the way Debbie writes family dramas just felt so pertinent to the novels. The characters in Poldark, as created by the author Winston Graham, are beautifully drawn and vivid, they almost leap off the page, just as Debbie's characters always do. And whilst the novels are steeped in an epic historical, social and political backdrop, it's the love stories and the characters' needs and passions, joys and despairs, that are at the very heart of the series. Although being a period piece, the people that populate Poldark are driven by the same feelings that we all have today – and Debbie writes this sort of drama with the greatest skill.

On a personal level, I desperately wanted to work with Debbie again, as early on in my TV career I had been lucky enough to work on one of her dramas. Debbie had spent a lot of time on set, absorbed in every detail of making the programme and it was her inspiration and sheer creative energy that led me to seek a career within the script department.

To our great relief, Debbie loved the books and wanted to adapt them. We then set out on the wonderful journey of series one and then straight into series two – which we are currently filming – with Debbie writing all eighteen hours of drama, which is a great achievement in itself.

From the outset, all of us involved in Poldark were keen to do justice to the novels. Prior to writing the screenplay, Debbie put in a lot of research, first reading all twelve of the Poldark novels, so she could get a sense of the full story-arc, the characters' journeys and the exquisite detail of the Poldark world. Set initially in the 1780s against a backdrop of historical, social and economic turbulence, Debbie also immersed herself in the history of the period, taking in everything from Cornish mining to shipwrecking, whilst also reacquainting herself with the literature of the period, its vocabulary, Cornish dialect, idioms and phrases, as well as its traditions and forms of etiquette.

The result is a script brimming with life, packed with an array of colourful characters, and a narrative that sometimes races along, but that also allows for a bit of breathing space here and there. We connect with the characters as they experience everything from love and ambition to hardship, betrayal and grief. Some scenes are comedic but also retain a sinister edge, and memorable lines are strewn throughout the scripts, some of them drawn from and some inspired by Winston Graham's own words in the Poldark novels.

A fantastic range of people also help with the creation of the scripts and the whole production of Poldark. Historical advisor Dr Hannah Greig looks at the scripts and flags any areas that might need revision. She also talks to the cast about general cultural trends, mannerisms and any queries they have about the period, and answers a host of random questions raised by the production crew as they attempt to recreate eighteenth-century Cornwall.

Winston Graham's son, Andrew Graham, also provides invaluable advice and feedback, helping us with specifics about the novels or locations in Cornwall. We also have a whole host of experts helping us, from food historians and dance instructors to specialists in Cornish dialect and language, even bringing in a Cornish folk-musician and musicologist, Mike O'Connor, to compose authentic-sounding folk tunes to weave in with Anne Dudley's incredible score.

Whilst Debbie's screenplay hits the mark perfectly, it is of course the cast that breathe life into the words. And central to it all is our hero, Captain Ross Poldark, as played by Aidan Turner, who takes on his leading-man responsibilities with real professionalism, bringing charisma and a strong physical presence to the screen. His character is that of a gentleman, but he also has a rebellious streak, and a real sense of social justice. He makes for the perfect romantic hero, torn between his first love, the genteel and elegant Elizabeth, played by Heida Reed, and the lowly-born Demelza. I'm not at all surprised that Aidan's portrayal of Ross has caused such a stir and gained a huge number of fans for both him and the series.

Eleanor Tomlinson similarly makes the role of Demelza her own as we follow her journey from street urchin to the wife of Ross Poldark. Eleanor not only captures Demelza's fearlessness and natural spirit, but she also worked hard to master the Cornish accent as she was keen that Demelza remained true to her roots despite her change of fortunes. A heavy dose of Cornish also flavours many of the words uttered by Phil Davis and Beatie Edney, who play the incorrigible and feckless servants Jud and Prudie.

Central to Poldark is also its gritty depiction of late eighteenth-century life in Cornwall: an economic depression has forced mines to close and poverty is rife amongst its workers and local villagers, while the bankers grow increasingly rich and more powerful. A situation that may well resonate with modern audiences today. Cornwall itself also has a major part to play in the books and our adaptation; the characters and events of Poldark are inextricably linked to Cornwall's unique character, wild beauty and rugged landscape. And, luckily for us, Cornwall's breathtaking scenery and wonderful palette of colours provide the perfect backdrop for filming, although we do have to cope with some extreme, windy weather on occasions!

Setting out on the journey of making Poldark, we were also aware that expectations ran high amongst existing fans: those who had read the novels or seen the previous television adaptation from the 1970s, as well as fans of Aidan Turner. We hoped that the new series of Poldark – with its high production values, expert crew, first-rate cast and wonderful scripts – would draw together all those fans, and also introduce a whole new audience to the series, just as Poldark enthralled me as a teenager and still does today.

I do hope you enjoy reading Debbie's wonderfully vivid adaptations. When I sit down to read a new script, or even a second draft of a script, I have to pinch myself to remind myself that I am actually working and not just reading for pleasure!

KAREN THRUSSELL
Executive Producer

POLDARK

The Complete Scripts
Series 1

A LIST OF TV SCRIPT ABBREVIATIONS

CU   *close up*

EXT *exterior*

GV   *General Views*

INT *interior*

OS   *off screen*

POV *point of view*

VO   *voice-over*

Episode 1

1: EXT. WOODLAND CLEARING – DAY 1

Caption: 1781, Virginia, America.

Shafts of sunlight slanting through trees. Drifting smoke from camp fires. Muskets stacked in tripods. Sounds of joking and laughter. A bedraggled group of young soldiers watching a card game. Among them a young British army ensign, unshaven, unscarred, long hair tied back. On his little finger a ring. Full of youthful bravado, 'one of the lads': Ross Poldark. A pompous young captain and lieutenant stand talking close by. Ross is playing French Ruff with a fellow-soldier.

ROSS Propose.

The soldier nods. They throw again. The soldier picks up.

ROSS *(cont'd)* Lay five.

SOLDIER Ten.

ROSS I'll take it.

They play the hand. The soldier wins. Suddenly, and without warning, Ross seizes the soldier by the throat as if to strangle him for winning the game. For a moment the soldier panics. Ross's eyes seem to blaze with hatred. Then he releases his grip and starts to laugh. It's all a huge joke. The soldier relaxes. Raucous laughter breaks out. The captain and lieutenant exchange a glance. They clearly regard Ross as a lost cause.

CAPTAIN Remind me why you enlisted, Poldark?

ROSS To escape the gallows, sir.

The soldiers laugh. The captain and lieutenant do not.

CAPTAIN Your crime?

ROSS Brawling, sir. Free trading, assaulting a customs official —

Everyone laughs. Ross's attention is drawn back to the cards where he is invited to play another game.

ROSS *(cont'd)* The stake?

SOLDIER Your ring?

Ross toys with the ring, as if considering the option, then shakes his head.

CAPTAIN Wastrels and thieves, the lot of you. But you'll soon have the honour of redeeming yourselves – in the service of king and country.

Ross's smile of derision does not go unnoticed.

CAPTAIN *(cont'd)* Do you doubt the justice of our cause, sir?

ROSS What cause would that be, sir? *(deliberately provocative)* Liberty or tyranny?

The captain, outraged, looks as if he's about to strike Ross across the face. Suddenly the sound of musket shot rings out. Blood spatters the cards. The captain falls to the ground, dead. Soldiers look round in panic. Another shot rings out. The lieutenant falls dead. Confusion. The firing continues. More men fall. All hell breaks loose. Soldiers scatter. The soldier Ross beat at cards is cowering on the ground, looking at him in panic. Other soldiers are sheltering from the musket shots, which are ricocheting past. Ross seizes four muskets from the tripods and flings them at each of four soldiers.

ROSS *(cont'd)* You want to leave here? Or die here?

Ross is already preparing to fire. Instinctively the others look to him for instruction.

ROSS *(cont'd)* On your feet, lads! On your feet!

The soldiers begin to scramble to their feet as, out of the smoke, American soldiers converge on them.

ROSS'S POV: Impressionistic images of noise, smoke, gunshot, rushing figures – and the onrush of an American soldier, who attacks him with an axe. Ross bayonets him. A second comes upon him. Ross despatches him too. A third rushes forward, flashing a tomahawk, catches Ross across the face.

Blackout.

Shafts of sunlight through the smoke. Sounds of girlish laughter . . .
CUT TO:

2: EXT. CLIFF-TOPS – DAY 2

Cornwall, 1780. Blazing sun, sound of wind, crashing waves, gulls crying. A girl's face appears, blocking the rays of sunlight for a split second: Elizabeth. Young. Carefree. Laughing. Hair loose, eyes dancing.

Cut wide to vast clifftop landscape. In the distance is a derelict mine. Two tiny figures – Ross and Elizabeth – chase along the headland, Elizabeth running away. Her silhouette dipping in and out of the blazing sun. Now she stops, turns to face him, surveys him. He's wearing a brand new ensign's uniform.

ROSS It won't be for long – six months at most?

They both laugh. Neither of them is taking this seriously.

ELIZABETH *(teasing)* You'll forget me.

ROSS How likely is that?

ELIZABETH *(teasing)* Men are fickle.

ROSS Not this one.

He takes a ring from her finger and puts it on his own little finger.

ELIZABETH Then, pray, do not be reckless. I wish you to return!

CUT TO:

3: EXT. WOODLAND CLEARING – DAY 1

Aerial shot of Ross spread-eagled on the battlefield, bleeding from a facial wound, the tomahawk beside him, eyes closed, apparently dead.

CUT TO:

4: EXT. MOOR, CORNWALL – DAY 3

Caption: Cornwall. Two years later.

A coach and horses gallop across a desolate, windswept moor. Below and beyond them, waves crash upon a deserted beach, spray cascades above hostile rocks and the gathering clouds seem to speak of some looming crisis.

CUT TO:

5: INT. COACH – DAY 3

A traveller sits hunched in the corner of the coach, apparently sleeping. Wrapped in a cloak, dressed in the uniform of a British army captain, his hat pulled down over his face. Gradually we become aware of excited whispering from his fellow-travellers: (later revealed to be Mrs Teague, Ruth Teague and Dr Choake). The following conversation is whispered.

RUTH'S VOICE Are you sure?

MRS TEAGUE'S VOICE I trust I may believe the evidence of my own eyes, dear.

RUTH'S VOICE But was he not reported dead?

DR CHOAKE'S VOICE Better if he had been! He's brought little credit to his family—

MRS TEAGUE'S VOICE His father was no different. A scoundrel—

DR CHOAKE'S VOICE And a libertine—

MRS TEAGUE'S VOICE Still the family name counts for something—

DR CHOAKE'S VOICE And now he's to inherit—

TRAVELLER (ROSS) Is my father dead?

The traveller slowly removes his hat . . . to reveal a deep scar down one cheek. The ladies give genteel gasps of surprise (at the scar). Though Ross looks exhausted, he's not lost his manners, nor his ability to shock.

MRS TEAGUE Oh! Sir! Bless me! We had no idea—

ROSS When did he die?

MRS TEAGUE Some six months past? You'd had no word?

ROSS None that reached me.

Ruth is daring herself to address him.

RUTH How was the war, sir?

Mrs Teague gives Ruth a sharp dig.

ROSS As any war, ma'am. A waste of good men.

Without warning, Ross reaches up and gives the coach ceiling a loud rap. The coach begins to slow down.

MRS TEAGUE You are not going home to Nampara?

ROSS To my uncle Charles first, ma'am. Since my father will evidently not be at home, I must look for a welcome elsewhere.

CUT TO:

6: EXT. BARGUS CROSSROADS – DUSK 3

The coach stops near a gibbet. Presently it drives off again, revealing Ross standing in the middle of deserted landscape. As he makes his way across fields, heading for Trenwith, we notice a slight limp.

CUT TO:

7: EXT. CLIFF-TOPS – DUSK 3

Making his way to Trenwith along the cliff-top path, Ross halts to let the news of his father's death sink in. He looks out to sea. The news is a blow, but he knows he must push on. After a pause, he continues on his way.

CUT TO:

8: EXT. TRENWITH HOUSE – DUSK 3

Ross arrives at the gates, sees the house lit up and hears the sounds of revelry inside.

CUT TO:

9: INT. TRENWITH HOUSE, GREAT HALL – DUSK 3

A feast is in progress. Elizabeth picks at her food, pausing occasionally to smile at a remark made by Francis Poldark. Charles Poldark and Great Aunt Agatha are entertaining guests: including Mrs Chynoweth

(Elizabeth's mother). Verity Poldark brings a tray of desserts from the sideboard to the table. Charles raps the table to hurry her along.

CHARLES Do the honours, Verity. And no half-measures!

Charles belches in anticipation. Verity serves. Elizabeth declines.

ELIZABETH I couldn't eat another morsel.

CHARLES Piffle, girl, you're as thin as a wraith. We must fatten you up!

MRS CHYNOWETH Perhaps Francis will be able to coax her.

FRANCIS I happen to like her just as she is.

Elizabeth and Francis exchange a smile.

VERITY Was that the door?

MRS CHYNOWETH Expecting someone, my dear?

Verity blushes.

CHARLES Don't encourage her! She's too valuable here to be thinking of gentlemen callers!

The door opens and Mrs Tabb the housekeeper comes in, looking as if she's seen a ghost. Before she can speak, Ross appears behind her. Absolute astonishment greets him. Verity and Francis leap to their feet. Charles looks quite perplexed, as if he'd never for a moment entertained the possibility of his nephew's return; Elizabeth seems frozen with shock; Mrs Chynoweth regards Ross with undisguised distaste.

ROSS I hope I'm not intruding.

VERITY Oh Ross— !

Ross limps forward. Verity rushes to him and clasps his hand in a firm embrace.

VERITY *(cont'd)* We'd given up all hope –

CHARLES Stap me, boy, you survived!

Francis rushes over and grasps him warmly.

FRANCIS To see you again, Cousin! – We'd quite despaired – hadn't we, Elizabeth?

ELIZABETH *(softly)* Yes—

For the first time Ross notices Elizabeth.

ROSS Elizabeth! I had no idea you'd be here.

As he makes his way to her, Mrs Chynoweth feels obliged to intervene.

MRS CHYNOWETH Do tell us, Ross, how we managed to lose the war?

ROSS By choosing the wrong side, ma'am.

Ross has been making his way round the table greeting people. Now he reaches Elizabeth.

ROSS I couldn't have wished for a better homecoming.

ELIZABETH I must speak with you, Ross.

ROSS Of course.

His hand lightly touches her shoulder. She shivers at his touch. Mrs Chynoweth bristles.

CHARLES And what will you do with yourself now, Nephew? You'll find Nampara's not as you left it.

Aunt Agatha has finally realized the newcomer is Ross.

AUNT AGATHA Damn me, boy! – if we hadn't thought you'd gone to join the Blest Above!

ROSS *(kissing her hand affectionately)* Great Aunt, I'm glad to see you are still of the Blest Below!

ELIZABETH We'd had no word from you, so I—

VERITY Sit here, Ross, you must be exhausted.

Verity guides him to a seat at the other end of the table.

MRS CHYNOWETH Elizabeth, fetch me my wrap.

It's the last thing Elizabeth wants to do – but Mrs Chynoweth's expression deters any argument.

ELIZABETH Yes, Mama.

She goes out. Mrs Chynoweth is glowering. This interruption is the very last thing she needs.

CUT TO:

10: INT. TRENWITH HOUSE, HALLWAY – DUSK 3

Elizabeth comes out into the hallway. She is breathless, excited, close to tears. In that moment all she can think of is Ross's return. Not its implications.

CUT TO:

11: INT. TRENWITH HOUSE, GREAT HALL – DUSK 3

Verity has been watching Ross closely. Now she brings him a plate of food. For the first time, he takes in the scale of the dinner.

ROSS I seem to have interrupted a party. Is it in honour of the peace or of the next war?

A few looks are exchanged between the family and guests. Ross is tucking into his food and doesn't immediately notice their reticence.

FRANCIS No – er – the occasion is—

CHARLES Something far more pleasant.

Ross looks up, ready to partake in the pleasure.

CHARLES *(cont'd)* My boy is to be married.

ROSS But that's tremendous! Who is to be— ?

MRS CHYNOWETH Elizabeth.

There is absolute silence in the room. For a moment Ross is unable to compute what he's heard.

ROSS Elizabeth— ?

MRS CHYNOWETH My daughter.

Elizabeth has just come back into the room with Mrs Chynoweth's wrap. Immediately she realizes what her mother has done.

ELIZABETH Mama – no—

ROSS Elizabeth— ?

He looks at her, uncomprehending. For what seems an eternity of anguish, Elizabeth and Ross stare at each other, as if neither can comprehend the situation they now find themselves in. Then . . .

MRS CHYNOWETH Naturally we're delighted that our two ancient and distinguished families will be united.

Ross is unable to speak. He and Elizabeth continue to stare at each other. Eventually, realising an awkward silence has fallen . . .

ROSS Did my father suffer much?

CHARLES A pitiful end. Affairs in tatters and next to nothing for you to inherit—

AUNT AGATHA Not that he ever thought you'd be back to claim it!

CHARLES It's a poor Cornwall you've returned to. Taxes sky high, wages in the gutter—

FRANCIS Mine closures every other week—

CHARLES Bad as you, lad! Scarred for life and on its knees!

FRANCIS If you want my help at Nampara, you've only to ask—

Without warning Ross gets to his feet.

ROSS I can't stay. I only called to let you know I've returned. *(then)* I must trouble you for a horse, Charles.

Charles nods. Around the table guests shuffle and stare at their hands. Ross rallies.

ROSS But first – a toast. To Elizabeth and Francis – *(still looking at Elizabeth)* May they find happiness together.

And as he raises his glass we – and Elizabeth – see the ring is still on his little finger.

CUT TO:

12: EXT. TRENWITH HOUSE, DRIVE – DUSK 3

Ross gallops down the drive at such break-neck speed that he can barely stay on his horse.

CUT TO:

13: EXT. CLIFF-TOP RIDE, CORNWALL – DUSK 3

Ross gallops wildly across the moors, the sea crashing below him, the wind tearing at his face.

CUT TO:

14: EXT. NAMPARA VALLEY, CORNWALL – DUSK 3

Ross only slows as he reaches the head of Nampara Valley. Here, as his pace decreases, he can contain his anguish no longer. There are tears on his face. He brushes them away, unable to admit them even to himself. He slows down as he passes the derelict mine Wheal Leisure, skeletal and broken in the moonlight. Glancing ahead, the distant sight of his family home, Nampara House, does little to cheer him. The house is in darkness, and as he rides slowly towards it, he notices the fences are broken, the walls are unmended and the track beneath his horse's hooves is rutted and puddled. The bleakness and devastation seem to mirror that of his own heart.

CUT TO:

15: EXT. NAMPARA HOUSE – NIGHT 3

Ross dismounts, tethers his horse to a straggly leafless tree. He notices further evidence of decay – broken windows, filthy window panes, torn curtains, neglected paintwork . . . He raps loudly on the front door with his riding crop. No one answers. Ross tries the handle. The door is not locked. He pushes it open. It goes creaking back, pushing a heap of refuse before it.

CUT TO:

16: INT. NAMPARA HOUSE, HALLWAY – NIGHT 3

Ross squints into the darkness of the house.

ROSS *(shouting)* Jud? *(no reply)* Prudie?

Absolute silence. As he gropes his way down the corridor he is momentarily startled to see a pair of eyes – pink,bloodshot – watching him from the far end of the hall. Deciding to avoid the encounter, he feels his way into the nearest room.

CUT TO:

17: INT. NAMPARA HOUSE, PARLOUR – CONTINUOUS

He is greeted by the sound of rats scuffling. His foot slips on something slimy. In putting out his hand to steady himself he knocks over a candlestick. He bends to retrieve it and sees that the floor is strewn with filth and animal droppings. He puts the candle back in its holder, gropes for flint and steel. After several attempts he succeeds in lighting the candle. The sight which greets him is not pleasing.

HIS POV: A large mahogany-panelled room with a huge, recessed fireplace, built round with low settles . . . on which roost a collection of mangy hens. The floor is thick with old straw and droppings. On a window sill are two dead chickens. Rats run across the table. Ross freezes at the sound of approaching hooves. He turns the candle to reveal the owner of the pink bloodshot eyes he saw earlier: a mangy-looking goat.

CUT TO:

18: INT. NAMPARA HOUSE – NIGHT 3

Ross holds the candle before him as he makes his way upstairs, peering into various rooms en route, finding all in a similar state. Eventually he halts, his attention transfixed by a peculiar rasping sound which seems to becoming from a room at the end of the landing. He approaches it cautiously. He opens the door into a pitch-black room. The sound becomes louder. Ross puts his candle down.

CUT TO:

19: EXT. NAMPARA HOUSE, COURTYARD – NIGHT 3

Ross fills a wooden pail with water from the pump and limps back inside.

CUT TO:

20: INT. NAMPARA HOUSE, ROSS'S BEDROOM – NIGHT 3

Ross pours the contents of the wooden pail into the bed from which the sound is coming . . . and from which now issue muffled groans. Ross brings the candle over to the bed – and for the first time we see its occupants: Jud (50s, scrawny, balding) and Prudie (40s, substantial, slovenly) – both drunk, soaked to the skin but barely stirring. Ross flings the contents of the pail into their faces – to be greeted by a shriek from Prudie and a groan from Jud, who presently whips out his pocket-knife and brandishes it at the darkness.

ROSS Give me an excuse and I'll break your miserable neck!

PRUDIE Judas! Is it Mister Ross— ?

Ross drags Jud out of bed by the collar.

ROSS Back from the grave!

CUT TO:

21: INT. NAMPARA HOUSE, PARLOUR – DAY 4

As dawn breaks Jud and Prudie are on their knees scrubbing and polishing floors, watched by Ross.

ROSS You were my father's personal servants! You were left in a position of trust.

JUD Well, pick me liver, what could us do? Left all alone wi' no master t' guide us!

ROSS I'll guide you with the side of my foot in future!

PRUDIE But see, 'twas rumoured 'ee were dead—

ROSS Perhaps you started the tale?

JUD In't no call t'accuse us, Mister Ross. 'Tidn' right – 'tidn' just – 'tidn' fit – 'tidn' friendly—

ROSS You'll get 'friendly' if I don't see my face reflected in this floor by the time you're done!

He goes out, leaving Jud mumbling behind him.

JUD *(muttering)* Well, boil me blasted, blatherin' buttocks – on'y have two pair of hands . . .

CUT TO:

22: EXT. NAMPARA HOUSE – DAY 4

Ross walks out across his land, past the apples in the leafless orchard lying unpicked or mouldering on the ground – and the hay barn empty and in need of repair.

CUT TO:

23: EXT. SAWLE CHURCHYARD – DAY 4

Ross kneels at a grave, the inscription of which reads: 'Sacred to the memory of Grace Mary, beloved wife of Joshua Poldark, who departed this life the 9th day of May 1770, aged 30 years'.

Below it is a newer inscription: 'Also of Joshua Poldark, Esqr, of Nampara, in the County of Cornwall, who died the 11th day of March 1783'.

CUT TO:

24: INT. TRENWITH HOUSE, GREAT HALL – DAY 4

Aunt Agatha, Verity and Francis are at breakfast. Aunt Agatha tucks in with gusto.

VERITY Ross looked well.

FRANCIS He did!

VERITY Better than one might have expected—

AUNT AGATHA Considering one thought him dead?

FRANCIS I'm glad he is not.

VERITY We all are!

They continue their breakfast. Then . . .

AUNT AGATHA Elizabeth will make a fine mistress of Trenwith.

VERITY Not for three months, Aunt.

AUNT AGATHA Your father thinks it should be sooner.

VERITY *(surprised)* Does he?

AUNT AGATHA His view is, if two young people wish to be together, what is there to wait for?

Francis looks pleased, Verity somewhat troubled.

CUT TO:

25: EXT. MELLIN COTTAGES – DAY 4

A rider approaches the cottages. Zacky, Paul, Mark and Jim are in conversation – along with Mrs Zacky and Jinny – around a fire.

Through the smoke of the fire they see the rider coming closer. At first they can't quite believe who they're seeing.

ZACKY Can it be?

PAUL Surely not—

They jump to their feet.

ZACKY 'Tid'n a ghost!

ROSS See for yourself!

Ross dismounts from his horse. They all erupt in expressions of shock and delight, rushing forward to greet him.

PAUL We 'eard 'ee took a bullet!

ROSS I dodged a few!

MARK An' got a title?

JIM *(mock salute)* Cap'n Poldark!

MRS ZACKY 'Is poor face! *(i.e. his scar)*

JINNY It did 'urt?

ROSS Only my vanity!

JIM An' the war?

ROSS An education, Jim.

Zacky observes Ross closely. Something in his tone, though light, betrays a wealth of unspoken horror. Ross takes in the dilapidated state of the cottages.

ROSS Well, what happened here?

ZACKY Since your father died, we've 'ad no repairs.

ROSS I'll remedy that. You were my father's tenants. Now you're mine.

ZACKY Nay, Ross, ye've enough to think on, wi' ruined 'ome an' barren land—

ROSS I have hands, do I not? A spade, a plough—

ZACKY We can 'elp 'ee.

ROSS I cannot pay you.

ZACKY We'd not expect it.

ROSS You labour long enough in my uncle's mine for a pittance. I'll not have you serve me for nothing.

He's about to walk on.

ZACKY Ross?

Ross halts.

ZACKY What did 'appen out there?

Ross looks him in the eye. He knows he means the war.

ROSS I grew up.

CUT TO:

26: EXT. CHYNOWETH HOUSE, GARDENS – DAY 4

Elizabeth is sitting, reading. She hears the approach of a horse. She gets to her feet in anticipation. She's excited. She knows it will be Ross. She prepares to receive him.

Trying to remain calm, she sits down again. A servant appears.

SERVANT Mr Poldark to see you, Miss Elizabeth.

Elizabeth nods her approval. The servant departs. Elizabeth can hardly conceal her excitement. She tries to contain herself, turns away as she hears footsteps approaching. But when she turns, she sees her visitor is Francis. She struggles to conceal her disappointment. And apparently succeeds. Francis is beaming.

FRANCIS My dear, I have great news.

CUT TO:

27: EXT. TRURO – DAY 4

Ross rides into Truro.

CUT TO:

28: INT. PASCOE'S OFFICE – DAY 4

Ross faces Pascoe.

ROSS Tell me the worst.

Pascoe has various papers spread across his desk which he now consults.

PASCOE Your father left little of value. The house – two derelict mines – a few decaying cottages. The land, I fear, has been left to rot?

ROSS Entirely.

PASCOE So you come to enquire as to credit? As your friend, I would back you to the hilt. As your banker, I'm obliged to disappoint. Your father had debts, your property is mortgaged, your land has no income.

ROSS I'm a poor risk.

PASCOE Quite so.

ROSS And my tenants? Can I do nothing for them?

PASCOE I know you have an affection for these people – but you can barely support yourself, let alone them.

ROSS Then you advise me—

PASCOE To look to your own devices. Seek your fortune as and where you may.

ROSS Beggars cannot be choosers?

PASCOE I hope you may rely on the friend, if not the banker.

ROSS I hope so too. For I need all the friends I can get!

CUT TO:

29: INT. WARLEGGAN HOUSE – DAY 4

George is playing with his coin-scales, idly clinking gold guineas. He seems rather excited by some news he's just received. Cary comes in, carrying some papers.

GEORGE Ross Poldark is alive.

CARY That wastrel?

Cary sits and begins to go through his papers.

GEORGE At school I rather admired him.

Cary looks surprised.

GEORGE *(cont'd)* He said what he thought, did what he liked.

CARY And where did it get him?

GEORGE It got him a following. Something we frequently fail to acquire.

CARY Except by bribery or bullying.

GEORGE Perhaps we should deploy charm.

CARY Charm is overrated.

He returns to his papers, George to his guineas.

GEORGE Still, I wonder if he might not be useful to us? *(no reply)* His father's dead. He's no obvious source of income. If we could rally him to our cause—

CARY To what purpose?

GEORGE He has an ancient family name. Doors that are closed to us might open for him.

Cary seems unconvinced, but George continues to think aloud.

GEORGE *(cont'd)* What inducements could we offer?

He idly piles up some guineas.

GEORGE *(cont'd)* His need at present must be severe.

CARY You mean to buy his friendship?

GEORGE I would rather he bestowed it willingly.

CARY I find people are very friendly when they cannot afford not to be.

He goes back to his papers. George continues to toy with his guineas. The expression on his face tells us he's still formulating his tactics.

CUT TO:

30: EXT. CHYNOWETH HOUSE – DAY 4

Elizabeth is walking (as if to the stables), when she is intercepted by Mrs Chynoweth.

MRS CHYNOWETH Where are you going, Elizabeth?

For a moment Elizabeth hesitates to own up. Then . . .

ELIZABETH I must speak with Ross, Mama.

MRS CHYNOWETH To what purpose?

ELIZABETH To explain. To ask him. What shall we do?

MRS CHYNOWETH There is nothing to do. You are engaged to Francis.

ELIZABETH But Ross and I—

MRS CHYNOWETH Are a thing of the past. *(seeing her about to argue)* Where is he now? Has he come to see you? Has he written to you? What does that suggest? *(no reply)* That he knows Francis is the better man. The better match. What can he offer except poverty – uncertainty – a dubious reputation—

ELIZABETH I do not care about reputation—

MRS CHYNOWETH But you should. And you will. *(then)* Francis adores you. You will be mistress of Trenwith. Had Ross not returned, would you have the slightest hesitation?

ELIZABETH But he has returned.

MRS CHYNOWETH And if he still cared for you, would he not have been at the door by now?

It's the final nail in the coffin of Elizabeth's hopes. She is defeated.

CUT TO:

31: EXT. NAMPARA VALLEY – DAY 4

Riding home across his derelict land, Ross hears raucous laughter and presently he sees Jud and Prudie lounging about by a hedge, near a patch of brambles, picnicking. When they see him, they spring up and make a great show of attacking the brambles. Ross isn't fooled for a moment.

PRUDIE Jus' clearin' the brambles, Mister Ross.

ROSS A cheering spectacle! And a needful one. Hard work is now required if we're to put food on the table.

JUD *(puzzled)* 'Ard work?

ROSS I can see you're unfamiliar with the concept. Let me clarify. We have nothing to live on beyond the fruits of our own labours. We shall need to tighten our belts. *(with a glance at Prudie)* In some cases that can only be to the good.

Prudie looks confused. Ross's sarcasm has fallen upon deaf ears. Then Ross notices a horse approaching. It's Verity.

ROSS *(cont'd – delighted)* Verity!

They greet each other warmly. Jud and Prudie scuttle away back to Nampara. After they've gone, Ross and Verity survey the scene before them.

VERITY Oh Ross, your poor land—

ROSS My poor Cornwall! *(laughs bitterly)* Seems we've both taken a battering!

Verity glances keenly at him. She can see he hasn't taken last night's news well.

VERITY You would be surprised to hear about Elizabeth.

ROSS I had no option on the girl.

VERITY It was strange how it happened. One moment she barely noticed Francis. The next—

ROSS She noticed his mine, his house, his estate— ? *(then)* That was uncalled for.

Ross looks out to sea. Verity watches him closely. She has further bad news for him.

VERITY The wedding's in a fortnight.

ROSS So soon?

Verity can see it's a blow to him.

VERITY I wish I could help you, my dear.

ROSS I must find my own way out of this.

CUT TO:

32: EXT. COASTLINE – DAY 5

The season is changing, the weather is worsening. Waves crash onto rocks.

CUT TO:

33: EXT. NAMPARA VALLEY – DAY 6

Torrential rain is pouring down as Ross mends a dry-stone wall. He curses silently as he skins his knuckles on a stone.

CUT TO:

34: EXT. NAMPARA VALLEY – DAY 7

Ross is drenched and covered in mud as he hammers in a fence post.

CUT TO:

35: EXT. MELLIN COTTAGES – DAY 7

Ross sits with Zacky, Paul, Mark and Jim round a fire. They sing a folk song: 'The Keenly Lode'. Zacky offers Ross a drink of brandy. He is lost in thought and doesn't notice.

CUT TO:

36: EXT. HEADLAND – DAY 7

Elizabeth stands on the headland where she had said goodbye to Ross before he went to war and wonders why he hasn't yet come to see her. The thought occurs: perhaps he never will.

CUT TO:

37: EXT. NAMPARA HOUSE – DAY 7

Ross limps home across his fields after a long day's labour.

CUT TO:

38: INT. NAMPARA HOUSE, KITCHEN – DAY 7

Exhausted from his labours, Ross sits alone by a meagre fire.

CUT TO:

39: EXT. CHYNOWETH HOUSE – DAY 8

Elizabeth is walking in the garden. Francis, unseen, watches her a while. He can see she's troubled. She turns, sees him, tries to look cheerful. He comes over, takes her hand.

FRANCIS *(trying to make a joke of it)* An alarming prospect, is it not? A lifetime with me! *(then, genuine)* I cannot promise to be as fascinating as some. Or as confident. Or as ambitious. But one thing I can promise you. *(beat)* My undying love. And gratitude.

Elizabeth's heart melts. Has she the heart to hurt him? Her hesitation makes Francis fear the worst.

FRANCIS *(cont'd)* But if something still troubles you? If there is something you wish to tell me?

ELIZABETH There is.

She hesitates. Will she choose Ross or Francis. Now is the moment to decide. Finally.

ELIZABETH *(cont'd)* I wish to tell you – that I cannot wait to be your wife.

Francis almost bursts into tears of relief. He kisses her hand gratefully. She smiles at him. They are reconciled.

CUT TO:

40: EXT. WHEAL LEISURE – DAY 8

Ross is dripping with sweat as he gathers stones from beside the derelict Wheal Leisure to mend his walls. As he pauses, he hears the sound of horse's hooves and sees Francis approaching.

FRANCIS Should you be doing this?

ROSS I cannot afford a farm-hand.

FRANCIS Your father would not have wished you to stoop—

ROSS My father would not have wished me to starve.

Francis dismounts, ties his horse beside Wheal Leisure, contemplates the derelict mine.

FRANCIS She's proved a poor legacy.

ROSS Certainly a fickle one.

Francis flushes. Is this a dig at Elizabeth?

ROSS *(cont'd)* Perhaps I should examine her.

FRANCIS Is that wise?

Ross shrugs. He's taken Francis's 'betrayal' to heart. He strides over to the mine shaft. Francis follows warily.

CUT TO:

41: INT. WHEAL LEISURE, SHAFT – DAY 8

Ross climbs down the ladder into the mine shaft. Once out of the wind, he lights a candle and sticks it to the front of his hat with melted wax. He begins to descend.

FRANCIS How deep did they drive it?

ROSS Thirty fathoms. Most of it will be under water by now.

Francis follows Ross down the ladder.

FRANCIS *(tentative)* Ross – my father's concerned—

No reply. Francis struggles to light his own candle.

FRANCIS *(cont'd)* That you should make the right choices—

Ross's candle flickers smokily and throws shadows against the walls. Above him Francis begins to descend.

FRANCIS *(cont'd)* Face certain realities—

Still no reply.

FRANCIS *(cont'd)* Accept that your future may lie elsewhere—

ROSS I thank him for his concern.

Ross begins to descend further, Francis above scrambling to keep up with him. The candles gutter fitfully and threaten to go out. There is a constant drip of water. Francis dislodges a stone, which clatters onto the next platform then falls with a plop into the water below. Ross looks round at the dank walls covered in green slime – then, to the side he sees, two feet deep in water, the opening to the first level. Ross steps down till he's up to his knees in water, then heads into the tunnel. As he walks along, he can hear Francis sloshing through the water behind him.

FRANCIS *(calling after him)* Ross – you do know I'm to be married next week?

ROSS And?

FRANCIS You've not yet accepted our invitation.

ROSS I've things to attend to – my house is a pig-sty – I'm not one for ceremonies—

FRANCIS But you must come. It's our dearest wish—

The flickering candlelight casts grotesque reflections on the dark, oily water. Ross continues to stride ahead, Francis struggling to keep up. The tunnel contracts, allowing passage only if Ross and Francis bow their heads. Francis begins to feel claustrophobic. His candle sputters.

Ross strides ahead towards a glimmer of light. He reaches an air shaft, full of water, crossed by a narrow plank.

FRANCIS *(cont'd – catching up)* Ross, you must understand – when I first met Elizabeth, there was no thought of my coming between you – but what could I do? My feelings – our feelings for each other—

Suddenly Ross turns, his face contorted with pent-up fury.

ROSS In God's name, must you rub my nose in it?

His expression is so menacing that Francis steps backwards – and in so doing inadvertently steps onto the wooden plank crossing the shaft.

It snaps. Francis plunges into the water and instantly disappears below the surface. Ross is momentarily transfixed with shock. There's no sign of Francis. Then he struggles to the surface, gasping for air. For a moment Ross seems unable to move. Francis screams at him before going under again—

FRANCIS Ross! For pity's sake—

As he disappears from view, Ross seems to come to himself. He drops onto his stomach, leans over the edge, tries to fish through the water to catch hold of Francis. But there's no sign of him. Ross leans further into the water, thrashes around trying to locate Francis. Finally a hand grasps Ross's sleeve. Ross seizes hold and hauls Francis to the surface. Francis is staring frantically at him, gasping for breath. Ross tenses his muscles and with a superhuman effort hauls Francis out of the shaft. Francis lies face down on the rock, choking and spitting out water. Eventually he turns and looks up at Ross. Ross is fuming.

ROSS Why the hell don't you learn to swim?

Francis stares at him, shivering at his narrow escape.

FRANCIS For a moment I thought you'd let me drown.

ROSS For a moment I thought so too.

Ross turns and makes his way back up the tunnel. Francis stares after him. If he'd had any doubt about the strength of Ross's feelings towards his forthcoming marriage, he's in doubt no longer.

CUT TO:

42: INT. NAMPARA HOUSE, ROSS'S BEDROOM – DAY 9

Ross dresses carefully for Elizabeth and Francis's wedding.

CUT TO:

43: INT. SAWLE CHURCH – DAY 9

Ross watches as Francis and Elizabeth stand at the altar. His face betrays no emotion, but the knuckles of his hands are white.

CUT TO:

44: EXT. TRENWITH HOUSE – DAY 9

Ross, Verity and other guests walk up the drive to Trenwith House. A coach drives up, almost running them over. It stops outside the front door and George and Cary get out. Ross hangs back so as to avoid meeting them.

ROSS *(surprised)* George Warleggan? He's done well for himself – judging by his waistcoat.

VERITY As you'll discover, the Warleggans are on the rise.

At that moment George spots Ross and gives an urbane smile. Ross nods in return.

CUT TO:

45: INT. TRENWITH HOUSE, GREAT HALL – DAY 9

The wedding festivities are in progress.

CHARLES Ladies and gentlemen, this is a proud day for the Poldarks.

Various couples are assembled for dancing. The musicians strike up and Francis leads off with Elizabeth. Ross watches silently from the sidelines. Presently he is approached by Verity.

VERITY I wish you could dance, Ross.

ROSS I thank an American musket for sparing me the ordeal!

(then, seeing her genuinely distressed) I trust I shall soon get the better of all my wounds.

Verity smiles sympathetically and goes off to tend to the wedding guests.

CUT TO:

46: INT. TRENWITH HOUSE, GREAT HALL – DAY 9

George and Cary are observing the bridal pair, in particular Elizabeth.

CARY Perhaps I should have purchased her for you, nephew.

GEORGE I broker my own business these days.

CARY She'll be wasted here. These Poldarks have nothing beyond the name. And with Charles's mine on its knees – and mortgaged to the hilt – Warleggan's Bank may send in the bailiffs as and when it chooses.

GEORGE This is elegant talk for a wedding, Uncle!

CARY Talk of a profit is always elegant, George.

ON ROSS: He's caught the gist of the conversation and his mood darkens further. He turns away from the dancing and makes his way out of the room.

CUT TO:

47: INT. TRENWITH HOUSE, HALLWAY – DAY 9

Ross is looking at the family portraits which adorn the walls. George comes in, strolls over.

GEORGE My compliments on the scratch! *(Ross's scar)* Was it got in any actual fighting or yet another gambling brawl?

ROSS *(smiles)* Old habits die hard.

GEORGE I was sorry to hear of your father.

Ross nods in acknowledgement.

GEORGE *(cont'd)* We have something in common.

Ross looks doubtful.

GEORGE *(cont'd)* Both fatherless? Hostages to our family fortunes?

ROSS And there the similarity ends.

GEORGE Cornwall is changing. These are difficult times. I trust you will feel you can rely on your friends.

ROSS For what?

GEORGE Whatever you might require.

It's a defining moment. Ross takes stock of George – and for the first time realizes he has a choice: to throw in his lot with the Warleggans or to go it alone. Eventually . . .

ROSS I believe I can manage, thank you, George.

From the next room comes the sound of cheering and Cary's voice shouting 'Go on, my beauty, do me proud! Rip its head off!' George hesitates, then . . .

GEORGE *(cont'd)* D'you believe that breeding can ever be bought?

ROSS You should ask your uncle.

George flushes, embarrassed by his uncle's vulgarity.

ROSS *(cont'd)* Elizabeth would be delighted by talk of bailiffs on her wedding day.

GEORGE Elizabeth's delight is surely no longer your concern?

It's as near the knuckle as George dares to go. Ross forces himself to smile. In the nick of time Verity appears.

VERITY There you are, Ross! I've been sent to find you.

Ross and George bow politely to each other then Verity walks Ross away towards the Great Hall . . .

CUT TO:

48: INT. TRENWITH HOUSE, GREAT HALL – CONTINUOUS

Ross and Verity come in to find a table being prepared for the cock-fighting. Charles is unveiling his own fighting cock, to the admiration of Aunt Agatha and Francis. Then Ross realizes he is being directed towards the Oak Room . . . and Elizabeth.

CUT TO:

49: INT. TRENWITH HOUSE, OAK ROOM – CONTINUOUS

VERITY *(to Elizabeth)* You see – he hadn't left after all!

Sensing there is much to be said between these two, Verity leaves them. Elizabeth smiles nervously at Ross. He forces a smile in return. The awkwardness between them is almost tangible.

ELIZABETH I was glad to see you at church. *(no reply)* You must wonder why I wished you there.

No reply. Ross is determined not to make this easy for her.

ELIZABETH *(cont'd)* After that night – when we had no chance to speak – I thought you would come to see me—

ROSS Why would I do that?

ELIZABETH To give me chance to explain – to apologize—

ROSS For what? There was no formal undertaking between us.

ELIZABETH Not officially, no, but – you know there was something – an understanding—

Ross stares at her, unable to believe that she's bringing up this subject, today of all days.

ELIZABETH *(cont'd)* But three years is a long time, Ross.

They are interrupted by the arrival of Mrs Chynoweth.

MRS CHYNOWETH Elizabeth, remember your duty as a bride is to all your guests?

ELIZABETH I've no taste for fighting, Mama.

MRS CHYNOWETH Are you a fan of the sport, Ross? Perhaps you'll instruct me in its finer points.

ROSS I doubt there are any subtleties of combat on which I can offer you advice, ma'am.

Mrs Chynoweth looks sharply at him – has she understood him correctly? – then at Elizabeth to see if she will take offence on her mother's behalf. But Elizabeth is resolute in wishing to be left alone with Ross.

MRS CHYNOWETH I'll send Francis to you.

With great reluctance, she leaves.

ELIZABETH You mustn't blame my mother. This was my decision—

ROSS And we must abide by it.

ELIZABETH And we shall be neighbours. *(beat)* And friends.

ROSS If you say so.

Francis has arrived.

FRANCIS Feeling neglected, my dear? *(takes her hand)* May I claim my bride, Ross?

He leads her away, back to the guests, leaving Ross struggling to put on a brave face.

CUT TO:

50: EXT/INT. NAMPARA HOUSE – NIGHT 9

Ross returns home from the wedding, kicks open the front door, slams it behind him. The house is dark except for a single candle.
CUT TO:

51: INT. NAMPARA HOUSE, STAIRS – NIGHT 9

Much the worse for drink, Ross seizes a decanter of rum and stumbles upstairs.
CUT TO:

52: INT. TRENWITH HOUSE, GREAT HALL – NIGHT 9

A hand puts down a tarot card: the Empress (Elizabeth).
CUT TO:

53: INT. NAMPARA HOUSE, ROSS'S BEDROOM – NIGHT 9

Ross sits on the bed, fully clothed. He has never felt more alone.
CUT TO:

54: INT. TRENWITH HOUSE, GREAT HALL – NIGHT 9

A hand puts down another card: The King of Swords (Ross).
CUT TO:

55: INT. NAMPARA HOUSE, ROSS'S BEDROOM – NIGHT 9

Ross takes a swig of brandy. And despairs.
CUT TO:

56: INT. TRENWITH HOUSE, GREAT HALL – NIGHT 9

The wedding celebrations are over. All the guests have gone. Aunt Agatha is tut-tutting over her tarot cards. Charles is seated at the table. Verity comes in, with a glass of wine, exhausted from the events of the day. She takes a seat beside Aunt Agatha, who lays another card: the Four of Cups (Francis).

VERITY *(as a joke)* Still a good day for the Poldarks?

CHARLES Don't encourage her!

AUNT AGATHA *(touching the King of Swords card)* The dark Poldark? *(touching the Four of Cups card)* Or the fair?

She deals another card: The Wheel of Fortune.

AUNT AGATHA *(cont'd)* The stronger rises as the weaker falls.

She deals more cards. The Lovers. The Devil. The Tower.

AUNT AGATHA *(cont'd)* For all is fair in love and war.

Charles suddenly looks anxious. Though he usually has no truck with Aunt Agatha's fortune-telling, this time her predictions fall alarmingly in line with his own fears. He knows he must take action.
CUT TO:

57: INT. NAMPARA HOUSE, ROSS'S BEDROOM –
NIGHT 9

As Ross stares at his hands, he realizes he is still wearing the ring Elizabeth gave him. The last vestige of hope now gone, he tears it from his finger and flings it across the room.

CUT TO:

58: EXT. NAMPARA HOUSE – DAY 10

Ross is repairing a trough in the yard. Jud is repairing a barn. Prudie is feeding chickens. The sound of hooves is heard. Charles approaches. Jud and Prudie slink away. They (and Ross) know that Charles is not a fan of theirs.

CHARLES Still feeding that pair of wastrels? If you turfed 'em out, you could afford to buy stock.

ROSS They were my father's friends.

Ross resumes his work. Charles glances round at the state of the farm and the land, still in disarray despite Ross's efforts.

CHARLES You drive yourself hard, boy.

ROSS It keeps me out of mischief.

Ross continues to work.

CHARLES I'm not unfeeling, Ross. I know your father had the worst of the land – and the property—

ROSS *(smiles)* The lot of a younger son—

CHARLES So I'd like to show you something.

CUT TO:

59: EXT. CLIFF-TOPS BY GRAMBLER – DAY 10

Charles and Ross, on horseback, survey the distant Grambler Mine.

CHARLES What do you see?

ROSS Grambler. Your family mine.

CHARLES Not so. What you see – is the past.

ROSS Does it not still produce?

CHARLES Precious little. And nothing to trouble the Welsh mines where they're dragging it out by the cart load. Meantime, we're sunk in debt, the bankers have us by the throat—

ROSS I'm sorry—

CHARLES And your mines? What of them? *(before Ross can reply)* Even worse than Grambler. Derelict, both of them. Your land? Barren. There's nothing for you here, boy. Your future lies elsewhere—

ROSS Well—

CHARLES A change of profession. The law, perhaps? – or even the church—

ROSS *(laughing)* D'you really not know me, Uncle?

CHARLES A move to London – or Oxford? *(beat)* I'll fund it.

Ross looks at him in amazement.

CHARLES *(cont'd)* Your education, your expenses. I believe it's what your father would have wanted.

Ross contemplates him narrowly. He suspects he can see what Charles's agenda is: to remove him from proximity to Trenwith and to Elizabeth.

ROSS And Francis? What d'you believe he would want?

CHARLES For you to prosper.

ROSS Away from here.

CHARLES I think that would be best for all concerned.

Ross smiles. He now knows how keen Charles and Francis are to get him away. And Charles's offer has a lot going for it.

ROSS I'll think on it.

CHARLES You should be biting my hand off!

ROSS And may yet do so. But till I've exhausted every possibility – of making a living on my own land, among my own people—

CHARLES Damn your stubbornness, boy! The land is useless, its people are starving – what possible reason is there to stay?

Ross says nothing. Thwarted, angry, Charles rides away. Ross watches him go. Presently Paul, Mark and Zacky approach, on their way to work. They see him looking down at Grambler.

PAUL Would 'ee ever think to re-open yer own mine?

ROSS Wheal Leisure? Without coal and wages? Am I a magician?

ZACKY If 'ee ever become one, 'ee know where t' find us!

Paul and Mark murmur their agreement. Ross rides off.

CUT TO:

60: EXT. NAMPARA HOUSE – DAY 10

Ross rides home. He realizes how much improved Nampara is since he first returned from the war.

CUT TO:

61: INT. NAMPARA HOUSE, KITCHEN – DAY 10

Ross comes in. (Jud and Prudie, caught napping in the box bed, now spring to life and start sweeping and scouring.) Ross seems to have come to a decision.

ROSS Tomorrow's market day?

JUD Aye, sur, 'tis, sur.

ROSS Well, don't stand there gawping, Jud! Fetch me my father's pocket watch!

Bemused Jud and Prudie exchange a puzzled glance, then scuttle off as directed.

CUT TO:

62: EXT. COUNTRY LANE – DAY 11

A bird's eye view of oxen being driven down a lane towards Truro. Ross, trailed by Jud, rides behind them. Up ahead he sees the throng and bustle of market day.

CUT TO:

63: EXT. TRURO, MARKET PLACE – DAY 11

Ross places his father's watch before a tradesman. The tradesman examines it – glances at Ross, then back at the watch. He hesitates. It's clearly a fine piece. Ross fixes him with a look which dares him to make a low offer. He doesn't dare.

CUT TO:

64: EXT. TRURO, MARKET PLACE – DAY 11

Ross is counting out money to pay for two oxen. He despatches Jud to take charge of them and heads towards the rest of the market.

CUT TO:

65: EXT. TRURO, MARKET PLACE – DAY 11

Ross strolls past a long row of pilchards in barrels. He weaves his way through various stalls, past a Methodist preacher who holds a placard which proclaims 'Set yourself on fire and all will come and watch you burn'.

He passes children watching a puppet show; past nosegay and sweet-meat sellers; hawkers accost him; he declines their wares. All human life is here, from beggars to gentry. In the distance he sees George and Cary Warleggan. They turn up their noses at the importunings of nosegay and sweetmeat sellers, they look with distaste at the beggars.

Ross walks on, intending to bypass them. Now he comes to the out-skirts of a crowd and as he advances further he realizes a dog-fighting arena has been set up and the spectators are eagerly awaiting the next bout. A fierce-looking fighting dog, a chain tied to its collar, is being restrained by a young gentleman.

Now another young gentleman is seen, dragging a trembling ragged mongrel towards the arena. The crowd begins to laugh, some begin to boo in derision at the inequality of contest between the mongrel and the fighting dog. As the mongrel is about to be attached to the other end of the chain, a scream is heard, a voice yells, 'Tha's my dog! Leave 'im be!' and a scrawny, ragged urchin rushes into the arena. The crowd cheers. This is an interesting turn of events. Two young gentlemen intercept the urchin and restrain him. He starts kicking and struggling. The crowd roars with laughter and cheers even more. They are joined by more spectators, including some ladies, who shriek with laughter at the struggling urchin. Playing up to the crowd now, the young gentlemen begin to shove the urchin from side to side, throwing him round the ring and into the mud like a rag doll.

ON ROSS: Unable to compute what he's seeing: members of his own class baiting a mere youth. He looks round at his fellow gentlemen. Will no one put a stop to this savagery? Evidently not.

ROSS'S POV: George, Cary and other gentry, all braying with laughter.

Something hardens in his expression. Calmly he moves forward, pushing through the crowd. Then he sees something which makes him hesitate:

ROSS'S POV: Elizabeth pushing forward to see what's going on, followed by Francis. As they get nearer, Elizabeth turns away in distress. This kind of baiting disgusts her.

ON ROSS: Knowing that if he steps forward he must eventually encounter Elizabeth. But how can he not step forward? Calmly he takes his riding crop from his boot and walks towards the young gentlemen. They are young, all of them fully convinced of their absolute right to do as they please.

ON THE CROWD: Some cheering, some curious, most expecting the newcomer (Ross) to join in with the tormenting.

ON THE YOUNG GENTLEMEN: Some of them notice Ross approaching. They see his expression and start to run.

ROSS Enough!

One – a young man with an arrogant face – stands his ground and sneers defiantly.

ROSS If you'll take my advice, you'll run.

YOUNG MAN Or else, sir?

Impassive, Ross hits him across the face with his whip. The man shrieks and flees, clutching his face.

ON THE CROWD: Gasping with shock – that a gentleman has attacked members of his own class for teasing a common urchin boy. George smiles to himself: Ross really has done it this time! But Elizabeth flushes with pleasure. Ross has done the right thing and she admires him for it.

ON ROSS: Daring anyone to intervene. No one dares.

Now he approaches the prostrate form of the urchin, lying face down in the mud. The urchin is clothed in breeches, shirt and coat that are far too big for him. On his head is a cap. His face is bleeding and bruised. Ross gently touches his shoulder.

ROSS Have they hurt you, child?

The urchin glares and squares up to hit him.

DEMELZA Dun't 'ee 'child' me, mister!

Ross tries to help the urchin to his feet, but he flings him off. Realizing they're still the focus of the crowd's attention, Ross seizes him firmly by the arm.

ROSS I think we've provided enough sport for one day.

He marches him off.

CUT TO:

66: INT. RED LION INN – DAY 11

Ross places a steaming bowl of stew in front of Demelza, who sits with her head slumped on a trestle table. She eyes it – and him – suspiciously. Then hunger gets the better of her and she shovels it into her mouth with her bare hands, as if she hasn't eaten in weeks. Still Ross hasn't realized she's a girl. A few people are hovering round, whispering, gawping at her.

ROSS Anyone know this child?

The landlord comes closer, peers into Demelza's face.

LANDLORD Tom Carne's daughter from 'Luggan. She'll get the strap if 'e catch 'er from 'ome an' in 'er brother's clo'es!

Demelza glares at him but continues to shovel food into her mouth with her hands, guarding her bowl as if expecting at any minute it will be taken away.

ROSS Easy, girl. No one will rob you.

He pushes a glass of rum towards her. She snatches it greedily, drinks it in one. Ross turns to fetch her another glass . . . and comes face to face with Elizabeth.

ELIZABETH I came to see if the boy was – *(then)* Oh!

She's realized that the urchin is a girl – and a rather striking one at that. Demelza and Elizabeth stare at each other, each taking the other in: Elizabeth delicate, beautiful, refined. Demelza filthy, ragged, uncouth, but strangely compelling. Elizabeth regains her composure.

ELIZABETH You were right to step in.

ROSS I'm glad you think so.

ELIZABETH I'm sure the child is grateful.

ROSS I doubt it.

For Demelza is still shovelling food into her mouth, careless of the attention she's creating. Elizabeth and Ross look at each other for a moment, then Elizabeth turns and walks away. Ross curses silently that he was not more civil to her. He makes to go after her, but Francis appears and steers Elizabeth back to their party. Now, alone again with Demelza, Ross takes her in fully for the first time. Her shirt has slipped from her shoulders and her back bears signs of bruising.

ROSS They did hurt you.

DEMELZA Not they.

ROSS Then who?

DEMELZA *(mumbling)* My father.

ROSS What?

DEMELZA Father.

ROSS Beats you?

DEMELZA Most days.

ROSS Family?

DEMELZA Six brothers.

ROSS You love your father?

DEMELZA Bible sez I must.

He contemplates her: bloodied and filthy, in her boy's clothes, her hair matted, her dark eyes staring at him resentfully.

ROSS What's your name?

DEMELZA *(mumbling)* 'Melzacarne.

ROSS Speak up, child.

DEMELZA Demelza Carne.

ROSS Ross Poldark.

They look at each other. In that moment something passes between them, a connection, a recognition of something in each other. It's not a connection either of them seek. The moment is broken by the sound of George's voice.

GEORGE'S VOICE Befriending the rabble, Ross?

George has come to order another drink.

GEORGE One would never guess you were a gentleman.

ROSS It takes one to know one, I believe, George.

Though George roars with laughter, we sense the insult has hit its mark. He nods briefly and rejoins Cary in another part of the inn.

GEORGE *(to Cary)* For a man so impecunious, he's very full of himself.

CARY Perhaps he considers us tradesmen.

GEORGE Which we are!

CARY Were.

GEORGE It's a pity he owns nothing worth having.

ON ROSS

ROSS *(to Demelza)* Come. I'm taking you home to Illuggan.

He ushers the unwilling Demelza out.

ON GEORGE & CARY

CARY He may do so, in future.

GEORGE *(smiling)* When he does, it will be my pleasure to take it from him.

ON ROSS: Ordering Demelza out.

ROSS Go.

CUT TO:

67: INT. TRENWITH HOUSE, GREAT HALL – DAY 11

Elizabeth and Francis return from the market. Elizabeth seems very distracted. Verity greets them.

VERITY You're back early. How was market day?

FRANCIS Not without incident.

Charles has also appeared. One look at Elizabeth tells him all he needs to know. Elizabeth heads straight upstairs. Francis and Charles exchange a glance.

CUT TO:

68: EXT. MOORS – DAY 11

Demelza sits astride the horse, in front of Ross. Her dog, Garrick, trots beside them. The day is fine and the ride is through scenery which is spectacular. Demelza, more relaxed now, begins to hum a song to herself.

DEMELZA *(sings, barely audible)* There was an old couple and they was poor . . . Tweedle, Tweedle, go twee . . . Oh, I have been sick since you have been gone . . . etc., etc.

Now they are approaching Bargus crossroads, where the road branches for Illuggan. Ross reins the horse to a halt.

ROSS 'Luggan's that way.

Demelza jumps down off the horse.

DEMELZA Thank 'ee, sur.

She whistles to Garrick – a loud, piercing whistle. He comes gambolling over. Demelza starts to walk off. Ross is about to ride off, when something – he has no idea what – makes him call back to her.

ROSS I'm in need of a kitchen maid.

Demelza halts, turns, looks at him, puzzled. Having made the suggestion before he even realized it, he's not sure how to go on.

ROSS *(cont'd)* You'd get food, lodging, proper clothing. I want someone strong for the work is hard.

Demelza stares at him, unsure what's being asked of her.

DEMELZA How far?

ROSS Too far to run home. *(then)* But perhaps you don't wish to come?

Demelza contemplates the offer. But now another thought occurs.

DEMELZA There be Garrick, sur – him an' me's friends. Where I go, he goes.

Ross contemplates the bedraggled dog and its no-less bedraggled owner. Ross shrugs, offers his hand for Demelza to get back on the horse. She takes it.

CUT TO:

69: EXT. NAMPARA HOUSE – DAY 11

Jud is leading the newly acquired oxen when he hears the approach of a horse, turns and sees Ross with the urchin Demelza sitting astride the horse, attended by the bedraggled Garrick. He is clearly unimpressed and looks at Demelza with disgust. She glares back at him. As Ross rides up to the house, dismounts and helps Demelza down, Prudie appears, eyes Demelza with suspicion.

PRUDIE 'Oo 'ee 'ave 'ere?

ROSS This is Demelza. She's to help in the kitchen.

JUD Pickin' up brats'll bring 'ee no end o' trouble—

ROSS See to the horse.

Jud stomps off, still muttering to himself.

JUD 'Tidn' right – 'tidn' fit – 'tidn' fair – 'tidn' proper—

PRUDIE She'll be seethin' with crawlers.

ROSS Not if I give her the same treatment I gave you.

CUT TO:

70: EXT. NAMPARA HOUSE, COURTYARD – DAY 11

Ross works the pump and holds Demelza's head under the cold water as it gushes all over her head and shoulders. Demelza gasps with shock but doesn't try to fight him.

ROSS If you work for me, you must be clean, d'you understand?

Demelza is choking from her drenching and is barely able to nod.

ROSS *(cont'd)* No lice—

DEMELZA *(choking)* No, sur—

Prudie watches with a scowl on her face.

PRUDIE Aren't no vittles f'r'er.

ROSS Find some.

Ross flings Demelza a cloth to dry herself.

PRUDIE Scarce feed us'selves, 'ow can 'ee feed another beside?

ROSS Leave that to me.

CUT TO:

71: INT. NAMPARA HOUSE, ROSS'S BEDROOM – DAY 11

Ross sits at his desk and begins to go through the drawers, looking for more things to sell. He finds a pair of candlesticks – obvious candidates. He sets them aside. He finds an intricately made compass. Another candidate. Then, as he searches for more saleable objects, something catches his eye.

HIS POV: In the corner of the room, on the floor, something is glinting, caught in the sunlight.

Ross goes to retrieve it. Almost before he gets there he knows what it is: the ring Elizabeth gave him the day he went to war.

CUT TO:

72: INT. NAMPARA HOUSE, KITCHEN – DAY 11

Demelza is standing by the stove, wrapped in a cloth. Though she's cold and shivering and on the receiving end of Jud and Prudie's glares, this is such an improvement on what she's left behind she can't help but look round in wide-eyed wonder. Prudie and Jud speak about her as if she wasn't there.

PRUDIE Wha' she be smirkin' at?

JUD Blatherin' blasted brat!

PRUDIE 'Ow old she be?

DEMELZA *(spirited defiance)* Old enough to know 'er own mind!

JUD Not too big to feel th' back o' my hand!

CUT TO:

73: INT. NAMPARA HOUSE, HALLWAY – DAY 11

Ross comes downstairs. As he passes a side-table, he notices a letter. He sees it's addressed to himself. He picks it up and examines it.

ROSS Prudie? When did this letter come?

PRUDIE'S VOICE Jus' now, sur – from your uncle Charles.

Ross opens the letter. It contains a great deal of money. He contemplates it thoughtfully.

CUT TO:

74 INT. NAMPARA HOUSE, PARLOUR/HALLWAY – NIGHT 11

Ross sits alone, eating an unappetizing pie (Prudie's creation). He becomes aware of someone watching him through the half-open door. It's Demelza. When she realizes she's been seen, she's about to scuttle off.

ROSS Don't lurk out there, girl. Come in.

Demelza edges into the room. Ross eyes her closely. She looks at him warily.

ROSS *(cont'd)* Have Jud and Prudie made you welcome? *(no reply)* Of course not. *(then)* You must learn to stand up for yourself. Show them you have a mind of your own and will not be dictated to.

Demelza nods warily. Ross – whose instruction to Demelza has articulated his own frustration towards Charles – now folds the money away. He takes a taste of the horrible pie and immediately abandons it.

ROSS *(cont'd)* Clear this away.

He points to the unappetizing-looking pie. As she begins to clear—

ROSS *(cont'd)* To Prudie. Not your dog.

DEMELZA Ais sur – *(hesitates, then)* I be thinkin', sur – 'bout Garrick, sur – 'e be outside, whinin' to come in—

ROSS Let him whine.

DEMELZA Ais, sur – *(then)* But see, sur – 'e'll get lonely out there, all by 'isself. *(no reply)* An' 'e be clean, sur – e' 'ave no cra-lers—

ROSS All dogs have crawlers. I'll have none of them in my house. Now go and do as I bid you.

She goes out.

CUT TO:

75: INT. NAMPARA HOUSE, KITCHEN – NIGHT 11

The kitchen is in darkness. Demelza is tossing and turning, trying to get to sleep in the box-bed. She's not succeeding. The house is strange and full of alarming noises. Then she hears something scratching at the back door. She gets up, opens the door. Garrick is there, wagging his tail. She's hushes' him. Dare she disobey her new master? She decides she dare. She lets Garrick in, urging him to be quiet. They curl up together on the floor in front of the hearth.

CUT TO:

76: EXT. TRENWITH HOUSE – DAY 12

Ross rides up the drive to Trenwith.

CUT TO:

77: INT. TRENWITH HOUSE, HALLWAY – DAY 12

Ross waits in the hall, contemplating the family portraits. His eye is drawn to a new one, just added – Elizabeth's. It does her justice. Foot-steps are heard on the stairs – and Elizabeth appears (carrying her book).

ELIZABETH Ross! I wasn't expecting—

ROSS Is my uncle in?

ELIZABETH He's gone to the mine with Francis.

They look at each other – both sense things are brewing which must now come to a head.

ELIZABETH *(cont'd)* Would you care to join me in the par-lour?

She leads the way into the parlour. Ross follows.

CUT TO:

78: EXT. CLIFF-TOPS – DAY 12

Demelza explores the countryside around Nampara – gathers flowers, admires the view, revels in her new-found freedom.

CUT TO:

79: EXT. NAMPARA HOUSE – DAY 12

Demelza stands at the front door looking out across the land of her new home, Nampara Valley. She is wide-eyed and excited by its wild beauty, and the promise of freedom it seems to hold out for her. Then, in the distance, too far away to be identified, the shapes of three well-built men appear on the horizon. Demelza's eyes widen in horror.

CUT TO:

80: INT. TRENWITH HOUSE, PARLOUR – DAY 12

The tension in the room is almost palpable. Elizabeth, pouring tea, makes a concerted effort to be normal. Ross is resolutely looking out of the window.

ELIZABETH Did you enjoy market day?

ROSS Not especially.

ELIZABETH We'd no thought of going but George was keen – and you know Francis—

ROSS Easily persuaded?

Elizabeth declines to be riled by his retort.

ELIZABETH You caused quite a stir. Though not everyone appreciated your intervention.

ROSS The child did.

ELIZABETH She got home safely?

ROSS What time will my uncle be back?

ELIZABETH Have you something to—

ROSS I thought to employ the girl as a kitchen maid. Her family appear to care little for her.

ELIZABETH How old is the girl?

ROSS She's of age but her family may want compensation—

ELIZABETH You should send her back to them. People are quick to judge—

ROSS Are you?

Elizabeth's demeanour has suddenly changed, as if she can no longer hide her feelings.

ROSS *(cont'd – seeing her distress)* I shouldn't have come. I can see it upsets you—

ELIZABETH Oh Ross, it's not your coming here—

ROSS What, then?

ELIZABETH It hurts to think how you must hate me.

ROSS Hate you? Good God, Elizabeth, you of all people should know—

He debates whether to go on. Elizabeth doesn't deter him, so he does.

ROSS *(cont'd)* From the moment I set eyes on you, no one else existed. While I was away, all I could think of was coming back to you—

ELIZABETH Don't say any more—

ROSS It's not pretty to be made a fool of by one's feelings. To take a childish promise and build a future out of it. And yet, did we really not mean those things we said— ?

ELIZABETH Ross—

ROSS That day I left – was there really nothing between us? *(no reply)* Is there really nothing between us now?

ELIZABETH I thought you were dead!

For a moment Ross is unable to speak.

ELIZABETH *(cont'd)* How can you come to me now and ask me things you know I can't answer?

ROSS Why can't you answer?

He's close to her now, seizes her hand.

ROSS *(cont'd)* Why can't you answer?

Elizabeth is on the verge of pouring out her feelings for him – but something makes her hold back and summon up all the strength she has left.

ELIZABETH There's nothing for you here, Ross. I love Francis. You must forget me and make your life elsewhere.

Ross looks at her coldly. He knows she's chickened out and he despises her for it.

ROSS You may rely upon it.

Ross turns and walks out of the house.

CUT TO:

81: EXT. TRENWITH HOUSE – DAY 12

Ross is mounting his horse when Elizabeth comes running out after him.

ELIZABETH At least let us part as friends.

ROSS We can never be friends.

He is about to ride off, then . . .

ROSS *(cont'd)* Tell my uncle he has his wish.

ELIZABETH What wish? Ross? What wish?

But he's already ridden off. We go with him. He can't believe he's allowed Elizabeth to get to him again. He's now determined to put her – and Cornwall – behind him.

CUT TO:

82: EXT. CLIFF-TOPS – DAY 12

Ross gallops along the cliff-tops by the sea on his way back to Nampara.

CUT TO:

83: EXT. NAMPARA HOUSE – DAY 12

Ross gallops up to the house, still furious, to be met by a scowling Prudie.

ROSS Tell the girl to fetch her belongings—

PRUDIE Eh— ?

ROSS She's leaving—

PRUDIE Leavin'— ?

ROSS As am I—

PRUDIE You, sur— ?

ROSS To London. She to her father.

PRUDIE But 'er father's 'ere—

ROSS What? Where?

Ross leaps off his horse and tethers it to the lilac tree.

PRUDIE Parlour, sur. Stank in without s'much as by' r leave—

Unimpressed, Ross walks past her into the house.

CUT TO:

84: INT. NAMPARA HOUSE, PARLOUR – DAY 12

Three men in working clothes, all powerfully built and belligerent, look up as Ross strides in. Tom Carne and his two younger brothers offer no deference, visibly squaring up as Ross enters. Beside them, Ross looks like a boy again.

ROSS What can I do for you?

TOM CARNE What can 'ee do? When 'ee've slocked my daughter an' 'ticed 'er away. Where is she?

ROSS No idea.

PRUDIE They searched the 'ouse—

ROSS By whose permission?

TOM CARNE I need no permission t' come after me own!

ROSS So you can take her home and beat her?

TOM CARNE That your business?

ROSS If I choose to make it so.

TOM CARNE *(to his brothers)* Right boys, scat 'un up!

PRUDIE *(shrieking)* Jud! Jud!—

She makes a quick exit. One of the brothers kicks over a table, the other upends a chair, Tom Carne seizes a candlestick.

ROSS That's why you bring your family. Not man enough to do the job yourself?

TOM CARNE I brought more'n we!

Suddenly Jud bursts in, out of breath.

JUD Sur, they be 'ordes ev 'em!

CUT TO:

85 EXT. NAMPARA VALLEY – DAY 12

Ten huge, brawny Illuggan miners (not the 'hordes' Jud promised, but still a formidable sight) are making their way down Nampara Valley. They are drunk, irate and on the rampage, some carrying sticks, all relishing the prospect of a large-scale brawl.

CUT TO:

86: INT. NAMPARA HOUSE, PARLOUR – DAY 12

Tom struts about as if he owns the place.

TOM CARNE 'Luggan folk dun' 'old wi' thievin'. We come fer justice—

ROSS An army against one man? That's brave!

TOM CARNE Afeared, are ye?

Tom Carne strips off his coat and waistcoat. His brothers follow suit.

ROSS On the contrary – you couldn't have come at a better time!

Ross strips off his coat and waistcoat. After the disappointment of this last encounter with Elizabeth, Ross realizes he's raging – and a fist-fight is exactly what he needs! He launches himself at Tom and the brothers.

PRUDIE Lord save 'im!

She runs out. The two Carne brothers are about to join in, but Tom intervenes.

TOM CARNE Nay, stand off, boys. I'll 'andle this m'self.

CUT TO:

87: EXT. NAMPARA HOUSE – DAY 12

Prudie runs out of the house, wailing, flapping her apron.

PRUDIE 'Elp 'im! 'Elp 'im! Lord save 'im!

She runs off towards Trenwith.

CUT TO:

88: EXT. NAMPARA VALLEY – DAY 12

The Illuggan miners rampage towards the opening of Nampara Valley . . . to be confronted by the (non-too-impressive) sight of Jud.

JUD Business 'ave 'ee 'ere?

ILLUGGAN MINER Naught with 'ee but wi' fancy gent 'oo's stole a 'Luggan maid! We're 'ere to take 'er back an' teach 'im a lesson!

JUD Good luck to 'ee!

The Illuggan miners look at Jud, uncomprehending. Then a low growl goes up and they rush at him. Jud turns tail and flees.

CUT TO:

89: INT. NAMPARA HOUSE, PARLOUR – DAY 12

Ross and Tom Carne are locked in battle. Ross being younger and less bulky than Tom, is taking a pounding. He is heaved and punched all round the room, scattering ornaments and tableware, colliding with furniture. When Ross is thrown towards one of the brothers, he is tossed back into the fray with Tom.

CUT TO:

90: EXT. TRENWITH HOUSE – DAY 12

Prudie hammers on the front door of Trenwith House.

PRUDIE *(shouting out)* Mister Francis! Mister Francis! They be killin' Mister Ross!

CUT TO:

91: INT. NAMPARA HOUSE, PARLOUR – DAY 12

Tom delivers a punch which sends Ross stumbling into a huge cupboard, which rocks precariously. Ross is bleeding, dazed, staggering, but comes back fighting.

CUT TO:

92: EXT. TRENWITH HOUSE – DAY 12

Francis is at the door, with Charles and Verity.

CHARLES Devil are you saying, woman?

PRUDIE They be murderin' 'im, sur! Mister Ross be fightin' f'r'is life!

Elizabeth rushes out, horrified.

ELIZABETH You must go to him, Francis – you must help him!

Caught up in Elizabeth's panic, Francis is about to go to help Ross, but Charles holds him back.

CHARLES The woman exaggerates.

ELIZABETH For pity's sake— !

CHARLES This is no business of yours, Elizabeth.

ELIZABETH But—

CHARLES *(to Francis)* Take Elizabeth inside.

Elizabeth knows that if she argues further, she will give herself away. She allows herself to be led back inside by Francis and Verity. Charles remains. Prudie looks at him expectantly.

PRUDIE 'Ee be meanin' t' 'elp 'im, sur?

Charles shuts the door on Prudie.

CUT TO:

93: EXT. NAMPARA VALLEY – DAY 12

The Illuggan miners have almost caught up with Jud – but as they round a corner they come face to face with Zacky, Jim, Paul and Mark. A moment's stand-off, then the two sides rush at each other.

CUT TO:

94: INT. NAMPARA HOUSE, PARLOUR – DAY 12

The fight between Ross and Tom Carne gets ever more vicious. Ross's lip is bleeding and he has a cut above the eye. But slowly he's coming into his own and we realize he is not the headstrong boy of three years ago. The war has given him strength and cunning and turned him into a veritable fighting machine! Soon it's Tom's turn to be whacked against the big cupboard, which rocks even more precariously.

CUT TO:

95: INT. TRENWITH HOUSE, PARLOUR – DAY 12

Elizabeth stands by the window, watching for Charles's departure.

ELIZABETH Where's your father? Why does he not leave?

Verity and Francis watch, uneasy. Despite Elizabeth's best efforts, they can see that this waiting, this not knowing what's happening to Ross, is torture for her.

CUT TO:

96: INT. NAMPARA HOUSE, PARLOUR – DAY 12

Tom launches himself at Ross and, locked in a wrestling hold, they collide with the big cupboard, which teeters and almost overbalances. Ross breaks free and sends Tom crashing into the fireplace, where he lies winded, chest heaving. Ross wipes blood from the cut on his lip. Tom staggers to his feet, launches himself at Ross, who delivers the coup de grâce, sending Tom crashing into a corner. Ross surveys a scene of utter devastation – but feels a sense of exhilaration, as if in beating Tom he's somehow begun to exorcise some demon. He looks down at Tom with grim satisfaction.

ROSS Be so good as to close the door on your way out.

Tom stumbles to his feet, glares at Ross, but knows he's beaten. He staggers out. The two brothers look at each other, as if debating what their next move should be. Then unexpectedly, first one, then the other comes over and shakes Ross by the hand, as if in grudging acknowledgement of his fighting prowess. Then they slink out after their brother. Ross remains, bruised, bloody and sore – but somehow transformed – as if he's thrown away the vestiges of boyhood and finally become the man. He opens the large cupboard to pour himself a drink. Prudie comes in. She's shocked to see him still in one piece.

PRUDIE Oh, sur! 'Ee be alive, sur!

ROSS It would appear so. *(then)* Any sign of the girl?

PRUDIE An't seen 'er since God knows when. 'Appen she's run away, sur.

Ross considers this, drinks from the bottle.

PRUDIE *(cont'd)* 'Appen that be fer th' best, sur.

As he reaches to put the bottle back, he turns away . . .

ROSS As things now stand, I'm inclined to agree with you.

She appears to be more trouble than she's worth. *(then, remembering)* Where's Jud?

PRUDIE Gone 'a fight 'em 'Luggan miners, sur—

Suddenly remembering the 'hordes' of miners, Ross puts the bottle back (and does not notice – peering out of the darkness from the top shelf of the cupboard, the dark eyes of Demelza Carne).

PRUDIE *(cont'd)* 'Appen 'e be dead 'isself by now. An' I left a widder, all forlorn.

Ignoring this plaintive lament, Ross rushes out. After he's gone, Prudie opens the cupboard to help herself to a drink. She brings it to the table, sits down, takes a swig. Then . . .

PRUDIE *(cont'd)* You 'eard 'im. He don't want thee 'ere.

Silence. Then the cupboard opens and Demelza gets out. She scowls at Prudie.

PRUDIE *(cont'd)* 'More trouble than she's worth'? His words not mine. Now hop it, girl. Back where 'ee b'long.

She gestures Demelza to leave then settles back in her chair and takes another swig of brandy. Demelza scowls defiantly and leaves.

CUT TO:

97: EXT. NAMPARA VALLEY – DAY 12

Ross gallops up to see Jud, Paul, Mark, Zacky and Jim limping home, battered and bruised.

ROSS In God's name, what happened?

CUT TO:

98: INT. TRENWITH HOUSE, TURRET ROOM – DAY 12

Elizabeth is reading by the window when she hears the front door slam and the voice of Charles.

CHARLES'S VOICE Francis! Where are you, boy?

Elizabeth tiptoes out of the room, onto the upstairs landing.

CUT TO:

99: INT. TRENWITH HOUSE, HALLWAY – DAY 12

Francis has appeared in answer to Charles's summons. Charles is beaming.

FRANCIS Half the village?

CHARLES They'll not thank him for dragging them into his folly. *(beat)* Which gives him even less reason to stay.

FRANCIS *(surprised)* He means to leave?

CHARLES He's been invited to leave.

The penny drops for Francis.

FRANCIS What have you done, Father?

Elizabeth is revealed, listening over the balcony, unseen by Francis and Charles.

CUT TO:

100: EXT. CLIFFS NEAR WHEAL LEISURE – DAY 12

Ross walks back with Jud, Mark, Paul, Jim and Zacky. No one looks happy, Ross least of all, but as the march continues, we gradually realize that all is not as it seems. Mark, Paul, Jud, Jim and Zacky are apparently struggling to hold back laughter. Eventually they can restrain themselves no longer.

JIM 'Twas better'n Michaelmas Fair!

MARK They'll be nursing their bruises till next back-end!

Ross looks at them in amazement. The five men burst out laughing and continue a long while, unable to stop, while Ross looks on. Eventually it begins to dawn on Ross: they've actually enjoyed the whole thing!

ROSS So you leave me at home to dispatch one man, while you treat yourselves to a full-scale brawl?

JIM *(nods happily)* Aye, sur.

JUD *(pleased with himself)* 'Tis the truth of it, sur.

ROSS It won't happen again.

MARK Don't say that!

They all burst out laughing again.

ROSS Quarrels of my own making, I'll fight my own way. Understand?

They all look at each other, momentarily puzzled.

MARK But Ross – 'twas a matter of pride.

PAUL Nay, of personal affront.

ROSS How? The quarrel was mine.

ZACKY Friends don't stand by when one of their own's at stake.

The words 'friends' and 'one of their own' hit Ross like a sledgehammer. He's astonished. Can they genuinely mean it? They have now reached the derelict mine Wheal Leisure.

ZACKY *(with a nod to the mine)* Come the day Wheal Leisure's fit, she can count on us an' all.

The others mutter their agreement. Still laughing and rubbing their bruises, Zacky and the other miners depart in the direction of their own homes, Jud heads off towards Nampara. Ross remains a moment, contemplating Wheal Leisure. The events of the day have given him pause for thought – in particular the response of Zacky and his fellow miners. Thoughtful, he turns his horse towards Nampara.

CUT TO:

101: INT. TRENWITH HOUSE, DINING ROOM – DAY 12

Charles pours Francis a glass of wine and toasts him. Francis seems reluctant to join in his father's celebrations.

FRANCIS I don't like it, Father.

CHARLES You'd like it less if you lost your wife.

FRANCIS You're assuming I can't keep her myself.

CHARLES Can you?

CUT TO:

102: EXT. CLIFF-TOP PATHWAY – DAY 12

The sun is beginning to set in a blaze of red and gold clouds over the sea. The landscape is windswept, bleak and utterly deserted . . . until a distant figure is seen wandering along the cliff-tops – with a dog at her heels.

CUT TO:

103: EXT. CLIFF-TOP PATHWAY – DAY 12

Demelza is wandering along the cliff-tops, singing to herself.

DEMELZA *(sings)*

The old man he went far from home . . .
Tweedle, Tweedle, go twee . . .

She's bruised and battered, she knows she's not wanted at Nampara, she has no intention of going home to her father – but she's a born survivor – a force of nature – and something will turn up, she's sure of it . . .

DEMELZA *(cont'd – sings)*

The old man he went far from home . . . *etc.*

Tweedle, Tweedle, go twee . . .

She's reached the crest of the cliff. As she's about to descend the other side, she grinds to a halt.

HER POV: Waiting for her, on horseback, is Ross. His stern expression gives nothing away.

ROSS What've you got to sing about?

CUT TO:

104: EXT. COUNTRY ROAD – DAY 12

The sun is setting lower as Ross rides with Demelza in the saddle in front of him. A gibbet is silhouetted against the setting sun. They have come to Bargus crossroads. One way points to Illuggan. One to Truro. One to Nampara. One to London. He's about to set off (though we can't tell the direction) when the sound of galloping catches his attention.

HIS POV: A horse in the distance, coming closer, being ridden at speed. There's an urgency about the approach which makes Ross curious to stay and see what's the matter. As the horse gets nearer, Ross's expression changes – from curiosity to astonishment. The rider is Elizabeth. She's dishevelled and breathless. She reins her horse in and comes to a standstill. She's shocked to see Demelza sitting in front of Ross, but it's too late for her to turn back now.

ELIZABETH You're making a mistake.

ROSS Am I?

ELIZABETH Your place is here. Your land – your mines—

Ross can't believe what he's hearing. He dares her to say what he knows she's come to say.

ROSS Are you asking me to stay, Elizabeth?

ELIZABETH I'm saying – that everything that matters to you – is in Cornwall.

ROSS Where did you think I was going?

ELIZABETH To London. Your uncle said—

Ross is silent. The full implications of her attempt to stop him begin to sink in. It's a huge moment between them. Demelza looks from one to the other – confused, an awkward wallflower in someone else's story. For what seems an eternity, Ross grapples with the temptation to give way to his own feelings. In the end, his honesty will not let him conceal the truth.

ROSS My uncle is mistaken.

ELIZABETH *(astonished)* Then – what are you doing?

ROSS I lost sight of something. I went in search of it. Having found it, I'm going home.

He turns his horse towards Nampara.

CUT TO:

105: EXT. DERELICT WHEAL LEISURE – DAY 12

Ross rides with Demelza up to the cliff-tops towards the setting sun.

He comes to a halt beside the derelict Wheal Leisure. He contemplates it a while. Demelza looks askance at the remnants of the mine.

DEMELZA What's that to you?

ROSS My inheritance.

Episode 2

1: EXT. WHEAL LEISURE – DAWN 13

Wheal Leisure mine lies dormant.

CUT TO:

2: INT. NAMPARA HOUSE, LIBRARY – DAWN 13

Ross is looking at maps of Wheal Leisure, thoughts beginning to form.

CUT TO:

3: EXT. WHEAL LEISURE – DAWN 13

Wheal Leisure sits overlooking the sea.

CUT TO:

4: INT. NAMPARA HOUSE, KITCHEN – DAWN 13

Ross is looking at a mining artefact. Jud is watching.

JUD 'Tis in the blood, yer father'd say. Mining is in th' blood.

CUT TO:

5: EXT. TRACK NEAR WHEAL REATH MINE – DAWN 13

A group of miners, chatting affably on their way to work, walk up a path beside the sea towards Wheal Reath mine.

JUD (*VO*) Like a vein o' copper. 'Tis th' bread o' life – Eat, sleep, live an' breathe it.

CUT TO:

6: EXT. WHEAL REATH MINE – DAWN 13

A glimpse of soldiers.

CUT TO:

7: EXT. WHEAL REATH MINE – DAWN 13

A notice of closure is nailed to a wall.

CUT TO:

8: INT. BASSET HOUSE – DAWN 13

An elderly man, Lord Basset, calmly studies his reflection in the mirror as he dresses. Urgent knocks at the door call out for 'Lord Basset!'

JUD (*VO*) 'Tis yer salvation – An' yer downfall—

CUT TO:

9: EXT. TRACK NEAR WHEAL REATH MINE – DAWN 13

The miners continue, still chatting, on their way to the mine. As they get nearer, a soldier appears over the crest of the hill (behind which is the mine). He is followed by another soldier. And another. The miners slow down, puzzled. Another soldier emerges. Then two bailiffs with clubs. The miners slow down further, perplexed.

JUD (*VO*) It d' make 'ee reckless – it d'make 'ee bold—

The miners look uneasy as the soldiers and bailiffs glare down at them. They continue to approach, but warily now. Then it begins to dawn on them what this is all about. One of them pushes to the front. It's Jim Carter.

JIM 'Tedn't right! 'Ee can't do this!

CUT TO:

10: INT. NAMPARA HOUSE, KITCHEN – DAWN 13

JUD Many a friend he seen did break. Many a more he know'd would follow.

CUT TO:

11: INT. BASSET HOUSE – DAWN 13

Lord Basset continues to dress, calmly and methodically.

CUT TO:

12: EXT. TRACK NEAR WHEAL REATH MINE – DAWN 13

Jim strides forward, but as he does so, one of the bailiffs calmly strikes him across the face with his riding crop.

JUD (*VO*) 'Tis a fool's game. Twill end in tears.

CUT TO:

13: INT. NAMPARA HOUSE, KITCHEN – DAWN 13

ROSS (*dry*) I admire your optimism.

JUD Yer father died afore 'is time—

ROSS In his bed—

JUD A brokken man. 'Tis mining did fer 'im. And he won't be the last neither.

CUT TO:

14: INT. BASSET HOUSE – DAWN 13

Lord Basset, now dressed, calmly takes something from a drawer in his desk. It's a pistol.

CUT TO:

15: INT. NAMPARA HOUSE, KITCHEN – DAWN 13

JUD Were he 'ere today, 'e'd tell 'ee to not t' make th' same mistake.

ROSS I wonder.

CUT TO:

16: EXT. BASSET HOUSE – DAWN 13

Silence. Then a gunshot rings out.

CUT TO:

17: EXT. NAMPARA VALLEY – DAWN 13

A spectacular thunderstorm breaks over the sea. Distant rain makes the horizon dark.

CUT TO:

18: EXT. NAMPARA HOUSE, HAY BARN – DAWN 13

Ross is shifting bundles of hay. He pauses to watch the breaking storm. He views his land with satisfaction. The back-breaking work of the past winter has at last started to show results. He is optimistic and hopeful. Suddenly his reverie is broken by the sound of curses, yelps, barking and gushing water from the yard below.

DEMELZA'S VOICE Ah Judas! That's cowd!

Ross looks out to see Demelza in the yard below working the pump and plunging her head, shoulders and arms under the cold gushing water. Garrick is barking as he watches.

Demelza scrubs and pummels at herself, in a mania to scour herself clean. Presently she shakes her mane of hair, looks up, sees Ross – and scowls.

DEMELZA Sa'isfied?

ROSS Shouldn't I be?

DEMELZA T'ain't enough not a' stink? A body must scrub 'erself raw as a buttock o' beef t' please some folk!

She stomps off inside, scrubbing her hair dry. Ross laughs out loud. Now he sees in the distance the scrawny and bedraggled figure of Jim Carter approaching. As Jim gets closer Ross realizes he's in some distress.

ROSS What happened?

JIM 'Tis the mine, Ross. They closed it. They closed Wheal Reath.

CUT TO:

19: INT. WARLEGGAN HOUSE, LIBRARY – DAWN 13

George comes in, wearing his dressing-gown, to find Cary already at breakfast.

GEORGE Is it true?

Cary glances at him, unconcerned.

GEORGE *(cont'd)* About Lord Basset?

CARY It would appear so.

GEORGE Will we be blamed?

CARY Did we furnish the pistol?

GEORGE We called in his loans.

CARY We declined to extend them.

George joins Cary at the table.

GEORGE Does it reflect poorly on us? – that we let his pleas fall upon deaf ears?

CARY Are we in the business of sentiment or profit?

George weighs this up. It's a defining moment for him: the choice between his better or darker side.

Margaret appears in the doorway, dishevelled, flirtatious, newly risen from George's bed.

MARGARET Will I be goin' now, Mister George?

GEORGE Have you been dismissed?

MARGARET No – but 'appen I 'ave other 'engagements'.

GEORGE None that reward you so well. *(then)* Return to my chamber. *(then)* And in future you will address me as 'sir'.

MARGARET Yes, sir.

She's not entirely sure if he's joking. And neither is he.

She does as she's told. He sits down and helps himself to breakfast. He reaches a conclusion:

GEORGE These ancient families lack backbone. I wonder they survive.

CUT TO:

20: EXT. NAMPARA HOUSE – DAY 13

Ross has come out to see Jim. Jim's breathing is wheezy.

JIM Why would they close it?

ROSS Believe me, this is the bank's doing, not the owner's.

JIM Now Grambler's the on'y mine left hereabouts—

ROSS Is my uncle taking on men?

JIM *(shakes head)* Even if he were, my breathin's that bad—

ROSS You'd welcome a few months 'above grass'?

JIM I need t' work, Ross. Or mother an' sisters'll starve. Can 'ee use a farm 'and?

Ross hesitates. He has no money to take on a farm-hand but the plight of Jim and his family excites his pity.

CUT TO:

21: INT. NAMPARA HOUSE, HALLWAY – DAY 13

Ross comes in, to be greeted by Prudie. Demelza lurks behind her.

PRUDIE So now we be 'ome to all the waifs n' strays o' th' county?

Ross ignores her, goes into the library and shuts the door.

PRUDIE *(cont'd)* Rags 'n' tatters o' Wheal Reath an' their beggin' bowls!

She stomps off. Demelza remains, looking at the closed door of the library, wondering what lies behind the door.

CUT TO:

22: INT. NAMPARA HOUSE, LIBRARY – DAY 13

The library contains shelves of books, several large chests and a spinet. It's by far the grandest room in the house though it's clear that it hasn't been used for some time. Ross's souvenirs from America have been dumped there. (Among the artefacts are several knives and a tomahawk). Ross is looking at the money Charles gave him. He now knows what he must do.

CUT TO:

23: EXT. CLIFF-TOP RIDE – DAY 13

Ross rides towards Trenwith. He looks determined.

CUT TO:

24: EXT. TRENWITH HOUSE, DRIVE – DAY 13

The skies are brightening as Ross rides up to Trenwith House. As he gets off his horse, he spots Elizabeth in an upstairs window. It's the first time they've seen each other since she rode after him to persuade him not to leave. Embarrassed at being caught watching him, she moves swiftly away from the window.

CUT TO:

25: INT. TRENWITH HOUSE, DINING ROOM – DAY 13

Verity is serving breakfast to Charles and Aunt Agatha when Ross is shown in.

VERITY Ross!

She takes his hands in hers and squeezes them warmly.

AUNT AGATHA Still here, boy? When d'you leave for London?

Ross smiles, half-apologetic. He's expecting this to be difficult. Verity continues to tend to her father's needs.

ROSS My uncle's been more than generous—

He hands over the letter (and money) Charles had sent him.

ROSS *(cont'd)* But I'm minded to stay and take my chances here.

Charles takes back the letter, checks inside to see that the money is untouched. He looks stern and we expect him to explode. But instead . . .

CHARLES As I expected. Stubborn as your father!

ROSS Little good it did him!

CHARLES *(to Ross)* I fancy you'll do better.

Ross glances sideways at Verity (who continues to clear the table). Charles raps the table to call for Verity's attention. She pours tea for him.

ROSS You heard about Wheal Reath?

CHARLES *(nods)* And the owner? Lord Basset shot himself. Bad business. Very bad.

ROSS Does Grambler have loans with the Warleggans?

CHARLES Everyone has loans with the Warleggans.

ROSS That doesn't alarm you?

CHARLES George is like a brother to Francis.

Another glance between Verity and Ross. Then, seeing Charles continue to demand Verity's attention . . .

ROSS *(to Verity)* You must visit me soon.

CHARLES And neglect her duties here?

Verity gives an apologetic smile.

CHARLES *(cont'd)* She's no time to go gadding about!

He signals her to provide him with milk and sugar.

CHARLES *(cont'd – to Ross)* Well, I trust you've learnt one lesson today? *(beat)* The hazards of owning a mine?

CUT TO:

26: EXT. TRENWITH HOUSE, DRIVE – DAY 13

Elizabeth watches Ross depart from the turret room.

CUT TO:

27: INT. TRENWITH HOUSE, ELIZABETH'S ROOM – DAY 13

Elizabeth paces her room, clearly in turmoil. Sitting at her dressing-table, she tries to compose herself. The sound of a footstep behind her alerts her that Francis has entered her sanctuary. She composes herself and turns to greet him.

FRANCIS Feeling tired, my dear?

ELIZABETH A little. Perhaps I should rest a while.

FRANCIS Shall I join you?

Francis leans over and nuzzles her neck. Elizabeth stiffens momentarily, then yields to her husband's desires.

CUT TO:

28: EXT. NAMPARA HOUSE – DAY 14

Demelza is scrubbing linens in a tub in the yard, really putting her back into it. Jud and Prudie appear. They nudge each other, silently egging each other on to torment Demelza. As she hauls the newly-washed linens out to dry, Prudie brings another gigantic pile and tips them into the tub. Demelza's face falls but she doesn't argue. Prudie looks to Jud for approval. He gestures back to her, and, to rub salt in the wound, Prudie removes her own apron and cap and throw them in as well. Jud is so tickled by this idea he now comes forward and starts to remove some of his own garments and throws them into the tub. But when he threatens to get carried away and remove all his clothes, Prudie is obliged to whack him sharply and chase him away.

CUT TO:

29: EXT. WHEAL LEISURE – DAY 14

Zacky is heading to Grambler (along with Paul and Mark) as Ross heads to Wheal Leisure.

ZACKY 'Ee 'ave a new farm-'and.

ROSS *(laughing)* Do I?

ZACKY 'Cordin' t' my Jinny.

PAUL 'Tis a fine thing 'ee done fer Jim.

ZACKY Ap'n 'ee could do same fer we? *(i.e. Zacky, Mark and Paul)* Below grass!

ROSS You have pitches already – at Grambler.

ZACKY Where it please yer uncle t' pay us starvation wages. *(then)* The owners 'ave we by th' throat, Ross. We can't go on like this.

Ross digests this. It's clear that Zacky & co are placing a lot of faith and hope in him.

ROSS I can promise nothing.

Zacky nods. He knows Ross will do his utmost.

CUT TO:

30: INT. WHEAL LEISURE – DAY 14

By the light of a candle Ross examines what looks like a glint of copper in the rock.

CUT TO:

31: EXT. WHEAL LEISURE – DAY 14

Ross emerges from the mine to find Francis waiting for him.

FRANCIS Father tells me you intend to remain.

ROSS Does that disappoint you?

FRANCIS Not at all. *(genuine)* We were always more friends than cousins. I'd be sorry if that changed.

Ross considers a remark about Francis's 'friendship' in marrying Elizabeth – but decides against. Instead . . .

ROSS I've been wondering if this mine was entirely worked out.

FRANCIS You don't think of reopening her?

ROSS I'll think of anything that might help those poor devils at Wheal Reath.

FRANCIS You consider them your responsibility?

ROSS You don't?

FRANCIS My father doesn't trust me with responsibility. He likes to keep the mysteries of mine-owning to himself.

ROSS Perhaps we should open Leisure together? Share the burden and the spoils?

CUT TO:

32: EXT. TRENWITH GROUNDS – DAY 14

A clutch of eggs nestles in a hollow. A hand reaches in and takes one. It's Elizabeth's. She is collecting eggs from round the garden. They are of all shapes, sizes and colours. She examines one. It's exquisitely freckled and delicately coloured. She smiles to herself, entranced by its beauty. It's a glimpse of the Elizabeth of earlier years – more girlish, less formal, less constrained. Her moment of reverie is interrupted.

VERITY'S VOICE Elizabeth?

Elizabeth turns to see Verity coming towards her.

VERITY *(surprised)* What are you doing?

Elizabeth holds out the egg to show Verity.

VERITY *(cont'd)* This is no task for you. Let me or Mrs Tabb—

Verity tries to take the basket of eggs but Elizabeth playfully whisks it away from her.

ELIZABETH *(teasing)* What may I do then?

VERITY There is much you may do, Elizabeth. You are the lady of the house. You may go out when you choose, pay calls, attend balls—

ELIZABETH And may you not?

VERITY *(smiles patiently)* I'm twenty-five. Unmarried. I spin, I bake, I make preserves, I drill the choir at Sawle church, I dose the servants with possets when they're ill. My life is not your life.

CUT TO:

33: EXT. TRURO STREET – DAY 14

Ross heads to Pascoe's bank.

CUT TO:

34: INT. PASCOE'S OFFICE – DAY 14

Ross faces Pascoe.

ROSS Suppose I wished to open a mine?

PASCOE I'd suppose you'd taken leave of your senses.

ROSS What in the least would I require?

PASCOE Capital?

ROSS I have none.

PASCOE Expertise?

ROSS A smattering.

PASCOE Allies?

ROSS None of means. My cousin would lend his name.

PASCOE So you'd require investors.

ROSS Can you find me any?

PASCOE In these uncertain times? With no experience, no bona fides, and a reputation somewhat tarnished?

ROSS Are you speaking as my banker or my friend?

PASCOE Both. I'd advise you to seek your future elsewhere.

CUT TO:

35: INT. RED LION INN – DAY 14

Ross is sitting, thoughtful, drinking. He is observed by Margaret. She comes over and sits at his table.

MARGARET Good day, me lord.

ROSS Are we acquainted, ma'am?

MARGARET We could be.

ROSS *(smiles politely)* I've neither the time nor the money to seek such diversions.

MARGARET What do you seek, me lord?

Ross smiles. It's a good question. Before he can protest, she takes his hand and proceeds to trace her finger across his palm.

MARGARET *(cont'd)* Better days ahead, I see. A prosperous business?

ROSS *(laughs)* Perhaps you should try a different profession!

She continues to trace her finger across his palm. Ross watches, amused. Finally she halts at the ring.

MARGARET A sweetheart perhaps?

ROSS *(smiles, shakes head)* I made the mistake of going to war.

MARGARET And when you returned she was pledged to another? *(she eyes him keenly)* Yet you still care for her. *(then)* But perhaps she loves you still.

ROSS If she had loved me at all, she would have waited for me.

It's said without bitterness, without sorrow. A simple statement of fact.

CUT TO:

36: EXT. CLIFF-TOP RIDE – DAY 14

Ross is riding home when the sound of horse's hooves draws his attention. He sees a rider coming after him. It's Verity.

VERITY Ross!

ROSS Verity—

He rides to meet her.

CUT TO:

37: EXT. NAMPARA HOUSE, FIELDS – DAY 14

Verity and Ross ride towards Nampara House. Jim and Jud are working in the fields. Verity can see how much progress has been made: walls and fences mended, Nampara House beginning to look neat and cared for again.

ROSS You escaped, then?

VERITY Father's gone to the mine for an hour. *(looking at the house)* I see you've not been idle!

ROSS I needed a distraction. The house reaped the benefit.

Now they see Demelza hanging out linens, attended by Garrick. When Demelza spots Verity, she tries to slink away.

ROSS *(cont'd)* Demelza! This is my cousin Verity.

Demelza gives a cursory nod, then scurries away into the house. Ross laughs.

VERITY Has she settled?

ROSS *(laughing)* Still somewhat feral.

They ride on a while, past Jud, who is instructing Jim. Then . . .

VERITY Does your wound still pain you?

ROSS Less than it did.

VERITY Then I wonder if I might ask you the greatest of favours?

CUT TO:

38: INT. NAMPARA HOUSE, LIBRARY – DAY 15

Close Up. The ring is being toyed with. Ross sits at his desk, dressed in formal attire, ready to go out – spruced, combed, handsome – and every inch the gentleman. He glances at his invitation to the assembly. He doesn't look at all keen on the idea of going. He toys with his ring. He decides against putting it on.

Demelza is revealed, peering though a crack in the doorway. She's been sweeping the hallway and has paused on the threshold.

CUT TO:

39: INT. TRENWITH HOUSE, GREAT HALL – DAY 15

Elizabeth enters and is surprised by Francis.

FRANCIS *(cont'd)* My dear, tonight's assembly, will you not reconsider? You know how I love to show off my wife to the world.

Elizabeth smiles reluctantly. We suspect she will give way.

CUT TO:

40: INT. NAMPARA HOUSE, LIBRARY – DAY 15

Ross gets up, puts the ring away, gathers his things and walks out of the room, past Demelza. After he's gone, Demelza is joined by Prudie.

DEMELZA Where's he goin'?

PRUDIE To the dance?

DEMELZA 'E don' look too glad about it.

PRUDIE Gentlefolks is strange.

CUT TO:

41: INT. ASSEMBLY ROOMS, STAIRCASE – NIGHT 15

The Assembly Rooms are a blaze of lights. Among the guests arriving are Ross and Verity.

Ross looks extremely handsome and wears his dress-clothes well, though it's clear he's not entirely delighted to be here. Verity is full of trepidation. She clutches his arm nervously.

VERITY I'm obliged to you, Ross.

ROSS For vanquishing my loathing of a gavotte?

VERITY For persuading Father to let me come.

ROSS As official escort, I'm entirely at your service.

VERITY Don't be! *(seeing him about to protest)* We neither of us come much into society. We should make the most of all it has to offer.

Ross forces a smile. He can see that Verity's delight at being here is tempered by nervousness. He squeezes her hand reassuringly.

CUT TO:

42: INT. ASSEMBLY ROOMS, MAIN HALL – NIGHT 15

Ross escorts Verity into the midst of a room which is not especially grand but which is ablaze with candles and is populated by a cross-section of Cornish society. The dancing has already begun. The air is vibrant with gossip and laughter, the tapping of heels, the rustle of silk. There is a strong nautical presence among the guests. Nervous as she is, it doesn't take long for Verity to notice the attention the handsome young Captain Poldark is attracting. Ross, of course, is oblivious.

VERITY Look to your liberty, Cousin.

ROSS Is it in danger?

VERITY From a great many girls who would be glad to acquire the name of Poldark!

Ross glances round. For the first time he sees what Verity can see: many girls and ladies (including Mrs Teague and her daughters Faith, Hope, Patience and Ruth) with their eyes on him, smiling, giggling, whispering behind their fans. Ruth Teague flashes Ross a dazzling smile. Ross forces a smile in return.

CUT TO:

43: INT. ASSEMBLY ROOMS, ANTE-ROOM – NIGHT 15

George Warleggan is playing cards and drinking with a coterie of wealthy men, including Dr Choake, and Francis.

DR CHOAKE Those ruffians at Wheal Reath made a nuisance of themselves.

GEORGE You'd hardly expect them to celebrate the closure.

DR CHOAKE They've no business to have an opinion at all!

Some of the other men roar with laughter. Francis is not amongst them.

FRANCIS Some would say that view is outdated.

George looks up with interest – he suspects this is something Francis picked up from Ross.

FRANCIS *(cont'd)* In America for instance – they have more liberal views—

GEORGE *(laughing)* All men created equal?

DR CHOAKE Preposterous! Distinctions of rank must be preserved.

FRANCIS Especially when they're so dearly bought?

CUT TO:

44: INT. NAMPARA HOUSE, DRAWING ROOM – NIGHT 15

Demelza is scrubbing the hearth while Prudie lounges in a chair. Jud goes to the big cupboard, gets out a bottle of brandy, pours some for himself and Prudie.

JUD T' th' 'Trade'!

PRUDIE An' t' Cap'n Ross! – providin' f'r our ease an' comfort!

Demelza looks up from her scouring to pass Prudie a cushion. Demelza returns to her chores, Prudie to her brandy.

PRUDIE *(cont'd)* This be the life!

CUT TO:

45: INT. ASSEMBLY ROOMS, ANTE-ROOM – NIGHT 15

Ross strolls out of the dancing room and immediately runs into George.

GEORGE Not dancing, Ross? Will none of the ladies have you?

Ross smiles. He has no wish to take offence so early in the evening. George wrinkles his nose and sniffs.

GEORGE *(cont'd)* The whiff of soil is hard to swill off – but if one communes with peasants—

ROSS D'you prescribe perfume?

GEORGE It covers a multitude of sins!

ROSS Like money.

GEORGE Indeed! For how else would a family of blacksmiths become bankers?

They both laugh. Beneath the lighthearted banter, an edge has crept in. But neither acknowledges it.

GEORGE *(cont'd – smiling)* One of these days you may come knocking.

ROSS *(smiling)* I would need to be desperate.

GEORGE *(smiling)* I look forward to the prospect.

Ross smiles pleasantly, bows and moves off. George watches him go, smiling in turn.

CUT TO:

46: INT. ASSEMBLY ROOMS, MAIN HALL – NIGHT 15

There's a hiatus in the dancing. Ross is watching Verity, who is sitting without a partner. They catch each other's eye across the room. Their attention is caught by an outburst of laughter as a group of naval men come in. Among them is a man in his late 30s: Captain Andrew Blamey.

Andrew spots Verity across the crowded room. He seems very taken by her.

ANDREW *(to one of his companions)* You know that lady?

Verity looks up, realizes she's the object of scrutiny, finds herself smiling at Andrew.

Meanwhile, Ruth Teague has contrived to pass by so close to Ross that he is forced to acknowledge her.

RUTH Captain Poldark.

ROSS Miss Teague. How do you find your first ball?

RUTH *(simpering)* Exceeding all expectations, sir!

Ross forces a smile. He suspects he is her target for the evening. A glance at Mrs Teague and the rest of her daughters, all watching avidly, confirms Ross's suspicions. Ross now looks round for Verity.

HIS POV: *Verity, now rather flushed, is being introduced to Andrew Blamey.*

ON VERITY & ANDREW: *Though their conversation is awkward, the attraction between them is obvious.*

VERITY A sea captain? How – invigorating!

ANDREW One is seldom – idle—

VERITY And so much to remember – the sails – the masts—

ANDREW Are you interested in rigging, ma'am?

VERITY Oh, exceedingly!

Ross catches Verity's eye, raises an eyebrow at her. She flushes. Both acknowledge the fact of the other's partner. Then Verity turns back, smiling shyly, to Andrew Blamey while Ross forces himself to smile at the gushing Ruth Teague.

RUTH Are you fond of dancing, Captain Poldark?

ROSS I fear I possess few of the refinements of polite society, ma'am.

CUT TO:

47: INT. NAMPARA HOUSE, CORRIDOR – NIGHT 15

An exhausted Demelza, carrying a candle, is on her way to bed when she notices the door to the library is ajar. Curious, she can't resist taking a peek inside.

CUT TO:

48: INT. NAMPARA HOUSE, LIBRARY – NIGHT 15

Demelza shines the candle round the library. The flickering flame catches various objects and throws up strange shapes against the walls. Her attention is caught by the spinet. Curious, she makes her way over to it.

CUT TO:

49: INT. NAMPARA HOUSE, HALLWAY – NIGHT 15

Jud and Prudie, roaring drunk, stagger up the stairs to bed, Jud carrying a bottle of rum, both of them singing raucously.

CUT TO:

50: INT. NAMPARA HOUSE, LIBRARY – NIGHT 15

Demelza hears the sounds of Jud and Prudie staggering off to bed, singing. She closes the spinet for fear of being caught red-handed. As she moves away from it, the candle light falls on a map of Wheal Leisure. She is fascinated by the books, the maps, the samples of copper ore on the table.

CUT TO:

51: INT. ASSEMBLY ROOMS, STAIRCASE – NIGHT 15

Ross encounters a group of men which includes Horace Treneglos, Mine Captain Henshawe and Harris Pascoe.

HORACE TRENEGLOS Ross Poldark! Seen you sniffing

round that old strumpet th' other day! *(roaring with laughter)* Wheal Leisure? You don't think of resurrecting her?

PASCOE It would take a brave man to open a mine now. Don't you agree, Henshawe?

HENSHAWE Depends on the mine.

ROSS *(recognizing him)* Mr Henshawe? You were mine captain at Leisure in my father's day?

HENSHAWE I was.

ROSS You worked her for tin?

HENSHAWE Aye.

ROSS But in the last samples taken, there were definite signs of copper.

HENSHAWE A pity she closed before we could dig further.

Ross suddenly becomes aware that George Warleggan is nearby – and though he's chatting to someone else, Ross has the distinct impression that he's listening in.

ROSS *(to Pascoe)* But if you know of anyone who'd be willing to chance a little speculation?

Pascoe's expression is a little more promising. The conversation between Ross and Henshawe tells him the cause may not be as hopeless as he'd first assumed.

PASCOE I'll see what can be done.

Ross moves closer to Pascoe so that George can't eavesdrop.

ROSS I'd require discretion.

PASCOE I fully comprehend you, sir.

They both glance towards George, and Ross is pleased to see that Pascoe at least understands his misgivings.

CUT TO:

52: INT. ASSEMBLY ROOMS, MAIN HALL – NIGHT 15

Verity is flushed and bright-eyed as she studies a sketch of a ship which Andrew has drawn her.

VERITY The – mizzenmast – you say?

ANDREW Which is part square-rigged and carries a gaff—

VERITY *(trying to memorize it)* A gaff—

ANDREW And a spanker boom—

VERITY So many names!—

ANDREW *(blurting it out)* When may I see you again— ?

VERITY Oh! – Captain Blamey – that I couldn't say.

CUT TO:

53: INT. NAMPARA HOUSE, CORRIDOR – NIGHT 15

The corridor is in darkness as Demelza emerges from the library, silently closes the door and begins to tiptoe away. Suddenly the floor creaks menacingly behind her. She gasps and wheels round . . . to be greeted by the leering face of the drunken Jud.

DEMELZA Judas!

JUD What 'ee be doin' in there?

DEMELZA Jus' lookin'.

JUD Jus' lookin'?

DEMELZA There's books – an' maps – an' knives – an' 'arpicord—

JUD Can 'ee read? Can 'ee play?

DEMELZA Can try—

JUD Be nothin' in there f'th' likes o' we. *(beat)* Less we be gettin' ideas above's station?

DEMELZA No!

JUD Go 'ome—

DEMELZA What?

JUD Back where 'ee come fr'm. 'Ee dun't b'long 'ere.

Demelza looks at him in dismay. He stomps off upstairs.

CUT TO:

54: INT. ASSEMBLY ROOMS, MAIN HALL – NIGHT 15

ANDREW Forgive me. I've no wish to appear forward but – I'd dearly like us to be better acquainted.

VERITY I too. *(then)* I should not have said that! What must you think of me?

ANDREW Can you be unaware of that, ma'am?

Verity blushes. Andrew smiles encouragingly. Their ineptitude at courtship is endearing.

ON ROSS: Standing in the doorway between the Main Hall and Hallway. Watching Verity from a distance. He's never seen her so vivacious and suspects at once that she has formed an attachment. Now he is accosted, as if by accident, by Ruth Teague.

RUTH Remind me, Captain Poldark, was I engaged to you for the next dance?

ROSS Er – not that I can recall – would you excuse me?

He bows and walks off. Ruth looks puzzled and very put out. Ross goes over to Elizabeth and Francis. (Andrew and Verity are following behind.)

FRANCIS Ah, Ross, are you come to take my wife off my hands?

ROSS If she's no objection.

Ross bows to Elizabeth. For a moment it seems Elizabeth will object.

ELIZABETH *(to Francis)* Did you not promise me this dance?

FRANCIS The cotillion. And I dare say Ross will return you to me in one piece!

He gives Elizabeth's hand to Ross. She shudders imperceptibly, as if Ross's touch has sent a tingle through her. He feels it too. Their eyes meet briefly, then she looks down, unable to trust herself not to give herself away. Ross leads Elizabeth to the dance – oblivious to the raised eyebrows, and murmured whispers from various bystanders.

ON VERITY: She's noticed – both Ross and Elizabeth together and the interest it's creating. She glances at Francis to see his reaction.

ON FRANCIS: Seemingly oblivious to the attention his wife and cousin are attracting. Now he is joined by George. Together they stand and watch the dancing a while.

ON GEORGE: Watching Ross and Elizabeth, then glancing at Francis to gauge his reaction.

ON ROSS AND ELIZABETH: Elizabeth, initially awkward, restrained, refusing to make eye contact. But every time the dance requires them to touch, her resistance seems to melt. Ross senses it too.

ON GEORGE: Watching Ross and Elizabeth. Again he glances at Francis. Again Francis seems oblivious.

GEORGE Your cousin is most attentive.

FRANCIS *(distracted)* Eh?

GEORGE To your wife.

FRANCIS Oh, I don't think he cares for dancing. He only came to please Verity.

They both look at Verity, who is now dancing with Andrew.

FRANCIS *(cont'd)* Who is that man?

GEORGE Captain Blamey? Master of the Lisbon packet. A pretty catch. *(beat)* And at her age—

FRANCIS She won't get many more chances? But Father couldn't spare her.

GEORGE And Elizabeth would miss her. *(beat)* Though doubtless your wife would find ways of distracting herself.

It's said lightly, but something in George's tone makes Francis look anew at Ross and Elizabeth.

HIS POV: Ross and Elizabeth dancing as if no one else in the room existed.

ON FRANCIS: Thoughtful. The idea planted by George has begun to take root.

Elizabeth's resistance has evaporated. It's clear to her – and Ross – that her feelings, their feelings for each other, are by no means a thing of the past.

As the dance ends, Ross and Elizabeth are flushed and smiling. Ross is oblivious to the many eyes which are now on them.

His feelings (and possibly the wine) make him heady and optimistic. As they leave the dance they run into Verity, who is still talking animatedly to Andrew Blamey.

VERITY *(flustered)* Oh! Ross – may I introduce – ? Captain Andrew Blamey – my cousin Ross – my sister-in-law, Elizabeth—

ANDREW Your servant, ma'am, sir.

He bows stiffly. Elizabeth and Ross, still giddy from the dance, stifle a giggle.

ELIZABETH I hope our boisterous spirits don't offend you, sir?

ANDREW Not in the least, ma'am. I've every reason to be happy myself.

As Ross and Elizabeth walk on . . .

ANDREW *(cont'd – low)* If I could dare to hope – that my interest was in the smallest way returned—

VERITY *(low)* I think you might dare to hope that, sir.

Verity is clearly smitten with Andrew – but seeing Ross continue with Elizabeth on his arm – and seeing the attention it continues to excite – she is distracted away from Andrew.

ANDREW May I speak with your father? You may think me presumptuous but – my attachment is sincere – and I would not wish to proceed without his approval—

Verity is only half-listening. She is distracted by the alarming spectacle of Ross paying Elizabeth such attentions.

ANDREW *(cont'd)* But first, there's something I must tell you—

VERITY *(distracted)* Forgive me – I must speak with my cousin—

She excuses herself from Andrew – who seems disappointed – and fights her way through the crowds towards them.

CUT TO:

55: INT. ASSEMBLY ROOMS, MAIN HALL – NIGHT 15

Ross and Elizabeth are smiling, whispering together, oblivious to the interest they are exciting. Verity now approaches.

VERITY *(to Elizabeth)* My dear, I believe Francis is looking for you.

Elizabeth flushes, conscious that her behaviour with Ross is dangerously close to impropriety. She bows to Ross and leaves.

ON ELIZABETH: *Visibly relieved – as if in separating herself from*

Ross, she's been given the chance to step out of her recklessness and back into normality.

Left alone with Ross, Verity struggles to get to the point without causing offence.

VERITY *(cont'd)* People love to gossip.

ROSS Isn't that why they come to such evenings?

VERITY But to give them cause? To make your attentions so pronounced?

Ross seems about to argue, but thinks better of it.

VERITY *(cont'd)* Whatever was between you, trust me, she has put it behind her. *(seeing him about to disagree)* So must you.

She draws his attention to Elizabeth, who has been detained by a group of attentive men.

ON ELIZABETH: Smiling graciously, enjoying the attention. Now Francis comes for her and leads her away.

Ross is brought down to earth with a bump. Verity notices and is sorry for him.

VERITY *(cont'd)* You'll take supper with us?

ROSS Thank you. I've no appetite.

He strides across the room towards the exit, leaving behind a flushed Elizabeth, a murmur of gossip and whispering, a dismayed Ruth and Mrs Teague – and Andrew and Verity.

ANDREW Miss Verity, I cannot go to your father without your being in full possession of the facts—

CUT TO:

56: INT. ASSEMBLY ROOMS, STAIRCASE – NIGHT 15

Ross is heading up the stairs towards the exit when George's voice accosts him from below.

GEORGE'S VOICE Ross Poldark in love?

Ross halts, turns to see George smiling at the bottom of the staircase.

GEORGE Quite the spectacle. *(beat)* Though may I say, an excellent choice. *(Ross makes to walk on without replying)* Ruth Teague is unlikely to remind one of a previous attachment.

It's the final straw. Not trusting himself to keep his temper, Ross abruptly leaves.

CUT TO:

57: EXT. TRURO STREET – NIGHT 15

Ross storms out of the Assembly Rooms, heading to the Red Lion.
CUT TO:

58: INT. RED LION INN – NIGHT 15

Ross barges into the inn. Customers look up in surprise as he enters. He orders rum, knocks it back in one, orders another. Now he scans the room – and soon finds what he's looking for: a scantily dressed woman. As she turns, he realizes it's Margaret. Better still. She flashes him a dazzling smile.

MARGARET May I be of service, me lord?

ROSS One service is all I require.

CUT TO:

59: INT. NAMPARA HOUSE, KITCHEN – NIGHT 15

The house is silent. Demelza, still smarting from Jud's verbal attack, is lying curled up on the floor beside Garrick.

CUT TO:

60: INT. MARGARET'S LODGING – DAWN 16

The first grey light of dawn reveals Ross's best boots, abandoned on the floor. Ross awakens and for a moment cannot remember where he is. Then a naked and dishevelled Margaret rises up from the bed beside him and he remembers all too well.

MARGARET You don't say much, me lord. *(no reply)* But p'raps you don't pay me for my conversation.

ROSS My apologies. I was not in a talkative mood last night.

One hand is lying across the pillow. Margaret takes it, traces her finger across it.

MARGARET A rare hand – *(tracing his palm)* Knows what it wants – *(tracing his palm)* But not always how to get it.

CUT TO:

61: EXT. CLIFF-TOPS – DAWN 16

Demelza is up early, gathering wild flowers. Garrick is with her. Below her, in Nampara Valley, she hears a horse approaching and presently sees a bleary-eyed Ross returning home after his night with Margaret.

CUT TO:

62: EXT. NAMPARA COVE – DAWN 16

Ross dismounts, strips off his clothes and dives into the sea. Presently he emerges from the waves, shaking himself as if to cleanse himself of the night before.

Demelza is revealed, watching him, unseen, from the cliffs above. As she watches the water glisten on his skin, she becomes aware of him – as a man, rather than an employer – for the first time. The thought is both exciting and disquieting to her. Ross is completely oblivious.

CUT TO:

63: INT. NAMPARA HOUSE, PARLOUR – DAY 16

Ross is studying the map of Wheal Leisure as Demelza brings his food. He barely notices her. There is a rap at the door. Demelza goes to answer it. Presently she returns with Charles.

ROSS Uncle – to what do I— ?

CHARLES Opening a mine? Despite our conversation?

ROSS Exploring the idea—

Charles contemplates Ross, shakes his head as if in dismay.

CHARLES Stubborn. Rash. Won't take no for an answer—

ROSS Well—

CHARLES The curse of the Poldarks. *(beat)* And our salvation! I salute you, boy. Take Francis with you. He needs to learn some initiative. When d'you meet?

ROSS Tomorrow – if Pascoe can drum up any interest—

CHARLES Francis will come. He must learn to stand on his own two feet. You must help him.

ROSS I will, Uncle, of course. *(a thought occurs)* But if you could urge discretion—

CHARLES Especially with regard to his good friend George?

Ross nods. He's glad to see that Charles understands the need for secrecy.

CUT TO:

64: EXT. NAMPARA HOUSE – DAY 17

Jim brings round Ross's horse. Ross comes out, carrying a travelling bag and a rolled-up map.

JIM 'E's ready fer 'ee, sur—

Ross prepares to leave. Now he looks round for Demelza.

ROSS *(shouts)* Demelza!

Demelza comes running from round the side of the house, carrying an armful of logs. She looks exhausted. Ross looks at her narrowly. In the doorway Jud and Prudie are slouching, making no attempt to help her.

ROSS *(cont'd)* What's the matter?

DEMELZA Sur— ?

ROSS You look weary to the bone. Have they been making you a beast of burden?

DEMELZA No sur, I be content, sur—

He eyes her narrowly. Is she telling the whole truth? Jud and Prudie slink further inside the doorway.

DEMELZA *(cont'd – suddenly)* It be tha' Jud? 'E be sayin' I got ideas? I an't got ideas!

ROSS No?

DEMELZA I d'know me place!

ROSS Your place is where I say it is. Fetch your cloak.

DEMELZA *(puzzled)* Sur— ?

Ross mounts his horse. Demelza considers a moment, then . . .

DEMELZA *(cont'd)* Never 'ad no cloak.

CUT TO:

65: EXT. COASTAL PATHWAY – DAY 17

Ross and Demelza ride to Truro. Tiny figures in a huge landscape. Demelza singing happily, enjoying the day, the landscape, her new life. Ross thoughtful, oblivious to Demelza though she sits behind him.

CUT TO:

66: EXT. HARBOUR, LOWER LEVEL – DAY 17

Ross rides towards Truro harbour with Demelza seated behind him. Ross looks alert and full of anticipation. He's unaware of Demelza shivering behind him (the wind is chilly and her arms are bare).

Several passers-by glance at them as they pass. Ross dismounts to deposit Demelza at the harbour.

ROSS This is an important day for us both. *(counts out some coins for her)* Let's see who can strike the better bargain.

Demelza heads for fish sellers. As Ross returns to his horse he sees, in the distance through a crowd of people, a figure he recognizes.

ROSS *(cont'd – calling out)* Verity?

Verity freezes, half-turns her head, then continues walking away. Ross mounts his horse. When he looks again Verity has disappeared. Puzzled – was it even Verity he saw? – Ross rides on.

CUT TO:

67: EXT. HABERDASHER'S – DAY 17

Elizabeth comes out of the haberdasher's – and runs straight into Ross.

ROSS Elizabeth—

ELIZABETH *(flustered)* Oh! – Ross! – is Francis with you?

ROSS At the inn. Can I be of service?

ELIZABETH I believe I can manage—

Nevertheless Ross takes from her the packages she's carrying. As their fingers touch, a frisson goes through them.

ELIZABETH *(cont'd)* Did you enjoy the assembly? Ruth Teague seemed very taken with you.

ROSS I scarcely remember her.

ELIZABETH How could that be?

ROSS There were distractions.

ELIZABETH Perhaps you should pursue her.

ROSS Would that please you?

ELIZABETH *(flustered)* I must go. Verity will be looking for me.

She hurries away. As Ross hangs back to let her go ahead, he becomes aware of George, who's just about to go into the Red Lion – and has witnessed this entire encounter. As George strolls indoors, Ross curses silently.

CUT TO:

68: EXT. HARBOUR – DAY 17

Demelza, haggling at the harbour with a fishmonger, sees something which surprises her:

HER POV: Verity emerging from a harbour-front house, followed by Andrew Blamey. He seems to be imploring her to stay, but she seems anxious and hurries away from him.

Demelza watches her go, then turns back to haggle with the fishmonger.

CUT TO:

69: INT. RED LION INN – DAY 17

George is whispering to Francis as Ross comes in. George smiles and walks away. Immediately Ross knows something has changed.

ROSS *(low)* Shall we go?

FRANCIS I'm in no mood to speculate.

ROSS May I ask why?

FRANCIS I need something I can depend on.

For a moment they look each other in the eye. Then Francis signals to George to bring over more rum. Full of regret, Ross leaves.

CUT TO:

70: EXT. STREET – DAY 17

Ross, carrying the travelling bag and rolled-up map, arrives at a door and goes inside.

CUT TO:

71: INT. PRIVATE ROOM, INN – DAY 17

Ross unfurls the map and spreads it out on a large table. It's the map of the workings of Wheal Leisure. In the middle he places a sample of copper ore. Presently the door opens and several men come in. They are: Captain Henshawe, Mr Renfrew (a mine chandler) Dr Choake, Horace Treneglos and 4 others.

HENSHAWE *(to Ross, low)* Are we expecting your cousin?

ROSS Francis has changed his mind.

HENSHAWE A pity. He would've lent a certain—

ROSS *(smiling)* Gravity? That I lack?

Henshawe is too polite to agree, but it's clear Ross is right. The rest of the men take their places round the table. Amidst them Ross looks callow and inexperienced. He knows he's going to have to step up if he wants to make an impression.

ROSS *(cont'd)* Gentlemen, welcome. You come here today to decide one thing: whether to risk good gold in the pursuit of copper.

He looks round at the other men. They look stern-faced and seem unlikely to be easily impressed.

DR CHOAKE The times could hardly be less auspicious. When Wheal Reath closes—

HORACE TRENEGLOS And Grambler's future hangs in the balance.

DR CHOAKE When Welsh mines prosper and Cornwall's on its knees – what chance has this meagre venture?

CUT TO:

72: INT. RED LION INN – DAY 17

George and Francis are playing cards, drinking brandy. Francis, moody and preoccupied, is watched keenly by George.

GEORGE Your cousin divides opinion. Some think him arrogant. Others observe a sense of – entitlement—

FRANCIS To what?

GEORGE Whatever takes his fancy. *(no reply)* But perhaps they misjudge him. *(no reply)* So what do I hear of his latest venture?

Francis hesitates. Then . . .

FRANCIS What do you hear?

CUT TO:

73: INT. PRIVATE ROOM, INN – DAY 17

Negotiations continue.

ROSS My thinking is this: the venture is small – so overheads will be low. Without Reath, supply to the markets will fall – so the price of copper should rise—

DR CHOAKE And if it doesn't?

CUT TO:

74: INT. RED LION INN – DAY 17

George and Francis continue to drink and play cards.

GEORGE Is he seeking investment?

FRANCIS I – really couldn't say.

George eyes Francis keenly and suppresses a smile. He suspects Francis is lying.

CUT TO:

75: INT. PRIVATE ROOM, INN – DAY 17

Negotiations continue.

HORACE TRENEGLOS So the question is: what will it cost us?

ROSS To begin with I propose to act as manager and head purser without salary.

Reactions of surprise from round the table.

ROSS *(cont'd)* If Captain Henshawe would oversee the works—

HENSHAWE Also without salary?

ROSS At a favourable rate – till we're up and running—

Captain Henshawe pulls a face, but doesn't give an outright refusal.

ROSS *(cont'd)* If Mr Renfrew would supply gear and tackle at nominal cost—

DR CHOAKE The man has impudence!

ROSS Pascoe's Bank will honour our drafts up to three hundred pounds—

DR CHOAKE Pascoe's Bank?

ROSS Yes?

DR CHOAKE Not Warleggan's?

CUT TO:

76: INT. RED LION INN – DAY 17

GEORGE Warleggan's would be happy to accommodate him. *(no reply)* Given the friendship between our families. *(no reply)* But perhaps he doesn't value friendship. *(beat)* Or family.

CUT TO:

77: INT. PRIVATE ROOM, INN – DAY 17

Negotiations continue.

ROSS Warleggan's will lend to a mine for as long as it prospers – but once it starts to struggle, they withdraw credit and see it go under. They could close Grambler tomorrow – as they closed Reath. Business is business but should profit be the be-all and end-all?

For a while no one speaks. Ross is beginning to lose hope. Then . . .

HENSHAWE I'm inclined to agree. We know Reath was struggling, but closing it cost the shareholders dear—

ROSS And the miners dearer.

HORACE TRENEGLOS And the owner his life.

A murmur of agreement round the table.

CUT TO:

78: INT. RED LION INN – DAY 17

George continues to work on Francis. The card game continues.

GEORGE We cannot choose our family. But we can choose our friends. And as a friend, I say to you, if ever you need my assistance—

FRANCIS What assistance might I need?

GEORGE What any man needs. Someone to alert him if he sees his friend being played for a fool.

FRANCIS A fool?

GEORGE In love – in business – at cards—

FRANCIS It's true – my losses of late have been considerable—

GEORGE Then may I prove our friendship by advancing whatever might defray them?

CUT TO:

79: INT. PRIVATE ROOM, INN – DAY 17

Discussions continue.

ROSS Gentlemen, I'll be straight with you. The rewards could be considerable but so are the risks. But if you like a wager – and which of us doesn't? – then I'd sooner gamble on a vein of copper and the sweat of fifty men than on the turn of a card.

No one speaks. Ross has no high hopes of success. Nevertheless . . .

ROSS *(cont'd)* Fifty guineas apiece will cover the first three months.

He gets a banker's draft out of his pocket and puts it on the table.

ROSS *(cont'd)* There's mine.

It's a big moment. The other men exchange glances. For a moment we think Ross will be the only one to make the commitment. But then : . .

HENSHAWE And mine.

HORACE TRENEGLOS And mine.

Silently the others all follow suit. Ross tries, and fails, to suppress a smile of satisfaction. After everyone round the table has pledged their fifty pounds . . .

ROSS If I may take the liberty of proposing a toast— ?

HENSHAWE A toast.

ROSS To Wheal Leisure!

They all raise their glasses and toast.

ALL Wheal Leisure!

They all rise and shake hands. Ross is feeling buoyant and full of optimism. As the others pack up to leave, Ross begins to roll up the map. As he does so he glances out of the window:

HIS POV: George Warleggan, walking down the street with his arm round Francis's shoulder, laughing.

ON ROSS: He is not happy. He suspects his venture is no longer safe from the long reach of George Warleggan.

CUT TO:

80: EXT. STREET – DAY 17

Ross comes out of a doorway (leading to the Private Room) – to be greeted by the sight of a shivering Demelza clutching a large barrel of pilchards.

DEMELZA 'E tried a' swizzle me but I beat 'im down!

ROSS I expected no less. *(then)* A good day's work for us both!

The other investors now come out. They give Demelza curious looks (they've heard rumours about Ross Poldark's kitchen maid – and the use he makes of her!) Henshawe raises his eyebrows appreciatively, Dr Choake also steals an approving glance when he thinks no one's looking. Demelza scowls at them defiantly.

DEMELZA What am I? A circus attraction?

ROSS A poorly dressed one!

Demelza looks affronted, but Ross is laughing.

ROSS *(cont'd)* Come with me.

He strides off down the street. Demelza follows, clutching her pilchards.

CUT TO:

81: EXT. HABERDASHER'S – DAY 17

A barrel of pilchards sits outside the haberdasher's shop. Presently the door opens and Demelza comes out, wearing a new red cloak. She is unable to stop grinning. Ross follows, picks up the pilchard barrel and walks beside her. As they walk past, several people turn to look at them, some begin whispering behind their hands.

Demelza struts proudly down the street, oblivious to the attention she's attracting. Ross barely seems to notice.

CUT TO:

82: INT. TRENWITH HOUSE, TURRET ROOM – DAY 17

Elizabeth looks thoughtful. She is toying with the invitation card to the assembly rooms. She becomes aware of raised voices from downstairs in the Great Hall.

CHARLES'S VOICE This cannot continue – she must be brought to her senses—

FRANCIS'S VOICE She must indeed. But what of him? Has he no sense of shame?

CHARLES'S VOICE I hold her most to blame! She must have encouraged him—

FRANCIS'S VOICE If you had seen her at the assembly!—

CHARLES'S VOICE But you were there! Could you not have put a stop to it?

FRANCIS'S VOICE I should not have needed to! She should be mistress of her own behaviour—

CHARLES'S VOICE Something must be done – at once – before our family name is dragged through the mud—

Horrified, Elizabeth gets up and goes out.

CUT TO:

83: EXT. COASTAL PATHWAY – DAY 17

Ross and Demelza return home on horseback. Demelza's red cloak is flapping in the wind. Demelza is singing. Not a care in the world, thrilled with her cloak. Ross is distracted, thinking of Elizabeth.

CUT TO:

84: INT. NAMPARA HOUSE, KITCHEN – DAY 18

The red cloak hangs on the back of a door. Demelza is preparing pilchards. She is hot, sweaty, dishevelled – and up to her elbows in fish scales. Presently she hears a knock at the front door. There's no sign of Jud or Prudie.

DEMELZA *(calling out)* Jud? *(no answer)* Prudie?

Another knock at the door. This time more urgent.

DEMELZA *(cont'd – louder)* Prudie? *(yelling)* Jud!

Still no answer. Another louder knock at the door.

CUT TO:

85: EXT. NAMPARA HOUSE – DAY 18

Demelza opens the door . . . to Elizabeth. For a moment Demelza is tongue-tied, staring at Elizabeth. The contrast could not be more striking. The glowing, beautiful, exquisitely dressed Elizabeth . . . and the hot, sweaty, dishevelled scullery maid Demelza! The two women, each momentarily caught off guard, eye each other. Then Demelza bobs a makeshift curtsey – the first she's ever attempted – and almost falls over!

DEMELZA 'Ee be lookin' fer Mister Ross?

ELIZABETH I am.

CUT TO:

86: INT. NAMPARA HOUSE, PARLOUR – DAY 18

Elizabeth is sitting in the parlour when Ross comes in (having been summoned by Demelza). She looks flushed and agitated.

ROSS Elizabeth—

He rushes to kiss her hands, but she pulls them back, seeing Demelza there.

ROSS *(cont'd)* You've been offered some refreshment?

ELIZABETH Your maid has done her best.

She indicates a small tray with a cracked glass of water, smeared with fish-scales, and a rough hunk of bread.

ROSS *(to Demelza)* You can go.

Demelza attempts another curtsey, then goes out. Elizabeth immediately dissolves into tears.

ELIZABETH Oh Ross—

ROSS What is it?

He takes her hands and pulls her towards him.

ELIZABETH How to even begin to put into words—

ROSS Don't try— *(before she can argue)* You love Francis, I love Francis. But this cannot be allowed to continue.

They're very close now. Ross leans towards Elizabeth. Before they can continue, Jud bursts in with a pile of logs which he drops all over the floor.

ROSS *(cont'd)* Out. Out.

JUD Damn me, if a body can't get about 'is sacred an' pro-fane duties wi'out a blastin' from 'is—

ROSS Out!

With a supreme effort Elizabeth composes herself.

ELIZABETH You must speak with Francis – and your uncle – you must speak with them both—

ROSS I'll follow directly.

Elizabeth leaves. Ross takes out his frustration on Jud.

ROSS *(cont'd – to Jud)* Saddle my horse. And remind me to thrash you when I return.

JUD In't no call for that, Mister Ross. 'Tidn' just, 'tidn' kind, 'tidn' civil, 'tidn' friendly . . .

Ross storms out.

CUT TO:

87: EXT. NAMPARA VALLEY – DAY 18

Ross gallops up the valley in the direction of Trenwith.
CUT TO:

88: INT. TRENWITH HOUSE, PARLOUR – DAY 18

Ross is shown into the parlour – where he is greeted by a stern-faced Charles, Francis and Aunt Agatha. Elizabeth is sitting as far away from Ross as possible, pretending to read. Nevertheless the tension between them is almost palpable. Francis and Charles exchange a glance. Then . . .

CHARLES It's a bad business, Ross—

AUNT AGATHA Very bad—

CHARLES But we must make the best of it.

Ross looks surprised. Does Charles really want it all out in the open?

CHARLES *(cont'd)* Verity has greatly disappointed us.

ROSS Verity— ?

CHARLES You're aware that she'd formed an attachment at the ball?

FRANCIS Who could fail to be aware? She was all over the man!

AUNT AGATHA All over—

ROSS The sea captain? Blamey?

FRANCIS He's been secretly paying court to her ever since.

CHARLES Hoping, no doubt, to secure her before she became aware of his appalling past.

AUNT AGATHA The varmint!—

FRANCIS He's a drunkard – who beat his wife to death – killing their unborn child.

Ross is open-mouthed with shock.

ROSS Is this certain?

FRANCIS Verity has confirmed it.

ELIZABETH And forgiven him.

ROSS Impossible—

CHARLES She's a plain girl – and that makes her easy prey—

FRANCIS So we must close ranks and protect her.

ROSS Of course – but how?

CHARLES She will not leave this house until she swears never to see him again.

CUT TO:

89: EXT. TRENWITH HOUSE, GARDENS – DAY 18

As Ross is leaving, Verity emerges from the back of the house and runs towards him.

VERITY Ross!

He waits for her to catch up with him.

VERITY *(cont'd)* I heard what they told you. It isn't true.

CUT TO:

90: EXT. TRENWITH HOUSE, GARDENS – DAY 18

Ross and Verity are walking, far from the house.

VERITY It was an accident. She tried to strike him. *(then)* He pushed her away – she fell and hit her head—

ROSS He told you this?

VERITY At the ball. But there was never any intent to harm her, none in the world. And he's paid for what he did. He lost his rank and went to prison. And I know he would never lift a finger to hurt me.

ROSS But still – how can you be sure he—

VERITY I'm sure. *(seeing him about to argue)* He loves me. I love him. *(then)* You of all people know what that feels like.

ROSS Yes. *(then)* Yes.

They walk on a while. Then . . .

ROSS *(cont'd)* What can I do?

CUT TO:

91: EXT. NAMPARA HOUSE – DAY 19

Two horses are tethered outside the house.

CUT TO:

92: INT. NAMPARA HOUSE, HALLWAY – DAY 19

ANDREW Captain Poldark – most generous – to allow us to meet here – in view of your concerns—

ROSS Verity trusts you. I trust Verity.

ANDREW She's my angel of redemption. You'll have no cause to regret it.

ROSS I believe you, sir.

He shakes Andrew's hand warmly.

CUT TO:

93: EXT. NAMPARA HOUSE – DAY 19

Two horses are tethered outside the house. Ross and Jim are working close by, bringing in the hay. Ross seems on edge. He keeps glancing towards the house.

JIM Sur—

He draws his attention to two people who are approaching. Ross recognizes Ruth and Mrs Teague.

ROSS Dammit! (*to Jim, low*) Tell our guests to keep to the parlour.

JIM 'Es, sur—

Ross walks forward to divert Ruth and Mrs Teague away from the house.

CUT TO:

94: EXT. NAMPARA VALLEY – DAY 19

Ross is walking with Mrs Teague and Ruth (who is dressed to kill and clearly on a mission to finish what she started at the ball).

MRS TEAGUE Farming is such an engaging hobby, is it not?

ROSS More than a hobby for me, ma'am.

RUTH But do you not hunt, Captain Poldark? Would it not be a fine thing to be mixing with people of your own station?

ROSS I'm kept very well occupied here.

Ruth taps her riding whip menacingly against her skirts. Having been forced to take matters into her own hands, she's clearly expecting Mrs Teague to support her campaign.

MRS TEAGUE Of course Ruth is an accomplished rider.

ROSS Of course.

MRS TEAGUE Not that it's her only accomplishment. One has only to taste her syllabubs to know their succulence.

ROSS Indeed.

Ruth raises her eyebrows suggestively to Ross – and for a moment he almost warms to her. Then . . .

MRS TEAGUE Is Miss Verity still meeting that blackguard in spite of her father?

ROSS I – er—

RUTH Of course, you're so out of the way here, you would not hear of it?

ROSS No indeed.

Now Demelza appears, hauling a basket of kindling from the orchard. Ruth and Mrs Teague eye her curiously. She's hot, sweaty and her face is streaked with mud. She stumbles as she passes, spilling some of the kindling. Ruth suppresses a smirk.

MRS TEAGUE Is this the young person you adopted?

ROSS I've adopted no one.

Demelza gathers up the spilt kindling, bobs a curtsey and leaves. Mrs Teague and Ruth eye her with intense curiosity.

ROSS *(cont'd)* I needed a kitchen wench – the girl is old enough to know her own mind—

MRS TEAGUE *(watching Demelza depart)* Yes, she looks as if she would know her own mind.

ROSS *(suddenly)* But I must beg your indulgence, ladies. There is much I must attend to.

MRS TEAGUE But you must take tea with us soon at Teague House? Perhaps we can show you what a woman's touch can do to a home.

ROSS I thank you, ma'am. But I fear your efforts would be wasted.

He kisses their hands dutifully. Highly disgruntled, they depart. Ross makes no attempt to conceal his haste to escape them.

CUT TO:

95: EXT. NAMPARA HOUSE – DAY 19

Seen through the window, Verity and Andrew sit sedately at a distance, engaged in genteel conversation.

CUT TO:

96: INT. NAMPARA HOUSE, HALLWAY – DAY 19

Ross has been listening in to Andrew and Verity's conversation.

ANDREW *(os)* My son James is fourteen – a midshipman with the fleet. I need hardly say how much I miss him. And you, who are no less attached to your family, would surely be loathe to quit them for my sake?

VERITY *(os)* I assure you I am quite willing to make the sacrifice.

Demelza passes. A thought occurs to Ross.

ROSS Have you had word of your family?

DEMELZA No sur, an' don' expect none.

Ross looks surprised.

DEMELZA *(cont'd)* Without I to skivvy f'r'em, they'll have no love o' me, nor care to 'ave news.

ROSS Particularly your father!

DEMELZA Too busy i' th' kiddleys or down th' mine.

ROSS And your brothers?

DEMELZA Soon be followin' in 'is footsteps.

ROSS Seems we both having mining in our blood.

DEMELZA Aye, sur. Though God knows if that be a blessing or a curse.

She goes off, leaving Ross to ponder the wisdom of her words.

CUT TO:

97: EXT. NAMPARA VALLEY – DAY 19

As Ross rides towards the head of Nampara Valley, an alarming sight greets him: Charles and Francis are riding towards him. He curses silently – but recovers quickly.

ROSS This is good timing! I was about to ride to Wheal Leisure.

Francis and Charles exchange a look of surprise.

ROSS *(cont'd – to Charles)* The investors' meeting went well. I still hope to persuade Francis to join.

CHARLES That will depend.

ROSS I take nothing for granted. And I still ask for George to be kept in the dark. *(to Francis)* I doubt your friendship would prevent him betraying you if the need arose.

FRANCIS Any more than our kinship has prevented you from betraying us?

Ross halts. He falls silent.

FRANCIS *(cont'd)* D'you deny that Verity is meeting that man at your house?

For a moment Ross considers denying it. But in the end . . .

ROSS I think you misjudge him.

FRANCIS I think I've misjudged you!

Francis rides off in a fury, followed by Charles. Ross wearily turns his horse and heads back to Nampara.

CUT TO:

98: INT. NAMPARA HOUSE, PARLOUR – DAY 19

Francis bursts into the parlour to find Verity and Andrew seated sedately by the fire, being served tea by Demelza.

FRANCIS Filthy skunk! Sneaking behind our backs to debauch my sister!

VERITY *(leaping to her feet)* Francis! No—

FRANCIS *(to Andrew)* Deceiving her family—

ANDREW If you and your father refuse to meet me—

FRANCIS We do not deal with wife murderers!

Now Ross strides into the parlour to see Andrew and Francis facing each other and Charles trying to restrain Verity.

VERITY I have a right to choose my own life!

ANDREW You heard your sister—

FRANCIS Honour means nothing to your sort! Perhaps a thrashing will!

ROSS Not in my house!

CHARLES You have the impudence to take his side?

ROSS I take no one's side – but you won't change the issue with this foolery.

ANDREW I've no wish to quarrel, but Verity is coming with me.

FRANCIS That she is not! There'll be no cleaning of your boots on this family!

ANDREW You insolent puppy!

FRANCIS Oh, 'puppy' is it?

He smacks Andrew across the cheek. Andrew hesitates a moment, then punches Francis in the face, sending him crashing to the floor. Verity screams. Ross shakes his head in disbelief. Francis wipes the blood from his mouth and gets to his feet.

FRANCIS *(cont'd)* When will it be convenient for you to meet me, Captain Blamey?

ANDREW As soon as you like, sir.

VERITY Andrew, no! Francis, please—

FRANCIS *(to Ross)* Get me a pistol.

ROSS Get one yourself.

Francis sees two pistols on the wall. He seizes them.

FRANCIS This fellow claims to be a gentleman. Let him step outside and prove it!

VERITY No! Francis! Ross, stop them!

Francis strips off his coat, Andrew does the same, though Verity is trying to stop both of them doing so. They both shrug her off and stride outside. Charles is undecided.

Does he intervene or does he let Francis stand on his own two feet?

ROSS Uncle, you must step in. Francis is out of his depth.

Charles admits the truth of it. He rushes out into the garden.

CUT TO:

99: EXT. NAMPARA HOUSE, GARDEN – DAY 19

Jud is visibly impressed by the scene unfolding before his eyes. Andrew and Francis stride into the garden, followed by Charles, the sobbing Verity, the resigned Ross.

CHARLES Francis, have no truck with this scoundrel! Verity will come home with us – won't you, Verity?

VERITY Yes, Father—

FRANCIS It's gone beyond that. The skunk insulted me!

CHARLES Fight it out with fists, then. He's not worth the risk of a pistol ball!

FRANCIS D'you want this family to be a laughing stock?

ROSS Francis, I urge you to consider—

FRANCIS Consider what? That anyone may abuse our trust and take advantage of us?

A brief moment between them. Now Ross knows exactly why Francis is so sensitive of his honour. Verity rushes forward.

VERITY Francis, I beg you—

FRANCIS *(looking Ross in the eye)* I will have satisfaction!

Verity tries to intervene but Francis pushes her away.

FRANCIS *(cont'd – to Jud)* You, there! Act as referee. Can you count?

JUD Aye, sur. One, two, six, four, sev'n, nine—

FRANCIS *(to Andrew)* We'll do it ourselves. One, two, three . . .

They begin to pace away from each other. Verity is wailing in horrified anticipation.

VERITY Stop them, Ross – please stop them—

Demelza and Prudie have come into the garden with Jim and are watching in horror.

FRANCIS Eight, nine, ten—

They turn and fire. Andrew is hit in the hand, Francis in the neck. He falls to the ground. Verity screams, Charles and Ross rush over to Francis. He appears lifeless.

CUT TO:

100: INT. NAMPARA HOUSE, ROSS'S BEDROOM – DAY 19

Ross, staggering under the weight, carries the apparently lifeless body of Francis into the room and lays him on the bed.

ROSS *(shouting)* Prudie! Fetch me some water—

He looks at Francis a long time. Francis appears to be dead. Going through Ross's mind is one thought: that Francis's death would be the answer to so many of his difficulties. And it would be so easy to simply let him go without a fight . . .

CUT TO:

101: EXT. NAMPARA HOUSE – DAY 19

A broken man, Andrew untethers his horse and prepares to leave. Verity appears, white as a ghost.

VERITY I know it was not your intention—

ANDREW God forbid!

CUT TO:

102: INT. NAMPARA HOUSE, ROSS'S BEDROOM – DAY 19

Prudie appears in the doorway, shielding her eyes with her hands.

ROSS Help me stop the bleeding—

PRUDIE *(still covering her eyes)* I can't, sur – I'm feared o' th' sight o' blood—

CUT TO:

103: EXT. NAMPARA HOUSE – DAY 19

VERITY But surely you must see how impossible it would be for us to be together now?

ANDREW I do see.

CUT TO:

104: INT. NAMPARA HOUSE, ROSS'S BEDROOM – DAY 19

Demelza appears behind Prudie with a bowl of water.

DEMELZA I'll 'elp, sur. I bain't afeared—

Against her will, Prudie is impressed by Demelza's no nonsense approach. Ross tries to stem the bleeding in Francis's neck. He is calm and methodical – tending this sort of wound is clearly something he's done in his army days. His expression is grimly determined.

Demelza assists by handing him new strips of torn linen when he beckons for them.

CUT TO:

105: EXT. NAMPARA HOUSE – DAY 19

Andrew gets on his horse.

ANDREW Goodbye, Verity.

He rides away. Tears stream down Verity's cheeks as she watches him go.

CUT TO:

106: INT. NAMPARA HOUSE, HALLWAY – DAY 19

A hysterical Elizabeth arrives. A shocked Charles, struggling for breath, is being tended to by Jud.

ELIZABETH Where is he?

Breathless, Charles signals that Francis is upstairs.

CUT TO:

107: INT. NAMPARA HOUSE, ROSS'S BEDROOM – DAY 19

Elizabeth bursts into the room – and gasps in horror. Francis is lying, white and apparently lifeless in Ross's bed. He is dressed in a night-shirt and there is no sign of blood. He looks like a corpse laid out. Elizabeth sinks to her knees beside the bed.

ELIZABETH Oh God, no – no – no—

Ross goes to comfort her but she waves him away.

ELIZABETH *(cont'd)* How could you let this happen?

ROSS *(gently)* Elizabeth—

ELIZABETH *(sobbing)* You let him die – how could you let him die?

ROSS Speak to him.

Elizabeth looks up, confused then at Francis. To her astonishment and relief, Francis opens his eyes. Elizabeth flings herself upon him in an outburst of weeping. Ross watches a while – then quietly tiptoes out of the room.

CUT TO:

108: INT. NAMPARA HOUSE, KITCHEN – DAY 19

Ross sits at the table, lost in his thoughts. Jud and Prudie dither in the corner, hapless, ineffectual, still in shock. Only Demelza seems in command of the situation. She puts a jug of ale and some bread and cheese on the table in front of Ross but he barely notices it or her.

DEMELZA Your cousin do owe 'ee 'is life.

Ross looks up, in a daze.

DEMELZA *(cont'd)* Where'd 'ee learn a' do sich things?

ROSS On the battlefields of Virginia.

A look of weariness that speaks volumes of the horrors Ross has witnessed. Demelza nods. Jud and Prudie are impressed with Ross and – reluctantly – with Demelza. Now the door opens and several Trenwith servants come from upstairs, carrying a stretcher on which Francis is being carried, sedated and barely conscious. Charles and Elizabeth accompany him, Elizabeth holding his hand. Charles is cold with fury.

CHARLES You're a disgrace to the name of Poldark.

ROSS I'm sorry you think so.

CHARLES I offer no thanks. I feel no gratitude. I hold you entirely to blame.

ROSS I understand.

They go out. Ross is about to follow when Elizabeth turns back.

ELIZABETH I do not blame you.

ROSS I wouldn't for the world wish him hurt.

ELIZABETH I know that. And I'm grateful for all you've done.

CHARLES *(trying to lead her away)* Come, Elizabeth—

ELIZABETH The more so now since, more than ever, I need him well and at my side.

Ross looks at her, confused.

ELIZABETH *(cont'd)* I'm with child.

A huge moment between them. In that moment Ross realizes all hope is gone. More than that, there never was any hope. All this time he'd been flattering himself that she entertained serious feelings for him, when in fact she'd continued to be intimate with her husband. A farewell look from Elizabeth, then she leaves, bustled away by Charles.

CUT TO:

109: INT. NAMPARA HOUSE, KITCHEN – DAY 19

Ross sits motionless at the table. He hasn't touched the ale. Demelza is sitting in a corner, quietly mending some clothes, watching him like a hawk. Ross is deep in thought. He comes to his senses. Suddenly he realizes that Elizabeth has always been teasing him – and this is the last time he's going to fall for it.

Demelza gets up and quietly begins to clear away the ale from the table. Suddenly, Ross – who up to this point has seemed totally oblivious to her presence – seizes her wrist to stop her removing the ale.

ROSS Do I look like an idiot?

DEMELZA Sur— ?

ROSS Do I have 'half-wit' branded across my forehead?

DEMELZA No—

ROSS Yet I fell for it! Again! Built a castle out of winks and smiles – and all the while—

He releases her wrist. She retracts it and continues to clear the table.

ROSS *(cont'd)* I should be grateful! What clearer proof is needed?

He seems suddenly reanimated, determined to move on.

ROSS *(cont'd)* Fetch Jim and Jud and Prudie. We have work to do!

He jumps up from the table and goes out. Demelza remains, utterly baffled.

CUT TO:

110: EXT. WHEAL LEISURE – DUSK 19

A driftwood fire glows warm and sparks fly up into the gathering dusk. Over the fire Demelza cooks pilchards. On a cloth on the ground, Prudie lays out plates, bread and other simple food. Jud pours ale. Jim is helping Ross resurrect the 'Wheal Leisure' sign outside the mine.

CUT TO:

111: INT. TRENWITH HOUSE, DINING ROOM – DUSK 19

Darkness is falling. In a dimly lit, cold, comfortless dining room, dinner is eaten in silence. Around the table sit a gloomy Charles, a distraught Verity, a nauseous Elizabeth – all lost in their own thoughts. Aunt Agatha, oblivious, tucks into her dinner voraciously. A fifth chair – Francis's – remains empty.

CUT TO:

112: EXT. WHEAL LEISURE – DUSK 19

The task completed, Ross stands back and surveys it with satisfaction. Demelza serves freshly cooked pilchards to all. Garrick lies at her feet. As they all eat, making murmurs of appreciation, Ross glances at Demelza. Her face is aglow with the light of the fire and the sunset. He watches her, as if truly seeing her for the first time. Eventually . . .

ROSS I wonder if I did the right thing – *(beat)* Taking you from your family.

DEMELZA Sur— ?

ROSS You did well today. I see how valuable you must be to them.

Demelza's face falls.

ROSS *(cont'd)* And if you miss them – if you feel their need is greater than mine—

Demelza looks horrified. A terrible thought occurs to her:

DEMELZA 'Ee be wantin' rid 'o me?

ROSS What?

DEMELZA 'Ee be wishin' me gone? *(then)* I'll work 'arder – I'll rise sooner – I'll scrub an' scour an' fettle an'—

ROSS Demelza!

DEMELZA Sur?

ROSS Your work is more than satisfactory.

DEMELZA Then, sur, why—

ROSS I was merely offering you the chance to return to your home. If that's where you feel you belong.

Demelza looks at him in disbelief. The very idea is preposterous to her.

DEMELZA I b'long 'ere.

She looks at him directly – and for the first time something passes between them – a moment of connection – not romantic or sexual – but the sense of a shared destiny.

DEMELZA *(cont'd)* I b'long 'ere.

As Ross glances round at this disparate group of people, another thought occurs to him: family and friendship are what you decide they are. As the sun sets – and the faces of this 'family' are lit by the glow of the fire – Ross finally feels he has reason to face the future with hope.

Episode 3

1: EXT. CLIFF-TOPS – DAY 20

Sunrise. The first rays of light pick out the towering hulk of the Wheal Leisure mine.

CUT TO:

2: EXT. WHEAL LEISURE – DAY 20

Sunrise. Ross explores the silent Wheal Leisure. He smiles to himself. This is a momentous day for him.

CUT TO:

3: EXT. MELLIN COTTAGES – DAY 20

Zacky Martin leaves his cottage. Presently he greets Mark Daniel, emerging from his own cottage. They in turn greet Paul Daniel, then Nick Vigus, who are both emerging from theirs. All four men are dressed for the mine. They seem expectant and hopeful, laughing and joking as they set off for work, followed by various women (including Mrs Zacky, her pregnant daughter Jinny) and assorted children.

CUT TO:

4: EXT. WHEAL LEISURE – DAY 20

Ross is greeted by Mine Captain Henshawe. They shake hands.

ROSS I thought this day would never come.

From their vantage point on the cliffs they can see down onto the neighbouring valleys, paths and by-ways.

THEIR POV: From all directions people are journeying towards the mine.

HENSHAWE Expectations are high.

ROSS Pray God we don't disappoint them.

The miners gather (about 30), along with their families, interested parties, casual onlookers, shareholders (Renfrew, Treneglos, Henshawe, Dr Choake), well-wishers (Jim). Jim is talking quietly to the pregnant Jinny. Demelza is going round handing out tots of rum from a tray.

HORACE TRENEGLOS A pleasant change – to see a mine opening!

DR CHOAKE For how long, I wonder?

Ross, seeing tots of rum being circulated, looks round to find Demelza at his elbow, ready to hand him one. A brief smile of acknowledgement, then he addresses the assembled crowd.

ROSS My friends, when my father closed this mine twenty years ago, he little thought it would have a future. Today, with your help, labour and good wishes, we aim to prove him wrong. Gentlemen, ladies, I declare Wheal Leisure mine open.

CUT TO:

5: EXT. WHEAL LEISURE – DAY 20

The bell rings for the first shift. The crowd begins to disperse. Jim parts from Jinny, who goes off with Mrs Zacky. Zacky, Paul, Mark, Nick and the other miners head cheerfully for the mine entrance. Some of them shake Ross by the hand as they go.

PAUL Grand thing 'ee done, Ross.

ZACKY Thank 'ee, Ross.

ROSS Zacky. *(then)* Mark!—

MARK Can't thank 'ee enough.

ROSS Then don't. If all goes well, it's I who'll be thanking you.

CUT TO:

6: EXT. WHEAL LEISURE – DAY 20

The shareholders take more rum from Demelza and continue to toast the new venture.

As Demelza walks off, some of the shareholders eye her appreciatively and raise their eyebrows at each other. Demelza walks over to Ross, unable to contain her excitement about the mine opening.

DEMELZA I'm that glad, sur! – for th' miners an' families – an' fer 'ee, sur!

ROSS *(laughing)* My neck's on the line. Are you glad about that?

DEMELZA *(laughing)* Oh, no, sur! For what shall I do if it come to grief?

They both laugh, then Demelza skips off back towards Nampara

House. As she goes, she is unaware that she and Ross have been observed by Dr Choake and Horace Treneglos.

DR CHOAKE *(low)* Are the rumours true, d'you think?

HORACE TRENEGLOS *(low)* He's a damned fool if they're not!

They all laugh. Demelza continues on her way, happily oblivious.

CUT TO:

7: EXT. CLIFF-TOPS – DAY 20

Charles and Francis look down at the scene below. Charles looks grudgingly impressed.

FRANCIS I take it you've forgiven him?

CHARLES He saved your life. Time for you to demonstrate it wasn't wasted.

FRANCIS I've no mine to resurrect.

CHARLES You've one to keep alive. *(then)* Start by stemming the leakage of workers from our mine to his!

FRANCIS Easier said than done. Our wages are hardly an incentive to stay!

Charles rides off, impatient. Francis lingers a moment longer, watching Ross, then spurs his horse after Charles.

CUT TO:

8: INT. TRENWITH HOUSE, TURRET ROOM – DAY 20

Elizabeth, heavily pregnant, sits reading by the window. She gets to her feet, feels the strain in her back, rubs it to ease the ache, then returns to her book.

CUT TO:

9: INT. WHEAL LEISURE, SHAFT – DAY 20

Ross descends the ladder into the shaft behind Henshawe. Though he's made the descent many times, today is an important day and he's full of anticipation. He is followed by Renfrew, Dr Choake and Horace Treneglos.

CUT TO:

10: INT. WHEAL LEISURE, 1ST LEVEL – DAY 20

Henshawe is waiting for Ross as he reaches the 1st Level. Ross looks up the way he's come, at the men climbing down the wooden ladders, at the distant patch of daylight at the head of the shaft. As the investors all reach the 1st Level . . .

ROSS We'll have iron ladders down the main shaft.

HORACE TRENEGLOS Iron?

ROSS Wood rots.

DR CHOAKE It'll cost you.

ROSS Better me than a man's life.

The investors grudgingly nod their agreement. Henshawe looks gratified. Now he leads the way towards the tunnel of the 1st Level. Ross follows, the others trail after.

CUT TO:

11: INT. WHEAL LEISURE, TUNNEL – DAY 20

Ross's eyes gleam in the reflected light of Henshawe's candle as they penetrate further into the mine along the 1st Level tunnel. Up ahead they can hear the sound of men working, the drip of water and the distant hacking of pick on rock. The mine itself seems to hum, to pulsate – as if it has a life of its own, and its own heartbeat.

ROSS *(to the investors)* Two shafts have been sunk, but it's hard going—

HENSHAWE We struck ironstone almost at once—

ROSS We've had to use steel borers – and may yet require gunpowder—

DR CHOAKE More expense?

HENSHAWE Aye, but don't be discouraged. Where there's ironstone, there's often copper.

As they reach the 1st level, they come upon the miners at work. Henshawe points out something in the rock.

HENSHAWE There. D'y'mark that?

The investors cluster round to get a better look.

HENSHAWE *(cont'd)* Chase that and we'll hope to catch copper.

The investors peer at it, shining their candles to examine the veins of tin which streak the rock. Ross and Henshawe exchange a glance. These men have taken a lot of convincing. Now Ross and Henshawe have to prove their faith is not misplaced.

CUT TO:

12: INT. WARLEGGAN HOUSE, LIBRARY – DAY 20

George sits weighing coins, but his mind is on Ross and Wheal Leisure.

CUT TO:

13: INT. NAMPARA HOUSE, HALLWAY – DAY 20

Coming into the house, with an armful of wild flowers, Demelza hears alarming sounds coming from the kitchen: the crash of breaking crockery, yelps of pain and muffled curses, the thud of bodies crashing to the floor.

CUT TO:

14: INT. NAMPARA HOUSE, KITCHEN – DAY 20

Demelza comes in to find Jud and Prudie, locked in combat, rolling around on the floor, surrounded by broken crockery.

DEMELZA Judas! I can 'ear 'ee kickin' up a dido three mile away!

PRUDIE 'Tis this g'eat buffle-'ead! 'Ee gi' me sich a colloppin'!—

JUD 'Ush yer creenin', woman! Y'd think cheese wud'n choke 'ee! *(to Demelza)* Be she 'oo started it!

PRUDIE 'E'll get 'is come-uppin' soon enough!

A telltale bottle of rum is upended on the table and two empty cups tell Demelza all she needs to know.

DEMELZA Mister Ross's rum again?

JUD 'E won't miss it! – 'is 'ead be fair full o' th' mine—

PRUDIE G'eat bladder! – 'ee's gone an' breeked me arm!

DEMELZA Let's see—

She goes to help Prudie. Prudie shrieks in pain as Demelza (rather capably) prods and pokes at it to assess the damage.

DEMELZA 'Tis on'y a sprain – but 'ee'll not be fit t' cook vittles this three week.

PRUDIE 'Ee mun' step into th' breach, then! *(seeing her look of alarm)* Don' worry, chile – ol' Prudie'll 'struct 'ee.

JUD Talk o' th' blind leadin' th' blind?

Jud upends the bottle into his mouth in the hope of catching the last dregs of rum, then stomps out.

PRUDIE Don' jus' stan' there – brew us a dish o' tea while I rest me brokken wing!

Prudie goes and reclines on a settle while Demelza affably puts the kettle on to boil then gets down on her hands and knees and begins to clear up the mess.

CUT TO:

15: EXT. WHEAL LEISURE – DAY 20

The bell rings for the end of the first shift. Miners for the next shift are assembling ready to take the place of those below. Ross and Henshawe emerge from the shaft, followed by Mark, Paul and Zacky and the rest of the shift. Mrs Zacky is waiting nearby with Jinny. Zacky approaches Ross.

ZACKY Can 'ee spare a minute?

ROSS By all means.

They walk away from the rest of the miners.

ZACKY Young Jim—

Ross can see from Zacky's expression that Jim's is trouble.

ROSS What's he been up to now?

ZACKY My Jinny.

CUT TO:

16: INT. WOODSHED – DAY 20

Two dead pheasants hang on a nail. Two pheasant nets lean against the wall. Jim is plucking a pheasant. Suddenly he becomes aware that he is not alone. He wheels round and sees Ross standing in the doorway.

ROSS Poaching's a capital offence. *(before he can reply)* Believe me, I'm acquainted with the niceties of the law!

JIM 'Tis not for my sake, Ross – 'tis me mother an' sisters. I can't see 'em starve'—

ROSS And Jinny?

JIM Sur?

ROSS Is her welfare of equal concern to you?

JIM Oh yes, sur – an' I mean a' do right by 'er – when I can afford it.

ROSS Dammit, man, the girl's frantic! Why didn't you come to me before?

JIM Why, Ross, but what could 'ee do?
CUT TO:

17: EXT. MELLIN COTTAGES – DAY 20

Ross holds open the door to an empty cottage and motions to Jim and Jinny to go inside. They dither awkwardly on the threshold, open-mouthed in disbelief.

ROSS It wants some small repairs.

JINNY But – nothin' a' pay— ?

ROSS You'd be doing me a favour – keeping it clean and dry.

JIM 'Tis more 'n we could ever 'ave 'oped—

ROSS Well then, that's settled.

Jim's mouth is opening and closing like a fish but no words come out.

ROSS *(cont'd)* So now what's your excuse?

JIM Sur?

ROSS Don't keep the girl waiting! Be off to her father – and while you're at it, see Reverend Odgers about getting the banns read.

He turns to go. Then, remembering . . .

ROSS *(to Jim)* And get rid of those nets. Let's have no more poaching.

CUT TO:

18: INT. NAMPARA HOUSE, KITCHEN – DAY 20

Demelza looks nervous as she labours over her first pie, crimping down the edges, pricking the centre and glazing it with beaten egg. She surveys it nervously, then puts it into the oven.

CUT TO:

19: INT. NAMPARA HOUSE, KITCHEN – DAY 20

Demelza places a jug of wild flowers on the table, which is neatly laid. Ross returns and sits down.

He helps himself to ale and barely seems aware of Demelza until she places his dinner – the well-made pie – in front of him. He glances at it suspiciously, then at her. She's on tenterhooks awaiting his verdict. He looks stern. He cuts a piece. He tastes it. He nods grimly.

ROSS So Prudie's recovery may take some time.

DEMELZA 'Ap'n a month or so, sur.

ROSS Have her delay it as long as possible.

He eats another mouthful. Demelza flushes with pleasure.

CUT TO:

20: EXT. MOORLAND – DAY 21

Demelza's red cloak is a flash of colour in a wild moorland landscape as she rides behind Ross to Jim and Jinny's wedding.

CUT TO:

21: EXT. MELLIN COTTAGES – DAY 21

Two fiddlers lead the way as newlyweds Jim and Jinny return from church, followed by a group of wedding guests including Jim's sisters as bridesmaids, Paul and Mark Daniel, Zacky and Mrs Zacky, Ross and Demelza.

CUT TO:

22: INT. TRENWITH HOUSE, PARLOUR – DAY 21

Elizabeth, heavily pregnant, is playing the harp. She is highly accomplished and puts herself wholeheartedly into her playing. A sad-faced Verity sits beside her, lost in her thoughts. As the piece ends, Verity gives a heavy sigh. Elizabeth glances at her with undisguised sympathy.

ELIZABETH I wish you could forget him, my dear.

VERITY Is love so easy to forget?

Elizabeth flushes self-consciously.

ELIZABETH Forgive me. I didn't mean to suggest—

She puts aside her harp and gets to her feet, to stretch her legs.

ELIZABETH *(cont'd)* For one thing I'm grateful. You're still here. And will be with me when—

She gives a soft gasp of pain. Does this mean what she thinks it means? She looks at Verity, suddenly afraid. Calmly Verity puts down her sewing, gets to her feet, rings the bell. Presently Mrs Tabb, the housekeeper, comes in.

VERITY *(calm)* Mrs Tabb, send for Dr Choake.

CUT TO:

23: EXT. MELLIN COTTAGES – DAY 21

Jim leads out his bride to begin the dancing. In view of Jinny's condition, her dancing is restrained, but it wins enthusiastic applause from the wedding guests (villagers, miners, peasants). Jim's mother, Connie Carter, struggles through tears to enjoy the spectacle. Reverend Odgers, who has joined them, now approaches Ross.

REVEREND ODGERS I wonder you don't think of marriage, Captain Poldark.

ROSS I dare say I shall in due course.

REVEREND ODGERS Always remembering the purpose for which it was ordained?

ROSS In particular— ?

REVEREND ODGERS *(with a glance at Demelza)* As a remedy against sin – and to avoid fornication?

Ross bites his tongue, bows and walks away. He sees Zacky and Mrs Zacky approaching. He knows what's coming and tries to avoid them. But in vain.

MRS ZACKY We can't thank 'ee enough—

ROSS Any man would do the same.

MRS ZACKY 'Any man' would not.

Connie Carter embraces Jim tenderly and with obvious distress at losing him. His sisters crowd round and hug him in turn. Ross can't help but notice.

MRS ZACKY Her on'y son—

ZACKY An' since his father bit the dust—

ROSS There's next to nothing coming into that household.

Zacky nods. He knows it's the truth. It's the only blot on an otherwise joyful day.

CUT TO:

24: INT. TRENWITH HOUSE, ELIZABETH'S ROOM – DAY 21

Elizabeth, attended by Verity and Dr Choake, is in the throes of labour. Verity dabs calmly at her forehead. Elizabeth makes very little sound though she's obviously in excruciating pain. Meanwhile Dr Choake seems more concerned with laying out his instruments, handling a pair of forceps with eager anticipation. Verity notices – and is eager to prevent their introduction into the proceedings. She grasps Elizabeth's hand and mouths her encouragement.

CUT TO:

25: EXT. MELLIN COTTAGES – DAY 21

The dancing is getting wilder and Demelza is flinging herself about with abandon. She's totally at home amongst her own class. But equally Ross is totally at home and accepted amongst these people.

From time to time Ross's eye strays towards Demelza. She's bright-eyed, glowing, flushed. It's not hard to appreciate what a force of nature she is or to admire the life-force which is strong in her.

As the dancing gets wilder, Demelza gets hotter and more flushed. She beckons Ross to join in – and he does.

Ross smiles at Demelza's antics. He's glad to see her enjoying herself.

CUT TO:

26: INT. TRENWITH HOUSE, PARLOUR – DAY 21

Charles raises a glass to Francis and Dr Choake.

CHARLES A grandson! Well done, my boy!

FRANCIS Thank Elizabeth. She did the work.

DR CHOAKE Ah, women – they make a song and dance about it, but if things are properly managed—

CHARLES *(toasting Francis)* A new Poldark! The line continues!

CUT TO:

27: EXT. NAMPARA HOUSE – NIGHT 21

A slightly merry Ross and a boisterously tipsy Demelza return home from the wedding. To Ross's amusement, Demelza is still dancing.

DEMELZA *(singing)*
There was an old couple
an' they was poor
Twee, Tweedle go twee . . .
Oh I have been sick
since you have been gone
Twee, Tweedle go twee . . .

CUT TO:

28: INT. NAMPARA HOUSE, KITCHEN – NIGHT 21

They burst into the kitchen, both laughing – to find Prudie asleep with her head on the kitchen table. She awakens with a jolt. Her head has been resting on a letter.

PRUDIE Letter come from Trenwith.

She hands it to Ross, who tears it open. For a moment his face falls. Then he recovers.

ROSS Francis and Elizabeth have a son.

He screws the letter up and tosses it at the fire. He seizes a bottle of rum and goes upstairs. Prudie raises her eyebrows. Demelza has stopped singing and seems to have sobered up instantly.

PRUDIE 'Ee be turnin' in?

DEMELZA Soon enough. I've bread to put on first.

She puts on an apron, gets out flour and starts preparing to make bread. Prudie cuffs Jud across the head. He awakens with a guilty start.

JUD *(confused)* 'Oo? – wha'? – where? -'ow? 'Tidn' I – 'tidn' 'ee – 'tidn' 'im – 'tidn' we!—

Prudie sends him reeling towards the stairs with a kick up the backside.

CUT TO:

29: EXT. TRENWITH HOUSE, DRIVE – DAY 22

A carriage delivers guests to the christening party.

CUT TO:

30: INT. TRENWITH HOUSE, GREAT HALL – DAY 22

Ross arrives, is greeted by a servant and directed towards the Great Hall. As he makes his way, he is struck, as if anew, by the sense of family history everywhere in this fine old house: in particular the family portraits lining the walls. One is of his father Joshua, his mother Grace and himself as a small child. Next to it, a portrait of himself and Francis as young adolescents. It gives him pause for thought. How their relationship has altered in recent years. Then he hears footsteps and turns to see Mrs Teague, Ruth Teague and Mrs Chynoweth arriving. He bows affably, ready to enter into conversation with them, but they return his greeting with marked coolness and walk off. He smiles to himself, more amused than offended and goes into the main reception room, which is full of christening guests . . .

As Ross comes into the room, he sees Verity listlessly attending to her guests.

He waves at her and is about to join her when George Warleggan (who's been talking to Cary) intercepts him.

GEORGE We were just saying, Ross, any man opening a mine these days must be exceptionally brave or extremely foolish!

ROSS *(pleasant)* How so?

CARY In these dire economic times—

ROSS Which might be less dire were they not in the hands of those whose only purpose is to make a profit.

CARY What other purpose is there?

ROSS Perhaps you should ask those who exist on starvation wages.

CARY Perhaps if you fraternized less with the lower orders you'd feel their woes less keenly.

MRS CHYNOWETH One does feel that the gentry and the vulgars should keep to themselves. Otherwise it just gets confusing.

ROSS Good day.

Ross bows politely and moves away. Aunt Agatha whacks Ross in the leg with her stick to grab his attention.

AUNT AGATHA Have we been introduced? I seem to recall you're related to me?

ROSS Forgive me, Aunt. I've had much to attend to of late. How are you?

AUNT AGATHA How should I be with Mistress Glumps for company? *(i.e. Verity)*

Charles approaches, passing Verity, noting her distress.

CHARLES Verity is well rid of that scoundrel Blamey. I trust you've learnt the folly of interference?

ROSS It won't be repeated, I assure you, Uncle.

Charles nods, satisfied.

CHARLES What d'you make of my grandson?

He directs Ross's attention to where Elizabeth and Francis are sitting together on a chaise, Elizabeth holding the baby. Seeing Ross, Francis waves him over. Ross goes.

FRANCIS A fine-looking boy, is he not?

ROSS Like his father.

ELIZABETH And his mother?

ROSS I congratulate you both.

Now Francis is called away by George. Ross, feeling slightly awkward, sits down beside Elizabeth.

ROSS You look pale.

ELIZABETH I've been stronger. *(then)* I'd hoped you'd be

named godfather. But Francis and George are inseparable these days – *(then)* Look at Geoffrey Charles. He's smiling at you!

ROSS I can't imagine why!

Suddenly they both become very self-conscious. As they glance at each other it's clear they're both thinking the same thing: could this (should this?) have been our child?

ON FRANCIS: Watching them, thinking exactly the same thing.

Francis goes over to Ross and Elizabeth.

FRANCIS Elizabeth?

He gestures for Elizabeth to take the baby over to Charles. She does so, standing beside Charles as he taps his glass for attention. A hush falls.

CHARLES Behold – the future: Geoffrey Charles Poldark – heir to the great Trenwith estate—

GEORGE *(aside to Cary)* What's left of it!

CHARLES When I have taken leave of this world – and Francis has taught the boy all he knows—

CARY *(aside to George)* That shouldn't take long.

CHARLES Our great Poldark dynasty will continue and – *(suddenly he doubles up as if in pain)* Damn me, this wind—

He clutches his chest, then collapses onto the floor with a resounding crash.

Ross, Francis, George and Dr Choake carry Charles up the stairs, attended by a distressed Verity.

AUNT AGATHA On a christening day? And the child named after him? 'Tis a sign, mark my words. A bad omen.

CUT TO:

31: INT. TRENWITH HOUSE, CHARLES'S ROOM – DAY 22

Ross and Francis watch in dismay as Charles lies in bed, panting for breath. Dr Choake bustles around full of self-importance, his instruments laid out, preparing to bleed his patient. Verity is sponging Charles's brow tenderly.

She flashes Ross a look of alarm as Dr Choake advances eagerly with a blood-letting instrument and a bowl.

CUT TO:

32: INT. TRENWITH HOUSE, UPSTAIRS LANDING – DAY 22

Ross comes out of Charles's room, clearly distressed. Through the door we glimpse Charles in bed, attended by Verity and Francis. Ross begins to make his way downstairs. Below he hears a murmur of voices.

MRS CHYNOWETH'S VOICE Of course a gentleman knows where to draw the line. Towards a lady of his own class his intentions should be strictly honourable—

CUT TO:

Mrs Chynoweth, Mrs Teague and Ruth Teague huddled together in the hallway, gossiping.

MRS CHYNOWETH Towards a woman of the lower class however—

MRS TEAGUE Oh indeed, it's all very disagreeable, but men are men—

RUTH We paid a call some months ago. There was the hussy – already beginning to put on airs—

MRS TEAGUE I saw her riding to church – bold as brass – all figged up in her scarlet cloak!

CUT TO:

Ross is no longer in doubt about the subjects of their conversation. He's seething, but he must remain still if he's to avoid drawing attention to his presence.

CUT TO:

MRS CHYNOWETH It's too bad! It tarnishes the family name – and my Elizabeth will undoubtedly suffer by association—

CUT TO:

Ross has had enough. Refusing to listen to this idiocy any longer, he thunders through into the hallway.

CUT TO:

Mrs Chynoweth, Mrs Teague and Ruth look startled and fall silent.

Ross makes no attempt to acknowledge them, instead heading straight for the front door, which he slams behind him as he leaves.

MRS TEAGUE Proof, if proof were needed, that Ross Poldark is no gentleman.

CUT TO:

33: EXT. TRENWITH HOUSE, DRIVE – DAY 22

Ross rides away, his expression seething with fury at what he's just overheard.

CUT TO:

34: INT. TRENWITH HOUSE, ELIZABETH'S ROOM – NIGHT 22

Elizabeth sits in bed with Geoffrey Charles in a cradle beside her. Presently Francis comes in.

FRANCIS My poor wife, neglected as usual.

ELIZABETH How is your father?

FRANCIS Rallying. Despite Choake's efforts!

He comes and sits beside her on the bed.

FRANCIS *(cont'd)* You look very lovely, my dear.

He leans over and gives her a lingering kiss. She returns it, but when he begins to caress her, she pulls back.

ELIZABETH Perhaps another night? I still feel a little weak—

FRANCIS *(irked by her rejection)* You seemed most animated this afternoon. With Ross.

ELIZABETH That's hardly fair.

FRANCIS *(impersonating her)* 'Oh Ross, look at my baby. See how he smiles at you. Don't you wish he was yours?'

ELIZABETH How can you say that?

FRANCIS Of course. Ross would never even think such a thing!

ELIZABETH No, I'm sure he would not!

The baby wakes and starts to cry. Elizabeth can't believe what's happening. Francis glares at her, then storms out of the room and slams the door.

CUT TO:

35: INT. TRENWITH HOUSE, UPSTAIRS LANDING – NIGHT 22

Francis storms out of Elizabeth's room and runs into Verity who has just come out of Charles's room. Having nowhere else to vent his frustration, she presents an easy target.

FRANCIS Listening at key-holes?

VERITY I've been tending to Father.

FRANCIS *(ignoring this)* No doubt you take Elizabeth's side!

VERITY Against whom?

FRANCIS Or Ross's!

VERITY I take no one's side.

FRANCIS Had it been left to him, you'd be in Falmouth now – living with that scoundrel in shame and misery!

VERITY I don't regard marriage as misery.

FRANCIS That's because you have yet to experience it!

Francis storms off downstairs.

VERITY *(low)* For which I have you to thank.

Verity takes out a locket. Inside is a portrait of Captain Andrew Blamey. She steels herself but the tears fall unbidden and without relief.

CUT TO:

36: INT. JIM & JINNY'S COTTAGE – NIGHT 22

It's late, but Jim is heading out.
CUT TO:

37: EXT. JIM & JINNY'S COTTAGE – NIGHT 22

As Jim emerges, a shadow appears from the darkness of another cottage. It's Nick Vigus. He carries a poaching net. Jim picks up his. The two of them tiptoe away into the darkness.
CUT TO:

38: INT. JIM & JINNY'S COTTAGE – NIGHT 22

Jinny is left alone.
CUT TO:

39: EXT. NAMPARA VALLEY, FIELDS – DAY 23

Demelza is out working in the fields. She attacks the task with vigour and is sweating from her efforts. As she takes a pause, she sees Jinny Carter (by now heavily pregnant) approaching. Demelza can see that all is not well.
CUT TO:

40: EXT. NAMPARA VALLEY, FIELDS – DAY 23

Demelza and Jinny walk through the fields together. Jinny seems close to tears.

JINNY Jim's a good man – an' it's good he should want to provide for 'is family – but not with poachin' – it's too dangerous! Could 'ee maybe ask Cap'n Ross to tell 'im to stop?

Demelza nods.

CUT TO:

41: INT. NAMPARA HOUSE – DAY 23

Demelza comes into the house, looking for Ross.

DEMELZA Sur? Mister Ross?

No answer. Demelza glances into the kitchen.

HER POV: Prudie with her feet up and her sprained wrist in a sling, snores loudly in a chair. Jud sits at the table, face down, also snoring, with a jug of ale and an empty glass beside him.

Demelza closes the door and looks into the parlour.

DEMELZA Mister Ross? Sur?

No answer. No sign of Ross. As she approaches the next door, she hesitates. Should she really be going in here after what Jud had said to her? It's the library. She pushes open the door and goes inside.

CUT TO:

42: INT. NAMPARA HOUSE, LIBRARY – DAY 23

The library is now being used as a mining office. Various

maps, mining artefacts and samples lie scattered about. Demelza examines them with interest. As she passes the map of Wheal Leisure, she traces some of the words and tries to spell them out.

DEMELZA *(to herself)* W-heal L-ee-i-sur. Wheal Leisure. U up-upper lev – upper level. Ea-east adit—

Now she turns her attention to something new: a great wooden chest, which sits in the corner of the room.

She opens it cautiously. Inside she finds some articles of fine clothing. It dawns on her that it's women's clothing. At first she doesn't dare to touch – then, gradually, she becomes braver, taking them out, feeling the texture, finally holding up one item – a beautiful pale blue silk dress. She gasps in admiration. It's the most beautiful thing she's ever seen. She holds it against herself. Then the sound of Ross's voice brings her to her senses.

ROSS'S VOICE Demelza?

Hurriedly she stuffs the dress back into the chest, closes the lid and rushes out.

DEMELZA Cap'n Poldark, sur? Do 'ee need me?

CUT TO:

43: INT. TRENWITH HOUSE, CHARLES'S ROOM – DAY 23

Charles is still in bed but sufficiently on the mend to be signalling impatiently to Verity to sponge his brow and bring him sips of water.

FRANCIS A heart stroke? Choake says you'll recover?

CHARLES Choake's a fool. And I am not immortal. *(then)* So this is your chance.

FRANCIS To do what?

CHARLES Step up to the mark. *(seeing Francis look confused)* You do recall that we have a mine?

FRANCIS Yes, but—

CHARLES It requires presence. Direction. Leadership. *(beat)* Yours.

FRANCIS But I know little of—

CHARLES Learn. Fast. If your cousin continues to pay decent wages, we'll soon have no one left at Grambler.

Francis is stunned.

CHARLES Take a leaf out of your cousin's book . . .

CUT TO:

44: EXT. GRAMBLER MINE – DAY 23

Francis rides towards Grambler Mine, but as he gets closer, he halts.

HIS POV: The mine looks run-down. A few miners are loitering about to no evident purpose. Some are arguing. Several, nursing injuries, are waiting in line to be seen by the mine surgeon, who has yet to appear.

CHARLES *(VO)* Does he keep his distance? Does he watch from afar?

CUT TO:

45: INT. WHEAL LEISURE – DAY 23

Ross joins his men in the mine.

CHARLES *(VO)* Or does he roll up his sleeves, and toil alongside his men?

CUT TO:

46: EXT. GRAMBLER MINE – DAY 23

Francis greets some of his workmen.

FRANCIS Good day to you all.

CUT TO:

47: INT. WHEAL LEISURE – DAY 23

Ross helps clear out heavy rocks as they mine deeper.

CHARLES *(VO)* Which do you think will yield the better result?

CUT TO:

48: EXT. GRAMBLER MINE – DAY 23

Suddenly Francis knows he can't face it. He turns his horse away and gallops in the opposite direction.

CUT TO:

49: INT. NAMPARA HOUSE, KITCHEN – DUSK 23

Ross sits at the table studying some papers.

ROSS *(without looking up)* How much longer, do you think, before we eat— ?

But she's already ahead of him and has placed a hearty bowl of stew in front of him. He tucks in appreciatively. Then . . .

ROSS *(without looking up)* And perhaps if there's some bread— ?

Again she's ahead of him – placing some bread beside him.

ROSS And maybe some— ?

Demelza sets the jug of ale she has in her other hand on the table. Ross tries not to laugh. She's so sharp, he can't keep up with her.

ROSS – Ale.

As she's about to go.

ROSS Have you eaten?

DEMELZA I d'sometimes forget to, sur.

ROSS Eat now. *(seeing her hesitate)* Sit.

She sits. He passes the dish of stew to her and pours her a glass of ale. She hesitates, but he seems to want her company so she begins to eat – warily at first – but when it becomes clear that he's unaware of her unease, she gradually relaxes.

ROSS You finished the lower field?

DEMELZA 'Es, sur. An' tomorrer I be startin' on the meadow.

ROSS You get through more in a day than Prudie in a month!

DEMELZA I be young, sur – an' strong—

ROSS And not bone idle.

They both laugh. Then . . .

ROSS *(cont'd)* I heard Jinny was over. How is she?

DEMELZA In truth, sur, she's that werrit—

ROSS About what?

DEMELZA Jim an' 'is poachin'. I thought p'r'aps 'ee could tell 'im to stop.

ROSS I'll do more than that. *(seeing her look of alarm)* I'll offer him a better job. Assistant Purser at the mine.

DEMELZA Oh, sur, Jinny'll be that glad!

Demelza smiles, excited. She can hardly wait to give Jinny the good news.

CUT TO:

50: INT. JIM & JINNY'S COTTAGE – DUSK 23

Jinny is getting ready for bed. Jim tries to sneak out but Jinny intervenes.

JINNY I dun' want 'ee t' go. We dun' need nothin' more. Cap'n Poldark d' give 'ee work an' this cottage an'—

JIM 'Tis not jus' for we, Jinny.

He comes and sits on the bed beside her, takes her hands and caresses it gently.

JIM *(cont'd)* Cap'n Poldark do 'elp us – but I can't ask 'im to 'elp mother an' sisters beside – an' since father be gone, 'oo else can put bread in their mouths but I?

Jinny nods, defeated. There's no way she can object to his argument. Except . . .

JINNY She'd not wish 'ee a' take sich risk—

JIM No more will I after t'night. 'Ee 'ave me word on it.

A moment between them. He kisses her and goes out. Jinny remains, close to tears.

CUT TO:

51: INT. NAMPARA HOUSE, LIBRARY – DUSK 23

Ross sits at the table, going through mining accounts. On the table are various copper samples. He picks one up and handles it thoughtfully. Then . . .

ROSS *(shouts)* Demelza? *(no reply)* Demelza, do we have any of that— ?

DEMELZA *(appearing in the doorway)* Brandy, sir? Last of that hid in th' cupboard, from France?

ROSS Exactly so.

She's already carrying it and puts it down on the table.

DEMELZA Anythin' else?

ROSS *(amused)* If you could somehow avoid the inference that I'm utterly predictable?

DEMELZA 'Es, sur. I'll try, sur.

Demelza practises a curtsey. Ross smiles, amused. A brief moment between them – then she leaves. Ross returns to his copper sample.

CUT TO:

52: INT. WOODS – NIGHT 23

Jim and Nick tiptoe through the undergrowth. Jim's breathing comes in short gasps. He's struggling not to cough. Nick stops short, signals to Jim to be absolutely still. Jim halts, hardly daring to move. Nick draws his attention to something up ahead: the shapes of sleeping pheasants roosting on the lower branches of trees. Nick signals him to move forward. They tiptoe ahead, slowly, nets at the ready. They're almost there . . . then Jim's coughing gets the better of him and the sound of a twig snapping behind them makes them wheel round. A gamekeeper emerges from the shadows – with a gun pointing. Jim and Nick drop their nets and sprint for cover. The gamekeeper fires. Jim stumbles and falls. Nick makes no attempt to help him and runs off. The gamekeeper catches up with Jim, who is clambering to his feet. He points the gun at Jim. Resigned, Jim raises his hands.

CUT TO:

53: EXT. NAMPARA HOUSE – DAY 24

Demelza opens the door to a Jinny who is too distraught to speak. She takes one look at Demelza and collapses in her arms in a flood of tears.

CUT TO:

54: EXT. NAMPARA HOUSE, STABLES – DAY 24

Ross is saddling his horse while Demelza holds the reins.

ROSS I shouldn't have waited, dammit! I should have made him the offer last night!

DEMELZA What will 'ee do?

ROSS Pay a visit to Sir Hugh Bodrugan. The owner of the pheasants.

Ross leaps on his horse and rides away.

CUT TO:

55: EXT. MOORLAND – DAY 24

Ross gallops urgently in the direction of Sir Hugh Bodrugan's house.

CUT TO:

56: EXT. STABLES – DAY 24

Ross gallops up to the stables. Sir Hugh Bodrugan, in hunting dress, surrounded by his hounds, is preparing to leave. He seems delighted to see Ross.

SIR HUGH Ross Poldark! Are you joining the hunt, sir?

ROSS Thank you, no. But I'd be grateful for five minutes of your time.

SIR HUGH What can I do for you?

ROSS The poacher taken last night on your land? As magistrate, you'll have hearing of the case? He's an employee of mine—

SIR HUGH Is he, by God!

ROSS It's a first offence – I've reason to think he's been led astray – and I'd happily make good any loss if he could be let off with a severe warning.

SIR HUGH *(erupting into laughter)* Blast me, sir, he's on his way to Truro Jail! I committed him for trial at eight o'clock this morning.

ROSS You were in haste, sir.

SIR HUGH There was no time to lose. The hunt starts at nine!

Ross's face gives away his feelings of disgust.

SIR HUGH *(cont'd)* And you must admit, it's a damned disgrace the amount of good game that's been lost of late. Hanging's barely good enough for the villain!

Ross bites his lip, bows politely, leaps onto his horse and rides away.

CUT TO:

57: INT. NAMPARA HOUSE, KITCHEN – NIGHT 24

Ross sits with Demelza having supper. He is brooding, thoughtful. She glances at him enquiringly. As if she had actually voiced the question, he replies.

ROSS Yes, they disgust me. My own class. Not all of them. But most.

DEMELZA How is it, sur, 'ee be not like 'em?

ROSS Perhaps I am.

DEMELZA No, sur. They don' see us like you do. As folk wi' 'urts an' feelin's same as they.

ROSS Sometimes I fail to see that too, Demelza. Sometime I barely see what's right in front of me.

She nods thoughtfully. He is silent too. They remain in companionable silence, eating their supper together.

CUT TO:

58: EXT. NAMPARA HOUSE – DAY 25

Establisher. Morning.

CUT TO:

59: INT. NAMPARA HOUSE, KITCHEN – DAY 25

The day of Jim's trial. Ross is preparing to leave.

DEMELZA He'm just a lad, sur. They mun' sure let 'im go.

ROSS You would think so.

He leaves. Demelza continues with her chores.

CUT TO:

60: EXT. MELLIN COTTAGES – DAY 25

Ross rides up to Mellin Cottages. Zacky emerges from one of the cottages.

ROSS Is Jinny ready?

ZACKY She can't go, Ross. 'Tis 'er time.

From inside the cottage come the sounds of a woman in the throes of labour.

ZACKY Bring 'im safe home, Ross.

ROSS I'll do my best.

A moment between the two men. They know Ross has a massive task on his hands. Then Ross rides off.

CUT TO:

61: EXT. TRURO – DAY 25

Ross rides into town.

CUT TO:

62: INT. COURT ROOM – DAY 25

Ross makes his way into the court room and looks for a seat among the spectators. He finds a seat behind Dr Choake.

HIS POV: Five magistrates preside over the court. Their chief is the Reverend Dr Halse.

The court, though small and cramped, is hot and airless and filled with boisterous spectators. The Reverend Dr Halse is pronouncing judgement on the current case.

REVEREND DR HALSE Sentenced for transportation. Take him away.

An uproar in the court. The convicted man struggles and protests but to no avail. Ross leans over to Dr Choake.

ROSS What was his crime?

DR CHOAKE Poaching.

As Ross settles in his seat, a thought occurs. He leans forward again.

ROSS A word, sir?

DR CHOAKE Don't tell me. More funds required?

ROSS No, sir. Another matter entirely. You treated Jim Carter when he worked at Wheal Reath?

DR CHOAKE Convulsive asthma – a morbid condition of the lungs. Did for his father, if I recall. Why d'you ask?

ROSS Only that with evidence of ill health and testament of good character, I'd hope we could get the charge dismissed.

DR CHOAKE Dismissed?

Dr Choake looks at Ross as if he's taken leave of his senses.

ROSS I doubt his lungs would survive a stint in jail.

DR CHOAKE *(cont'd)* To be frank with you, sir, I've not much sympathy for your aims. No good will come of being sentimental about such folk. They're a different breed, sir. A different breed.

A voice calls out: 'Call James Carter.' Jim is brought in. He looks pale and scared. He gives Ross a feeble smile.

CUT TO:

63: EXT. STREET – DAY 25

Francis cuts a lonely figure as he walks through the town. Up ahead is the Red Lion Inn. George appears. He sees Francis.

GEORGE Will you join me?

FRANCIS I have an estate to run.

GEORGE One game won't hurt.

He goes into the Red Lion. Francis continues down the street. He passes the Red Lion. He keeps walking. Then he stops. He's fighting the urge to succumb to his old ways. We see the moment when he loses the battle. He turns and walks back.

CUT TO:

64: INT. COURT ROOM – DAY 25

The Reverend Dr Halse is questioning the gamekeeper.

REVEREND DR HALSE So he was caught red-handed? And according to Sir Hugh, there's scarcely a pheasant left in his woods?

The gamekeeper nods humbly.

REVEREND DR HALSE *(cont'd)* You may stand down. *(then)* Is there any defence in the case? No one speaks.

ON ROSS: Looking surprised. Surely Jim is going to say something in his own defence? But apparently not.

REVEREND DR HALSE *(cont'd)* Very well, then—

Ross, realising that Jim isn't going to defend himself, gets to his feet.

ROSS If I might ask the indulgence of the court?

The Reverend Dr Halse peers at Ross, nods slightly in recognition. Ross returns his nod.

REVEREND DR HALSE You have some evidence you wish to give in this man's defence?

ROSS I wish to give evidence of his good character. He's my servant.

A murmur of interest from the spectators. A gentleman defending his servant is a rare event. There's a whispered conference amongst the magistrates. Then . . .

REVEREND DR HALSE Take the witness stand, sir.

Ross walks across to the witness stand.

ROSS No doubt, on the evidence you've heard, you will see nothing exceptional in this case. In your long experience there must be many such cases – especially in times when hunger, poverty and sickness prevail amongst the poor—

REVEREND DR HALSE Keep to the matter in hand, sir.

Ross is on the verge of making a sharp retort, but he restrains himself and does as instructed.

ROSS I've reason to believe that the accused fell into bad company with an older man who's so far escaped punishment. He has a wife, a mother and four sisters to support, he's in failing health—

REVEREND DR HALSE Evidence, sir? Pertaining to the crime itself?

Again Ross is forced to bite back a retort. It's becoming clear to him that the Reverend Dr Halse is not interested in anything which may extenuate Jim's guilt.

ROSS I have it on the authority of Dr Choake of Sawle that Jim Carter is suffering from a chronic lung condition which may prove fatal. I myself am prepared to stand surety for his future employ and good behaviour—

REVEREND DR HALSE Is it your contention that the prisoner is not in a fit state of health to go to prison?

ROSS It is, sir. Furthermore, this very day he will become a father for the first time.

Jim gasps and bursts into tears. There is a murmur of sympathy from the spectators in the court.

REVEREND DR HALSE The prisoner was ill when he went poaching?

ROSS He's been ill for some time.

REVEREND DR HALSE And his wife has been with child 'for some time'?

Ross bites back a sarcastic retort.

REVEREND DR HALSE *(cont'd)* It appears to me that if a man is well enough to go poaching he's well enough to take the consequences – whether or not they adversely affect his wife and child.

Ross's face falls. Jim's likewise. They can see their hopes evaporating.

CUT TO:

65: EXT. NAMPARA VALLEY, FIELDS – DAY 25

Demelza is working in the field with Jud. Prudie is lounging in a chair with her arm in a sling, fanning herself and directing the workers in their tasks.

PRUDIE When 'ee finish that, there be turnips t' thin – an' calves t' be meated – an' . . .

JUD 'Oo be this now?

PRUDIE It be the maid's father.

Demelza turns and looks in the direction Prudie's looking.

DEMELZA Why, what can he be wantin'?

HER POV: A man in the distance walking across the fields towards them. As the man approaches, we recognize Tom Carne, Demelza's father. Demelza's face falls. This is an unwelcome visit. Tom Carne greets his daughter.

TOM CARNE So 'ee be 'ere still.

DEMELZA An' content too, father. An' I 'ope you're the same.

TOM CARNE Take a look at me, daughter. What do 'ee see?

He turns full circle so she can take in his clothes and appearance (respectable, neat, clean).

DEMELZA What's happened?

TOM CARNE I be married. The Widow Chegwidden 'ave raised me up an' brought me out to meet the Lord—

DEMELZA Meanin' what?

TOM CARNE Meanin' farewell drink an' livin' in sin. We d' live a good life now, daughter. An' we be fixin' to 'ave 'ee back.

Demelza's face falls.

TOM CARNE 'Tis a fine woman I've married, chile! An' Nelly d'feel ye be better wi' we than stayin' 'ere exposed to all temptations o' flesh an' the devil—

DEMELZA Temptations?

TOM CARNE 'Ee d'know of what I speak.

Demelza looks blank.

TOM CARNE *(cont'd)* Confess, daughter – what sin there is 'twixt you an' Poldark.

Tom looks smug and self-righteous. Demelza is outraged.

DEMELZA There's no sin! 'E's my master, I'm 'is servant—

TOM CARNE An' more besides, if tales be true!

DEMELZA What's it to me what folks say?

TOM CARNE Naught to thee maybe, but I want no daughter o' mine mixed up in such talk!

DEMELZA Since when were 'ee so tender o' me?

TOM CARNE Since the Lord 'ope'd my 'eart an' shone 'is light! *(then, firm)* So I give 'ee a day to make it right wi' Poldark – then I'll be back 'ere again to fetch 'ee 'ome!

He walks off. Stunned and horrified, Demelza watches him leave. Without warning she bursts into tears. Jud and Prudie exchange a look of alarm.

CUT TO:

66: INT. COURTHOUSE – DAY 25

The trial continues. The Reverend Dr Halse now sums up.

REVEREND DR HALSE You paint a vivid picture of the hardships endured by the poor, sir. Still, a man's need should not determine his honesty, else all beggars would be thieves.

Murmurs of disagreement from the spectators.

REVEREND DR HALSE *(cont'd)* However, in view of these extenuating circumstances and your testimony of Carter's good character, the court is prepared to take a more lenient view.

Ross and Jim exchange a hopeful glance. The whole court seems to hold its breath, waiting for a lenient sentence.

REVEREND DR HALSE *(cont'd – to Jim)* Sentenced to two years imprisonment.

Jim gasps in dismay. An outburst of disgust from the spectators. Ross shakes his head in disbelief.

ROSS I trust I shall never have the misfortune to have the 'leniency' of the court extended to me!

REVEREND DR HALSE Have a care, Mr Poldark. Such remarks are not entirely outside our jurisdiction.

ROSS No, sir. Only mercy enjoys that privilege.

As Jim is led away, Ross prepares to leave the box. But the Reverend Dr Halse is not yet finished with him.

REVEREND DR HALSE One moment, sir. *(Ross halts)* You take issue with the laws of this land?

ROSS I can't help but feel that in this case justice would have best been served by clemency.

REVEREND DR HALSE Happily for justice, this court is better able to interpret the law than you.

ROSS *(exploding)* Then the law is savage and you interpret it without charity! The book from which you preach says that man shall not live by bread alone. These days you're asking him to live without even that!

REVEREND DR HALSE Step down, Mr Poldark, or we'll have you committed for contempt of court.

ROSS I can assure you, such a committal would be an entirely accurate reading of my thoughts!

Ross walks out of the court room. A murmur of agreement and appreciation breaks out.

Various spectators slap him on the back but it's no consolation to him. He feels entirely wretched.

CUT TO:

67: INT. NAMPARA HOUSE, KITCHEN – DAY 25

Demelza is quietly distraught as she prepares Ross's supper. Prudie, watching from the side, is surprisingly sympathetic.

DEMELZA How can I go? I cud'n live nowhere else. Till I came, I never lived at all. I can't leave 'ere. *(beat)* I can't leave him.

Prudie nods sympathetically. Then a horrible thought occurs.

DEMELZA *(cont'd)* 'E'll make me go. 'E won't care. I'm not so important to 'im as he is to me.

Prudie watches her as she prepares the dinner.

PRUDIE Spare 'ee'self th' trouble, girl. 'E'll not be 'ome t'night.

CUT TO:

68: INT. RED LION INN – DAY 25

Ross sits with a bottle of rum in front of him. He pours himself a final glass. He's had the entire bottle. A woman seats herself at his table. It's Margaret.

MARGARET What cheer, Captain Poldark?

ROSS Precious little.

MARGARET I could remedy that.

He looks at her – and is reminded of that night once before when he availed himself of her 'cheer'. He's almost tempted. Then . . .

ROSS You could not.

MARGARET Sure?

ROSS Nobody could.

Margaret seems as if she might press him further but his expression makes her realize she'd be wasting her time.

MARGARET Then I shall take my consolation where it's more appreciated.

She gets up and goes over to another table, where she slides her hand round the neck of the man sitting there and whispers in his ear. The man is clearly inebriated and his head is bowed. Only as Ross gets up to leave does he realize it's Francis. Francis is oblivious. Margaret smiles at Ross over Francis's shoulder as Ross walks out. Then she turns her attention back to Francis.

MARGARET A 'Poldark' you say?

FRANCIS Not a Poldark. The Poldark. Of Trenwith House—

MARGARET Lord bless you, sir. What other Poldark is there?

CUT TO:

69: INT. NAMPARA HOUSE, LIBRARY – DAY 25

Demelza opens the chest which contains the pale blue dress. She knows now that she will never have another chance to try it on.

CUT TO:

70: INT. BODMIN JAIL – DAY 25

Jim is thrown into the dark, cramped, squalid depths of Bodmin Jail. His fellow prisoners are an appalling sight: filthy, weak, hacking coughs, hair and beards matted, skin mottled and festering. Beside them, Jim looks like a new-born babe: pure and helpless. This glimpse into his future horrifies him.

JIM Oh, Jinny . . .

CUT TO:

71: EXT. MELLIN COTTAGES – DUSK 25

Jinny weeps softly with her newborn baby in her arms. Beside her, Zacky looks grim. Ross, close to tears himself, has just told them the news.

ZACKY 'Twas more'n good of 'ee t' try, Ross.

ROSS Don't thank me. I failed miserably.

Without another word he leaps on his horse and rides away. Jinny continues to weep. Zacky puts his arm round her shoulders and leads her back inside.

CUT TO:

72: INT. NAMPARA HOUSE, LIBRARY – DUSK 25

Demelza is wearing the pale blue dress. It rustles as she walks about the room. She touches various items as she passes them – maps, copper samples, books, mining artefacts, candlesticks, the tomahawk – as if taking her leave of them one by one.

DEMELZA *(to herself, barely audible)* Goodbye – goodbye – goodbye – goodbye – *(then, dissolving into tears)* I can't leave 'im – I can't – I can't – *(pulling herself together)* But I must—

Suddenly the sound of approaching horse's hooves jolts her back to the present. And then she hears a voice.

ROSS'S VOICE Demelza!

She gasps, horrified. To be caught like this, wearing this dress? She'll be in so much trouble . . .

ROSS'S VOICE *(louder)* Demelza!

Almost without thinking – and with no time to take off the dress – she runs out of the room.

CUT TO:

73: INT. NAMPARA HOUSE, PARLOUR – DUSK 25

Ross flings himself into a chair, throws off his coat and begins to pull off his boots. Presently Demelza comes in with his supper, which she puts on the table. Ross is so distracted, he doesn't even look at her. She's about to sneak out again.

ROSS *(without looking up)* Demelza? Close the windows.

DEMELZA Yes, sur.

Demelza closes them one by one, trying to move slowly so that the rustling of her dress won't be noticed. Ross sits, head in hands, the events of the day churning over in his head.

ROSS Jud and Prudie abed?

DEMELZA Yes, sur, long since.

ROSS Fetch me the rum.

Ross sits at the table but doesn't touch his supper. Demelza is acutely aware of the rustling of the dress, but Ross seems oblivious, locked in his thoughts. Demelza places the rum and a glass on the table. Ross pours, downs the rum in one, pours another. Demelza is heading for the door again.

ROSS Light the candles.

She begins to light the candles. It seems incredible that he hasn't noticed the rustling of her dress. But he's still preoccupied with the events of the day.

ROSS Jim Carter got two years.

DEMELZA I fear'd it might be worse.

ROSS I doubt he'll survive.

DEMELZA 'Ee did all 'ee could.

ROSS Did I? I doubt it. I was too concerned with my own dignity. Grovelling and compliments were the order of the day – and I made the mistake of trying to teach them their business. A schoolboy error – and Jim paid dearly for it.

Demelza, having lit the candles, is about to sneak out of the room, but as she's going through the door, Ross becomes aware of the rustle of her dress and takes in her appearance for the first time.

ROSS *(cont'd)* Demelza?

She halts in the doorway, hardly daring to move.

ROSS What are you wearing?

She turns back into the room, squirming with shame.

DEMELZA I – I found it in one o' the chests – in the library—

ROSS You dare to go rifling through those things?

DEMELZA I – I'm sorry, sur – 'ee never told me I shouldn't look—

ROSS That was surely obvious?

Demelza is crimson with embarrassment. Ross is looking at her in utter disbelief.

ROSS *(cont'd)* You're employed as a maid—

DEMELZA I know, sur—

ROSS And you've been a good one. And for that you've been allowed certain liberties. But dressing up in fine clothes is not one of them.

DEMELZA I meant no 'arm, sur. 'Twas jus' rottin' away in that ol' box – I thought 'ee might let me wear it sometimes—

ROSS Take it off.

DEMELZA Sur—

ROSS Take it off now!

Demelza's mouth trembles, but she doesn't move. Ross starts to lose patience.

ROSS *(cont'd)* If you don't take it off this minute, you can pack your things and go back to your father!

Demelza suddenly dissolves into tears. To Ross this seems totally out of proportion to his threat. To Demelza his threat is confirmation that she has no choice but to return home. She continues to cry. Feeling he's been a little harsh, Ross modifies his tone.

ROSS *(cont'd – more gently)* Demelza—

When she still doesn't stop crying, Ross gets to his feet and goes over to her.

ROSS *(cont'd)* Enough now. I shouldn't have spoken so harshly.

Demelza continues to sob, seemingly inconsolable.

ROSS *(cont'd)* Don't take it to heart. It's been a hellish day and I'm not myself—

She stops sobbing. He's standing close to her now. Tear-drops glisten on her eyelashes. One escapes and runs down her cheek. Almost without thinking, Ross reaches out and smudges it away. She looks up at him – imploring. For the first time he becomes aware of her fragility. And her undeniable loveliness. She's so close to him now, he can almost breathe her in. Desire surges in him. Scarcely knowing what he's doing, he seizes her and kisses her. She is only momentarily surprised, then she surrenders wholeheartedly. He devours her hungrily. Then, without warning, he pushes her away. She looks at him, confused.

DEMELZA What've I done?

ROSS I didn't take you from your father for this.

DEMELZA What do it matter what you took me for?

ROSS Go to bed.

DEMELZA But—

ROSS Go to bed, now.

As if he can no longer trust himself to keep his hands off her, he walks out of the room. Demelza sinks to her knees in despair. For a long time she remains there, distraught. Then finally, resigned, she gets to her feet and begins to blow out the candles one by one.

CUT TO:

74: INT. NAMPARA HOUSE, ROSS'S BEDROOM – NIGHT 25

Ross lies awake a long while, tormented by his thoughts. Then, just as he's about to blow out the candle, the door opens and Demelza comes in. She is still wearing the dress. She closes the door behind her. He looks at her, uncomprehending.

ROSS What is it?

DEMELZA The dress. *(beat)* It unfastens down the back.

Ross sits up in bed. For a moment he's confused by what she's asking. She sits on the edge of the bed. Now her meaning is clear to him. He hesitates. So many reasons not to do this. And then he begins to unhook the dress. Slowly. Carefully. One hook at a time. Demelza doesn't move. She can hardly breathe. Hook after hook, until the last is undone. She's absolutely still, as if the slightest move would break the spell. He's so close now, she can feel his breath on the back of her neck. She shivers.

ROSS You know what people say of us?

DEMELZA Yes.

ROSS If we behave like this, it will be true.

DEMELZA Then let it be true.

And finally he can resist her no longer. He slides his hands inside the dress. It falls from her shoulders. He pulls her head back towards him and kisses her until the room goes dark.

CUT TO:

75: EXT. NAMPARA VALLEY – DAY 26

Before sunrise. Absolute silence broken by the first notes of bird song.

CUT TO:

76: INT. NAMPARA HOUSE, ROSS'S BEDROOM – DAY 26

Demelza opens her eyes. For a moment she doesn't remember where she is. Then she catches sight of Ross's head on the pillow beside her – and remembers everything. Unsure of how she's feeling, anxious to be away before he wakes up, she slides quietly out of bed. The dress lies in a heap on the floor. She gathers it quietly, wraps it around her and tiptoes from the room. Only when the door closes does Ross open his eyes. He's been awake all the time. His face is impassive. It's impossible to tell what he's thinking.

CUT TO:

77: EXT. NAMPARA VALLEY, FIELDS – DAY 26

Demelza is lying on her back in a corn field, surrounded by cornflowers. She stretches out her limbs and smiles.

CUT TO:

78: INT. TRENWITH HOUSE, DRAWING ROOM – DAY 26

Charles is helped into the drawing room by Verity. Elizabeth, with Geoffrey Charles beside her, is playing the harp. Aunt Agatha watches, eagle-eyed.

CHARLES Where's Francis?

Elizabeth stops playing. She debates whether to tell the truth and decides that she will.

ELIZABETH He did not come home last night.

VERITY He'll have stayed in town with George—

AUNT AGATHA *(a snort of derision)* That upstart?

CHARLES Has he been going to the mine?

VERITY I'm sure he has.

CHARLES *(ignoring her)* Elizabeth? Is he attending to his duties?

Again Elizabeth debates whether to tell the truth. She decides against.

ELIZABETH Of course he is, sir.

But it's clear that she knows exactly what's going on – and that Charles isn't fooled either.

CUT TO:

79: INT. NAMPARA HOUSE, KITCHEN – DAY 26

Ross comes into the kitchen to find Prudie making tea. She is using both hands, but when she sees him, she reverts to using only one, hurriedly returning her 'sprained' arm to its sling. He's not in a great mood.

ROSS Where's Demelza?

PRUDIE An't seen 'er.

ROSS When she appears, tell her to start on the barley field. *(to Jud)* You and I will set to with the hay.

JUD Aye, sur. *(then)* I, sur?

ROSS You, sir. Without Jim to cover your idleness you may be forced to break a sweat occasionally.

Ross goes out without taking any breakfast. Prudie raises her eyebrows. He's clearly in a touchy mood.

JUD 'Tidn' right.

CUT TO:

80: EXT. NAMPARA VALLEY, FIELDS – DAY 26

Ross and Jud are scything. The sun is overhead now and the heat is shimmering in a haze over the fields.

JUD They be sayin' Jim Carter won' last five minutes in Bodmin Jail—

Ross says nothing. He continues to scythe the meadow.

JUD *(cont'd)* If th' fever don' get 'em, starvation will—

Still no answer. Ross continues to work.

JUD *(cont'd)* Still, they say that if 'Someone We Know' 'an't spoke up f'r'him, 'e'd be on's way to seven years transportation.

Ross still doesn't reply.

CUT TO:

81: EXT. NAMPARA VALLEY, FIELDS – DAY 26

Demelza lies on her stomach in the long grass, with Garrick beside her, watching Ross and Jud scything the meadow below. They can't see her. She watches Ross thoughtfully. He's stripped to the waist and his torso is glistening with sweat. Demelza shivers, as if remembering the events of the night before.

CUT TO:

82: EXT. NAMPARA VALLEY, FIELDS – DAY 26

Exhausted, Ross takes a swig of water. As he does so he sees, through the shimmering heat haze, as if gliding through the fields, a woman on horseback. His heart leaps. It's Elizabeth. Slowly he hands his scythe to Jud, picks up his shirt and walks towards the house.

CUT TO:

83: INT. NAMPARA HOUSE, PARLOUR – DAY 26

Ross tries to make himself look presentable as he walks into the parlour. Elizabeth is sitting in a chair. She looks cool, beautiful and every inch a lady.

ROSS An unexpected pleasure.

ELIZABETH I was passing this way and—

They both know this isn't true.

ELIZABETH *(cont'd)* I was sorry to hear about your farm boy. *(then)* Reverend Halse plays cards with the Warleggans.

ROSS And?

ELIZABETH Perhaps if you'd approached George things could have been arranged?

ROSS Is that how justice works?

ELIZABETH We both know it, Ross.

A moment between them. He knows it's true. It's also the last thing he wants to hear right now.

ROSS *(to change the subject)* How's Geoffrey Charles?

ELIZABETH He's my joy. *(correcting herself)* Our joy. *(then)* I heard blasting as I came by Wheal Leisure. Have you hit ironstone?

ROSS This is a new interest?

ELIZABETH Francis thinks it unladylike but how else can I understand the business on which our fortunes, and those of our tenants, depends.

ROSS You always had an enquiring mind!

ELIZABETH Marriage discourages such a thing.

ROSS Always?

ELIZABETH Perhaps it depends on the partners.

A moment between them. Is Elizabeth just playing with the thought or is she encouraging him again? Suddenly the door opens and Demelza walks in. She looks wild and unkempt, with grass stalks in her hair. She carries a bunch of cornflowers. She sees at once that she's intruding.

DEMELZA Oh! – beg pardon, sur, ma'am – I—

She looks at Ross and flushes. Involuntarily he flushes back. Elizabeth catches the look that passes between them. She feels ice in the pit of her stomach. She knows beyond all doubt that the rumours are true – there is something between Ross and Demelza.

DEMELZA Can I get you anything, ma'am – sur?

ROSS *(brusque)* Prudie's served us. Her arm seems recovered.

DEMELZA Oh – yes, sur – I'll just see t' these flowers, sur—

ELIZABETH They're very pretty.

Demelza halts. She senses that Elizabeth is making an effort to be kind to her.

DEMELZA *(impulsively)* Would ye like 'em?

ELIZABETH Oh! Thank you. But I'm afraid they won't last. See they're fading already. Cornflowers are like that.

Demelza looks at the cornflowers in her hand. They are indeed beginning to droop.

ELIZABETH *(cont'd – to Ross)* I must go.

ROSS I'll see you out.

Elizabeth picks up her riding gloves and crop. Ross escorts her out of the room. He can't bring himself to look at Demelza as he passes her. It's all Demelza needs to know. She realizes that their relationship is changed (spoiled) forever. She goes out, leaving behind on the table the bunch of drooping cornflowers.

CUT TO:

84: EXT. NAMPARA COVE – DAY 26

Demelza walks barefoot down to the sea. At the water's edge she paddles a while through the surf. She seems troubled. What has she done? And what is she to do now?

CUT TO:

85: EXT. NAMPARA HOUSE, COURTYARD – DAY 26

Ross sits in the courtyard peening his scythe. He is lost in thought. Elizabeth's appearance has consolidated something in his mind. He does the job methodically, painstakingly. Presently he finishes and gets to his feet. His expression is solemn. He's reached a decision. Now he must communicate it.

ROSS *(shouts)* Demelza!

CUT TO:

86: INT. NAMPARA HOUSE, KITCHEN – DAY 26

Ross comes into the kitchen, where Prudie is making a fuss about having to use her injured arm.

PRUDIE An' me ailin' an' still barely fit a' stand!

JUD 'Ee can stand well enough wi' a gill o' brandy in 'er fist!

ROSS Where's Demelza?

JUD Las' I seen 'er she were 'eadin' t'wards Sawle wi' that blatherin' dog at 'er 'eels.

Ross halts. Surely Demelza hasn't done what he thinks she's done? He grabs his riding crop and goes out.

CUT TO:

87: EXT. COUNTRY ROAD – DAY 26

Demelza walks briskly, a knapsack over her back and Garrick at her heels. She looks tearful but determined. She must return to her family and that's all there is to it. She doesn't look round when she hears the sound of galloping hooves approaching. She hasn't the least expectation that the rider is after her. But he is. Ross pulls up alongside her. He looks stern.

ROSS I engaged you for two years. What d'you mean by running away?

Demelza looks at him in astonishment. He dismounts. He seems so angry she's almost afraid of him.

DEMELZA Sur, I—

ROSS Haven't you been well treated? Aren't you grown used to the house – and your tasks – and my moods?

DEMELZA Yes, sur, but—

ROSS Can you not give me what I want before I even ask?

DEMELZA Yes, sur – but I thought – after what happened—

ROSS You thought you would no longer be my servant.

DEMELZA Not from choice, sur, but—

ROSS You're right. You can no longer be my servant.

CUT TO:

88: INT. SAWLE CHURCH – DAY 27

Reverend Odgers conducts the service through pursed lips, his expression pinched and severe.

REVEREND ODGERS Dearly beloved, we are gathered together here in the sight of God, and of this congregation to join together this man and this woman in holy matrimony . . .

Only now do we reveal the 'congregation' is Jud and Prudie, and 'this man and this woman' are Ross and Demelza. Demelza seems to be in shock. She keeps glancing at Ross as if expecting him to say it's all a huge joke. Ross, stern-faced, looks back at her, as if he too can hardly believe what he's doing. They're in a daze. The words of the marriage service seem to come and go – Reverend Odgers is opening and closing his mouth but the sounds are distorted and distant. Until . . .

REVEREND ODGERS *(cont'd)* Ross Vennor Poldark, do you take this woman to be your lawful wedded wife?

Episode 4

1: EXT. CLIFF-TOPS – DUSK 28

Sunset. Bare feet pick their way through the evening dew. Demelza is revealed, gathering wild flowers, Garrick at her heels. She halts on the cliff-tops looking out to sea.
CUT TO:

2: INT. NAMPARA HOUSE, KITCHEN – DUSK 28

Jud and Prudie potter about bemoaning their changed circumstances.
JUD 'Tidn' right—
PRUDIE 'Tidn' fair—
JUD 'Tidn' fit—
PRUDIE 'Tidn' proper—
JUD Won' last—
PRUDIE Won' work—
JUD 'Oo d' she think she is?
PRUDIE 'Oo d' 'e think she is?
CUT TO:

3: EXT. NAMPARA VALLEY, FIELDS – DUSK 28

Ross rides home to Nampara.

CUT TO:

4: INT. NAMPARA HOUSE, KITCHEN – DUSK 28

JUD Chit of a girl. She'll be too grand t' skivvy—

PRUDIE Too common t' curtsey—

JUD 'Tis all cocky-eyed—

PRUDIE My head fair 'urts with it!

CUT TO:

5: EXT. NAMPARA HOUSE – DUSK 28

Demelza returns home as dusk is falling, Garrick trotting beside her. She looks up the valley, but there's no sign of Ross.

DEMELZA *(to Garrick)* 'E's late t'night, Garrick. So where can 'e be?

CUT TO:

6: INT. NAMPARA HOUSE, KITCHEN – NIGHT 28

Ross comes in to find Demelza shaping dough into loaves ready to put in the oven. He stands for a moment, unnoticed, watching her.

DEMELZA *(sings)*

As pretty a piece of mischief as never I saw . . .

She breaks off as she sees him, almost stands to attention, as if awaiting instructions.

DEMELZA *(cont'd)* Oh! Sur! – *(correcting herself)* Ross – *(then)* I was thinking 'ee might stay o'er in town—

ROSS I have a home, do I not? And a wife?

DEMELZA Sometimes I d' forget.

ROSS That I live here?

DEMELZA That I'm your wife.

ROSS Let this be a reminder.

He seizes her and kisses her hungrily. Then, releasing her . . .

ROSS *(cont'd)* Why are you up so late?

DEMELZA I 'ave chores—

ROSS Suppose I have other plans for you?

DEMELZA Tell me.

She looks at him seriously as if trying to read his mind. His face is impassive – but suddenly she knows exactly what he's thinking.

DEMELZA Yes, Ross.

ROSS *(laughing)* I think I prefer 'sir'!

He takes her hand and leads her out of the kitchen towards the stairs.
CUT TO:

7: INT. NAMPARA HOUSE, ROSS & DEMELZA'S ROOM – NIGHT 28

Ross and Demelza lie naked, flushed from lovemaking. Ross seems thoughtful. For a while they lie in silence. Then . . .

DEMELZA Folks'll wonder. *(no reply)* They'll not understand. *(no reply)* I don' rightly understand.

ROSS What?

DEMELZA How it came t' happen. This. We.

ROSS You're not required to understand. You're required to accept it as a fact of life.

Demelza considers this a moment. Then . . .

DEMELZA So it's not t' be a secret?

ROSS Why should it?

CUT TO:

8: EXT. CLIFF-TOP RIDE – DAY 29

Ross rides along the cliff-tops towards Grambler Mine. In the distance he sees small groups of women looking out over the sea. As he approaches one such group, he recognizes Mrs Zacky, Connie Carter and several young Carter girls.

ROSS Good day, ladies. Are we expecting a storm?

MRS ZACKY Storm o' pilchards, God willin'!

ROSS They're late this year.

MRS ZACKY An we d' fear they miss'd us entire an' swung away t' Ireland.

ROSS If that happens you'll have nothing to see you through the winter—

MRS ZACKY An' we'll starve. Simple as that.

They both look worried. It's a very real possibility.

CUT TO:

9: EXT. GRAMBLER MINE – DAY 29

Francis emerges from the engine house of the mine, followed by an angry mine captain.

FRANCIS I'm not a magician, sir! I cannot conjure wages out of thin air! The men must wait.

As Francis mounts his horse and prepares to ride away, he sees Ross approaching.

FRANCIS Did my father send you?

ROSS Why would he?

FRANCIS To read me the riot act? Tell me what I'm doing wrong? Or perhaps it was my wife. Does she fear I'm falling short of the mark?

ROSS Is she wrong to be concerned?

FRANCIS What she doesn't know won't hurt her.

ROSS What she suspects might.

FRANCIS Gaming? Whoring? What gentleman doesn't occasionally indulge?

ROSS This one.

FRANCIS *(laughing)* Since when?

ROSS Since my wedding.

Francis is open-mouthed with shock.

CUT TO:

10: INT. NAMPARA HOUSE, PARLOUR – DAY 29

Demelza's wedding posy, now faded, stands in a jug on a table. Demelza takes out the posy and replaces it with a bunch of fresh wild flowers. One of the blossoms in the posy is still fresh. She breaks it off and puts it in her apron pocket, singing softly to herself.

DEMELZA *(sings)*

I suspicion'd she was pretty
I suspicion'd she was wed . . .

She picks up the broom and continues her chores.

CUT TO:

11: EXT. GRAMBLER MINE – DAY 29

Francis stares at Ross as if he's taken leave of his senses.

FRANCIS Your – kitchen maid?

Ross merely smiles.

FRANCIS *(cont'd)* But Ross, you must surely see—

He struggles to find a polite way of expressing himself. Eventually he realizes there is no polite way.

FRANCIS *(cont'd)* With such a wife you cannot hope to have entry into any respectable gathering? You'll cut yourself out of society – consign yourself to—

ROSS A life of peace and seclusion? I must try to bear it as best I can.

Francis continues to stare at Ross in astonishment – much to Ross's amusement.

ROSS *(cont'd)* May I leave you to share the glad tidings at Trenwith?

CUT TO:

12: INT. TRENWITH HOUSE, OAK ROOM – DAY 29

Elizabeth is trembling with shock. Charles explodes into a coughing fit.

ELIZABETH Demelza?

CHARLES *(through his coughing fit)* Damn me, he's done it now!

FRANCIS What the devil can he mean by it?

Verity says nothing but smiles quietly to herself.

CUT TO:

13: INT. RED LION INN – DAY 29

Ross sits at a table, hunched over some mine papers.

MARGARET I never thought you the marrying kind. Is she wealthy?

ROSS Not at all.

CUT TO:

14: INT. WARLEGGAN HOUSE, LIBRARY – DAY 29

George and Cary are busy with their paperwork.

GEORGE He could've had his pick. Any number of eligible girls from rising families. Instead of which – he marries his serving wench?

CARY It beggars belief.

GEORGE It may beggar him.

CUT TO:

15: INT. TRENWITH HOUSE, OAK ROOM – DAY 29

Elizabeth is playing the harp, concentrating hard to try and block out her mother Mrs Chynoweth, who is pacing up and down.

MRS CHYNOWETH He must be deranged. How else could he lower his sights so abominably?

CUT TO:

16: INT. RED LION INN – DAY 29

MARGARET Is she beautiful?

ROSS In a way.

CUT TO:

17: INT. WARLEGGAN HOUSE, LIBRARY – DAY 29

GEORGE In spite of all our assets, we Warleggans struggle to pass muster. How will he fare with a scullery maid on his arm?

CUT TO:

18: INT. TRENWITH HOUSE, OAK ROOM – DAY 29

MRS CHYNOWETH His family will never forgive him. Society will never forgive him.

CUT TO:

19: INT. WARLEGGAN HOUSE, LIBRARY – DAY 29

CARY Doors which were open will be slammed in his face. His ventures will fail—

George is thoughtful.

CARY *(cont'd)* And you can enjoy the sight of him in the gutter, along with his slut.

CUT TO:

20: INT. RED LION INN – DAY 29

Ross gathers up his papers, finishes his rum, heads for the door.

MARGARET So you love her?

He halts, considers her question, smiles.

ROSS We get on.

He goes out. Margaret remains, intrigued by this response.

CUT TO:

21: INT. TRENWITH HOUSE, OAK ROOM – DAY 29

VERITY *(VO)* My dear Ross, I am the last person to criticize your attachment . . .

CLOSE ON: *Verity's handwriting.*

VERITY *(VO)* But I would like to be the first to write to you . . .

CUT TO:

22: INT. NAMPARA HOUSE, PARLOUR – DAY 30

Ross reads Verity's letter of congratulation aloud to Demelza.

ROSS *(reads)* '. . . and wish you joy. I am presently taken up with attending father, but I hope soon to call to offer my felicitations in person'. *(to Demelza)* There. We have at least one friend.

DEMELZA Why— ?

ROSS Why?

DEMELZA Does she need to come? 'Tis kind of her t' wish us well – but why mus' she call?

ROSS Because 'calling' is the favoured pursuit of polite society. Of which you are now a member. So you'd better get used to it!

CUT TO:

23: INT. NAMPARA HOUSE, KITCHEN – DAY 30

Demelza whacks a piece of dough onto the table.

DEMELZA 'Callin'?

She thrashes the dough into shape, as if taking out her frustration on it.

DEMELZA *(cont'd)* 'Oo 'as time t' call? What do 'ey mean by it? 'Callin'? I'll call 'em!

Now we realize she's not alone. Jud and Prudie have paused from their chores and are looking at her in amazement. She seems to notice them for the first time.

DEMELZA *(cont'd)* What?

No reply. Jud and Prudie glance at each other and shuffle awkwardly.

DEMELZA *(cont'd)* 'Ee bin givin' me squinny-eye ever since I got back from church.

PRUDIE 'Ow else we mun look? We don' rightly know 'oo we lookin' at!

JUD One minute she Miss Skivvily-Scullery-Kitchen-Maid – next she be Mistress 'Igh n' Mighty!

Demelza looks at them as if they've gone mad. Then . . .

DEMELZA *(cont'd)* Do 'ee think it's not as strange to me as it is to you? Do 'ee 'magine I ever looked for or 'spected it?

And now I think on it, 'tis more your fault than mine!

JUD 'Ow be that, then?

DEMELZA 'Tis you 'ave raised me up an' taught me all I know. If I'm fit for better than I'd 'oped, blame 'ee'selves for eddycatin' me!

She says it in a threatening tone and strides out. After she's gone . . .

PRUDIE We?

They consider it further.

JUD Eddycators?

Now they're seeing themselves in a new light.

PRUDIE We made 'er what she is.

JUD She 'ave we a' thank ferrit.

Then another thought occurs . . .

PRUDIE An' she d' still do all her chores—

JUD An' most o' yourn—

PRUDIE An' after all, 'tis better'n takin' orders from some fudgy-faced baggage wi' drop-curls!

They strut about the kitchen, full of self-importance and self-congratulation.

CUT TO:

24: INT. WHEAL LEISURE – DAY 30

Ross is working alongside Henshawe (and Mark, Paul and Zacky) by the mine entrance.

ROSS Damn this ironstone. Is there no end to it? How long till we strike copper?

HENSHAWE If we strike copper? Could be months.

ROSS Can we last?

HENSHAWE With good will and good men—

ROSS And a power of luck beside—

HENSHAWE We'll need a rise in the price of ore – else we're all wasting our time.

Ross nods in acknowledgement. They've always known this won't be easy.

CUT TO:

25: INT. NAMPARA HOUSE, ROSS & DEMELZA'S ROOM – NIGHT 30

As Demelza sleeps, Ross is working. The bed is covered with papers.

CUT TO:

26: EXT. NAMPARA HOUSE – DAY 31

Ross is saddling up his horse as Demelza holds his travelling bag. She's trying hard to understand his business.

DEMELZA This shareholders' meetin'—

ROSS Not a prospect I relish. We're no closer to copper – so I must appeal for further investment if we're to keep blasting.

DEMELZA But – are they not friends o' yourn?

ROSS *(laughing)* If ever they were, they're reconsidering the connection!

CUT TO:

27: EXT. HARBOUR – DAY 31

Ross rides into town. Is it his imagination or do several groups of people give him odd looks and start whispering as he rides past? As he passes the harbour he sees Choake, Pascoe, Renfrew and Horace Treneglos. Groups of villagers are seen on the cliff-tops looking out to sea.

DR CHOAKE I would I had nothing better to do than admire the view!

ROSS They'd happily swap places with you, sir. *(in response to Choake's glare)* You have means to last the winter. Without the pilchards, they do not.

DR CHOAKE Those who cannot feed, should not breed.

Pascoe, seeing that Ross is about to lose his temper, intervenes.

PASCOE I believe felicitations are in order. *(to Horace Treneglos)* Your son John? Recently wed?

HORACE TRENEGLOS To Miss Ruth Teague. A determined girl.

ROSS My best wishes to them both.

HORACE TRENEGLOS But are we not remiss to celebrate the absent and overlook the bridegroom in our midst?

Renfrew and Choake look baffled until, after a series of nods and winks from Pascoe in Ross's direction, the penny drops.

DR CHOAKE Oh – indeed, indeed—

HORACE TRENEGLOS Congratulations Captain Poldark, you have our best wishes for you and your young bride.

Renfrew seems rather embarrassed by the subject, Dr Choake outraged, but Ross smiles affably.

ROSS I thank you gentlemen. *(then)* If you'll excuse me, I must consult with Captain Henshawe before our meeting.

He strolls off, conscious of Choake's continuing outrage.

CUT TO:

28: EXT. HARBOUR WALL – DAY 31

Dr Choake, Horace Treneglos and Renfrew stroll along the harbour wall.

DR CHOAKE I confess myself uneasy. *(pause)* His early skirmishes with the law. His contempt of court at the last assizes—

Renfrew nods, as if sharing his concern.

DR CHOAKE *(cont'd)* Now this marriage to his serving wench—

HORACE TRENEGLOS You think him foolish?

DR CHOAKE I think him reckless in the extreme. Is a man who demonstrates such spectacular lack of judgement to be trusted? Is he fit to helm a venture of such risk as a mine? More to the point, am I prepared to trust him with more of my capital?

CUT TO:

29: INT. PRIVATE ROOM, INN – DAY 31

Henshawe has joined Choake, Horace Treneglos, Renfrew and Ross. Dr Choake delivers his verdict.

DR CHOAKE I am not, sir. I can see no reason for pouring good money after bad. Come to me when you've struck copper and I may reconsider. Till then you'll see no more of me or my guineas.

Ross is barely surprised. He looks round the table at the other investors.

ROSS The rest of you share his opinion?

There's an awkward silence. Ross fears he has lost all his investors. Eventually . . .

HENSHAWE I do not.

HORACE TRENEGLOS *(after a struggle)* Nor I, damn you!

He puts down a banker's order. Ross and Henshawe do the same. Renfrew and the other investors remain silent, staring at the table. Eventually . . .

ROSS Gentlemen. Thank you. I'm sorry we could not bring you better reports.

CUT TO:

30: EXT. NAMPARA VALLEY, FIELDS – DAY 31

Ross rides home slowly, disheartened.
CUT TO:

31: INT. NAMPARA HOUSE, KITCHEN – DAY 31

Ross arrives home, disheartened. Demelza is doing chores. He makes a determined effort to look cheerful. He is carrying a parcel which he hands to her.

DEMELZA You got the candles an' twine? An' muslin for the cheese?

ROSS Open it.

Demelza opens the parcel. It contains a copybook and a pen, and some lengths of ribbon. Demelza looks at him, puzzled.

ROSS For you. To practise your letters. *(the book)* And to tie up that unruly mane. *(the ribbons)* I know little of these things. If they don't suit, give them to Prudie.

Demelza snatches back the ribbons protectively and tries them in her hair.

ROSS Did I mention I wrote to your father?

DEMELZA Oh! No, Ross, ye never! He'll be that vexed, thinkin' I'll never come 'ome.

ROSS I told him your duty lay here.

DEMELZA Well, so it do, Ross. For nothin's changed.

ROSS Nothing?

DEMELZA I d' get less sleep!

ROSS That's your only complaint?

DEMELZA I 'ave no complaints.

ROSS I do, however.

DEMELZA: (immediately worried) Tell me— ?

ROSS You have yet to make an official visit to the mine.

It dawns on Demelza what Ross is saying.

DEMELZA Oh no, Ross – I couldn't. 'Ow would it look?

ROSS 'Look'?

DEMELZA A kitchen maid givin' 'erself airs—

ROSS I see no kitchen maid. I see a wife – whose duty is to take an interest in her husband's work.

DEMELZA I do take an interest!

ROSS Excellent. First thing tomorrow, then.

CUT TO:

32: EXT. TRENWITH HOUSE – DAY 32

Verity, Tabb and another servant, watched by Elizabeth (holding Geoffrey Charles) are trying to haul the frail-looking Charles onto his horse.

CHARLES Harder, dammit. Push harder.

ELIZABETH Is this wise, sir? Can Grambler not wait till you're stronger?

VERITY Dr Choake ordered bed-rest—

CHARLES Choake does not have a failing mine – or a son who's neither use nor ornament!

Francis is revealed in the doorway.

FRANCIS I'm touched by your faith, Father.

CHARLES Not sufficiently touched to behave like a man and the heir of Trenwith?

Straining to mount his horse, Charles is taken by another seizure and collapses in groans of pain. Francis, Verity, Elizabeth and the servants rush to his aid.

CUT TO:

33: EXT. WHEAL LEISURE – DAY 32

Ross emerges from the mine office with Henshawe.

HENSHAWE I never knew such ironstone. It's impenetrable.

ROSS Our luck has deserted us.

HENSHAWE Let's hope the pilchards don't do likewise!

They look over to where Demelza is standing on the cliffs talking to Jinny Carter, who's crying over Jim's plight. As Demelza tries to comfort her, Mrs Zacky and Connie Carter keep watch for the arrival of the pilchards. Their poverty, and that of all the families, is plain to see. Now Demelza sees Ross, waves and makes her way towards him. As she does so, the miners nod respectfully and the bal-maidens bob curtseys to her. Demelza's puzzled – are they actually deferring to her? When she realizes they are, she feels uncomfortable. Ross notices – and makes a point of treating her as if she were the grandest lady in the land.

ROSS Captain Henshawe, you know my wife Demelza?

HENSHAWE A pleasure to see you, ma'am.

Demelza, on the verge of curtseying, checks herself.

DEMELZA G'day to 'ee, sir. *(to Ross)* No sight 'o th' shoals yet.

ROSS *(to Henshawe)* Demelza's of mining stock herself. Her father's a tributer at Illuggan.

HENSHAWE Perhaps you'd like him to join us here, ma'am?

DEMELZA I'd as lief stick forks in my eye! *(correcting herself)* We d' get on better from a distance, sir. *(then, feeling she's out-stayed her welcome)* I must be gettin' back. The pies'll be burnin'.

HENSHAWE We hope to see you here often, ma'am.

Demelza is on the verge of curtseying again, but Ross links her arm and escorts her away.

CUT TO:

34: EXT. NAMPARA VALLEY – DAY 32

Ross escorts Demelza back towards Nampara House.

ROSS Was it such an ordeal?

DEMELZA I was that werrit I'd show 'ee up!

ROSS Why would you?

DEMELZA I've no notion 'ow to be.

ROSS As you are.

DEMELZA What am I?

ROSS A lady—

DEMELZA I'm not – an' I don't know 'ow.

ROSS You're a quick learner.

DEMELZA Nay, Ross, I came a'day at your behest, but I shan't venture again. Miners are my own kind – but I'd not be so kindly received by yours. *(then, suddenly)* Judas! I'll fetch 'im such a doostin'!

Without warning she tears off before Ross can stop her.

ROSS'S POV: Demelza running towards Jud, who is tiptoeing from the house, carrying a large, fresh-baked pie.

DEMELZA *(yelling)* Oi! Guts! Get back 'ere, 'ee good fer-nothin' viper!

JUD Garl!

Realizing the game is up, he breaks into a trot in an attempt to flee.

DEMELZA Filthy, sneakin', thievin' connivin'—

She chases after him. Garrick appears, joins in, thinking it's a huge game.

ROSS *(shouting)* Demelza! Come back this minute!

Demelza ignores Ross and continues to chase Jud. She launches herself at him, rugby-tackles him. They go sprawling. The pie flies out of Jud's grasp. Demelza pins him to the ground.

DEMELZA 'Alf a morn I labour'd at that pie, y'lizard!

ROSS Demelza, leave him be!

DEMELZA Think to fox me, would 'ee? 'Ee'll 'ave to be quicker 'n that!

Garrick seizes the pie and runs off with it. Jud lies, face down in the dust, Demelza still sitting on him, pinning him to the ground.

JUD Damn me if a body can't take a fair morsel now 'n then—

Ross runs up. He looks down at Demelza. He looks distinctly unimpressed. (Jud daren't move – as if by not moving he thinks he'll escape notice.)

ROSS I told you to stop. Did you not hear me?

DEMELZA Yes, but—

ROSS I cannot have my wife wrestling a manservant. It's unbecoming.

Demelza clambers to her feet, brushing the dust and dried mud from her dress.

DEMELZA No, Ross. I see 'tis not dignified. I'll 'member next time.

ROSS There'll be no next time. Come with me.

They walk off. Jud peeks out from beneath his arm. He can hardly believe his luck in avoiding punishment. Then . . .

ROSS'S VOICE *(calling back to Jud)* Tell Prudie to prepare a poultice.

JUD For what, sur?

ROSS'S VOICE Your backside – after I've lashed it to 'Luggan and back.

Jud grimaces at the thought.

CUT TO:

35: EXT. MOORLAND – DAY 32

Ross and Demelza (now tidied up and changed) walk across the moors.

ROSS There's only one way to remind you you're no longer a servant.

DEMELZA But you'll do all th' arrangin'?

ROSS I will not. You are mistress of Nampara. It's for you to engage your own servants.

CUT TO:

36: INT. JIM & JINNY'S COTTAGE – DAY 32

Jinny stands amazed, hardly able to believe her change in fortune.

JINNY I'll serve 'ee gladly, ma'am. When shall 'ee want me?

Demelza shoots a panicked glance at Ross – then remembers his instructions and forces herself to behave as the mistress of Nampara.

DEMELZA Tomorrow'd be quite convenient.

JINNY *(curtseying)* Yes, ma'am – thank 'ee, ma'am.

CUT TO:

37: INT. NAMPARA HOUSE, KITCHEN – DAY 32

Ross and Demelza return from Jinny's.

DEMELZA She curtsey'd me.

ROSS Get used to it.

DEMELZA I never will.

A thought occurs to Ross.

ROSS I must visit my uncle. Perhaps it's time for you to come with me.

DEMELZA Oh, I cud'n – *(already sidling off)* There's calves t' be meated – an' pastry t' make—

Before he can stop her, she launches into her chores

ROSS From tomorrow, that excuse won't avail you!

But she's already rushed off. Ross laughs.

CUT TO:

38: EXT. CLIFF-TOPS – DAY 32

Ross rides to Trenwith.

CUT TO:

39: INT. TRENWITH HOUSE, CHARLES'S ROOM – DAY 32

Ross comes in to find Dr Choake in the process of bleeding Charles and Verity on hand to tend to Charles's needs.

ROSS How does the patient fare?

CHARLES Lucky to have any blood left!

DR CHOAKE Progress is excellent. If he continues with my treatment, he can expect to eat a hearty Christmas dinner!

CHARLES But how will you manage, Ross, without a kitchen maid?

ROSS *(cheerful)* My wife has this very day engaged another.

CHARLES *(roaring with laughter)* The cheek of the devil – but your father was no different!

DR CHOAKE *(on his way out)* The Nampara Poldarks were renowned for their disregard of convention.

After he's gone, Verity comes over to embrace Ross warmly.

VERITY We're so delighted by the news, Ross.

CHARLES Francis especially was quick to see the advantage!

VERITY Father—

ROSS Of what?

CHARLES A wife to divert you! He feels it marginally less likely you'll ride over and steal Elizabeth from him!

Delighted by his own wit, he explodes into roars of laughter.

VERITY Father—

Charles's laughter becomes more hysterical.

VERITY *(cont'd)* Father – compose yourself—

The hysterical laughter becomes grunts then gasps of pain. Soon Charles is panting and clutching his chest.

CHARLES My heart – my heart! Damn Choake! – he promised me Christmas dinner!

Charles falls, apparently lifeless, onto his pillow.

CUT TO:

40: INT. TRENWITH HOUSE, CHARLES'S ROOM – DAY 32

Ross waits outside the closed door of Charles's room. Presently the door opens and Francis comes out. He's close to tears.

FRANCIS He's asked to see you.

A moment between Francis and Ross. We see the genuine depth of affection between these two. Then Francis stands aside to let Ross go in.

CUT TO:

41: INT. TRENWITH HOUSE, CHARLES'S ROOM – DAY 32

Ross sits at Charles's bedside, holding Charles's hand. Charles is barely alive.

CHARLES I've lost all faith – in this world of ours – and my legacy – *(then)* We both know Francis is not the man you are.

ROSS Uncle—

CHARLES Look after him for me—

ROSS Of course—

CHARLES And our family—

ROSS Yes—

CHARLES And our good name.

ROSS You have my word, Uncle.

CUT TO:

42: EXT. SAWLE CHURCHYARD – DAY 33

Francis stands at Charles's grave. Ross appears beside him.

ROSS He'll be missed.

FRANCIS Not by me. *(beat)* Is it terrible to feel nothing but relief?

Ross look sympathetic.

FRANCIS *(cont'd)* Nothing I ever did pleased him.

ROSS Not even your choice of wife?

FRANCIS He always said she'd make a fine mistress of Trenwith. *(bitterly)* And I an indifferent master.

ROSS You can still prove him wrong.

FRANCIS Now I've come into my estate? *(beat)* Half of it's mortgaged, the other half soon will be. *(false jollity)* But apparently I'm now one of the most important men in the county!

CUT TO:

43: INT. NAMPARA HOUSE, KITCHEN – DAY 33

Demelza is showing Jinny how to make bread. She is patient with Jinny, who is not exactly a quick learner. After a while . . .

JINNY How is it 'ee be not at the buryin'?

DEMELZA 'Tis for fancy folks an' family – not for the likes of me!

JINNY But – are ye not family?

DEMELZA Ross might say so. But I d' know 'tis not my place.

JINNY What is your place?

DEMELZA *(smiles)* Betwixt an' between? Neither one thing nor th' other.

She continues to show Jinny how to make bread.

DEMELZA Need more flour, keeps it from sticking. See?

CUT TO:

44: INT. TRENWITH HOUSE, GREAT HALL – DAY 33

Aunt Agatha is being settled in her chair by Ross. Francis looks worn and prematurely aged. Amongst the other mourners are George and Cary.

ON ROSS AND AUNT AGATHA

AUNT AGATHA I warned Charles. Too many capons and custards. Look at me – poached egg, a little broth – fit as a fiddle!

ON THE WARLEGGANS

GEORGE *(low)* Fitter than Francis by the look of it.

CARY Grambler must be taking its toll.

GEORGE Not to mention a young morsel by the name of Margaret!

CARY Have you dined there yourself of late?

GEORGE My tastes are more refined these days.

CUT TO:

45: INT. TRENWITH HOUSE, ELIZABETH'S ROOM – DAY 33

Elizabeth stands at the window, thoughtful. Verity comes in.

VERITY Are you not coming down?

ELIZABETH I really cannot face it.

VERITY Nor I, but one of us must play the hostess.

ELIZABETH She didn't come. *(beat)* His wife.

VERITY This isn't the occasion.

ELIZABETH Will you give him my good wishes?

VERITY Shouldn't you do that yourself?

ELIZABETH I wouldn't know where to begin.

A moment between them. Verity can see that Elizabeth is struggling to come to terms with the news of Ross's marriage. She declines to press the matter further. Verity goes out.

CUT TO:

46: INT. TRENWITH HOUSE, GREAT HALL – DAY 33

Verity comes in and whispers something in Francis's ear.

FRANCIS 'Unwell'? And not even the thought of a tête-à-tête with Ross could persuade her?

VERITY Francis—

FRANCIS She'll have less opportunities with a Mistress Poldark to amuse him. *(then)* You must be relieved.

VERITY How?

FRANCIS You're not the only one to disgrace the family by an unsuitable attachment.

VERITY Francis—

FRANCIS Consider yourself fortunate. See what you've missed.

He draws her attention to Ross, who has just entered the room.

THEIR POV: Ross goes to engage with Dr Choake, Ruth and John Treneglos, but they all greet him coldly and turn away immediately to avoid further engagement. Other guests go out of their way to avoid him. Ross is surprised by such behaviour. He glances round, looking for Elizabeth, but there's no sign of her. Now he is accosted by George.

GEORGE I've puzzled you out.

ROSS Was I so hard to fathom?

GEORGE I thought so, but your recent nuptials have made everything clear. *(beat)* It delights you to thumb your nose at society, because you consider yourself above the niceties by which it operates.

ROSS *(smiles)* Not above. Just indifferent.

He bows politely and walks off. George intercepts Dr Choake.

GEORGE Are you pleased with Wheal Leisure?

DR CHOAKE Pray do not mention it to me.

GEORGE Mining's always a gamble. And the gamester rarely meets a Good Samaritan.

DR CHOAKE As in— ?

GEORGE Someone willing to take a worthless bet off his hands? *(beat)* But should I hear of anyone, would you be interested?

CUT TO:

47: INT. WHEAL LEISURE, TUNNEL (MONTAGE)

The miners continue to try and break through the ironstone.

CUT TO:

48: EXT. WHEAL LEISURE (MONTAGE)

Ross stands looking out to sea. He sees the ladies still looking for the pilchards from the cliff-tops.

CUT TO:

49: EXT. CLIFF-TOPS (MONTAGE)

Francis stands looking out to sea. His face is impassive. Is he grieving or is he relieved? It is impossible to tell what he's thinking.

CUT TO:

50: EXT. NAMPARA HOUSE – DAY 34

Autumn leaves fall from the elm trees. Rows of logs, cut from the fallen tree, lie neatly stacked, ready to be brought in for winter. Demelza, laden with logs, is met by Ross.

ROSS What have I told you?

He divests her of the armful of logs.

ROSS *(cont'd)* I don't require my wife to crochet and sip tea, but I do require her to remember she's not a beast of burden.

He gives her a light kiss on the lips. She smiles.

ROSS Are you happy?

DEMELZA I am.

ROSS Then I hope you'll be even more so when I tell you who's coming to stay.

Demelza's face falls. Ross has just ruined her day.

CUT TO:

51: INT. NAMPARA HOUSE, HALLWAY – DAY 35

Ross opens the door to Verity, who is carrying two valises. He and Verity embrace warmly. Demelza loiters in the hallway. Already she feels an outsider. Though Verity is plainly dressed and totally unthreatening, Demelza feels like an awkward serving girl again. As Verity comes towards her, she involuntarily curtseys.

ROSS Come through.

VERITY It's so kind of you to invite me, my dear.

DEMELZA *(with exaggerated politeness)* You would care for some refreshment?

VERITY Oh, no, please! Let me take care of myself. The last thing I want is to give you any trouble.

ROSS *(putting his arm round Verity and leading her to the parlour)* No trouble at all. We've been looking forward to your visit – haven't we, Demelza?

As Ross and Verity go into the parlour . . .

DEMELZA *(unconvincing)* Yes, Ross.

CUT TO:

52: INT. NAMPARA HOUSE, PARLOUR – DAY 35

Demelza sits silent and awkward at luncheon as Ross and Verity chat. Jinny serves. Demelza is fidgeting, wishing she had an excuse to help her and leave the room.

VERITY It's a quiet house since Father died – though Elizabeth plays the harp – and speaks French to Geoffrey Charles. And I have my needlework – Aunt Agatha her spinning—

ROSS And Francis— ?

VERITY Is – often away. *(to Demelza, eager to change the subject)* This pie is delicious, my dear. Did you bake it yourself?

Demelza leaps to her feet, grateful for the opportunity to escape.

DEMELZA Custard! I'll go an' see if it's set.

She makes a hurried exit. Ross and Verity exchange a glance.

ROSS She thinks you a great lady – who will show me what a mistake I made in marrying her.

VERITY What can I do?

ROSS *(getting up)* I'm sure you'll think of something.

He prepares to leave. Verity looks panic-stricken.

VERITY Ross! No – where are you going? You cannot just – Ross!—

Ross waves amicably and departs, leaving Verity dreading the thought of managing Demelza alone.

CUT TO:

53: INT. WHEAL LEISURE, TUNNEL – DAY 35

Henshawe, Zacky and Mark are conferring at the head of the mine shaft, preparing to take down gunpowder for another attempt to blast through the ironstone. Ross arrives.

ZACKY Blasted copper, it is proving a devil to find.

ROSS Blasting is the word.

HENSHAWE It seems to be our only hope.

Ross and Henshawe make the final preparations for the blasting. The powder is laid, the fuse set. Ross signals to Zacky and Mark to withdraw further away.

HENSHAWE Right, boys.

CUT TO:

54: INT. NAMPARA HOUSE, PARLOUR – DAY 35

Demelza and Verity sit stiffly, in silence, both sewing, stealing awkward glances at each other.

DEMELZA Some – tea?

VERITY Oh! Thank you! No. It's a little early.

DEMELZA Oh – so 'tis—

She blushes and bends low over her sewing, feeling she's revealed her-

self to be ignorant and unladylike. Verity can see what Demelza's thinking, and could kick herself for being the cause of it. After what seems an endless silence, Verity realizes she will have to make the first move.

VERITY You know, Ross is very dear to me—

Demelza fears she's about to get a telling off.

VERITY *(cont'd)* What woman should ever deserve him, I couldn't imagine. So when I heard he'd married you, I was—

DEMELZA Horrified.

VERITY *(after a pause)* Relieved.

Demelza suspicious. Surely Verity is mocking her?

VERITY Before he met you – he was broken – lost. So I was relieved to think he'd found someone to console him – to save him from his loneliness.

Demelza is listening, uncomprehending, still expecting a lecture.

VERITY *(cont'd)* But now I see it's more than consolation. *(beat)* You've given him hope.

It's beginning to dawn on Demelza that Verity is not against her.

VERITY A life without hope is bleak. And a life without love—

DEMELZA Oh, 'tis not that—

VERITY You do not— ?

DEMELZA Love 'im? Oh, beyond anything – but I could never 'ope that he – that he would ever – *(struggling to find the words)* 'E's kind to me – and when we're abed – I 'ave reason to think I d' please 'im—

VERITY I'm sure you do.

DEMELZA But I'd never call it love. E've never used the word t' me – and I misdoubt 'e ever shall.

Verity nods. She takes a different view but knows Demelza will not yet be convinced.

VERITY It's life's greatest treasure – to love – and be loved in return.

She is thoughtful. Demelza suddenly sees immense sadness in Verity's eyes. Her heart melts.

VERITY My dear, d'you think I care a jot where you come from – or who your father is – or how well you curtsey?

DEMELZA I've often wished I could curtsey. *(summoning up her courage)* Will you teach me, Verity?

The sound of an underground explosion shakes the room and makes the fixtures and fittings rattle. Verity and Demelza, both used to such things, don't bat an eyelid.

CUT TO:

55: EXT. NAMPARA HOUSE – DAY 35

Ross is astonished to hear shrieks of laughter coming from the house as he returns home to Nampara.

CUT TO:

56: INT. NAMPARA HOUSE, HALLWAY – DAY 35

Demelza and Verity shriek with laughter as they, together with Jud, struggle to move the spinet out of the library into the parlour.

DEMELZA Left! – to the left!—

VERITY No, to the right a little—

JUD Well, make up yer blasted blatherin' minds!—

ROSS What in God's name are you doing?

They all halt and Verity and Demelza dissolve into giggles.

VERITY We thought we should move it into the parlour so Demelza may learn to dance.

Ross raises his eyebrows at Verity. He's surprised and impressed by her progress. Verity smiles. Demelza is fanning herself after her exertions.

ROSS If you ladies would give us leave?

He takes over from Demelza and Verity and he and Jud heave the spinet towards the parlour.

CUT TO:

57: INT. NAMPARA HOUSE (MONTAGE) – DAY 36

Verity teaches Demelza some dance steps. Verity shows Demelza which knives and forks to use at dinner. Verity teaches Demelza to curtsey. Verity teaches Demelza how to walk. Verity teaches Demelza how to use a fan. Demelza feels faint from all the activity and has to use her fan to cool herself.

CUT TO:

58: INT. NAMPARA HOUSE, ROSS & DEMELZA'S ROOM – NIGHT 36

Demelza lies in bed while Ross prepares for bed.

DEMELZA That man who used to meet Verity here— ?

ROSS Captain Blamey?

DEMELZA Has nothin' bin heard of 'im?

ROSS Thankfully, no.

DEMELZA Oh Ross, the shame on you!

ROSS What d'you mean?

DEMELZA How could you let 'em part like that?

ROSS What the devil could I do?

He gets into bed beside her.

DEMELZA You should've stood up t'yer uncle f'r'er! Even now in 'er heart she still hankers f'r him—

ROSS Then she must stop.

DEMELZA Why should she? Must hope be buried an' love denied?

ROSS What do you know of love?

DEMELZA A little.

ROSS Is that all? *(pulling her towards him)* Then you must practise more.

He kisses her hungrily. She eagerly responds.

CUT TO:

59: INT. MARGARET'S LODGING – DAY 37

Margaret's lodging is considerably more luxurious than when we last saw it. Margaret is lounging in bed. Francis is getting dressed. He looks thoughtful and somewhat guilty.

CUT TO:

60: INT. TRENWITH HOUSE, GREAT HALL – DAY 37

Elizabeth cuddles with baby Geoffrey Charles.

CUT TO:

61: EXT. CLIFF-TOPS – DAY 37

The women continue to look out to sea for the pilchards.

CUT TO:

62: EXT. HABERDASHERS – DAY 37

Verity leads the way to the haberdasher's. Demelza hesitates on the threshold. Seeing her reluctance, Verity links her arm and steers her inside.

CUT TO:

63: EXT. NAMPARA VALLEY – DUSK 37

Demelza and Verity, heavily laden with purchases, ride towards Nampara House.

DEMELZA Must you go home tomorrow?

VERITY Francis needs me, but I'll come again soon.

They ride on a while. Verity notices that Demelza seems preoccupied.

VERITY Did you really hate it today?

DEMELZA Oh, no! I'm just afeared we spent too much money – and 'twill all be wasted.

VERITY How could it?

DEMELZA On'y that – p'raps my measuring won't be the same for long—

For a moment Verity doesn't grasp what she means. But then . . .

VERITY My dear, d'you mean— ?

Demelza nods shyly.

VERITY *(cont'd)* Oh, my dear! Ross will be delighted!

DEMELZA Don' tell 'im! Not yet – *(seeing Verity hasn't understood)* See, e's not liked me fer long. And when I get to waddlin' about like an old duck, he'll mebbe forget he ever liked me at all.

VERITY Ross forgets nothing.

CUT TO:

64: EXT. WHEAL LEISURE – DAY 38

Henshawe, Zacky and Mark are conferring at the head of the mine shaft, preparing to take down gunpowder for another attempt to blast through the ironstone. Ross arrives.

ZACKY Come t' watch us set our final fuse?

ROSS *(hopeful)* Will one more blast get us through?

HENSHAWE One more blast is all we can afford.

Ross's face falls. This the moment he'd been dreading. Their funds are about to run out – and the ironstone has not been breached.

CUT TO:

65: EXT. CLIFF-TOPS – DAY 38

Ross is riding home. Up ahead he notices a commotion on the cliff-tops beside Wheal Leisure. The mine bell starts to ring. A huer is beginning to call out, 'Heva! Heva!'

High angle shot at top of slipway looking out to sea. Tiny specks seen on the horizon. Crowds of villagers run towards the water's edge.

CUT TO:

66: EXT. NAMPARA HOUSE – DAY 38

As Ross rides towards Nampara House, Demelza comes running out, looking worried.

DEMELZA I 'eard the bell! What's amiss?

ROSS We must leave at once. *(seeing her hesitate)* Quickly now!

He sees the troubled expression on her face.

ROSS *(cont'd)* What is it?

DEMELZA Nothin', sur. *(corrects herself)* Ross. Just—

ROSS What is the matter?

DEMELZA *(hesitates, then)* Sometimes I d' think I displease you.

He's about to dismiss her fears, but something in her expression stops him. He realizes she has reason to be fearful. In that moment, he knows he must do better.

ROSS I'm used to giving orders. And having no one to suit but myself. *(then)* But you are far from displeasing to me.

DEMELZA See, how would I know that?

ROSS I'll endeavour to make it clearer.

A moment of connection between them. Then . . .

ROSS We must go! Make haste!

Demelza jumps up onto the horse.

DEMELZA Where are we going?

CUT TO:

67: EXT. NAMPARA COVE – DAY 38

Expectant faces line up at the water's edge.

The tiny specks on the horizon are now rowing boats coming towards the shore. Through the scrum of villagers crowding the shoreline Demelza and Ross are seen running towards the beach.

The people rush forward into the shore break to pull the boats up on the shore.

The sailors jump from the boats and drag them onto the beach.

As one, the villagers, fishermen, Ross and Demelza set about landing the catch.

Large buckets are produced which are passed to the boats. Huge scoops of fish are gulped into the buckets then passed back up the beach.

Joy and relief is etched on the face of every villager.

Ross and Demelza are in the thick of the activity, sleeves rolled up, heaping fish into baskets and passing them along. Their faces are bright with joy and relief. The entire event is a celebration of life, love and community!

CUT TO:

68: EXT. NAMPARA COVE – DUSK 38

The sun is setting as the beach empties. Ross and Demelza help to pull one of the last boats ashore. It's Mark Daniel's.

ROSS Good catch, eh, Mark?

MARK 'Andsome, Ross. More'n a quarter million, they reckon, afore they're done.

ROSS I'm very glad. It'll make the difference this winter.

MARK 'Twill indeed! 'Night, Ross, 'night, ma'am.

ROSS 'Night, Mark.

Other stragglers bid Ross and Demelza goodnight as they leave. 'Night, Ross', 'Night, ma'am'.

CUT TO:

69: EXT. CLIFF-TOPS BY NAMPARA COVE – DUSK 38

In the fading light two tiny figures in a sea of heather walk along the cliff path. The embers of a few fires glow here and there along the cliffs. Ross and Demelza are greeted by other villagers heading home. 'Night, Ross', 'Night, ma'am'. Ross smiles contentedly to himself.

ROSS *(almost to himself)* Everyone's happy tonight.

They stop to watch the last rays of the dying light. The dying fires glow. Demelza is thoughtful.

DEMELZA They like you.

ROSS Nonsense.

DEMELZA 'Tis the truth. I know 'cos I'm one o' 'em. You're a gent, but you don' despise 'em. You help 'em, give 'em food, an' work, an—

ROSS Marry you?

DEMELZA No, not that. They don' know what t' make o' that. But they like you jus' the same.

He looks down at her – her eyes bright with happiness and love. He kisses her – not passionately, not out of desire, but with tenderness.

ROSS And you? Do you like me?

DEMELZA I could learn to!

ROSS And I, you.

It's said teasingly, but it carries the promise of something more. Some-

thing has shifted in their relationship, has brought them closer to each other. They both know it, but the realization remains unspoken.

CUT TO:

70: EXT. WHEAL LEISURE – DAY 39

Establisher.

CUT TO:

71: INT. WHEAL LEISURE, TUNNEL – DAY 39

Henshawe and Ross are examining the results of the blasting.

ROSS We are still not through.

HENSHAWE I could swear we're almost there.

ROSS But we're out of gunpowder. And capital. And invest-ors. *(then)* How long can we continue?

HENSHAWE An optimist would say – three months?

ROSS And a realist?

HENSHAWE Two.

Ross nods. He knows what this means.

ROSS I must find more capital.

CUT TO:

72: EXT. TRURO STREET – DAY 39

Ross rides into town.

CUT TO:

73: INT. PASCOE'S BANK – DAY 39

Ross is sitting with Pascoe in his office.

PASCOE It gives me no pleasure to tell you this, but capital's short.

ROSS I understand.

PASCOE Though I've kept my ear to the ground – in case other speculators could be found—

ROSS And?

PASCOE *(shakes head)* Tom Choake has done you no favours, Ross. His views on your marriage—

ROSS 'Ross Poldark, the loose cannon? – too much of a risk for the prudent investor'?

PASCOE Quite so, quite so.

CUT TO:

74: EXT. WHEAL LEISURE – DUSK 39

Ross confers with Henshawe and Zacky.

ROSS I blame myself.

ZACKY You couldn't foresee as we'd 'it such rock—

ROSS But I could foresee that in marrying my kitchen maid, I'd scandalize all I might look to for capital.

HENSHAWE Well, short of jilting her and wedding a rich heiress—

ROSS Perhaps I was over-hasty. But it's done now. *(then)* So how shall we order things?

HENSHAWE We can last till the week before Christmas.

ROSS Let it be the week after. If I have to sell half my house, I'll not ruin Christmas for them.

CUT TO:

75: EXT. NAMPARA VALLEY, CORNWALL – DAY 40

Winter on the valley.
CUT TO:

76: EXT. NAMPARA HOUSE – DAY 40

Establisher.
CUT TO:

77: INT. NAMPARA HOUSE, PARLOUR – DAY 40

Demelza is making Christmas garlands, helped by Prudie and Jinny. Jud is singing tunelessly to himself (the Boar's Head carol) and doing a little caper.

JUD *(sing)*
An' I prithee masters, be merree
Quod estes in convivio
Caput apri defero—

JUD/PRUDIE/JINNY *(sing)*
Reddens laudes Domino –
Caput apri—

As Demelza stretches to hang one up, she suddenly feels nauseous and rushes out.

CUT TO:

78: INT. NAMPARA HOUSE, KITCHEN – DAY 40

Demelza comes in to find Ross reading a letter. He seems surprised by its contents.

ROSS From Francis. Inviting us to spend Christmas at Trenwith.

Demelza's face falls.

DEMELZA Oh—

ROSS What's the matter?

DEMELZA I – I couldn't. You go—

ROSS Naturally we both go or we both stay.

DEMELZA Ross, I aren't their sort. They'll look down their noses and send me t' eat wi' th' servants—

Ross contemplates her a moment as she squirms with discomfort. After a pause . . .

ROSS Do you think I ought to be ashamed of you?

DEMELZA 'Tis not that but—

ROSS You think they are so much better than you?

DEMELZA I don' – but they'll think so. *(then)* Mebbe not Verity, but – *(she hesitates, then)* Elizabeth—

ROSS You do her an injustice. *(beat)* And me.

DEMELZA You?

ROSS To think I could admire someone who thought meanly of you.

DEMELZA Do you admire her?

ROSS Elizabeth was born to be admired.

DEMELZA An' I was born to pull turnips?

Ross laughs, takes a piece of paper and starts writing.

DEMELZA *(cont'd – alarmed)* What are you doing?

ROSS *(cheerfully)* Accepting the invitation.

CUT TO:

79: EXT. WHEAL LEISURE – DAY 41

Work continues at the mine.

CUT TO:

80: INT. WHEAL LEISURE, TUNNEL – DAY 41

Work continues in the tunnel.

CUT TO:

81: EXT. NAMPARA VALLEY – DAY 41

With heavy heart, Demelza sets off to accompany Ross to walk to Trenwith. She is feeling nauseous but is determined to keep her pregnancy secret. As they walk towards Wheal Leisure, Ross can't disguise his despair as they see the miners gathering for the next shift, and their ragged families who hang about the mine.

ROSS A sorry Christmas I've handed them.

DEMELZA No. You've handed them near-on a twelve month o' work they'd not otherwise 'ave.

Ross squeezes her hand, grateful for this reminder.

CUT TO:

82: EXT. TRENWITH HOUSE, DRIVE – DAY 41

As they approach the gates of Trenwith, Demelza is full of trepidation. Ross glances at her. He knows it's make or break for her – and even he is unsure that she will come through unscathed. Verity is waiting at the door. She greets them warmly. Demelza holds her tight for a moment – then she takes a deep breath and walks in.

VERITY Welcome.

CUT TO:

83: INT. TRENWITH HOUSE, GREAT HALL – DAY 41

Demelza looks around her in awe. The paintings, the furnishings, the size and scale of Trenwith House all conspire to render her speechless. Then Elizabeth appears. For a moment both women look warily at each other. Elizabeth glances at Ross. It's the first time they've met formally since Charles's funeral. Then Elizabeth smiles at Demelza and puts out both hands to welcome her.

ELIZABETH My dear, it's so good of you to come to us. May I take you to meet Aunt Agatha?

Completely disarmed by the warmth of Elizabeth's welcome, Demelza allows herself to be led into the Oak Room. Ross, who had expected some coolness towards Demelza, is profoundly impressed by Elizabeth's behaviour. It stirs in him feelings he'd hoped were dead. Verity recognizes this and glances sideways at Ross as they go into the Oak Room.

CUT TO:

84: INT. TRENWITH HOUSE, OAK ROOM – DAY 41

Aunt Agatha has taken possession of Demelza, who is sitting beside her. Much to the amusement of Ross, Francis and Verity, she declines to let go of Demelza's hand.

AUNT AGATHA Married, you say? To my nephew? Why wasn't I told of this?

FRANCIS You were, Aunt. I told you myself!

AUNT AGATHA *(to Demelza)* Nobody tells me anything. And you, bud, where are you from?

DEMELZA 'Luggan, ma'am.

Involuntarily Ross and Elizabeth exchange a glance.

AUNT AGATHA Who do we know from Illuggan? The Cardews? You'll know Sir John, of course. And the Perrins of Helston Hall?

DEMELZA No, ma'am, I—

AUNT AGATHA Six generations of Poldarks I've seen. Now what d'you think of that? You think I don't look old enough? Quite right too. Now go and sit by Elizabeth so I may see how you measure up.

VERITY Aunt Agatha—

AUNT AGATHA *(ignoring Verity)* Go on, child. Off you go!

Demelza does as she's told. Elizabeth smiles and welcomes her warmly, but Demelza feels gauche and coarse beside the cool beauty of her rival.

ON ROSS: Unable to suppress the strange mixture of feelings this evokes: his new bride and his old love sitting side by side.

Everyone seems conscious of it. Everyone, it seems, except Aunt Agatha.

AUNT AGATHA Hmmmmm. A pretty little thing. A mite coarse beside Elizabeth – but doubtless she'll polish up sufficient when the need arises.

Elizabeth takes Demelza's hand and squeezes it reassuringly. Demelza is astonished.

CUT TO:

85: INT. TRENWITH HOUSE, GUEST BEDROOM – DAY 41

Demelza and Ross have returned to their room to get changed. Demelza is still marvelling at her reception from Elizabeth.

DEMELZA I thought she'd hate me.

Ross doesn't reply.

DEMELZA *(cont'd)* I wouldn't blame 'er. I probably should in 'er shoes.

ROSS Then you've less sense than I credit you with.

Demelza glances at Ross. He's staring absently out of the window and it's not hard to guess where his thoughts lie.

CUT TO:

86: INT. TRENWITH HOUSE, ELIZABETH'S ROOM – DAY 41

Francis is pacing restlessly as Elizabeth gets ready for Christmas Eve.

FRANCIS You think I don't know what you're about?

Elizabeth glances at him through the mirror. She knows what's coming and declines to engage.

FRANCIS *(cont'd)* Taking her under your wing? Making her your friend?

ELIZABETH *(wearily)* Francis—

FRANCIS 'Oh Ross, see how kind and generous I am!' 'Look what a pearl you've lost!'

ELIZABETH You're being ridiculous—

FRANCIS Am I?

They look at each other for a moment, then Francis goes out.
CUT TO:

87: INT. TRENWITH HOUSE, GUEST BEDROOM – DAY 41

Demelza is trying to coax her mane of hair into a presentable style when there's a knock on the door. Ross opens it – and a servant delivers a large box.

ROSS What's this?

DEMELZA Jus' something I ordered from town.

Ross goes to open the box.

DEMELZA *(cont'd)* No, Ross! 'Tis meant as a surprise!

ROSS It's just a family party. No need to flig yourself up for it.

DEMELZA *(crestfallen)* I asked Verity. She said it was right t' change fer Christmas Eve.

ROSS Well, don't lace your stays too tight. They feed you well here and I know your appetite!

Demelza's face falls. She is beginning to fear she will never pass muster in this society. As Ross is about to go out . . .

DEMELZA Ross— ?

ROSS Yes?

DEMELZA Will I polish up?

ROSS What does it matter? I didn't marry you so I could see my own reflection!

He goes out. Unreassured Demelza contemplates her own reflection in the mirror. She does indeed look unpolished and gauche. And then there's the nausea, which is rising again . . .

CUT TO:

88: INT. TRENWITH HOUSE, OAK ROOM – NIGHT 41

Ross comes into the Oak Room to find Elizabeth alone.

ROSS You were very kind to Demelza.

ELIZABETH Who wouldn't be? She looks like a startled faun.

Ross sits down beside her. She's looking very lovely tonight – cool, refined, delicately beautiful. It's impossible for Ross not to be reminded of his old feelings for her.

ELIZABETH *(cont'd)* She's young. And this must seem very daunting to her.

ROSS You don't despise my choice, then.

ELIZABETH What right have I to despise anyone? Besides I've too much to distract me here. Grambler failing, Francis gambling away his inheritance—

ROSS I'm sad to hear it.

ELIZABETH Oh, and worse! Rumours – no, reports – that he has another woman.

Ross looks at her sharply. She gives him a searching look.

ELIZABETH *(cont'd)* Has he?

For a moment we think Ross might tell what he knows.

ROSS If he does, he's an idiot.

A moment between them. Broken by the arrival of Francis.

FRANCIS I'm ravenous! When do we dine?

CUT TO:

89: INT. TRENWITH HOUSE, GUEST BEDROOM – NIGHT 41

Demelza sits at the dressing-table feeling so nauseous and nervous she hasn't even begun to get dressed. Presently there's a tap on the door and Verity comes in.

VERITY My dear? Are you coming down?

DEMELZA I can scarce stand up. Lord knows 'ow I'll keep my food down. An' they'll think I'm that vulgar an' simple – an' Ross'll be sorry he ever wed me.

VERITY Here, let me help you.

DEMELZA *(touched)* Thank you.

VERITY Trust your husband, my dear. And yourself.

As she continues to fasten the buttons, there is a loud hammering on the front door below.

VERITY Visitors? At this hour?

CUT TO:

90: INT. TRENWITH HOUSE, OAK ROOM – NIGHT 41

Ross, Francis and Elizabeth are surprised (and not overly delighted) to be ambushed by George and Cary Warleggan, John Treneglos and Ruth Treneglos. John is already drunk.

CARY We were just passing, Francis. Thought we'd come and offer the compliments of the season.

GEORGE *(to Elizabeth)* If we're intruding, we can easily depart.

JOHN TRENEGLOS *(sniffing)* Damn me nostrils, though! What do I scent? Swan? Partridge?

Elizabeth glances at Francis, who nods, resigned.

ELIZABETH Mrs Tabb, lay four more places for dinner.

George smiles gratitude to Elizabeth. John Treneglos accosts Ross.

JOHN TRENEGLOS Ross Poldark, the famed recluse! For all we see you, you might be Robinson Crusoe!

RUTH Oh, but he has his Man Friday, dear. *(looking round)* Is she hereabout? *(aside, to Cary)* Or should we seek her in the scullery?

CUT TO:

91: INT. TRENWITH HOUSE, BALCONY – NIGHT 41

Fighting back nausea, Demelza listens nervously from the upstairs landing to the loud chatter of the visitors. We only see her face, which is pale and wide-eyed with anxiety.

RUTH'S VOICE An attempt on the king's life?

CUT TO:

92: INT. TRENWITH HOUSE, OAK ROOM – NIGHT 41

The conversation continues. Cary, John and Ruth have made themselves completely at home. George, to his credit, less so.

JOHN TRENEGLOS Ambushed for his waistcoat, no doubt.

ELIZABETH I'm told it's worth more than half the mines in Cornwall.

RUTH And the royal household servants not paid for twelve months.

CARY I'm amazed no one's attempted to sharpen a knife on the king of France!

GEORGE Give them time, sir. Give them time!

Francis and Ross exchange a glance. They're not exactly delighted by this intrusion into their family circle. Now Verity appears.

VERITY Dinner is served.

JOHN TRENEGLOS Excellent!

He belches loudly. Ruth glares at him.

RUTH John is so full of the Christmas spirit, he won't require any claret.

JOHN TRENEGLOS I assure you he will!

They all begin to filter out into the hallway.

CUT TO:

93: INT. TRENWITH HOUSE, GREAT HALL – CONTINUOUS

As they all come the Great Hall, Demelza appears at the other end. She is wearing a silk dress, not expensive but exquisitely suited to her. She has dressed her hair, her eyes are bright and her pale skin glows. She forces a smile and comes forward nervously. The surprised reactions of the other guests are nothing to what Ross is feeling. It's as if he's seeing her, if not for the first time, at least in a new light. Her beauty, though not conventional, is luminous, striking. He steps forward and offers her his hand.

ROSS Demelza, let me introduce you.

CUT TO:

94: INT. TRENWITH HOUSE, GREAT HALL – NIGHT 41

A sumptuous dinner is almost at an end. Demelza is seated between Francis and John Treneglos, who are both vying for her attention. Opposite her sits Ross, between Verity and Aunt Agatha. Elizabeth is partnered with George and Ruth with Cary. Ross watches Demelza for any signs of unease, but she seems to be managing admirably.

JOHN TRENEGLOS Damn you, Ross, for keeping this rosebud a secret!

RUTH Hardly secret, John. All the county was talking of her in June!

She gives Demelza a superior smile.

DEMELZA Oh yes, ma'am. People dearly love t' gossip, don't they?

JOHN TRENEGLOS Ha! Well answered, Mistress! A merry Christmas and damnation to all gossips!

VERITY *(low, to Ross)* She's on her mettle tonight.

ROSS *(low, to Verity)* Overdoing the manners a bit! Look at her plate – she's hardly touched a morsel.

VERITY Too busy making conquests!

CARY *(loud)* What news of the mine, Ross? Are we swimming in copper yet!

JOHN TRENEGLOS Not according to my father!

ROSS We have reason for optimism.

FRANCIS *(genuine)* Glad to hear it, Ross. At least one of us is prospering!

CARY *(aside to George)* You believe him?

GEORGE *(aside to Cary)* Each way, we win. Enjoy his ruin – or the fruits of his labours. *(seeing Cary's look of surprise)* Our friend Choake saw the wisdom of my offer. And sold me his shares in Wheal Leisure.

They are brought back to the present by an outburst of drunken laughter from John Treneglos, who is salivating over Demelza.

ON RUTH: Furious that her pointed glares at her husband are being ignored.

RUTH *(loudly)* And how d'you manage for servants, Elizabeth? Mama and I were only saying, young girls these days have such ideas – always trying to rise above their station!

She is clearly expecting Elizabeth to join in against Demelza. However . . .

ELIZABETH I haven't noticed that. Perhaps you've been unlucky.

RUTH Well, at least I have my own household. My poor sisters all lack husbands. And truly, beyond the age of twenty-three, what hope is there?

Verity flushes and looks steadfastly down at her plate. Demelza notices at once and springs to her aid.

DEMELZA I don't believe there's ever cause to give up hope.

She halts, conscious that everyone is looking at her. But for Verity's sake, she persists.

DEMELZA *(cont'd)* 'Tis sometimes a question of waiting—

RUTH And seizing the opportunity when it comes? I bow before your expertise, ma'am.

Anxious to diffuse the mounting tension, Elizabeth rises from the table.

ELIZABETH Ladies, shall we?

Demelza, grateful for the opportunity to escape, quickly flees the room. Ross looks anxiously after her, exchanges a glance with Verity.

CUT TO:

95: INT. TRENWITH HOUSE, GUEST BEDROOM CLOSET – NIGHT 41

Sounds of retching. Presently Demelza emerges from the closet, pale and trembling.

CUT TO:

96: INT. TRENWITH HOUSE, OAK ROOM – NIGHT 41

Demelza slips back to join the others in time to hear Elizabeth complete a performance on the harp, to enthusiastic applause. Demelza tries to slide into a chair unnoticed, but sharp-eyed Ruth sees her. Rushing forward she links Demelza's arm.

RUTH Mistress Poldark, now you must play for us.

DEMELZA Oh – no – I don't—

RUTH Not musical, ma'am? Did your governess not teach you?

ROSS Demelza sings.

Demelza shoots him a panic-stricken look.

RUTH Oh? Then we must hear her.

JOHN TRENEGLOS We surely must!

Demelza looks at Ross in horror. He nods encouragingly at her. A moment of connection between them. Suddenly she feels brave. She goes to the harp and plucks a single note. Then she begins to sing.

DEMELZA *(sings)*

I'd pluck a fair rose for my love
I'd pluck a red rose blowing
Love's in my heart, a-trying so to prove
What your heart's knowing.

Her voice is not strong, but clear and sweet-toned. Surprised looks from Francis, Elizabeth, George and Cary. Admiration from John Treneglos. Francis glances at Elizabeth. A moment between them.

DEMELZA *(sings)*

I'd pluck a finger on a thorn
I'd pluck a finger bleeding
Red is my heart, a-wounded and forlorn
And your heart needing.

As Demelza begins the third verse she looks at Ross – and he at her. It's as if she's singing just for him – and no one else exists, for either of them.

DEMELZA *(sings)*

I'd hold a finger to my tongue
I'd hold a finger waiting
My heart is sore, until it joins in song
Wi' your heart mating.

The song ends. For a moment there is silence. Demelza and Ross don't notice. They have eyes only for each other. Then applause breaks out, started by John Treneglos and Verity. The spell is broken. Demelza and Ross look away from each other. Elizabeth and Francis, for different reasons, look uncomfortable. Both find it hard to deal with the intensity of connection they've just witnessed between Ross and Demelza.

CUT TO:

97: INT. TRENWITH HOUSE, HALLWAY – NIGHT 41

Francis has just bidden good night to the guests. He closes the door with a sigh of relief. Now he sees Ross.

FRANCIS It's a curious thing—

They are both looking through into the parlour, where Elizabeth and Demelza are seated side by side talking quietly.

FRANCIS *(cont'd)* We envy a man for something he has. Yet the truth may be, he hasn't got it after all. *(beat)* And we have.

Ross looks at him curiously. Does Francis mean what Ross thinks he means?

FRANCIS Am I rambling? Ignore me. Merry Christmas, Cousin.

ROSS Merry Christmas.

CUT TO:

98: INT. TRENWITH HOUSE, GUEST BEDROOM – NIGHT 41

Ross contemplates the head of the sleeping Demelza on the pillow beside him.

ROSS *(softly)* Merry Christmas, my love.

CUT TO:

99: EXT. TRENWITH HOUSE – DAY 42

Ross and Demelza take their leave of Elizabeth, Francis and Verity, embracing them warmly.

ROSS Thank you, Francis.

FRANCIS Merry Christmas.

ROSS Merry Christmas.

They walk away. Elizabeth remains at the door, watching them go.

CUT TO:

100: EXT. CLIFF-TOPS – DAY 42

Ross and Demelza walk along the cliff-top path. Something has happened to their relationship. It's as if they've come through the ordeal at Trenwith with their closeness cemented. Ross takes Demelza's hand. She says nothing. But she smiles. Noticing, Ross hesitates to spoil her happiness.

ROSS I hope you won't live to regret your choice of husband.

DEMELZA Why would I?

ROSS We may soon be destitute.

DEMELZA There's other kinds of treasure.

Ross smiles and squeezes her hand. They walk on, neither looking at the other. Finally it dawns on Ross that, despite everything, he too is happy. He allows himself to surrender to the feeling . . .

And then suddenly – up ahead – the Wheal Leisure bell starts to ring out – loud, urgent, incessant.

DEMELZA What is it? A rock-fall?

ROSS I dread to think.

He starts to run towards Wheal Leisure.

CUT TO:

101: EXT. WHEAL LEISURE – DAY 42

Wheal Leisure is a flurry of hysterical activity: miners and bal-maidens rushing about, some in tears, some on their knees, some hugging each other. As Ross rushes up, panic stricken.

ROSS What's happened?

He is greeted by a near-hysterical Zacky.

ZACKY Copper! Copper's bin struck! A monstrous lode!

Ross sinks to his knees with gratitude. As Demelza runs up she is treated to the sight of her husband disappearing beneath a scrum of euphoric miners.

CUT TO:

102: INT. NAMPARA HOUSE, ROSS & DEMELZA'S ROOM – NIGHT 42

Ross looks out of their bedroom window at the bright lights of Wheal Leisure. As he turns and closes the window, he's smiling. Now he sees Demelza lying in bed, watching him. She seems thoughtful.

DEMELZA So how did I do, Ross? You were not too ashamed of me?

He halts, wondering how to answer her. The question is more profound than she knows. Eventually he comes to sit on the bed beside her.

ROSS Why d'you think I married you?

DEMELZA I don' rightly know.

ROSS To satisfy an appetite? To save myself from being alone? Because it was the right thing to do? *(no answer)* I had few expectations. At best you'd be a distraction. A bandage to ease a wound. I was mistaken. You have redeemed me. I am your humble servant and I love you.

He takes her face between his hands and kisses her tenderly. Then he looks at her lovingly, wonderingly.

DEMELZA I hope you will have a little love t' spare.

ROSS For what?

DEMELZA Our child.

Episode 5

1: INT. WHEAL LEISURE, TUNNEL – DAY 43

Pickaxe splinters rock. Miners' shadows dance across the walls of the tunnel, flickering in the light of their candles. The clank of metal being driven into rock reverberates through the darkness. The air is full of noises: clanking, hacking, hissing, dripping.

CUT TO:

2: EXT. WHEAL LEISURE – DAY 43

A figure on horseback is seen riding towards the mine. Ross emerges from the mine office. The mine is bustling and thriving. The rider arrives and is revealed to be a handsome, earnest young doctor – Dwight Enys. He dismounts and greets Ross.

DWIGHT *(salutes)* Captain Poldark.

ROSS Dr Enys! You survived the journey?

DWIGHT Missed the riots in London, but caught them in Exeter!

Ross embraces Dwight warmly.

ROSS We're uncivilized here – didn't they warn you?

DWIGHT *(laughing)* I've seen worse.

ROSS You've saved worse! *(then)* Come and meet my friends. Paul, Zacky, Mark, this is Dwight Enys. I have him to thank for patching me up!

DWIGHT I trust my skill's improved since then.

ROSS Dr Enys is here to make a study of mine diseases.

MARK There's no shortage o' subjects!

DWIGHT D'you suffer yourself?

MARK *(proudly)* 'Eart an' lungs of an ox!

DWIGHT Then I hope we'll have no call to meet except socially.

Everyone laughs. It's all very amicable.

ROSS *(to Dwight)* You must meet my wife.

CUT TO:

3: EXT. FIELDS – DAY 43

Ross and Dwight greet Demelza, who has walked from Nampara to meet Ross. She is 8 months pregnant.

ROSS Demelza, my friend Dr Dwight Enys.

DWIGHT Ma'am.

DEMELZA 'Twas you that mended his face?

ROSS Your fame precedes you!

DWIGHT My infamy you mean!

They all laugh.

DWIGHT Well, I intend keep my head down here. I've no wish to become notorious!

They walk on.

CUT TO:

4: EXT. FIELDS – DAY 43

We reveal various miners, villagers and assorted local gentry begin-ning to gather. Ross, Demelza and Dwight stroll up. As Dwight breaks off (to be introduced by Zacky to Mrs Zacky), Ross links Demelza's arm and walks her towards Francis, Elizabeth and Verity, who are seen approaching.

FRANCIS A picture of conjugal bliss! *(aside, to Ross)* Make the most of it!

Elizabeth goes to greet Demelza.

ELIZABETH You look well.

DEMELZA A month to go and I'm fatter than Prudie!

They both laugh together. Verity comes to embrace Demelza, then all five stroll on past Dr Choake, who is holding forth to an audience of assorted gentlemen and ladies (including Ruth & John Treneglos).

DR CHOAKE If in doubt, purge. That's our motto. Bleed, boil, blister, sweat – *(seeing Ruth grimace)* Healing is a science, ma'am. Few comprehend its mysteries.

DWIGHT'S VOICE Or its fees.

The group turns to see the newcomer. Suddenly Dwight seems con-scious of the fact that everyone is staring at him.

DWIGHT I merely meant – not everyone can afford expen-sive treatments. And sometimes – does it not do better to work with nature's remedies?

DR CHOAKE And you are— ?

ROSS *(making the introduction)* Dr Dwight Enys. He's making a study of lung diseases.

FRANCIS He's come to the right place.

DR CHOAKE Not if he cares to eat. The cases are miners — and they rarely pay.

DWIGHT I wonder if healing is not its own reward?

DR CHOAKE When you're living under a hedge and dining off thistles, perhaps you'll care to revisit the question, sir.

He bows abruptly and stalks off.

ROSS How's Grambler?

FRANCIS *(cheerfully)* Mortgaged to the hilt, running out of ore, the price of copper tumbling—

ROSS Perhaps we'll all be sleeping under hedges soon!

They go to take their seats.

Mark Daniel is arm-wrestling. As his opponent's arm goes down, a girl of 20 is revealed: pretty young actress Keren Smith. She is helping to set up a stage for 'The Aaron Otway Players' of which she's the youngest member. The elderly Aaron Otway himself is slobbering over her. She pushes him away, her revulsion all too evident, but he persists with his attentions. Keren catches Mark's eye. It's easy to see what she's thinking: if that was my man, I wouldn't need to put up with Aaron Otway's fumbling. She smiles at Mark. He flushes.

ZACKY Stop playing with him Mark. Come on.

Mark wins the arm wrestle with ease.

CUT TO:

5: EXT. FIELDS – DAY 43

The plays is in progress – an adaptation of All's Well that Ends Well. *Mark Daniel squeezes onto a row at the front. He can't take his eyes off Keren. Alone of all the company, she speaks her lines with conviction and passion.*

KEREN I am undone, there be no living. None. If Bertram be away. 'Twere all one that I should love a bright particular star and think to wed it—

She locks eyes boldly with Mark. Mark gazes back at her, mesmerized. It's as if she's speaking only to him.

KEREN *(cont'd)* He is so above me. In his bright radiance and collateral light must I be comforted, not in his sphere—

ON ROSS: Observing this exchange with some amusement. Beside him Demelza is fidgeting, in some discomfort.

ROSS *(to Demelza)*

My love?

DEMELZA 'Tis on'y an ache. I'll mebbe stretch my legs a while.

She gets up and leaves the audience as the play continues. Verity notices, discreetly gets up and follows her. Their departure is noted by Dwight.

CUT TO:

6: EXT. NAMPARA HOUSE – DAY 43

Establisher.

CUT TO:

7: INT. NAMPARA HOUSE, KITCHEN – DAY 43

Demelza and Verity enter the kitchen. Prudie and Jinny are surprised to see Demelza back.

PRUDIE Back so soon?

Demelza doesn't answer, but Verity's expression tells Prudie and Jinny all they need to know. Demelza has gone into a world of her own. She is walking up and down, having mild contractions and trying to convince herself she's not in actual labour. Verity, Prudie and Jinny exchange a glance.

Though the only sign of her oncoming contraction is a sharp intake of breath, a wince and the fact that her knuckles whiten as she holds on to a chair, Prudie and Jinny recognize the signs of progressing labour.

VERITY I hate to see your pain, my dear.

DEMELZA I hate to see yours.

Verity flushes, knowing exactly what Demelza's referring to. Prudie raises an eyebrow and Jinny nods.

PRUDIE *(low, to Jinny)* Get the linen.

Prudie puts on water to boil and Jinny begins to gather linen.

DEMELZA *(cont'd)* I could prescribe a remedy. *(beat)* One that lives in Truro and captains a ship.

VERITY I never think of him, Demelza. I pray you do likewise.

DEMELZA I must have somethin' to divert me!

Prudie and Jinny go upstairs to prepare the bedroom, Verity joins Demelza in her determined walk around the kitchen.

DEMELZA *(cont'd)* Judas Mary Joseph! Where's that brandy-wine?

She takes a quick nip of brandy as the contraction strengthens and she winces at the increasing pain.

VERITY Perhaps we should go upstairs?

CUT TO:

8: EXT. FIELDS – DAY 43

The final moments of the play. Keren is smiling and posturing as she utters her final lines.

KEREN All yet seems well; and if it end so meet, the bitter past, more welcome is the sweet.

Mark Daniel is enthusiastic in his applause. Keren smiles at him. Ross notices Elizabeth, applauding enthusiastically to make up for Francis's lack-lustre response. For a moment their eyes meet, then Elizabeth looks away. As Ross gets up – and looks around for Demelza – he notices Mark still gazing after Keren.

ROSS *(jokes)* Should we expect an announcement soon?

Mark grins bashfully and heads off in pursuit of Keren. Dwight approaches Ross.

DWIGHT You may soon find you've an announcement of your own.

Ross looks at him, for a moment uncomprehending. Then the penny drops. He races off.

CUT TO:

9: EXT. NAMPARA VALLEY – DAY 43

Ross gallops home to Nampara.

CUT TO:

10: INT. NAMPARA HOUSE, HALLWAY – DAY 43

Ross bursts into the house. All is peaceful and quiet and there is no one to be seen.

Then from upstairs comes the unmistakable cry of a newborn baby. Ross rushes upstairs.

CUT TO:

11: EXT. COAST – DAY 43

Establisher.

12: INT. NAMPARA HOUSE, ROSS & DEMELZA'S BEDROOM – NIGHT 43

Ross and Demelza snuggle up in bed as Demelza cradles their newborn baby Julia and both contemplate their child with disbelief. He examines her tiny fingers with amazement.

ROSS *(cont'd)* How did we make something so perfect?

DEMELZA *(after a pause)* I'm a feared, Ross.

Ross looks at her, puzzled.

DEMELZA *(cont'd)* That I love her too much. That I will hurt so much more if things go amiss.

ROSS I promise you, my love – I will make the world a better place for her. *(then)* I will be a better man for her sake.

DEMELZA And for mine?

ROSS I'm already a better man because of you.

He kisses her tenderly. Reassured, she snuggles closer to him and closes her eyes in peaceful bliss.

CUT TO:

13: EXT. NAMPARA COVE – DAWN 44

Ross stands on a rocky outcrop with Julia in his arms, watching the sun rise. Everything seems crisp and clear and vibrant with colour. Ross looks down at his newborn child, turns her so that she's facing the sea and the sunrise. As we pull back, Wheal Leisure mine is revealed in the distance – a silent reminder of Ross's heritage – and Julia's.

CUT TO:

14: INT. TRENWITH HOUSE, STUDY – NIGHT 44

CU: Elizabeth reading at her desk. A hand gives her an opened letter.

FRANCIS'S VOICE Ross and Demelza have a daughter.

Elizabeth takes the letter and glances at it. She struggles to remain calm and smile. This announcement brings up feelings she is unable to deny.

ELIZABETH I wish them well.

And she's genuine. But not without regrets.

CUT TO:

15: EXT. NAMPARA VALLEY – DAWN 45

Establisher.

CUT TO:

16: INT. NAMPARA HOUSE, KITCHEN – DAY 45

CU Ribbon. Demelza is embroidering a ribbon with the name 'Julia Grace'. It is only days after she's given birth and she looks tousled and dishevelled. There is a knock at the door. Jinny gets up to answer it. Presently she comes back.

JINNY 'Tis Mistress Poldark from Trenwith.

Before Demelza can compose herself, Elizabeth comes in. Demelza jumps to her feet.

ELIZABETH Please – don't get up—

DEMELZA Ross an't here. An' Julia's sleeping—

ELIZABETH 'Tis you I came to see.

DEMELZA *(surprised)* I? Er . . . some – refreshment—

ELIZABETH I beg you, do not trouble yourself – *(then, seeing Demelza's ribbon)* That's very pretty.

DEMELZA Oh – 'tis just a fancy I had – to make her a keepsake. I know 'tis not made of gold – or silver – *(laughs)* Or even copper—

ELIZABETH It's made of something more precious. *(then)* A mother's love for her child surpasses all other loves, does it not?

DEMELZA I'm not sure Ross'd care to hear that!

ELIZABETH Nor Francis!

A moment between Demelza and Elizabeth. Then . . .

ELIZABETH *(cont'd – smiles)* Men do not understand such things.

CUT TO:

17: INT. SAWLE CHURCH – DAY 46

Six weeks later. Ross, Demelza, and godparents Francis and Verity gather round the font as the Reverend Odgers trickles water on Julia's forehead.

REVEREND ODGERS Julia Grace Poldark, I baptize thee in the name of the Father, and of the Son, and of the Holy Ghost. Amen.

ALL Amen.

CUT TO:

18: EXT. NAMPARA HOUSE – DAY 46

Establisher. (Guests arriving back from the christening.)

CUT TO:

19: INT. NAMPARA HOUSE, KITCHEN – DAY 46

Demelza tries to pull in her stomach and force her posture upright as she glances through into the parlour, where the christening guests are gathering. She can see Ross chatting to Horace Treneglos, George chatting to Elizabeth, Dwight chatting to Henshawe. Other guests include Zacky & Mrs Zacky, Paul & Beth Daniel, Connie Carter – and Mark Daniel. Verity appears at Demelza's shoulder, gives her arm a reassuring squeeze.

DEMELZA This is Ross's doing. I wanted two christenings. One f'r'his sort, one for mine.

VERITY And where do I fit in?

DEMELZA You fit in everywhere. Like Ross. Whereas I – *(then)* I can scarce breathe.

VERITY What's there to fear?

DEMELZA *(laughs)* That my stays are so tight they'll burst?

Verity gives her arm a reassuring squeeze. Ruth Treneglos and John Treneglos have just arrived and sweep past into the parlour.

RUTH *(low, but not low enough to escape Demelza's ears)* I'm surprised Captain Poldark allows such riffraff in his house. But perhaps he's been obliged to lower his standards of late.

Verity and Demelza exchange a glance. This is precisely the kind of attitude Demelza fears.

CUT TO:

20: INT. NAMPARA HOUSE, PARLOUR – DAY 46

Ross pours himself a drink. Francis appears beside him.

FRANCIS Getting much sleep, Ross?

ROSS I've no complaints.

FRANCIS *(sour)* A child changes everything.

ROSS So does owning a mine. Neither can be ignored!

FRANCIS Much as one tries!

They watch Demelza and Elizabeth talking.

FRANCIS *(cont'd)* My wife is perfection, is she not? God knows what I've done to deserve her.

A moment between Ross and Francis. Ross can see that behind Francis's bitterness is genuine sadness. Francis walks off. Ross remains. Verity appears at his shoulder.

VERITY The curse of the Poldarks. Once given, our hearts are not easily withdrawn.

Ross nods thoughtfully. They contemplate Elizabeth and Demelza talking.

VERITY *(cont'd)* They're very different.

ROSS Yes. *(beat)* Yet each has something the other lacks.

VERITY *(as a joke)* Perhaps you'd like them both?

ROSS Perhaps I would.

Verity glances at him. Neither are entirely sure he's joking. Watching Demelza and Elizabeth talking together, the contrast between them is noticeable. Elizabeth refined, exquisitely lovely. Demelza, tousled, earthy, pretty but less delicate. Ross is shocked to realize he is not yet immune to Elizabeth's charms.

CUT TO:

21: EXT. NAMPARA HOUSE – DAY 46

Some of the guests are outside. George is chatting to a group of gentry. Ross and Dwight are talking together. Dwight is thoughtful as he contemplates Ross's home, family and friends. Ross, observing him, knows exactly what he's thinking.

DWIGHT I envy you.

ROSS My 'charmed' life?

DWIGHT Is it not charmed? Has it not comfort? – and purpose? – and certainty?

ROSS *(laughs)* This is Cornwall, Dwight. Nothing is certain!

As if to prove him right, Henshawe approaches.

HENSHAWE *(low)* As we feared. Choake's sold his shares in Leisure.

ROSS To whom?

Henshawe nods in the direction of George.

ROSS *(cont'd – low)* Damn him!

George now strolls past. George toasts Ross.

GEORGE Your health and prosperity, Ross!

ROSS *(affably)* And yours, George. *(unable to resist)* Particularly in the light of your recent acquisition.

GEORGE My shares in Wheal Leisure? You must take that as a compliment.

ROSS Oh, I do. Clearly you know a fine investment when you see it!

George returns Ross's affable smile and walks off. Ross rejoins Henshawe.

ROSS *(cont'd)* What of the other shareholders?

HENSHAWE Two or three more wish to sell.

ROSS We must buy them out.

HENSHAWE How?

ROSS No idea. But I'll starve before I see another piece of Leisure in his hands.

CUT TO:

22: INT. NAMPARA HOUSE, KITCHEN – DAY 46

Demelza is feeding Julia. She gazes down at her child, for a moment lost in the moment of mother-and-daughter bonding. Verity comes in, pauses at the sight of mother and child. Demelza looks up, sees her.

DEMELZA Has Ruth Treneglos finished dissecting me?

VERITY Don't mind her, dear. She cannot spoil a splendid day.

Something in Verity's tone makes Demelza look at her more closely. She guesses that Verity envies her.

DEMELZA I wish you could have this too, Verity.

VERITY *(smiling)* My dear, don't waste another moment on such thoughts. I assure you I'm quite reconciled to my lot.

But despite Verity's smile, Demelza suspects she's only putting on a brave face. Prudie comes in with some empty plates.

PRUDIE *(looking out of the window)* 'Oo be this, just as we run out o' likky pie?

Jinny and Jud (who have been busy with the refreshments) join her at the window.

THEIR POV: Two figures, one very tall, one very short, dressed in black, too far away to be distinguishable, make their way down the valley towards the house. (It's Tom Carne and Nelly Chegwidden-Carne.)

JUD 'Tis a blatherin' funeral procession!

PRUDIE Tell 'em 'ey come too soon. The mistress an't throttled Madam Ruth yet!

Now Demelza joins them at the window. Her face goes white.

DEMELZA It can't be . . .

CUT TO:

23: EXT. NAMPARA HOUSE – DAY 46

Suddenly Ross becomes aware of the approach of two new guests: it's Tom Carne and Nelly Chegwidden-Carne (45, sour, like a fat black hen). Ross rapidly computes the implications of this arrival. He knows it could spell disaster for Demelza but no one would guess it as he calmly goes to greet his in-laws.

ROSS *(cont'd)* Mr Carne, how d'you do, sir? Mrs Carne. I'm glad you were able to join us, ma'am. This way.

CUT TO:

24: INT. NAMPARA HOUSE, HALLWAY – DAY 46

Ross leads the way into the hallway. Tom seems determined to be displeased. He glances round, seeing the gentlemen in their finery, the women in their gaudy dresses and low-cut bodices, the port and rum, which are being drunk by all.

TOM CARNE Step no further, Nelly. This be a place of filth and abomination.

A silence descends. All guests – whether gentry or miners – are aware that this arrival is something out of the ordinary. They wait on tenterhooks to see how things develop. Demelza appears, carrying Julia.

TOM CARNE *(cont'd)* Shame on 'ee, daughter! To mingle wi' such dandical folk when yer own flesh an' blood should take precedence.

ROSS And so they shall, sir. Allow me to introduce you to my friends and family. Beginning with your granddaughter.

He takes Julia from Demelza, then escorts Tom and Nelly into the parlour, introducing them to the guests.

ROSS This way, Mr Carne.

Ross approaches Francis, Dwight and John Treneglos with the Carnes. Ruth joins John and thrusts out her low-cut dress provocatively.

ROSS My cousin Francis, my friends John and Ruth Treneglos, Dr Dwight Enys.

FRANCIS Your servant, sir.

TOM CARNE No servant o' mine! And no friend neither. *(to Ruth Treneglos)* Cover yerself, missy. Your place is to be decent an' modest – not layin' out wares for men to slaver o'er—

John Treneglos stifles a smirk. Ruth, however, is outraged.

RUTH Damn your insolence! John, did you hear what he said?

Stung by her reprimand, John has no choice but to take action.

JOHN TRENEGLOS You impudent swine! Make apology or I'll have the coat off your back!

ROSS Have a care, John. You are both my guests. And I couldn't permit you to strike my father-in-law.

A frisson of shock from the guests at hearing Ross publicly affirm his relationship to Tom.

TOM CARNE Nay, let him come! I've been in the ring, I can 'old me own!

ROSS Hold your tongue, sir! If we want your opinion, we'll ask. *(to John Treneglos)* Will you allow me as host to apologize for any offence caused?

JOHN TRENEGLOS Well, if Ruth is satisfied—

RUTH *(sneering)* Naturally if Ross wishes to protect his new relative—

Ross bows graciously. Dwight stifles the impulse to weigh in on Ross's behalf.

RUTH *(cont'd)* Allowances should be made for those who don't know any better.

She looks up and locks eyes with Demelza, who is watching aghast.

CUT TO:

25: EXT. NAMPARA HOUSE – DAY 46

The distant figures of Tom and Nelly can be seen retreating. Crossing them, coming towards Nampara, is Keren.

Ross with Zacky and Mark are revealed outside Nampara House.

ROSS I thought the players had moved on?

Mark's face breaks into a smile.

MARK They 'ad! An' she did tell me she'd return – but I niver thought she would.

ROSS *(as a joke)* You must catch her while you can.

MARK I mean to. *Mark rushes out greet Keren.*

MARK Keren . . .

ZACKY Like a lamb to the slaughter.

Ross and Zacky smile resignedly. Then Ross goes inside.

CUT TO:

26: INT. NAMPARA HOUSE, KITCHEN – DAY 46

Ross comes in to find Demelza in despair, cradling Julia, being comforted by Verity and Prudie. Jud is scowling in the corner. Dwight is also there, lending support.

ROSS They've gone.

PRUDIE *(muttering)* An' good riddance!

JUD Blasted 'ippocreets!

DEMELZA Oh why did they come?

ROSS Because I invited them?

DEMELZA They meant t' shame an' disgrace me.

ROSS Then they failed.

DWIGHT And in a week it will all be forgot.

DEMELZA Not by me.

CUT TO:

27: EXT. NAMPARA VALLEY, FIELDS – DAY 46

Mark sits with Keren like a lovestruck puppy.

MARK I did miss 'ee.

KEREN How much?

MARK Scarce did eat.

KEREN They all say that.

Mark looks crestfallen. Keren continues to toy with him.

KEREN *(cont'd)* I can't stay long. An' tomorrow I'll be gone.

MARK An' when return?

KEREN 'Appen I shan't.

MARK Not ever?

KEREN What's to keep me here?

She gives him a pointed look – a challenge. He falls for it.
CUT TO:

28: INT. NAMPARA HOUSE, KITCHEN – DAY 46

Demelza looks up from tending Julia as Jinny and Verity bustle round clearing up after the party. Ross has just informed them of an extraordinary request.

DEMELZA Find her a home? Within a week?

VERITY How?

DEMELZA Why?

ROSS It's the condition of her agreeing to marry him.

DEMELZA You could help 'em? There's a cottage at Mellin—

ROSS It's in no fit state to live in. And besides . . .

His hesitation reveals just how sure he is about the wisdom of this match. Demelza, however, has other ideas.

DEMELZA Does she love him?

ROSS She says so.

VERITY Does he love her?

ROSS Besotted.

DEMELZA Then they mus' marry.

ROSS Because?

DEMELZA Love should conquer all. *(a pointed look at Verity)* Even if it requires a little help.

ROSS On the contrary. *(beat)* Some obstacles cannot be overcome. *(with a look at Verity)* And should not – for the peace of all concerned.

Verity nods stoically. She knows it makes sense. And yet . . . It's the final straw for Demelza. Though Ross doesn't notice, the expression on Demelza's face tells us she's about to take matters into her own hands.

CUT TO:

29: EXT. TRENWITH HOUSE – DUSK 46

Establisher.

CUT TO:

30: INT. TRENWITH HOUSE, GREAT HALL – DUSK 46

Elizabeth and Francis return from the christening. Elizabeth notices that Francis has paused by a portrait of Charles.

ELIZABETH He would have enjoyed today.

FRANCIS He'd have revelled in it. The great patriarch and leader of men!

ELIZABETH Is that to be disdained?

FRANCIS It's to be lived up to.

ELIZABETH And can you not?

It's said gently but Francis takes it as a challenge and walks off.

ELIZABETH *(cont'd)* It was a question not a judgement.

CUT TO:

31: EXT. THE SEA – DUSK 46

Establisher.

CUT TO:

32: EXT. CLIFF-TOP, CORNWALL – DUSK 46

Verity stands looking at the drawing of the ship Captain Blamey gave her.

CUT TO:

33: INT. TRENWITH HOUSE, OAK ROOM – NIGHT 46

In contrast to the warm bustling household she's just left at Nampara, Verity comes in to an atmosphere of listless formality. Aunt Agatha is snoring in her chair, Elizabeth reading quietly to Geoffrey Charles and Francis prowling restlessly. Verity stands a moment observing this sad tableau. Then she comes in and takes up her needlework. Francis continues to prowl. It's clear he'd much rather be elsewhere. Elizabeth knows it too, and in an attempt to detain him longer . . .

ELIZABETH *(to Geoffrey Charles)* Shall Papa read to you now?

FRANCIS *(abruptly)* Papa has business to attend to.

Elizabeth bites her tongue and doesn't look at Francis as he walks out without taking his leave. Geoffrey Charles looks crestfallen. Aunt Agatha snores. Verity sees all and continues to sew in silence.

CUT TO:

34: EXT. NAMPARA HOUSE – DAY 47

Early morning.

CUT TO:

35: INT. NAMPARA HOUSE, PARLOUR – DAY 47

Demelza is feeding Julia as Ross comes in to say goodbye.

DEMELZA Will you be gone long?

ROSS As long as it takes to raise capital to buy out our nervous shareholders?

He kisses her and Julia and goes out. Demelza settles back in her chair, to all appearances with no intention of moving for the entire day.

CUT TO:

36: EXT. NAMPARA HOUSE – DAY 47

Jud brings Ross's horse round to the front door, saddled and ready to depart.

CUT TO:

37: EXT. NAMPARA HOUSE – DAY 47

As Jud watches Ross mount his horse and gallop away, Demelza appears in the doorway behind him.

DEMELZA Are you ready?

JUD Well, pick me liver! What's the blatherin' rush? *(muttering to himself)* Sneakin' an' slidin' an' slitherin' about – 'tedn't right, 'tedn't fit, tedn't proper—

DEMELZA *(ignoring this)* We must be done and back by five or Julia will suffer. Now let's get gone.

CUT TO:

38: EXT. COUNTRY ROAD – DAY 47

Ross arrives on the outskirts of Truro. He is met by a group of beggars. He shares out a few coins.

CUT TO:

39: INT. RED LION INN – DAY 47

Ross is taking refreshment with Dwight. At the next table is Harry

Blewitt (45, manager and shareholder of Wheal Maid mine), who for now goes unnoticed, both by us and by Ross.

DWIGHT What brings you to town?

ROSS *(laughs)* Insane optimism? *(then)* The fond hope that my banker can drum up sufficient capital for me to buy out our discontented shareholders. *(beat)* Before they sell to the Warleggans.

DWIGHT I wish you well.

ROSS *(laughs)* Let us change the subject.

DWIGHT By all means. Did you hear of the riots in Launceston?

ROSS Are you surprised? People can only starve for so long while the rich get fat.

DWIGHT In France they make their feelings known with hatchets and pikes.

ROSS They may do so here soon. Copper prices have fallen again. God knows when Grambler last paid full wages. The industry's on its knees.

DWIGHT What's to be done?

ROSS Sit tight and wait for the price to rise?

DWIGHT And if it does not?

CUT TO:

40: EXT. ANDREW BLAMEY'S HOUSE – DAY 47

Jud waits impatiently as, with trepidation, Demelza knocks at a door.
CUT TO:

41: INT. ANDREW BLAMEY'S HOUSE – DAY 47

An old housekeeper shows Demelza into a well-furnished though not luxurious suite of rooms. She sits down to wait then immediately stands up. She's clearly very nervous and cannot settle.

DEMELZA Thank you.

CUT TO:

42: INT. RED LION INN – DAY 47

Ross and Dwight continue their luncheon. Blewitt continues to eavesdrop.

ROSS We're all committed to short-term loan repayments. If we don't sell cheap, we don't sell at all. *(then)* Of course, if the smelting companies were honestly run—

DWIGHT Are they not?

ROSS It's a ring. They don't bid against each other so the price they pay us is rock-bottom. *(then)* A pity the mines are not in similar unity. We could band together and withhold supplies till a decent price was paid.

Ross and Dwight continue their luncheon. Blewitt continues to eavesdrop.

DWIGHT No remedy, then?

ROSS *(an idle thought)* Unless the mines were to form a company of their own—

At the next table Blewitt pricks up his ears.

ROSS *(cont'd)* Bid independently, purchase the ore, build a smelting works – that would keep the shareholders happy.

An excited Blewitt interrupts.

BLEWITT I couldn't help but overhear. You intend to form a smelting company—

ROSS I intend nothing, sir. I merely say that were the mines to unite and create a company – one that would bid, buy, refine and sell their own products – they might keep the profit for themselves instead of handing it to the Warleggans.

Ross walks out with Dwight, unaware that what was intended as a casual remark has been taken utterly seriously.

BLEWITT Absolute genius.

CUT TO:

43: INT. ANDREW BLAMEY'S HOUSE – DAY 47

Demelza, waiting nervously, gets to her feet, paces anxiously. Her courage failing, she's finally made up her mind to leave when she hears a door slam and angry footsteps hasten upstairs. Panicking, she heads for the door, but before she can get there, it opens and Andrew Blamey storms in. He stops short in amazement, struggles to collect himself. He has no recollection of Demelza (who was only a serving-girl last time he saw her).

ANDREW May I be of service to you, ma'am?

Demelza's courage almost fails. Then . . .

DEMELZA My name is Poldark.

Andrew is glaring at Demelza with undisguised hostility.

ANDREW Did Verity send you?

DEMELZA No. She's no idea I've come. No one does.

ANDREW It was made clear long ago that Verity was not for me. I've since moved on, set my sights elsewhere—

DEMELZA You're married?

ANDREW To my ship, to my profession. And all the better for it.

DEMELZA But—

ANDREW I never think of her now. I'm sorry you've had a wasted journey.

He opens the door to let her leave.

CUT TO:

44: EXT. TRURO STREET – DAY 47

On Ross as he walks down the street to Pascoe's office.

CUT TO:

45: INT. PASCOE'S OFFICE – DAY 47

Pascoe shows Ross into his office.

PASCOE If you wish to realize the money to buy out your shareholders, you have only one option. Raise a mortgage on Nampara.

Ross nods thoughtfully, digesting the implications of this.

ROSS And risk the very roof over my head.

PASCOE And with a wife and young child to support—

ROSS You'd advise against.

PASCOE Most emphatically.

Ross looks resigned.

CUT TO:

46: EXT. NAMPARA HOUSE – DAY 47

Establisher.

47: INT. NAMPARA HOUSE, PARLOUR – DAY 47

A picture of domestic bliss: Demelza is in exactly the same chair, in exactly the same position, feeding Julia, when Ross returns home. To all appearances, she hasn't moved since he left.

DEMELZA A good day?

ROSS A frustrating day. *(kisses her)* At least Julia's content.

DEMELZA She is.

ROSS But you seem very confined here. Can you bear it?

DEMELZA Oh, I find it suits me well enough.

Behind Ross, Jud raises his eyebrows. Demelza glares him into silence. Now Prudie comes in.

PRUDIE Mark Daniel sent for 'ee, Cap'n.

Ross raises his eyebrows.

ROSS It seems to be catching.

DEMELZA What?

ROSS Recklessness.

DEMELZA How so?

ROSS I open a mine. Dwight Enys takes on its diseases. And God knows what Mark's taking on!

He goes out.

CUT TO:

48: EXT. MARK & KEREN'S COTTAGE – DAY 47

The cottage is semi-derelict. Paul, Zacky and Nick are busy patching it up. As Ross walks up, they greet him warmly. He surveys the cottage.

ROSS She's a fortunate girl.

PAUL A plaguey d'mandin' one!

ZACKY What kind o' woman d' make such conditions?

PAUL Ap'n she niver thought 'e'd do it.

ZACKY She don' know Mark, then.

Now Mark appears – exhausted but beaming with pride.

ROSS Looks like you are making progress.

MARK *(proudly)* No sleep fer four nights!

ROSS *(taking Mark aside)* And you're set on this girl, Mark? You barely know her.

MARK Mebbe so, Ross, but truly she be my 'eart's desire.

Ross nods. He hopes, rather than believes, that Mark's made the right choice.

ROSS I hope she deserves you.

He picks up tools and joins in with the work on the house.

CUT TO:

49: EXT. NEAR MARK & KEREN'S COTTAGE – DAY 48

A fiddler leads newly-weds Keren and Mark home from church. Ross and Demelza join the other guests. Mark is beaming, Keren strutting, preening and tossing her hair. Demelza notices Mrs Zacky, Beth Daniel and Connie Carter looking askance at Keren.

DEMELZA *(to Ross)* They don' like her.

ROSS They like Mark. She's an outsider.

DEMELZA So am I.

ROSS They like me. They make allowances for you!

Demelza hits him playfully. Now, as Mark and Keren approach, the guests disperse from in front of the cottage, leaving it visible to Mark and Keren. A lick of limewash and some rough plaster has improved its condition since we last saw it, but it's still very basic.

ON KEREN: Struggling to suppress her dismay as she contemplates the rough exterior of her new home.

KEREN Is that it?

MARK Yes.

KEREN Oh.

MARK We'll make it fitty, Keren, once we livin' 'ere – 'twill soon be a palace, ee'll see—

Keren forces a smile, but only Mark is convinced by it.

CUT TO:

50: EXT. MARK & KEREN'S COTTAGE – DAY 48

Ross is chatting to Dwight.

ROSS I've secured lodgings for you.

DWIGHT That's tremendous. Where?

ROSS Mingoose Cottage. It's not grand, but I hope it'll serve.

KEREN'S VOICE 'Twill serve me—

They turn to see Keren standing behind them, smiling archly.

KEREN To know who my neighbour is!

ROSS *(to Dwight)* Have you been introduced to the bride?

KEREN If he'd dance with her, she might introduce herself.

DWIGHT Oh – er – at your service, ma'am.

Clearly struck by Keren's wild beauty, he walks off with her. Mark returns to Ross.

MARK I been thinkin', Ross – Keren do 'ave finer tastes than I can easy stretch to—

ROSS Yes?

MARK So could 'ee mebbe find me extra work at th' mine?

ROSS I'd like to say yes, Mark. But it depends how we fare at the auction tomorrow.

CUT TO:

51: INT. NAMPARA HOUSE, PARLOUR – NIGHT 48

Ross and Demelza sit by the fire. It's late. Julia sleeps in Demelza's arms.

ROSS So there you have it. The copper auction is tomorrow. As usual the price will be fixed by the smelting companies. I've no means to buy out the shareholders without risking all we have. This house, our land, our very livelihood—

Demelza is silent, thoughtful. Ross misinterprets her silence.

ROSS *(cont'd)* You must be regretting your marriage to such a destitute rogue!

DEMELZA *(amused)* Must I? After what 'e brought me to? Am I now such a great lady as to forget where I'd be if we'd never met?

Ross considers this, laughs to himself.

DEMELZA *(cont'd)* What?

ROSS *(laughs)* Women! *(then)* Not all are created equal. Some are never satisfied. Some could never be brought so low. And some thumb their nose at adversity and roll up their sleeves!

DEMELZA P'raps you wish you'd wed a rich lady!

Ross smiles, shakes his head.

ROSS I'm quite aware of my good fortune, I assure you.

CUT TO:

52: INT. TRENWITH HOUSE, GREAT HALL – DAY 49

Francis is preparing to leave for the auction in Truro. Elizabeth is breakfasting with Geoffrey Charles and Verity. Elizabeth is determined to remain positive.

ELIZABETH *(to Geoffrey Charles)* Shall we ask Papa how much copper we sent?

FRANCIS 'We'?

ELIZABETH Our mine? Grambler? To the auction. One, parcel, or two?

FRANCIS *(to Geoffrey Charles)* Mama's becoming quite the expert.

ELIZABETH *(to Geoffrey Charles)* We must hope for a good price.

FRANCIS Though we know we shan't get it!

He addresses Geoffrey Charles directly.

FRANCIS *(cont'd – to Geoffrey Charles)* And unless the price goes sky-high, Papa will have to start pawning the family jewels!

ELIZABETH *(gently)* Francis—

FRANCIS *(to Geoffrey Charles)* Perhaps someone will make a bid for Mama!

Verity looks down at her plate. Elizabeth declines to be provoked. Francis leaves.

CUT TO:

53: EXT. RED LION INN – DAY 49

Establisher.

CUT TO:

54: INT. RED LION INN – DAY 49

Ross, Francis and other mine owners and managers – including Blewitt and Richard Tonkin (mine owner) gather for the copper auction. The mine owners look tense.

CHAIRMAN Gentlemen. Gentlemen. The auction is now open. I have first to dispose of a dole of ore from Grambler. Forty-five tons.

CUT TO:

55: INT. RED LION INN – DAY 49

Ross, Francis and the other owners and managers leave the auction room. Faces are grim.

FRANCIS Disastrous.

TONKIN A scandal.

BLEWITT Disgrace!

TONKIN Every single parcel gone for half its true value.

ROSS We'll be paying them to take it off us next.

Francis takes a consolatory swig from a hip-flask. Ross doesn't bat an eyelid but Francis, feeling defensive, goes on the attack.

FRANCIS You realize you're been uncommonly dull since you became a father?

ROSS *(laughs)* My apologies!

FRANCIS No matter, I've a remedy. Seeing what little entertainment your life affords, I've procured you an invitation.

ROSS To what?

FRANCIS The ultimate house-party! And if that doesn't put a smile on your face . . .

Though Ross clearly doesn't require such entertainments, he's happy to humour Francis if it will make him feel better. Now they are accosted by Blewitt.

BLEWITT Gentlemen? I take it you feel no satisfaction at the business done today?

FRANCIS Who the devil could?

BLEWITT Then may I trouble you to step this way a moment?

He indicates for them to follow him. Puzzled but intrigued, they do so. In a corner of the room Ross and Francis see a group of mine managers and shareholders – including Tonkin.

BLEWITT We'd like your word that nothing that passes between us goes any further.

Ross and Francis nod their agreement.

CUT TO:

56: INT. NAMPARA HOUSE, PARLOUR – DAY 49

A letter, addressed to 'Captain Ross Poldark of Nampara' lies on the table. Presently it is snatched up by Demelza, who has Julia wrapped inside a shawl and is ready to go out walking.

DEMELZA *(cont'd)* Jinny, put the tetty pie to cool. I'll walk out to meet Ross.

Demelza goes out with Julia.

CUT TO:

57: INT. RED LION INN – DAY 49

Ross and Francis have joined the gathering. Tonkin has just explained the purpose of it.

FRANCIS A smelting company? Formed by the mines themselves? Well, it all rings very agreeable – but you'd be biting off no end of trouble—

TONKIN We know that, sir. The smelting companies will want no competition—

ROSS And the banks will be behind 'em—

BLEWITT But all of us here are willing to stand together – and between us we can lay our hands on a measure of cash.

TONKIN But it requires secrecy. So before we proceed – who wishes to join us?

He looks round at them all. No one speaks. Eventually . . .

FRANCIS What d'you say, Ross? Too risky a venture?

TONKIN It was your cousin who first suggested it.

FRANCIS *(surprised)* Did he?

People are now looking at Ross for his verdict. Feeling he can no longer remain uncommitted . . .

ROSS We can't go on as we are. And I'd rather fail fighting than throw up my hands and wait for the end.

A murmur of relief and appreciation greets his decision.

TONKIN And Mr Francis Poldark?

FRANCIS My finances are at present – somewhat compli-
cated. So I cannot at this time join you. But I wish you well,
gentlemen. I do indeed. *(then)* And who's to be your leader?
Is it you, Tonkin?

TONKIN Oh no, sir. I'm not at all the right man. But we're all
agreed on who is.

All eyes turn to Ross.

CUT TO:

58: EXT. COASTAL PATH – DAY 49

Demelza walks across the cliff-tops with Julia, reading the letter.

DEMELZA *(to Julia, referring to the letter)* A house-party! At
George Warleggan's. Think of that, my lamb. Your mother's
a lady – your father's a gent – his name goes back hundreds
of years and a good name it is – and now 'tis yours too, my
sweet—

VOICE Mistress Poldark!

Demelza freezes. She is horrified to see Andrew Blamey.

ANDREW Forgive me, I don't mean to alarm you – but I must
speak.

CUT TO:

59: EXT. NAMPARA VALLEY – DAY 49

Returning from Truro, Ross encounters Zacky on his way home.

ZACKY Good news or bad?

ROSS Both. The auction was dismal, but—

ZACKY I still 'ave a job?

ROSS *(nods)* And I have a new one.

He dismounts and walks with Zacky, to tell him about the new copper-smelting company.

CUT TO:

60: EXT. COASTAL PATH – DAY 49

Demelza is looking nervous, Andrew placatory.

ANDREW When you saw me in Truro I was unmannerly. I'm a man of strong temper. To control it has been the work of a lifetime. But God forbid I should quarrel with those who wish me well.

DEMELZA Captain Blamey, I cannot stay—

She begins to walk off.

ANDREW Hear me out, I beg you. Since your visit, I've been in torment. What you spoke – of Verity – I thought I'd put her behind me. *(beat)* But I had not.

Demelza halts.

CUT TO:

61: EXT. NAMPARA VALLEY – DAY 49

Ross, leading his horse, walks on with Zacky.

ZACKY Mister Francis cannot be part of the new smelting company?

ROSS Will not. Nor others who bank at Warleggan's. If their names were known, George would call in their debts. To a man, they'd be ruined. But I may have found a compromise.

Those who bank with Warleggan's will keep their names secret. Those who bank elsewhere will let their names be known. I bank with Pascoe. George cannot touch me.

CUT TO:

62: EXT. COASTAL PATH – DAY 49

Demelza has halted.

DEMELZA What d'you want o' me?

ANDREW To ask you – am I to hope? With her father deceased, do I have a chance? May I see her? How? When?

DEMELZA *(flustered)* I don't know. My husband – he mustn't see you here—

ANDREW Is he against me too? He wasn't before.

DEMELZA He's against me – stirring up what should be left alone. *(then)* He'll be on his way home soon. I must go.

ANDREW Will you tell Verity?

DEMELZA No! I think – not yet – I'll send word—

ANDREW Bless you, ma'am. I'll not fail you. Or her.

He kisses her hand then runs quickly away.

CUT TO:

63: EXT. COASTAL PATH – DAY 49

Demelza is walking along the path when she sees Ross riding towards her. Ross leaps off his horse and greets Demelza and Julia with a kiss. He looks closely at Demelza and seems suspicious.

ROSS You seem very excitable. Is something amiss?

DEMELZA Nothing – no! – on'y – *(a sudden brainwave)* A letter came – *(shows him)* Inviting us to George Warleggan's party. *(he takes it)* I'm that glad! It'll make up for the christening. Now I'll show I can wear fine clothes an' behave all genteel along with the best of 'em.

ROSS That you will not.

DEMELZA Why?

ROSS It's not that kind of party.

DEMELZA *(disappointed)* Oh.

ROSS Don't look so sorry for yourself. It'll be nothing but gaming and toping and dawn-to-dusk business talk.

DEMELZA Will you go, then?

ROSS If only to please Francis and throw George off the scent of Carnmore. But you at least may be spared.

CUT TO:

64: INT. NAMPARA HOUSE, LIBRARY – DAY 49

Demelza sits at the desk looking with disappointment at the invitation to George Warleggan's party. She notes the date of the party. Then a thought occurs. She gets out a sheet of paper and starts to compose a letter of her own: 'Dear Capten Blamy . . .'

CUT TO:

65: INT. NAMPARA HOUSE, KITCHEN – DAY 50

Ross is getting ready to leave for Truro. Demelza comes in, dressed to go out, but with Julia at the breast. She bustles about, one-handed, breakfasting, doing small chores, preparing to leave. Ross looks at her in surprise.

ROSS Going somewhere?

DEMELZA To town.

ROSS To what purpose?

DEMELZA Urgent business. I need a new cloak – and Verity must help me choose.

Ross begins to laugh. Demelza looks at him defiantly.

DEMELZA *(cont'd)* What?

ROSS *(laughing)* The choosing of cloaks? May that always be the worst of your worries! Now don't delay me, I have a party to attend. Jud! Bring the horses.

Ross goes out, laughing. But as Demelza hands Julia to Jinny and prepares to leave, we know she has other plans afoot.

CUT TO:

66: INT. MARGARET'S LODGING – DAY 50

A jewelled necklace is laid onto a table. A delicate hand, weighed down by rings and bracelets, takes it up. The giver is revealed to be Francis. The recipient Margaret. He fastens it gently round her neck.

MARGARET You spoil me.

FRANCIS You like it?

MARGARET I like to be appreciated.

FRANCIS Who doesn't?

He leans down and kisses the back of her neck.

MARGARET Does your wife not appreciate you?

FRANCIS My wife tries to make me a better man.

MARGARET Like your father.

FRANCIS I will never be that man.

His hand is on her shoulder. She reaches up and caresses it. Francis is desperate for approval – and will seemingly pay any price for it.

CUT TO:

67: INT. TRENWITH HOUSE, GREAT HALL – DAY 50

Ross and Demelza are shown into the hallway.

DEMELZA Could you take me to Miss Verity?

SERVANT This way, ma'am.

Demelza goes off. Ross remains. Presently Elizabeth appears. She looks fragile – but determined to put on a brave face.

ROSS Are you joining this 'urgent' trip to the dressmakers?

ELIZABETH *(smiling)* Because shopping and dressing up are the only things of matter to us women?

ROSS Not at all, but—

ELIZABETH They are, of course! But I hesitate to buy ribbons when our copper can scarce be given away! Besides, Francis has more urgent calls on his purse.

ROSS Such as?

ELIZABETH Gaming? Entertaining? Oh, himself, not his wife. Nor his workers. They're not remotely entertained. Though I dare say she is. Lavishly.

It's said with a smile but Ross knows the depth of pain beneath.

ROSS Elizabeth, I wish—

ELIZABETH There was something you could do? Oh, I wish it too, Ross. But we are beyond wishing, are we not?

It's all said very lightheartedly, but Ross isn't remotely fooled. Demelza now reappears with Verity. Elizabeth avoids looking at Ross and gives Demelza a welcoming smile.

ELIZABETH *(cont'd)* Next time I hope to join you.

CUT TO:

68: EXT. COUNTRY ROAD – DAY 50

Riding along the road to Truro, Demelza is struggling to contain her excitement. Ross and Verity are oblivious. Presently they spot a crowd of people in the distance, spilling out across the road. From this distance it's impossible to tell who they are or what they're doing.

As they get closer they realize the crowd is a group of destitute miners and their families.

The miners stare coldly at Ross, Demelza and Verity and only reluctantly move out of the way. Ross glances at them but Demelza and Verity look straight ahead as they ride through. Though the miners make no attempt to accost the riders, the atmosphere is hostile. Verity is deeply rattled. After they've passed . . .

VERITY *(to Demelza)* My dear, were you not afraid? The look in their eyes—

DEMELZA I seen the like before. In Illuggan once, when we were out of corn. Empty bellies make for such looks.

ROSS And worse.

They ride on.

CUT TO:

69: EXT. WARLEGGAN HOUSE – DAY 50

Ross jumps down from his horse and hands it to a groom.

CUT TO:

70: INT. WARLEGGAN HOUSE, GAMING ROOM – DAY 50

As Ross comes in the first person he sees is Dwight Enys. They greet each other warmly. Dwight seems overawed by sight of the splendidly dressed George, playing the host, enjoying the trappings of wealth and status.

DWIGHT And his grandfather was a blacksmith? How is it possible?

ROSS To leap from poverty to wealth in two generations?

DWIGHT And maintain it in the midst of a slump! While men like you and Francis face ruin!

Ross shrugs good-humouredly.

ROSS We have different ways of doing business.

He draws Dwight's attention to Francis, who is playing cards with Matthew Sanson. As they watch, Francis loses again. Sanson prepares to gather up his winnings and encourages Francis to play another game. Ross spots Margaret on her way to rejoin Francis and detains her.

ROSS Who is that?

MARGARET The infamous Matthew Sanson? Mill owner and corn merchant.

ROSS Does his infamy extend beyond bankrupting Francis?

MARGARET It extends almost everywhere! And he has George's endorsement. Which makes him—

ROSS A force to be reckoned with.

MARGARET A man of means. Though, sadly, not of generosity.

She fingers her necklace provocatively, as if to tease him.

ROSS That collar is not a gift of his?

MARGARET No indeed. The giver was a man of taste.

Ross has heard enough. He now knows that Sanson is a threat and that Francis has emptied his coffers for Margaret not Elizabeth. Margaret smiles at him – and at Dwight – then goes to rejoin Francis.
CUT TO:

71: INT. HABERDASHER'S – DAY 50

Demelza seems on edge as she tries to select material for a new cloak. She lingers so long over fabrics, fingering them, standing back, debating with herself, that even Verity starts to lose patience.

VERITY Could you manage without me while I visit the chandler?

DEMELZA On no account. You must help me choose. What do you think of this one? Or this one, perhaps?

Just as Verity is pouring over the fabrics again . . .

ANDREW'S VOICE Miss Verity?

Verity freezes. She does not turn round, but the colour drains from her cheeks.

CUT TO:

72: INT. WARLEGGAN HOUSE, GAMING ROOM – DAY 50

Ross is watching Francis lose again. George saunters over to Dwight.

GEORGE A physician, sir? Pray, what d'you prescribe for boredom?

DWIGHT It's not a condition I'm familiar with, sir.

GEORGE Doubtless you'll have opportunities to study it.

DWIGHT I suspect not, sir. The patients I tend rarely suffer from that affliction.

George smiles affably. Dwight bows politely. Margaret strolls over to Ross. Together they watch Francis play cards a while.

MARGARET A pity he hasn't your skill at cards. *(beat)* Or in other ways.

Ross ignores her suggestive glance. He watches Francis, who is ashen-faced and perspiring.

MARGARET *(cont'd)* He'll shortly be ruined.

ROSS And you will have done with him.

MARGARET As his wife did long ago.

Ross is about to retort, but decides against.

MARGARET *(cont'd)* Do all men come to regret their choice?

ROSS I couldn't say.

MARGARET Do you?

ROSS I regret nothing.

MARGARET Come the day, you know where to find me. *(in her 'old' voice)* You was always my weakness, me lord.

She lets the offer hang there a moment, then she returns to Francis. As Ross watches, Francis loses again. He mops his brow, which is beaded with sweat. He hesitates. Then gambles again.

CUT TO:

73: INT. HABERDASHER'S – DAY 50

Verity is staring at Andrew Blamey as if she's seen a ghost. Demelza is trying to look as if she has never seen the man in her life.

ANDREW Miss Verity – for so long I never dared to hope – but such a chance as this—

VERITY *(forced calm)* Captain Blamey, may I introduce you to my cousin, Mistress Demelza Poldark, Ross's wife.

ANDREW I'm honoured, ma'am.

DEMELZA And I, sir.

ANDREW May I beg the pleasure of your company? – for a cordial or coffee?

DEMELZA That would be most—

VERITY No! *(as if shocked at her own outburst)* Thank you, sir – we cannot. No good can come of it. I bid you good day.

Without warning she rushes out of the shop and disappears down the street. Demelza stares helplessly at Andrew a moment, then follows.

CUT TO:

74: INT. WARLEGGAN HOUSE, GAMING ROOM – DAY 50

Ross watches from a distance as Francis continues his card game.

ON FRANCIS: Getting increasingly rattled, becoming more and more desperate. He's at his last gasp now. Dwight has stationed himself near Ross. Margaret has detached herself from Francis's side and is watching his demise from a distance. George is lounging back in his chair, watching every card that's played. Francis loses again. Ross can bear it no longer. He walks across to the table.

ROSS What are the stakes?

GEORGE You wouldn't wish to know.

ROSS On the contrary.

FRANCIS You'll find out soon enough.

Before Ross can take issue with George, a servant whispers in Sanson's ear. Sanson nods, smiles and gets to his feet.

SANSON Pray excuse me, gentlemen. *(to Francis)* A pleasure, as always.

He bows and takes his leave. Now Francis gets up from the table. He's unsteady on his feet but he brushes aside Ross's attempts to support him. Margaret, tellingly, makes no attempt to do so. Francis stumbles out of the room. He looks a sorry sight. George and Ross exchange a glance. To Ross's surprise, there is a trace of pity on George's face.

CUT TO:

75: EXT. TRURO STREET – DAY 50

Demelza catches up with Verity. Verity's face is wet with tears and she looks distraught.

DEMELZA Would it have been so very bad to hear him out?

VERITY He can have nothing to say that I wish to hear.

DEMELZA Nothing?

They have been moving forward, lost in conversation, but now become aware of footsteps behind them and people beginning to stride past them. At first this barely registers, but as more people stride past, it begins to dawn on Demelza who they are.

DEMELZA Oh! Verity – the miners—

Now more people come past. They look ragged, dishevelled, angry, aggressive. Their paces quickens. Demelza and Verity are momentarily trapped in the middle as miners barge past them on either side. Verity is beginning to panic. As Demelza pulls Verity closer, an arm reaches out and grabs her.

CUT TO:

76: INT. WARLEGGAN HOUSE, GAMING ROOM – DAY 50

Ross and Dwight are about to leave when George detains Ross.

GEORGE Will you believe me if I say it gives me no pleasure to see Francis beggar himself?

ROSS *(shrugs)* Business is business.

GEORGE It's not my business to bankrupt a friend.

ROSS So you leave it to a third party. And so your conscience is clear. *(beat)* I thank you for your hospitality.

Ross bows politely and leaves. Dwight does likewise. George watches Ross go, torn between anger and respect.

CUT TO:

77: EXT. TRURO STREET – DAY 50

Andrew pushes Demelza and Verity into a doorway as protesting miners continue to flood past, angrily shouting, brandishing weapons. Demelza watches anxiously. Andrew, however, has seized the opportunity to renew his pleas to Verity.

ANDREW Miss Verity – I beg you – if you would only hear me out—

VERITY I cannot – I cannot—

Without warning Verity dashes off into the stream of passing miners. Andrew runs after her. Demelza remains, trapped by the miners. As she watches, Andrew pulls Verity into another place of safety. Now she notices miners beginning to come back the opposite way, some carrying sacks of flour or pushing wheelbarrows full of it. Demelza sees this, but Andrew and Verity seem oblivious.

Demelza continues to watch the miners. Now, as more miners run past carrying corn, the mill owner himself strides through the throng, escorted by two henchmen. It is Matthew Sanson.

SANSON *(to his henchmen)* These people should be flogged!

He tries to seize a sack of flour from a miner. His henchmen try to do likewise. A tussle breaks out.

SANSON Pay for it, damn you! Fifteen shillings a bushel is the price! Fifteen shillings a bushel – and not a penny less!

Sanson seizes the sack of corn from one of the miners. Then he stops another miner who is wheeling a barrow full of sacks of corn, hits the miner and seizes the barrow. More miners come, carrying sacks of corn. Sanson and his henchmen try to stem the tide. A brawl breaks out. Andrew and Verity seem oblivious.

ANDREW All these years I've thought of none but you – I've waited – in the hope that one day—

VERITY I cannot bear it, Andrew. Are we to endure it all again? The parting – and the heartache—

ANDREW *(to Verity)* Not the parting – I swear to you, never the parting—

They continue to talk. They appear to have become reconciled. Alarmed by the escalating situation, Demelza inches her way over to them.

DEMELZA We should go. Tid'n safe here.

Andrew and Verity come to their senses.

ANDREW Of course. Come with me.

He puts his arm protectively round Verity and shepherds her and Demelza away. The tussle between Sanson, his henchmen and the miners gets more violent.

SANSON I know who you are!

CUT TO:

78: INT. TRENWITH HOUSE, TURRET ROOM – DAY 50

A butterfly is trapped, its wings beating against the window pane. Elizabeth shows it to Geoffrey Charles. She's trying to remain positive but it's a struggle. The sound of approaching hooves makes her look up.

HER POV: Shoulders slumped, Francis rides towards Trenwith House. He looks a broken man.

CUT TO:

79: EXT. COUNTRY ROAD – DAY 50

Demelza, Verity and Ross ride home. Verity is bright-eyed and tremulous. Demelza too is struggling to contain her excitement and appear matter-of-fact. Only Ross seems preoccupied and low.

DEMELZA And I could not for the life o' me choose between the blue and the grey so I came away with none—

ROSS I'm sorry you had a wasted journey. Did you hear anything of the riots?

DEMELZA With our heads full o' muslin and calico? Oh, Verity, we must try again next week. Can you spare the time?

VERITY I can.

Demelza smiles to herself. Ross glances at her. He senses something afoot but he has no idea what it is. Demelza becomes aware of his scrutiny.

DEMELZA And how was the party? Dull as you feared?

ROSS Duller.

CUT TO:

80: EXT. NAMPARA HOUSE – DUSK 50

Establisher.

CUT TO:

81: INT. NAMPARA HOUSE, KITCHEN – DUSK 50

Demelza is feeding Julia. Demelza seems flushed and excited. She smiles to herself (thinking of Verity and Andrew). Ross is drinking brandy. He seems thoughtful and preoccupied.

ROSS I don't imagine we've seen the last of the unrest.

DEMELZA I wonder how Verity and I missed it. But we'd so much to talk of, we barely noticed another soul.

ROSS Verity seemed in high spirits.

DEMELZA She did indeed. I'm that glad. She deserves to be content.

ROSS She should make the most of it.

DEMELZA Why?

ROSS Her life is about to change. And not for the better.

DEMELZA *(alarmed)* How d'you know that?

ROSS I know her brother.

DEMELZA Why, what's he done?

CUT TO:

82: INT. TRENWITH HOUSE, OAK ROOM – DUSK 50

Francis, Elizabeth and Aunt Agatha are deep in discussion as Verity comes in. She's still bright-eyed and tremulous, struggling to contain her feelings, but they barely acknowledge her, so preoccupied are they by their own conversation.

VERITY It was monstrous crowded in Truro. Kenwyn Street was a boiling of miners, and there was talk of a riot.

FRANCIS *(muttering)* There'll be rioting closer to home soon.

AUNT AGATHA All these years – damm me, 'twas old afore I was born.

Verity sits down and takes up her needlework. She's so preoccupied, she barely registers the conversation of the others.

AUNT AGATHA *(cont'd)* Old John Trenwith cut the first goffin the year afore he died—

ELIZABETH Two hundred years ago—

AUNT AGATHA An' never closed – not once—

ELIZABETH And not long since it yielded thousands a year—

AUNT AGATHA It don't seem right – it don't seem right at all.

VERITY *(finally registering)* What's this?

Verity looks at Francis, Elizabeth and Aunt Agatha with alarm. Something catastrophic has happened.

ELIZABETH *(to Francis)* Shall you tell her?

FRANCIS Or shall I let you have the pleasure?

A tense moment between Francis and Elizabeth. Then, seeing Francis make no move to explain . . .

ELIZABETH For months now you know that Grambler has been failing—

FRANCIS She means 'Francis has been failing'!

ELIZABETH *(ignoring this)* We could no longer afford the repayments on the loans—

FRANCIS Thanks to his 'profligacy and mismanagement'!

ELIZABETH So in an attempt to recoup these losses, Francis today staked—

FRANCIS Gambled—

ELIZABETH The mine. On a game of cards.

Verity looks at Francis in horror.

FRANCIS He lost.

CUT TO:

83: INT. NAMPARA HOUSE, KITCHEN – DUSK 50

Ross has just told Demelza the news about the loss of Grambler. She is horrified.

DEMELZA What d' this mean?

ROSS For Francis? Loss of income. Loss of pride. Loss of family inheritance. For Verity and Elizabeth? A sharp decline in their standard of living. For the Warleggans? A chance to tighten their stranglehold by closing down a rival mine. And for the poor souls who worked there? Unimaginable hardship. *(beat)* And all because one man was weak and others were greedy.

Silence. Both lost in their thoughts. Then . . .

DEMELZA So often I've envied Elizabeth—

ROSS Why?

DEMELZA Why did you envy Francis?

Ross nods in acknowledgement. He knows exactly what she means.

ROSS I envy him no longer. No more should you Elizabeth.

DEMELZA I've never envied her less than I do tonight.

It's said without triumph or bitterness. A simple statement of fact, tinged with compassion. They remain, silent, lost in their own thoughts.

CUT TO:

84: EXT. TRENWITH HOUSE – DAY 51

Elizabeth comes out of the house, followed by Francis.

FRANCIS There's no need for you to come. Elizabeth! Elizabeth – *(hesitates, then)* What I did – was unforgivable – *(no reply)* But my love for you – my love will always—

He's floundering. And suddenly Elizabeth has no more patience. She walks off down the drive. Behind her Francis is joined by Verity. He looks desolate.

CUT TO:

85: EXT. GRAMBLER MINE – DAY 51

Grambler looks forlorn and decrepit. People gather to witness its demise. Ross and Demelza stand at a respectful distance, along with crowds of miners and their families (among them Zacky, Mark, Beth Daniel, Connie Carter, Mrs Zacky, Jinny, Nick, etc), also Dwight Enys. Keren is there too. Though Mark clasps her hand tightly, she keeps stealing glances at Dwight Enys. Dwight tries to keep his eyes off her but finds himself glancing involuntarily at her. Francis, stony-faced, stands with Verity and Elizabeth. He feels – and looks – thoroughly ashamed of himself. Now he steps forward.

FRANCIS My friends, this has been a Poldark mine for over two hundred years. Generations of all our families have worked it side by side. It was my dearest wish that my own son take it up. But time and circumstance have ruined that hope.

A low murmur from the assembled crowds. It's clear that many people hold Francis responsible for the closure.

FRANCIS *(cont'd)* It may be that we shall all meet here again – to see her resurrection. But for the present – *(consults his watch)* It is now twelve noon.

He turns and starts to ring a bell. Single note, mournful, slow. No one moves. A few women sob, Verity amongst them. Elizabeth's face gives nothing away. On impulse Francis takes a piece of chalk and scrawls something on the side of the mine entrance. It reads 'Resurgam'. Then he walks away. He looks a pitiful figure. Elizabeth makes no attempt to detain him. Ross hesitates, then, leaving Demelza, goes after her.

Demelza watches him go, knowing herself to be powerless at this moment. As Ross himself is powerless in the face of his feelings.

CUT TO:

86: EXT. GRAMBLER MINE – DAY 51

Elizabeth is walking away. She senses that Ross is following.

ROSS Elizabeth!

She stops.

ROSS *(cont'd)* What can I do?

ELIZABETH Not once has Francis asked me that question.

ROSS He's afraid to. You must know this was never what he intended for you.

ELIZABETH And yet it is how it is. *(beat)* And we shall weather it – retrench, make economies. There are many worse off than we. Let Francis feel sorry for himself. I will not do so.

Ross is impressed by Elizabeth's fortitude and pragmatism. A moment between them. Then Elizabeth turns and walks away. Presently Demelza appears beside Ross. She waits. In this moment she knows that his feelings for Elizabeth are in the ascendent. Eventually Ross turns back to her. A moment between them. Ross is grateful for her understanding and her silence.

The crowds are dispersing. Dwight Enys is amongst them. He waves goodbye to Ross and Demelza, who have remained where they are. Keren catches Dwight's eye. She gives him an encouraging glance, then runs to join Mark. A group of young village girls converge on Dwight.

ROSS He'll need to watch his step.

DEMELZA He's young – and handsome!

ROSS And green.

DEMELZA And free.

Ross laughs.

DEMELZA *(cont'd)* You envy him?

ROSS *(laughs)* Sometimes.

They stand together in silence, both thoughtful. Eventually . . .

ROSS *(cont'd)* You were right. The world is a harder place now. Thanks to Julia. *(seeing her look of surprise)* Stakes are higher. Losses more painful. *(then)* Yet I would not change places with him.

They glance back at Dwight and his gaggle of adoring village girls.

ROSS *(cont'd)* My life is more precious for being less certain. And richer, for being poorer.

They stand together, with Grambler behind them in the distance. After a while . . .

DEMELZA What does it mean? 'Resurgam'?

ROSS 'I shall rise again'.

DEMELZA Shall we?

ROSS I hope so.

He takes her hand.

Episode 6

1: INT. BODMIN JAIL – DAY 52

Establishers of the squalid conditions.

CUT TO:

2: EXT. NAMPARA HOUSE, COURTYARD – DAY 52

Jinny Carter, with her baby on her hip, is humming happily to herself as she crosses off a mark on the wall (the rest of the wall has marks in groups of 7. There are only 4 more groups to cross off). Demelza, who has Julia on her hip, takes dry linens off the line.

DEMELZA Jim'll soon be home.

JINNY God willin'.

Jinny takes down dry linens from the line.

JINNY *(cont'd)* Will I find 'im changed?

DEMELZA He's come through this far. That's what matters.

A look between them. They both know that if Jim does 'come through' it will be against all the odds. Jinny grabs another sheet from the line.

CUT TO:

3: INT. TRENWITH HOUSE, FIELDS – DAY 52

Francis is scything in the fields. In the distance a figure on horseback approaches. It's Ross.

ON ROSS: Profoundly affected by the sight of the once-boyish, fine featured Francis now reduced to tending his own land. He slows to a trot.

ON FRANCIS: Seeing Ross approaching, holds out his scythe to make sure the full extent of his ignominy is clear.

FRANCIS A pretty sight, is it not?

ROSS No shame in it.

FRANCIS As we sow, so shall we reap! *(beat)* As my wife would no doubt remind me.

Elizabeth appears (though with no sign of the reproach Francis attributes to her). She's carrying a basket of herbs and vegetables and seems far more sanguine about their fall from grace.

She and Ross exchange a glance. He's moved by her determined cheerfulness.

ROSS If I can be of service—

FRANCIS You can. Find a way to restore me my mines, my estate, my dignity—

ELIZABETH *(gently)* Francis—

FRANCIS But today is your day! The first auction for Carnmore.

ROSS I wish you could join us.

FRANCIS George would disapprove. *(before Ross can retort)* Oh, I know how little you care for his opinion. But you should.

ROSS I care for those he seeks to ruin.

Ross is about to ride on.

FRANCIS *(calling after him)* You'll never get it, Ross.

ROSS What?

FRANCIS *(sarcastic)* Justice for all!

ROSS Fair wages would be a start!

Ross rides off. Francis returns to his task. Presently Verity appears. She's nervous, steeling herself to approach Francis. Just as she's summoned up the courage . . .

FRANCIS Damn these blisters!

He abandons his task and stalks off, sucking his blistered hand. Verity opens her mouth to speak but doesn't get the chance. Elizabeth notices her frustration.

ELIZABETH You would speak with him?

VERITY It will keep.

She turns and walks back to the house. Elizabeth remains – determined to stay cheerful despite their fall from grace.

CUT TO:

4: EXT. CLIFF-TOPS – DAY 52

Ross rides to town.

CUT TO:

5: EXT. RED LION INN – DAY 52

Ross joins agents, managers and mine owners congregating outside the inn. He is joined by Henshawe, who raises his eyebrows but says nothing. They go inside.

CUT TO:

6: INT. RED LION INN – DAY 52

The auction begins. Amongst those present are Ross, Henshawe, Tonkin, Blewitt, Zacky Martin and Blight (Warleggan agent).

CHAIRMAN Gentlemen. Gentlemen. The auction is now open. I have first to dispose of a dole of ore from Wheal Busy.

He surveys the first lot of tickets (the bids). A clerk enters the bids in a ledger. Several people look expectant. Tension mounts. Presently . . .

CHAIRMAN Wheal Busy ore is sold to the Carnmore Copper Company for six pounds seventeen shillings and sixpence a ton.

A moment's silence. Several men look round. One man frowns, is about to speak, then thinks better of it. The chairman continues.

CHAIRMAN Wheal Leisure. Parcel of red copper. Forty-five tons.

Several men glance at Ross. Ross looks at the end of his riding crop and smooths down a piece of frayed leather. The chairman opens the tickets. The clerk enters the bids in a ledger.

CHAIRMAN Sold to the Carnmore Copper Company for eight pounds two shillings a ton.

BLIGHT *(stands up)* What name did you say?

CHAIRMAN Wheal Leisure.

BLIGHT No sir, the buyers.

CHAIRMAN Carnmore Copper Company?

Blight looks as if he would like to say more but instead sits down again. The chairman moves on.

CHAIRMAN United Mines. Three doles of ore. Fifty tons apiece.

The tickets are unfolded, the bids entered in the ledger. People are now straining forward to see.

CHAIRMAN First parcel to Carnmore at seven pounds one shilling a ton. Second parcel to Carnmore at six pounds, nineteen shillings.

Murmuring from the floor. Blight leaps to his feet.

BLIGHT Sir, I dislike to intervene but may I say I've never heard of the Carnmore Copper Company.

CHAIRMAN I'm assured it exists, sir.

BLIGHT What proof have you of its good faith? Who stands guarantor for it? Who is its agent? *(no reply)* As I thought. There's something here not—

ZACKY'S VOICE I'm the agent.

Everyone turns to see Zacky Martin sitting at the back. Blight looks him up and down and decides he's dealing with a person of inferior class.

BLIGHT I've never heard of your company.

ZACKY That's odd, since chairman's bin talkin' o' little else since noon.

BLIGHT What is your purpose in bidding for this quantity of copper?

ZACKY Same as yours, sir. To smelt and sell it in the open market.

BLIGHT And who are the men behind your company? What are their names?

BLEWITT *(leaping to his feet)* Do we know the names behind the South Wales Smelting Company?

BLIGHT You know full well we came in vouched for by the Warleggans!

HENSHAWE *(low)* Because you are the Warleggans!

 BLIGHT *(to Zacky)* You, sir – I don't know what your game is – but it reeks—

CHAIRMAN Gentlemen! Gentlemen! Please! Let the auction continue.

Blight sits down, hardly able to contain his fury. Ross continues to idly examine the end of his riding crop. Not once have he and Zacky looked at each other.

CUT TO:

7: EXT. MARK & KEREN'S COTTAGE – DAY 52

Mark is laying a trail of crumbs for a starling which he is taming. Keren comes and sits beside him. He takes her hand, puts a crumb in it and holds it out for the starling.

MARK Here 'e come. See, Keren? I tamed 'im for 'ee.

Keren lets the bird hop on to her hand. Almost against her will she's touched. A brief moment of tenderness between them has Mark glowing with pleasure. But not for long . . .

KEREN An' Zacky Martin? Do he waste his days 'ticing starlings? Or do he swagger round the county on Cap'n Poldark's business?

MARK Zacky's eddicated. 'E can read—

KEREN Any fool can read!

MARK Oh, I know you can. 'Tis no secret 'ee could've done better f'r 'ee'self. So I'm on'y glad 'ee pick'd me an' not some high fallutin' scholary chap.

He gets up and goes into the house. Keren continues to feed crumbs to the starling. Then she sees Dwight riding past in the distance on his way to the mine. A ladder is leaning against the house, where Mark has been mending the roof. Keren eyes it thoughtfully.

CUT TO:

8: INT. RED LION INN – DAY 52

The auction has ended. Agents, managers and mine owners begin to emerge from the auction room. Ross and Henshawe go ahead of Zacky. Zacky is about to follow when Blight bars his way.

BLIGHT You may think you've done well today—

ZACKY Sir— ?

BLIGHT But we're on to you – and believe me, you won't have it your own way next time.

He barges past Zacky, and joins the others in the main room. Ross and Henshawe exchange a glance. They stand at some distance from Zacky and continue to avoid eye contact with him. To avoid further discussion of the auction, Tonkin changes the subject.

TONKIN Riots in Bodmin now?

BLEWITT Looting in Truro—

TONKIN Every week another mine closes—

BLIGHT No excuse to take the law into their own hands. Examples must be made.

BLEWITT And are. Bodmin Jail's now fit to burst—

For the first time Ross and Zacky exchange a glance.

TONKIN And rife with fever—

A look of anxiety crosses both their faces.

BLEWITT *(to Blight)* 'Tis as plain a death sentence as you could wish, sir.

A brief moment between Ross and Zacky. The same thought has occurred to both of them: what will this mean for Jim Carter?

CUT TO:

9: EXT. MARK & KEREN'S COTTAGE – DAY 52

Mark departs for his shift. Keren allows herself to be kissed, as if she's conferring the greatest of favours upon her husband. She sees a child passing, along a nearby footpath. An idea occurs to Keren. She climbs up the ladder. When Mark is safely out of sight – and the child is close by – she looks down at the ground below, deliberates, makes a decision. We go in closer as she prepares to jump but cut before the fatal moment.

CUT TO:

10: EXT. WHEAL LEISURE – DAY 52

Dwight is tending to a queue of miners and their families, who are lining up near the mine to see him. He is examining a young miner who is coughing.

DWIGHT *(to the miner)* Both lungs are afflicted – but with a strict regime of goat's milk, walking four miles a day, sleeping out in the open when it's fine—

The child runs up and whispers something in Dwight's ear.

DWIGHT Is she badly hurt?

CUT TO:

11: EXT. RED LION INN – DAY 52

As Ross exits the Red Lion, he runs into Ruth Treneglos and her sister Patience.

RUTH Captain Poldark! I can guess why you're here.

ROSS I should imagine not, ma'am.

RUTH You've heard the rumours attaching to Miss Verity's name again?

She seems pleased at being able to offer Ross unwelcome news.
CUT TO:

12: INT. NAMPARA HOUSE, KITCHEN – DAY 52

Demelza, Prudie and Jinny are baking when Jud appears.

JUD 'Tis 'er – from ower there – come t' see—

Unable to communicate even the simplest announcement, he shrugs and gives up – just as Verity comes in.

VERITY Have you heard? The Warleggans are giving a ball.

DEMELZA Are we invited?

VERITY We are! *(then)* What a way to mark your entrance into society!

Demelza's face falls.

VERITY *(cont'd)* What is it?

DEMELZA What would I wear? What will I say? How shall I know the new dances?

VERITY I'll help you—

Demelza clasps Verity's hands with gratitude.

VERITY *(cont'd)* When I return from town. I'm expected there tomorrow.

DEMELZA *(teasing)* 'Expected'?

Verity blushes and looks coy.

DEMELZA *(cont'd)* But you've spoken to Francis? *(no reply)* You must.

VERITY I will. *(before Demelza can insist)* I will.

But it's clear that Verity is finding it difficult to do so.

CUT TO:

13: EXT. COUNTRY ROAD – DAY 52

Ross and Zacky ride out of Truro.

ZACKY Did well today. We did indeed.

ROSS That was the easy part.

They continue to ride out of town. Soon they are passing a large house on the edge of the town. It's Warleggan House. They break into a canter.

CARY *(OS)* You underestimated him.

CUT TO:

14: INT. WARLEGGAN HOUSE, LIBRARY – DAY 52

Cary and George watch from the window as Ross canters past with Zacky.

GEORGE I did no such thing. You took him for one of those overbred idiots who trade on their name instead of their wits.

CARY Like his cousin.

GEORGE Ross is made of harder metal.

CARY And his company's a threat. But if we knew the names of its shareholders—

They exchange a glance. It's clear George is not averse to foul means and Cary positively advocates them.

CUT TO:

15: INT. MARK & KEREN'S COTTAGE – DAY 52

Keren is lying on the bed as Dwight bandages her arm. She winces as if in excruciating pain.

DWIGHT You're being very brave.

Keren gasps as if to demonstrate just how brave she's being.

DWIGHT *(cont'd)* You must stay in bed. If you get up it may raise a fever.

KEREN Of course, sir, I'll do anything you say, sir.

She turns the full force of her smile on him.

KEREN *(cont'd)* I never knew anyone could be so kind.

CUT TO:

16: EXT. HARBOUR WALL – DAY 52

Verity and Andrew are walking together along the harbour wall.

VERITY Lisbon? I long to see it—

ANDREW It will enchant you, my love. The orange trees, the olive groves, the endless sunlight—

VERITY Will you take me?

ANDREW Are you a good sailor?

VERITY Oh yes! Indeed! Though – I have never actually been to sea—

They both laugh. Joy gives rise to optimism.

ANDREW My quarters aboard are not lavish—

VERITY I need no luxury. To be free – to live my own life – to be with you – is all the riches I could wish.

ANDREW So you will tell Francis? Before the ball?

The mood changes instantly. Verity hesitates.

VERITY Perhaps we should not be seen there together – unless I speak to him first—

ANDREW Or let me.

VERITY No! It must be me. I must find the right moment—

ANDREW Then let it be soon, my love. Let it be soon.

CUT TO:

17: EXT. NAMPARA HOUSE – DAY 52

As Ross rides home the distant sounds of the spinet being played drift up the valley towards him. He smiles to himself. He dismounts, ties up his horse and walks the rest of the way so as to catch Demelza unawares.

CUT TO:

18: INT. NAMPARA HOUSE, PARLOUR – DAY 52

Demelza concentrates on her playing, with Julia sleeping in the crib beside her. Demelza's face is furrowed with concentration. Ross sneaks in and surprises her.

DEMELZA Judas! This is a new device! Creepin' in like a tomcat!

Ross kisses the back of her neck. She squirms with pleasure. Ross takes Julia out of her crib.

ROSS *(to Julia)* And how's my fair maiden?

DEMELZA The one invited to the Warleggan ball?

ROSS That one too. Would it please you to go?

DEMELZA Oh, Ross! Can we?

He grabs her and pulls her towards him and kisses her. Jinny comes in.

JINNY Beg pardon, sur, ma'am. Shall I serve supper?

ROSS Thank you, Jinny. *(as she's about to go)* Have you heard from Jim?

JINNY Not since last month, sur. But he was fair then.

Ross smiles. Jinny doesn't notice the flicker of anxiety which crosses his face. But Demelza does.

CUT TO:

19: INT. TRENWITH HOUSE, OAK ROOM – DAY 52

Verity takes a deep breath and enters the Oak Room, intending to tell Francis about Andrew. But the sight of Aunt Agatha at her tarot cards and Elizabeth trying to placate Francis stops her in her tracks.

FRANCIS So I'm to go to the ball without a mine to my name, my estate in ruins and my wife in a made-over dress?

ELIZABETH For heaven's sake, Francis, who can afford new clothes these days? Truly? You imagine Demelza won't be trotting out her one good dress – and not care a feather what people say?

FRANCIS Well she should care. And if she does not, she shows her ignorance. Dammit, if Ross wants to marry beneath him, that's his affair but at least his wife should make the effort!

ELIZABETH You like Demelza.

FRANCIS I do, but that doesn't alter the fact that the connection does our family no credit. *(with a glare at Verity)* I'm grateful it's the only unsuitable match we're forced to endure.

Verity wilts beneath his scowl – and knows she can't possibly bring up the subject of Andrew now.

CUT TO:

20: INT. NAMPARA HOUSE, ROSS & DEMELZA'S BEDROOM – NIGHT 52

Ross and Demelza lie in bed wide awake. Ross seems preoccupied.

DEMELZA What keeps you awake?

ROSS The mine. The smelting company. Jim.

DEMELZA Is there news?

ROSS Rumours. *(then, another thought occurs)* Has Verity said anything? About Andrew Blamey?

DEMELZA Why?

ROSS There's a rumour she's meeting him again. *(no reply)* Is she?

DEMELZA I wouldn't like to say she is. *(beat)* And I wouldn't like to say she isn't.

ROSS In other words, you wouldn't like to say anything at all!

DEMELZA Well, Ross, what's given in confidence isn't fair to repeat.

ROSS I can't pretend I'm not disturbed. *(no reply)* I wonder how she met him again. *(no reply)* I'm only glad I had nothing to do with it.

Demelza stares guiltily at the ceiling.

CUT TO:

21: EXT. NAMPARA HOUSE – DAY 53

Julia is sleeping under a tree of blossom and Demelza is practising her new dance steps as Ross comes out, dressed for a journey.

DEMELZA I wish you would not go.

ROSS It's the very least I can do. *(kissing her)* Practise your steps. I claim first dance at the ball.

He rides off. Demelza, anxious, watches him go. She forces herself to return to her dance steps but it's with a heart filled with foreboding.

CUT TO:

22: INT. WHEAL LEISURE, TUNNEL – DAY 53

The miners are hard at work.

CUT TO:

23: EXT. WHEAL LEISURE – DAY 53

The shifts are changing. The mine is bustling with activity and productivity. Ross arrives and is greeted by Zacky.

ZACKY 'Tis as we feared. Fever's rife at Bodmin an' they're droppin' like flies.

ROSS Say nothing to Jinny.

Without another word Ross rides off.

CUT TO:

24: EXT. FIELDS NEAR MINGOOSE COTTAGE – DAY 53

Ross gallops in the direction of Mingoose Cottage. He sees someone loitering nearby. It's Keren. She flashes an encouraging smile at him. He nods politely. As he rides on, a thought crosses his mind. Is something going on between Dwight and Keren?

CUT TO:

25: EXT. MINGOOSE COTTAGE – DAY 53

Ross knocks impatiently at the door. Presently Dwight opens it.

CUT TO:

26: EXT. MOORS – DAY 53

Ross and Dwight ride across the wild and windy moors. Ross is thoughtful and clearly worried.

DWIGHT You're close to Jim?

ROSS I've known him since he was a boy. But were he my worst enemy I'd not wish jail pestilence on him.

They ride on.

CUT TO:

27: EXT. MINGOOSE COTTAGE – DAY 53

Keren knocks at the door of Mingoose Cottage but gets no answer. She knocks again. Same result. Feeling thwarted, she walks away. She sees

Demelza walking through the fields. Demelza sees her and waves. Reluctantly Keren makes her way towards her.

DEMELZA Your arm is mending?

KEREN I came to see what Dr Enys could prescribe.

DEMELZA He's away with my husband till tomorrow.

Keren is about to walk off, judging Demelza not worth engaging in conversation. Demelza hesitates, then—

DEMELZA Mrs Daniel? A word?

Keren halts, bristles. She's no great liking for Demelza, envious as she is of Demelza's great fortune in securing a man like Ross.

DEMELZA *(cont'd)* Folk d' love a gossip – an' it's not wise to give 'em cause—

KEREN *(defiant)* What cause?

DEMELZA 'Tis said you have – a roving eye—

KEREN And whose business is it where my eye d' light?

DEMELZA Some might say it is their business if it light on their husbands—

KEREN There's not a man in fifty miles I'd look twice at! *(then)* Excepting one—

DEMELZA Mark?

Keren and Demelza look each other in the eye. In that moment Demelza knows she doesn't mean Mark. And Keren knows she knows.

DEMELZA Pardon my interference. 'Twas kindly meant.

Demelza walks away. Keren heads in the other direction.

CUT TO:

28: EXT. BODMIN JAIL – DAY 53

Ross and Dwight stand outside the great doors of the jail. Dwight glances at Ross.

DWIGHT You have a plan?

ROSS None whatsoever.

Ross raps loudly on the door. Dwight glances anxiously at him. Has he really no actual plan? Ross knocks again. Still no reply. Dwight's beginning to get worried. Ross is about to hammer on the door again when a small grate opens and a pock-marked, bedraggled jailer peers out. To Dwight's amazement (and admiration), Ross springs into action.

ROSS Good evening t'you, sir. Dr Enys is here to attend on James Carter.

JAILER Eh? Wassat?

ROSS James Carter? The typhus? Be so good as to let us in so we may show our papers.

The Jailer hesitates.

ROSS There's not a moment to lose, sir!

Dwight shows his doctor's bag, Ross pretends to rummage in his bag for some papers. The Jailer slams shut the grate.

Dwight fears they have been defeated at the first hurdle, but Ross knows better. Presently the small pass-door creaks open a fraction. Ross immediately shoulders his way inside. Dwight follows.

ROSS *(cont'd)* This way if you please, Dr Enys. *(to the Jailer)* We're much obliged t'you . . .

CUT TO:

29: INT. BODMIN JAIL, LOWER CORRIDOR – DUSK 53

The jailer leads Ross and Dwight down the corridor.

JAILER Now look 'ee here, I say there be fever down here. We be sick ourselves if we don't . . .

ROSS Is this his cell?

DWIGHT What an affront to human dignity.

Ross, Dwight and the Jailer stand in front of a large cage-like cell crammed with filthy, ragged prisoners whose hollow eyes stare out at them. Ross peers into the cell.

ROSS Is Jim Carter among you?

JAILER Where's yer authority? Ye mun show yer papers—

ROSS *(ignoring him)* Jim, can you hear me?

DWIGHT Perhaps he's been moved, or—

ROSS *(louder)* Are you there, Jim?

A low moan issues from somewhere inside the cell. Some men who had been clutching at the bars now move aside to reveal a figure lying on the floor. It doesn't move.

It's Jim, with a long straggly beard and skin covered with red blotches. Jim is delirious and barely alive.

DWIGHT Dear God, look at his arm.

Ross looks more closely. Jim's arm is hideously festered.

ROSS *(to the Jailer)* Open this cell.

JAILER Eh?

ROSS This man needs urgent medical attention. We're taking him away.

JAILER Nay, but he be servin' a sentence—

ROSS Dammit, man! Open this cell before I have you dismissed for neglecting your duty. Give me the keys.

The Jailer tries to back away but Ross corners him, grabs his keys and proceeds to unlock the cell door.

JAILER You can't go in there! It ain't safe. There's fever.

CUT TO:

30: INT. TRENWITH HOUSE, ELIZABETH'S ROOM – NIGHT 53

Elizabeth is holding up an old gown for Verity to assess.

VERITY I could make over the bodice – maybe add a little lace?

ELIZABETH Just as you please. So long as Francis thinks it's new.

She gives the dress to Verity and is about to go out.

VERITY I'm sorry.

Elizabeth halts.

VERITY *(cont'd)* That he's been a disappointment.

ELIZABETH You – speak to me of disappointment?

Verity says nothing. She's grateful for Elizabeth's sympathy and doesn't seek to disabuse her.

ELIZABETH *(cont'd)* Perhaps it's always the way. In the first flush of love we think anything's possible. *(then)* We must both learn to lower our expectations.

Verity says nothing. But her eyes sparkle and we know she would contradict Elizabeth if she dared tell her the truth. Elizabeth goes out.

CUT TO:

31: INT. DISUSED BARN – NIGHT 53

Ross and Dwight carry a delirious Jim into the barn.

DWIGHT Avoid his breath. It will be deadly at this stage.

Dwight and Ross put handkerchiefs over their mouths as Dwight examines Jim's festered arm.

ROSS What chance does he have?

DWIGHT He might survive the fever, but this arm—

ROSS Is it gangrene?

Dwight nods grimly.

ROSS *(cont'd)* It must come off.

DWIGHT He won't survive.

ROSS I beg you to try. *(seeing him hesitate)* I'll help you.

Dwight nods. Ross cradles Jim's head on his lap. He pours brandy down Jim's throat. Jim splutters and coughs. Ross hands the bottle to Dwight, who declines. Dwight opens his bag of instruments. Ross takes a swig of brandy, then pours some on Jim's wound.

ROSS *(cont'd)* *(to Jim)* Be brave now, Jim. Think of Jinny, waiting at home—

JIM S'aright, Jinny – I'm comin' 'ome I'm comin' 'ome—

CUT TO:

32: INT. NAMPARA HOUSE, PARLOUR – NIGHT 53

Baby Kate (Jinny & Jim's baby) is crying. Demelza, cradling the sleeping Julia, and Jinny, cradling Kate, sit by the fire. Jinny's only concern is her child, but Demelza, thinking of Jim (and Ross's mission) is fraught with anxiety. Jud and Prudie exchange a glance with

Demelza. It seems everyone is aware of what's afoot with Jim, except Jinny.

CUT TO:

33: EXT. CLIFFS ABOVE NAMPARA COVE – DAWN 54

The sun rises in the morning sky.

CUT TO:

34: EXT. NAMPARA COVE – DAWN 54

Ross is tearing off his bloodied shirt and throwing it onto a fire he's made of other of his infected garments. He's consumed with despair at the thought of the news which will shortly reach Jinny.

CUT TO:

35: INT. JIM & JINNY'S COTTAGE – DAWN 54

With a heartrending cry of anguish, Jinny falls to her knees. Zacky (who has brought the news from Ross) and Mrs Zacky rush to comfort her, but she is beyond consolation.

CUT TO:

36: EXT. CLIFF-TOPS – DAWN 54

A makeshift grave.

ROSS *(OS)* We buried him by the sea.

CUT TO:

37: INT. NAMPARA HOUSE, LIBRARY – DAY 54

Demelza watches helplessly as Ross tries to contain his grief and anger.

ROSS If you'd seen his face, Demelza. I think he knew me – at the end – he smiled and tried to speak, but – *(then)* The magistrates should have been there. Smug, self-satisfied upholders of the law – and so-called gentlemen who prize game above honest working men. He tried to feed his family! How is that a crime? By God, I could commit murder myself—

DEMELZA But will there not be trouble? That you broke the jail and helped a prisoner escape?

ROSS Let there be! I welcome it. I could almost be induced to go amongst 'em tonight at the ball if I thought I might infect them!

DEMELZA You mean – not to go, then?

ROSS How could we? To dance and smile with the very men to blame for Jim's death – when all I want to do is to wring their damned necks?

DEMELZA No. No, we could not go. I do see that.

A knock on the door. Prudie enters with a large box.

PRUDIE Parcel come for mistress.

She leaves the box on the table and makes a hasty retreat. Demelza stares at the package suspiciously. It comes from Trelask's.

DEMELZA From the dressmaker's? 'Tis a mistake.

ROSS No mistake. I called on my way to Bodmin to order it. It seems like a hundred years ago.

DEMELZA *(eyes widening)* Oh.

For a moment she daren't move. Then, hesitant . . .

DEMELZA *(cont'd)* Could I – see it?

ROSS If you've the interest. It will do for some time in the future.

Hardly daring, Demelza opens the box, peels back the delicate wrappings to reveal shimmering scarlet and silver silk.

DEMELZA Oh Ross.

She bursts into tears.

CUT TO:

38: INT. MINGOOSE COTTAGE – DAWN 54

Dwight, still ashen-faced from the horrors of Bodmin, is unpacking his instruments.

CUT TO:

39: EXT. MINGOOSE COTTAGE – DAWN 54

Keren arrives at the cottage.

CUT TO:

40: EXT. MINGOOSE COTTAGE – DAWN 54

There's a knock on the door. Dwight opens it to Keren.

KEREN I couldn't sleep. All last night – I was thinking of you – *(coming closer)* Giving me something. To ease the pain.

She holds out her bandaged arm. In a daze, it takes Dwight a while to digest what she's asking. Eventually . . .

DWIGHT Please wait here. I'll fetch you something.

He goes inside and, to Keren's irritation, closes the door on her.
CUT TO:

41: EXT. NAMPARA HOUSE – DAY 54

Establisher.
CUT TO:

42: INT. NAMPARA HOUSE, PARLOUR – DAY 54

Jud is whittling by the fire, scowling as he contemplates Demelza, who is trying, unsuccessfully, to coax Ross to eat. Losing patience, Jud gets up, pours a large glass of rum, puts it in front of Ross – who drinks it without looking up. Jud gives Demelza a 'that's what he needs' look and returns to his whittling. Prudie appears.

PRUDIE Miss Verity, sur—

Verity comes in.

VERITY Oh my dears, I heard about Jim.

Jud growls to himself and goes out.

ROSS Say nothing, Verity. If I'm forced to re-live it, I'm like to explode!

Verity and Demelza exchange a glance.

VERITY You must compose yourself before the ball.

Ross is momentarily speechless. He looks at Verity in disbelief.

ROSS You know who will attend this ball?

VERITY Every single one of those men who condemned Jim to die.

ROSS So how d'you imagine I could go among them— ?

VERITY Because you must go among them. *(seeing him about to argue)* Your move in forcing the jail was reckless and unlawful. Your presence among these people tonight will remind them that you are one of them – a gentleman. It may make them think twice before moving against you.

ROSS Your arguments disgust me.

VERITY They disgust me too – but you have more than yourself to consider now.

For a moment the significance of what she's saying doesn't occur to Ross. But then . . .

ROSS My wife and child—

VERITY Would suffer—

ROSS As Jinny suffers. 'Justice' is a fine thing, is it not?

He heads out, taking the bottle with him. Demelza and Verity exchange a glance.

CUT TO:

43: EXT. WARLEGGAN HOUSE – DUSK 54

Demelza, Ross and Verity arrive outside the house.

CUT TO:

44: INT. WARLEGGAN HOUSE, BALCONY/STAIRS/HALL-WAY – NIGHT 54 44

Demelza, Ross and Verity are standing at the top of a staircase and balcony, looking down at the splendour of the gathering in the hallway below. Neither Demelza, Ross nor Verity are at ease. Ross, simmering with suppressed rage, is more than a little intoxicated. Demelza is nervous, overawed by the obvious opulence of the house. Verity is glancing anxiously around, hoping to reassure herself that Andrew is not there. Ross spots Francis and Elizabeth and immediately heads off down the stairs.

DEMELZA Ross? Where are you going?

ROSS To acquaint myself with as much brandy as George can supply.

Demelza looks dismayed.

DEMELZA We shouldn't've come. Ross an't been sober since he got back from Bodmin.

A lady's maid now approaches, whispers something in Verity's ear and hands her a small box. Verity reads the inscription.

VERITY For you, I think.

She hands the box to Demelza. It has the mark of the goldsmith's shop in Truro. It's addressed to 'R. Poldark Esq' but Ross has crossed it out and scribbled 'For delivery to Mistress Demelza Poldark'. Puzzled, Demelza unwraps and opens the box. Inside is a pearl and ruby brooch fastened to a ribbon (so it can be worn round the neck as a choker). Demelza gasps with surprise.

DEMELZA From Ross. But – how can I wear it? *(seeing Verity hasn't understood)* With Jim in the ground – and Jinny bereft—

VERITY You cannot help them, my dear. But you can try to keep a lid on that powder keg below!

She draws Demelza's attention to Ross, who is downstairs talking to Francis and Elizabeth.

ON ROSS, FRANCIS AND ELIZABETH: *Ross's face is like thunder. Francis's (for different reasons) is not dissimilar. Elizabeth, resolutely smiling, is trying to coax them into better moods. Without success.*

CUT TO:

45: INT. WARLEGGAN HOUSE, HALLWAY – NIGHT 54

George is beaming broadly as he spots Ross, Francis and Elizabeth through the other guests. As George weaves his way towards them, affably greeting guests on either hand, Francis, in no mood for George's pleasantries, detaches himself from Elizabeth, grabs Ross's arm and steers him away. George's surprise is matched only by his delight at being left alone with Elizabeth.

GEORGE Is there a war on? The Poldark cousins seem hell-bent on battle.

ELIZABETH I cannot speak for Ross – but Francis is most definitely at odds with all the world.

George graciously offers Elizabeth his arm and leads her away to the ballroom.

CUT TO:

46: INT. WARLEGGAN HOUSE, BALCONY/STAIRS/ HALLWAY – NIGHT 54

Verity ties the choker/brooch round Demelza's neck.

VERITY There now. How lovely you look. *(then)* Let us go down. It will take us both to keep Ross in check.

DEMELZA You won't desert me?

VERITY I would not dream of such a – *(suddenly)* Oh dear God—

For a moment Demelza doesn't understand, then she sees what Verity has seen:

Andrew Blamey in the hall below.

VERITY *(cont'd)* I must go to him. He must leave at once.

Without another word, she abandons Demelza and heads down the stairs towards Andrew. Andrew sees Verity. Verity begs him to follow her. They disappear into the crowd of guests.

ON DEMELZA: Abandoned at the top of the stairs. Horrified. Panic rising.

HER POV: Gaudily dressed guests, milling about, greeting each other, laughing, smiling, gossiping, drinking, braying with laughter . . .

Struggling to calm herself down, Demelza begins gingerly to descend the stairs. Now we see her in her full glory for the first time: in her scarlet and silver gown, her hair piled up, her brooch sparkling. She has never looked more like a lady – nor felt less able to appreciate her new status. As she descends further, her eyes scan the room in panic, in search of a familiar, friendly face. To her immense relief, she sees Dwight coming towards her.

DEMELZA Oh, Dwight – I fear'd I wouldn't know a soul—

DWIGHT Here is a gentlemen eager to make your acquaintance.

Demelza is taken aback. It's the first time this has ever happened to her.

DWIGHT *(cont'd)* Sir Hugh Bodrugan. May I present Mistress Demelza Poldark.

SIR HUGH BODRUGAN 'Cod, ma'am, Enys tells me we're neighbours. How did I come to overlook such a bloom?

DEMELZA I – cannot account for it, sir.

SIR HUGH BODRUGAN D'you hunt, ma'am?

DEMELZA No, sir. I have some sympathy for the foxes.

Sir Hugh roars with laughter.

We cut to Verity, who has caught up with Andrew.

VERITY Please, Andrew!

CUT TO:

47: INT. WARLEGGAN HOUSE, BALLROOM – NIGHT 54

Ross and Francis are talking and drinking apart. They are being watched by George. Something is obviously brewing in his mind. As Ross moves away, in search of another drink, George intercepts him.

GEORGE I've been singing your praises.

ROSS To whom?

GEORGE Mr Matthew Sanson?

He introduces them. Ross bows stiffly. Sanson smiles.

GEORGE *(cont'd)* He's keen to test his mettle against you.

ROSS Thank you, I've no taste for gaming tonight.

GEORGE That's a pity. Last time he played, he had the better of the Poldarks. I thought you might care to level the scores.

SANSON He may try!

ROSS I'm here to escort my wife. That being so, it wouldn't suit my purpose to spend the evening in a card room.

SANSON Which is your wife? I should like the pleasure.

ROSS She is over there.

He indicates where Demelza is surrounded by admirers.

GEORGE She seems very well attended by Sir Hugh Bodrugan. Might I suggest a short game, just while the evening warms up?

Ross notices Cary approaching with the Reverend Dr Halse. Not trusting himself to be civil to them, he acquiesces to George.

ROSS As you wish. Please.

They go into the card room together, passing Ruth Treneglos and her sister Patience. Francis trails after them. After he's gone . . .

RUTH Did you not hear? Since Francis lost the mine, that woman has thrown him over—

She indicates Margaret, who is escorted by her latest conquest Luke Vosper, a foppish, besotted young man.

RUTH *(cont'd)* Now he can't even afford a new dress for his wife!

Elizabeth is revealed, talking to Dwight, having heard the entire conversation, struggling to retain her composure and dignity.

RUTH And as for Ross – no doubt regretting his marriage to that hussy who's showing herself up something fearful!

Demelza looks flushed and is fanning herself as she is led forward by Sir Hugh for her first dance. Only as we get closer do we realize her fan is actually a crib-sheet, with the instructions for each dance written on it.

DEMELZA *(under her breath, rehearsing her steps)* Step, bow – turn – step – step, step, turn—

The dance begins. Demelza takes a deep breath and takes her first steps.

CUT TO:

48: INT. WARLEGGAN TOWN HOUSE, HALLWAY – NIGHT 54

Verity is trying to persuade Andrew to leave.

VERITY Andrew, I beg you to leave. Francis will see you.

ANDREW That's exactly what I wish. To have it all out in the open. I will not be ashamed of our love.

VERITY Nor I, but if we're seen together, it will be a disaster.

ANDREW But who's to say Francis would make difficulties? Has he not grown up? Might he not have mellowed?

VERITY Let him once catch sight of you and you will see how much he's mellowed!

CUT TO:

49: INT. WARLEGGAN HOUSE, BALLROOM – NIGHT 54

Demelza continues her dance with Sir Hugh. He seems besotted with her. She is more concerned with her fan and continues to talk herself through the dance under her breath. Elizabeth, neglected by Francis, is watching with Mrs Chynoweth.

MRS CHYNOWETH Who is that young person dancing with Sir Hugh? She's quite lovely, don't you think?

Elizabeth now takes in Demelza's appearance for the first time. She's unable to conceal her shock at Demelza's splendour (made finer by comparison with her own refurbished gown).

ELIZABETH That's Demelza, Mama. Ross's wife.

MRS CHYNOWETH The scullery maid?

ELIZABETH I see no scullery maid, Mama.

CUT TO:

50: INT. WARLEGGAN HOUSE, CARD ROOM – NIGHT 54

George is watching Ross and Francis play cards with Sanson and Vosper. Vosper loses and gets up to leave. He is joined by Margaret, who smiles with ironic good humour at Francis and Ross. Now Sanson signals to someone who has just entered the card room. It's the

Reverend Dr Halse. As he comes over, he sees Ross and hesitates. Ross's face hardens. Francis, oblivious, is eager to continue playing.

FRANCIS Reverend Halse, will you join us?

REVEREND DR HALSE What are the stakes?

FRANCIS A guinea?

REVEREND DR HALSE It's more than my customary stake.

ROSS Perhaps you'd prefer to wait for another table.

REVEREND DR HALSE *(bristling)* I think not. I have as much right to call the stakes as any here. Half a guinea let it be.

He sits down. Ross scowls and bites his tongue.

CUT TO:

51: INT. WARLEGGAN TOWN HOUSE, BALLROOM – NIGHT 54

The dance continues. Demelza is growing in confidence but is still anxious over Ross. Sir Hugh continues to slaver over her. Dwight, standing watching, notes that John Treneglos and several other young men dancing close by are neglecting their own partners and attempting to converse with Demelza whenever the dance brings them close to her. Her popularity is again noted by Elizabeth, who just at this moment is passing Mr and Mrs Chynoweth.

MRS CHYNOWETH Still not dancing, Elizabeth? What will people say? Your first outing in months and to be so neglected by Francis?

Now George appears.

GEORGE Elizabeth, grant me the favour of the next dance.

Elizabeth smiles and gives him her hand.

GEORGE *(cont'd – to Mrs Chynoweth)* How charming you look

tonight, ma'am. I swear, Elizabeth's seat will be taken the moment I lead her away.

Mrs Chynoweth simpers as George leads Elizabeth away.

MRS CHYNOWETH A wicked shame to have thrown her away on a Poldark. What a match she would have made with George.

CUT TO:

52: INT. WARLEGGAN TOWN HOUSE, CARD ROOM – NIGHT 54

The card game continues. Ross and Francis are winning. Ross is still glowering but so far reining himself in. Sanson is becoming irritated with the Reverend Dr Halse.

SANSON *(to Reverend Dr Halse)* You did not return my trump lead, sir. 'Tis an elementary principle to return one's partner's lead.

REVEREND DR HALSE Thank you. I'm acquainted with elementary principles.

ROSS *(to Sanson, unable to resist)* No doubt your partner has all the principles at his finger tips. It's a general misfortune that he does not make better use of them.

REVEREND DR HALSE Manners were never your strong suit, Poldark. One can only guess at the bad humours which come of an ill-spent life.

ROSS 'Ill-spent'? And this from a justice of the peace who combines all the virtues of office except perhaps justice and peace?

REVEREND DR HALSE No doubt the common people you mix with have blunted your faculties as to what may and may not be said in polite society.

ROSS I agree that they alter one's perspective, sir. You should try mixing with such people, it might enlarge your outlook.

REVEREND DR HALSE *(rising to his feet)* I think I will find another table.

ROSS *(also rising)* Have you ever been in a jail, sir? It's surprising the stench that thirty or forty of God's creatures can give off when confined to a squalid pit for months on end without drains, water or a physician's care—

REVEREND DR HALSE The matter of your performance at Bodmin Jail has not gone unnoticed, sir. There will shortly be a meeting of the justices – of whom, may I say, I am one—

ROSS Then pray convey this message: that it will give me great pleasure to meet any of you who can spare the time from your high offices and holy livings – especially those responsible for the upkeep of Bodmin Jail!

REVEREND DR HALSE You offensive young drunkard! You will be hearing from us presently!

The Reverend Dr Halse gets up and stalks out. Margaret breaks into ironic applause.

ROSS *(to Francis)* Continue.

MARGARET *(to Francis)* Come, Mr Francis, follow your cousin's lead. Lay a stake on the queen of spades.

FRANCIS Thank you, I've learnt never to stake on women. *(to Ross and Sanson)* Excuse me, I will take a breath of air.

He goes out.

CUT TO:

53: INT. WARLEGGAN HOUSE, BALLROOM – NIGHT 54

George and Elizabeth have finished dancing. George leads Elizabeth from the floor.

GEORGE You look ravishing tonight, Elizabeth. If I were a poet or a painter I could do you justice.

ELIZABETH You're very kind, George, but I'm afraid you have little reward for your attentions. I'm a dull creature these days.

GEORGE That which is treasured can never be dull.

Elizabeth smiles but it's clear she thinks this is mere gallantry.

GEORGE *(cont'd)* You should venture out more. Bring Francis if you will—

ELIZABETH To the gaming tables? It's the only reward for the end of Grambler – that he sees less of the green cloths and more of his family.

GEORGE If I were to promise never to encourage – or even play with Francis again? Would that please you?

ELIZABETH We both know he will continue to play, whether you encourage him or not. He cannot help himself.

GEORGE Any more than I can.

Elizabeth looks quizzically at George. Was that actually some kind of declaration? Now is the moment for George to follow it up and make it clear. At the last moment he loses his nerve.

GEORGE *(cont'd)* Some – refreshment?

As he leads her away he's cursing himself for not daring to be more explicit. But something tells him this is not the time.

CUT TO:

54: EXT. WARLEGGAN HOUSE, GARDEN – NIGHT 54

Francis is pacing, trying to calm himself down. He is close to tears – of rage, frustration and humiliation. Finally he walks back into the house.

CUT TO:

55: INT. WARLEGGAN HOUSE, HALLWAY – CONTINUOUS

Francis walks in – and comes face to face with Verity and Andrew, who are leaving. Verity almost faints with horror. Francis looks as if he will strike her. Andrew steps forward to shield her.

ANDREW I hope you will do me the honour of allowing me to—

FRANCIS How dare you address me?

VERITY Francis—

ANDREW Your sister deserves better. I beg you, let us resolve this peaceably—

FRANCIS Step aside.

ANDREW Your sister is not to be commanded. And nor am I.

FRANCIS Then perhaps you'll take this as an inducement.

He aims a punch at Andrew but fortunately misses. Verity gasps.

Andrew seems about to unleash his fury at Francis – who wilts at the prospect – but by a supreme act of will, Andrew reins himself in, gives Francis a look of utter contempt, and – without even a glance at Verity – walks out. Verity watches him go in absolute horror.

FRANCIS I forbid you ever to see him again.

Without another word, Verity rushes off.

CUT TO:

56: INT. WARLEGGAN HOUSE, BALLROOM – NIGHT 54

The group of admirers around Demelza has grown and she is now battling to keep them – and their offerings of wine and refreshments – at bay. Scanning the room for Ross, Demelza sees an ashen-faced Verity. She knows instantly that something is wrong.

DEMELZA Your pardon, sirs, I must speak with my cousin.

SIR HUGH BODRUGAN Oh no, no. Not so fast, missy. I've not had the pleasure of my second dance!

JOHN TRENEGLOS Nor I, indeed!

DEMELZA Excuse me, sirs – I cannot stay.

To the dismay and disgruntlement of her admirers, Demelza leaves them and makes her way towards the hallway to meet Verity. But as she reaches the exit, she is intercepted by Elizabeth, who is talking to Ruth Treneglos and Mrs Chynoweth.

ELIZABETH We've been admiring your gown, Demelza. Mama thought it had come from London – till Mrs Treneglos assured her to the contrary.

Demelza flashes a glance at Ruth, who smiles icily.

RUTH And how is your father, dear? We've not seen him since the christening.

For a moment we think Demelza will flush with shame and be tongue-tied. But instead . . .

DEMELZA No, ma'am. I'm very sorry, but father is over particular who he meets.

She bows to the ladies and walks off, leaving Ruth furious – and Elizabeth turning aside so that Ruth will not see her smile of amusement.

CUT TO:

57: INT. WARLEGGAN HOUSE, HALLWAY – NIGHT 54

Verity is pulling a lace handkerchief to shreds. Demelza is fanning her to cool down.

VERITY He despises me.

DEMELZA No—

VERITY And so he should. I'm to blame. I should have told Francis when I had the chance. But I was timid. It's the one weakness Andrew cannot abide.

DEMELZA He will forgive you.

VERITY He left. Without a backward glance. I shall never see him again.

CUT TO:

58: INT. WARLEGGAN HOUSE, CARD ROOM – NIGHT 54

Francis, grey-faced with anger, returns to the card room to find Ross playing cards with Sanson. He sits down without a word and continues drinking. Margaret detaches herself from Vosper and comes and perches behind him. At that moment Elizabeth comes in, in search of Francis. She takes one look at Margaret, then Francis – then, mustering all the dignity she can manage, walks over to Ross instead.

ELIZABETH *(smiling)* I hope you're as well entertained as your wife.

Ross looks up at her, surprised.

ELIZABETH *(cont'd)* Had you forgot her existence? A dangerous mistake! *(ignoring Francis and flirting with Ross)* Absentee husbands make for wandering wives. If you wish to retain our favour, you do well to pay us attention.

She sweeps out again before Ross – or Francis – can respond. Margaret seems rather impressed by her rival's spirited performance.

CUT TO:

59: INT. WARLEGGAN HOUSE, HALLWAY – NIGHT 54

Demelza is coming down the stairs when she sees a cluster of her admirers waiting for her, vying for her attention. Dwight is also there.

SIR HUGH BODRUGAN I'm determined, ma'am – the next dance is mine.

Demelza doesn't know whether to be flattered or overwhelmed. Then she sees someone else approaching.

ROSS Forgive me – Pardon me – *(to Demelza)* I came to see if you require anything.

SIR HUGH BODRUGAN It's a bit late to be showing a lively concern for your wife.

ROSS Better a belated conscience than none at all.

He offers Demelza his arm and walks her towards the ballroom.

CUT TO:

60: INT. WARLEGGAN HOUSE, BALLROOM – NIGHT 54

Ross steers Demelza away from the other guests. She is furious at his interruption and rudeness.

DEMELZA Perhaps I should ask for an introduction as it's so long since we met.

ROSS I hear you've been well consoled in my absence.

He looks at the other guests, who are gossiping, laughing, preening, posturing.

ROSS *(cont'd)* Look at 'em all! Over-dressed, over over-painted, over-stuffed! If these are my people, I'm ashamed to belong to 'em!

DEMELZA Well, if you think all the stupid, fat ignorants are in your class, you're mistook! I've lived long enough to know they're everywhere! *(Ross ignores her)* An' you'll not right wrongs by blaming just these folks for Jim dyin'—

ROSS They are to blame! For their ignorance, their selfishness – their arrogance.

DEMELZA And you'll not right any wrongs by drinking an' gaming an' leaving me to fend for myself at my very first ball!

ROSS If you behave like this you'll not come to another!

DEMELZA If you behave like this, I'll not want to!

They stop short and look at each other, suddenly conscious of how out of hand things have got. Then Ross strides away and heads for the card room. Demelza watches him, furious. Then she is ambushed by admirers, eager to replace Ross.

MALE ADMIRER Would you care to dance?

DEMELZA No, thank you.

CUT TO:

61: EXT. WARLEGGAN TOWN HOUSE – NIGHT 54

Establisher.

CUT TO:

62: INT. WARLEGGAN HOUSE, CARD ROOM – NIGHT 54

Ross, with Francis getting ever more drunk beside him, is playing French Ruff with Sanson. Margaret and Vosper, along with Dwight, are watching. George is standing near the door with Cary.

CARY Poldark's losing badly.

Demelza is revealed, standing in the doorway.

HER POV: Ross playing, his expression utterly inscrutable. Someone brings him a drink and he knocks it back in one.

Demelza has the distinct impression that at some point soon he will explode and all hell will break loose. Forcing herself to remain calm, she makes her way over to where Ross and Sanson are attracting a growing crowd of spectators. She takes a seat behind Ross. He's locked in his own world and seems unaware of her. Sanson wins. Ross puts his gold watch on the table.

ROSS Fifty guineas?

SANSON Agreed.

Ross deals, turns up diamonds as trumps, picks up the 9, 10, ace of diamonds, the knave and 10 of spades.

SANSON I propose.

ROSS How many?

SANSON The book.

ROSS I'll take two.

Sanson changes all his cards for new ones. Ross throws his spades and picks up the king of hearts and 8 of spades.

SANSON Propose.

ROSS Accept.

SANSON Two.

Ross nods. They throw again, Sanson two and Ross one. Ross picks up the king of spades.

SANSON I'll lay ten guineas.

ROSS Twenty.

SANSON I'll take it.

They play the hand. Sanson has the king, queen, eight of trumps and two of clubs and makes four tricks to Ross's one.

DWIGHT The luck of the devil!

Sanson takes up the gold watch.

SANSON A decent little piece, if somewhat high-priced. I trust it keeps good time.

ROSS It never failed my grandfather.

A footman comes in with more drinks but Ross declines. This alarms Demelza more than his drinking. His expression is cold and steely.

ROSS Shall we continue?

SANSON What do you intend to play with?

ROSS Assets I can realize.

DEMELZA Ross, no!

They both know he means his shares in Wheal Leisure. Ross ignores her and continues to address only Sanson.

Demelza takes off her brooch and puts it on the table.

DEMELZA Play for this if you must.

SANSON What is its worth?

ROSS About a hundred.

DEMELZA Oh Ross—

She's touched by the generosity of his gift.

ROSS *(to Sanson)* Well? *(then)* Deal.

Sanson glances at George and Cary. Then he deals. He continues his winning streak.

GEORGE He has met his match in Matthew.

Sanson picks up the brooch, examines it briefly then puts it in his pocket. Demelza fights back tears.

SANSON Shall we retire?

ROSS Another hour.

SANSON With what?

ROSS My stake in Wheal Leisure.

DEMELZA *(barely a whisper)* Ross, no—

A glance between Cary and George. Dwight and Francis are horrified. Demelza is struggling not to cry.

Ross is expressionless. He deals: the seven, eight, nine of diamonds and the nine, ten of spades.

SANSON Propose.

ROSS How many?

SANSON One.

ROSS I'll take the book.

He throws away all five cards. Sanson is about to draw a card when Ross reaches across and catches his wrist. As Ross turns Sanson's hand up he reveals, in Sanson's palm, the king of trumps. No one speaks. In the silence you could hear a pin drop. Sanson tenses his arm to try and release it, but Ross's grip remains firm.

ROSS *(calm)* Can you explain how you come to have a card in your hand before you drew one from the pack?

SANSON You're mistaken! I'd already drawn—

GEORGE I rather think he had, Ross.

DWIGHT Oh no he had not!

FRANCIS Most certainly he had not!

Outnumbered, Sanson glances at Cary and George. They offer no support, but neither do they offer condemnation. Sanson tries again to escape Ross's grip – and for a moment thinks he has succeeded: Ross releases him – only to seize him by the ruffles of his shirt and, pulling him out of his seat, drags him across the table.

GEORGE What the hell are you doing? Ross, you would not dare!

Suddenly the place is in uproar. The table is overturned, sovereigns and guineas are scattered across the floor. Ross wrestles Sanson to the floor and rips his coat off.

SANSON George! Cary! Will you permit this?

Ross shakes out Sanson's coat. Three cards fall from an inner pocket. Ross now empties the other pockets, taking out the brooch, the watch. Sanson lies on the floor, dishevelled, grovelling, reaches out to retrieve his coat. Ross places his foot on Sanson's hand. Sanson howls in pain. Ross locks eyes with George.

ROSS I'm sorry for assaulting your friend, but if you insist on entertaining such fellows, you should at least keep them on a leash. *(grinding his foot into Sanson's hand)* Or perhaps you prefer your guests to be ruined in silence.

Ross releases Sanson's hand, collects his belongings and walks out. The rest of the room remains in shocked silence. George and Cary's expressions are like thunder.

CUT TO:

63: EXT. THE SEA – MORNING 55

Establisher.

CUT TO:

64: EXT. WARLEGGAN HOUSE – DAY 55

Dwight's horse and a carriage are brought round and Ross, Francis, Elizabeth, Demelza, Verity and Dwight prepare to leave. Verity is silent and tearful. Francis glares and refuses to speak to her. Elizabeth is silent and wistful, watching Ross and Demelza talking quietly to each other.

DEMELZA *(low, to Ross)* When did you first know he was cheating?

ROSS Almost at once, but I wanted to be sure before I challenged him.

He goes to assist Verity into the carriage. As Demelza waits, a servant approaches and hands her a note.

DEMELZA Thank you.

She glances round, is relieved to see that no one has noticed, takes a cursory glance at the handwriting, seems to recognize it, then thrusts the note into her pocket.

Dwight prepares to ride beside them. Ross assists Demelza into the carriage. Francis and Elizabeth remain.

ELIZABETH Your exploits at Bodmin Jail were much discussed.

ROSS No doubt.

ELIZABETH There was some sympathy for your intentions—

DWIGHT Though not our actions?

FRANCIS A pity some of your partners at Carnmore should be on the other side of the bench.

ROSS How d'you mean?

FRANCIS St Aubyn Tresize, Alfred Barbery – they're magistrates, are they not? They may feel compelled to take a stand?

Ross shrugs, impatient. 'Let them'. Elizabeth gets into the carriage.

FRANCIS *(cont'd)* Then there's the matter of Matthew Sanson—

ROSS What of him?

FRANCIS Once the tale gets out, George may feel obliged to respond.

ROSS Why should he?

FRANCIS Matthew's a cousin. Did you not know?

The implications of this now begin to sink in.

ROSS No. I did not.

CUT TO:

65: EXT. NAMPARA HOUSE – DAY 55

Establisher.

CUT TO:

66: EXT. NAMPARA HOUSE – DAY 55

Ross and Demelza walk up to the house. Jud comes out to greet them.

JUD Ol' tripe-fer-brains be within.

ROSS Who?

JUD Mark Daniel? Mopin' an moanin' fit t' make yer lugs bleed!

Jud slopes off. After he's gone . . .

DEMELZA There's talk o' Keren. An' Dwight.

ROSS Any truth in it?

DEMELZA I couldn't say.

ROSS Anything else you can't say? *(beat)* About Verity? Blamey?

DEMELZA I know as much as you.

CUT TO:

67: INT. NAMPARA HOUSE, KITCHEN – DAY 55

Demelza, sitting by the fire, surreptitiously opens the letter, unnoticed by Ross who sits at the table with Mark.

ON DEMELZA: Scanning the letter.

ANDREW *(VO)* Since you brought Verity and me together this second time, I must turn to you for further help . . . Francis is impossible. There can never be a reconciliation. Therefore Verity must choose between us . . .

ON ROSS AND MARK

MARK Folk say she's brazen. That she d' fling 'erself at other men.

ROSS Have you asked her if it's true?

MARK I 'aven't the heart, Ross. I can't put myself to believe it. But if a man can't trust 'is wife—

Jud comes in from outside, bringing logs for the kitchen fire.

ON ROSS AND MARK

ROSS You must have faith, Mark. Without that, there's no hope for a marriage.

JUD 'Ope fer marriage? Pick me liver! Best 'ee can 'ope fer, is not 'a be cuckolded thrice a day by ev'ry man, dog n' mule i' th' county!

Having delivered his optimistic assessment, Jud departs.

CUT TO:

68: EXT. MINGOOSE LODGE – DAY 55

Dwight opens the door to Keren.

KEREN I come to offer myself—

Dwight looks at her, alarmed.

KEREN *(cont'd)* As your assistant. To help you with your work. I can write, I can take notes—

DWIGHT But—

KEREN Oh, don't refuse me. You've been so kind – and I must use my wits for something or I'll go mad.

Before he can protest, she slips past him and goes inside.

CUT TO:

69: INT. TRENWITH HOUSE, OAK ROOM – DUSK 55

Elizabeth is spinning, but with little relish for the task. Francis watches as Verity sighs over her embroidery and Aunt Agatha mutters at her spread of tarot cards.

AUNT AGATHA *(barely audible)* 'Tis an omen, mark my words – a fiendish black omen . . .

FRANCIS What's the matter with the women of this family?

AUNT AGATHA *(without looking up)* The men?

FRANCIS You think you could do better?

Elizabeth, Verity and Aunt Agatha all stop what they're doing and look at him. He challenges them to say what they're thinking. For a moment we think they might. In the end, they don't. They resume their activities.

CUT TO:

70: INT. WARLEGGAN HOUSE, LIBRARY – DAY 55

Cary and George sit round a large table spread with papers.

CARY So. What do we know?

GEORGE What we know – is that Ross Poldark, though clever, has a weakness—

CARY Just the one?

GEORGE He plays it straight – and trusts others to do the same. But 'others' have eyes and ears—

CARY And they report— ?

GEORGE What we've been trying for some time to find out. The site of the Carnmore Copper Company Smelting Works.

CARY And?

GEORGE Trevaunance land – they've struck a deal with Tresidder's Mill.

CUT TO:

71: EXT. TRESIDDER'S ROLLING MILL – DAY 55

Jonathan Tresidder is seen standing outside the Rolling Mill. Ross, Sir John Trevaunance, Zacky and Tonkin walk towards him. Loud noises of clanking machinery. Blight, the Warleggan agent, is revealed, watching from a distance, unseen.

GEORGE *(VO)* For now they've enough copper to keep going. But come the next auction—

CARY *(VO)* We'll see they come away empty-handed.

CUT TO:

72: INT. WARLEGGAN HOUSE, LIBRARY – DAY 55

Back in the library.

GEORGE The question is: will that be enough to ruin them?

CARY What more can we do? Since they deliberately withhold the names of their shareholders—

GEORGE There's no law against that.

CARY But it makes it considerably more difficult for us to 'exert pressure'.

GEORGE So let's begin with the one name we do know.

CUT TO:

73: EXT. TRESIDDER ROLLING MILL – DAY 55

Brandy is poured into glasses. Five glasses chink. Ross, Zacky, Sir John and Tonkin stand and share the toast with Jonathan Tresidder.

GEORGE *(VO)* Jonathan Tresidder – banks with us, does he not?

CARY *(VO)* Does indeed.

GEORGE *(VO)* *(raises his glass)* And has substantial loans. So, here's to the first chink . . .

CUT TO:

74: INT. WARLEGGAN HOUSE, LIBRARY – DAY 55

Back in the library.

GEORGE *(raises his glass)* . . . in the Poldark armour.

They toast each other.

CUT TO:

75: EXT. CLIFF-TOPS – DAY 56

A tiny group of figures seems lost in the sweep and scale of the landscape. As we go closer we recognize Jinny and her child, kneeling by a rough wooden cross, supported by Connie Carter, Zacky and Mrs Zacky. Standing apart are Paul, Mark and Keren. Also, at a distance, Dwight. Then further still, Ross and Demelza. She carries a handful of wild flowers.

ROSS I wish Jim could've seen his child grow up.

DEMELZA You did all you could.

ROSS I wonder.

DEMELZA *(gently)* Ross – you cannot fight all the world. You can only make your own small corner a fairer place.

As the wind howls around them, Ross puts his arm round Demelza to protect her from the cold. Jinny walks away from Jim's makeshift grave, supported by Zacky and Mrs Zacky. Connie Carter and the others follow. As Dwight moves away, Ross notices Keren look back and steal a look at Dwight – who, almost against his will, flushes and returns it. Finally Ross and Demelza come to stand at the wooden cross.

DEMELZA Will anything come of what you did?

ROSS It may. It may not. *(then)* Lay your flowers. This is the first time I've been sober in five days.

Demelza lays the flowers. She and Ross remain, staring at Jim's grave.

Episode 7

1: EXT. MOORLAND – DAY 57

A rider gallops across the moors.

CUT TO:

2: EXT. COUNTRY ROAD – DAY 57

The rider canters down a country road, comes to a halt, dismounts beside a dry-stone wall. He is revealed to be Andrew Blamey. He takes a loose stone from the wall and into the cavity puts a letter. He replaces the stone and rides away. We watch him go. Then: CU A hand removes the stone, extricates the letter. The hand belongs to Demelza.

CUT TO:

3: EXT. WOODED GARDEN – DAY 57

Verity and Geoffrey Charles walk in the garden towards the wooded garden. Demelza appears in the distance. They meet. Demelza surreptitiously passes Verity the letter. They whisper conspiratorially. Only as they part do we reveal Mrs Tabb, feeding chickens in another part of the garden. Has she noticed? We can't be sure.

CUT TO:

4: INT. WARLEGGAN HOUSE, ENTRANCE – DAY 57

Mr Tresidder is leaving the house after a meeting with George. As they get to the door George stops him.

GEORGE Your mill provides rolling and cutting services for the Carnmore Copper Company?

Tresidder nods nervously.

MR TRESIDDER Yes.

GEORGE In these difficult times, we urge all who bank with us to consider where their best interests lie – *(beat)* Particularly when they have several outstanding loans with us.

Tresidder is devastated. He can't afford to lose Carnmore's business, but he knows he has no choice.

CUT TO:

5: INT. RED LION INN – DAY 57

Ross is sat at a table alone working through some papers. One document, poking out from amongst the rest, reads: The Carnmore Copper Smelting Company: Lord Devoran; Sir John Michael Trevaunance, Bart.; Alfred Barbary, Esq; Ray Penvenen, Esq; Ross Vennor Poldark, Esq; Peter St Aubyn Tresize, Esq; Richard Paul Cowdray Tonkin; Henry Blewitt; William Trencrom; Thomas Johnson.

Ross looks up as Francis comes and sits down beside him.

FRANCIS Still building your empire Ross? And you bought all the copper.

ROSS All we could afford while the price was low. Next time they'll be wise to us and the price will rise.

FRANCIS Which is good news for the mines. And your shareholders.

Ross sees that Francis is trying to read the papers and quickly starts to roll them up out of sight.

ROSS In the short term, yes. And in the long term – anything which breaks the Warleggan stranglehold and stops them keeping prices artificially low—

FRANCIS Benefits Leisure and Carnmore—

ROSS Benefits miners, smelters and shareholders alike. The Warleggans seek only to benefit themselves.

FRANCIS I hope you know what you're taking on.

ROSS I would I had your support.

Ross keeps eye contact with his cousin.

ROSS *(cont'd)* I know I have your discretion.

FRANCIS Of course.

Ross, having packed his papers away, leaves.
CUT TO:

6: EXT. MARK & KEREN'S COTTAGE – DAY 57

Establisher.
CUT TO:

7: INT. MARK & KEREN'S COTTAGE – DAY 57

Keren is feeding crumbs to the starling Mark tamed for her. Mark sits at the table awaiting breakfast. Karen, her thoughts elsewhere, absent-mindedly puts a few scraps of bread and cheese in front of him. He looks at them, unimpressed.

KEREN I bin too busy to bake.

MARK 'Ow's that?

KEREN I told you – I bin helping Dr Enys with his work. 'Tis a worthier cause than your stomach I'd say.

MARK Enys bain't yer 'usband.

KEREN No. But people hereabout depend on him. *(before he can argue)* I'm proud to serve him. And you should be proud I'm able.

She goes out before he can reply, leaving him to simmer in silence.

CUT TO:

8: EXT. WHEAL LEISURE – DAY 57

A miner coughs up black mucus into a cloth. Dwight is using percussion to sound the miner's chest. His manner is concerned and caring.

DWIGHT Damp and dust – no friend to the lungs. *(then)* Fresh air and exercise. A little sea bathing. Fennel root and ginger in warm water. Come and see me in a month.

The miner nods and departs. Other miners, men, women and children, wait to be seen. Now Jud appears, rolling a barrel of rum from the direction of the distant derelict mine – Wheal Grace. Ross appears from the mine office.

JUD Trencrom's finest!

ROSS Need you inform half of Cornwall?

JUD Tuck'd 'er away, I did – down yer father's ol' mine!

ROSS *(surprised)* Wheal Grace?

JUD Best 'idin' place there be. Tek a brave man t' venture down there. Folk say 'tis haunted!

ROSS You'll be haunted if that barrel's not intact by the time I return home!

JUD 'Es, sur – 'ee know me, sur.

Jud continues on his way, rolling the barrel. Dwight approaches Ross.

DWIGHT Trencrom?

ROSS Supplier of fine goods, direct from France—

DWIGHT Without troubling the excise men?

They both laugh. Now Mark appears for his shift. He nods at Ross and glowers at Dwight. Dwight senses Mark's animosity and seeks to divert attention from it.

DWIGHT *(to Ross)* Will you break even this month?

ROSS With luck – and a fair auction.

DWIGHT You must be relieved.

ROSS Yes.

DWIGHT *(with a glance at Mark)* I should get back to my patients.

He's about to return to the miners but Ross detains him.

ROSS Dwight, have a care.

Ross nods in Mark's direction.

DWIGHT Of course.

He goes back to his patients. Ross strolls over to Mark.

ROSS You look weary.

MARK Keren do 'ave me up all hours, mendin' roof.

ROSS Mind you don't exhaust yourself.

MARK Tes'n I as wants mindin', Ross.

He seems as if he wants to elaborate, but they are interrupted by the sound of an approaching horse. Zacky rides up.

ZACKY Ross, I bring word from Tresidder's Mill.

Ross can tell from Zacky's face that there's a problem.

ZACKY (cont'd) As of next week, we mus' look elsewhere f'r our rolling and cutting.

Ross digests the implications of this. He suspects George is behind this.

ROSS So be it. We shall take our business elsewhere.

CUT TO:

9: EXT. NAMPARA HOUSE – DAY 57

Establisher.

CUT TO:

10: INT. NAMPARA HOUSE, PARLOUR – DAY 57

Distant church bells can be heard ringing. Demelza glances nervously at the clock. She seems on edge but tries to distract herself by helping Julia to toddle across the room.

DEMELZA To Prudie? Shall we go to Prudie?

Julia laughs as Demelza helps her to toddle towards Prudie.

PRUDIE An' where be that buffle-'ead? 'E's bin quiet too long—

Both women look round suddenly at the sound of a heavy thud presently followed by the soaring strains of drunken singing:

JUD'S VOICE (sings)

Blessed are the pure in 'eart –
For they shall see our Lord—

Demelza and Prudie exchange a glance.

CUT TO:

11: INT. NAMPARA HOUSE, LIBRARY – DAY 57

Demelza and Prudie cautiously push open the library door.

Their POV: A drunken Jud, feet on the table, wearing one of Ross's hats, lounging back in Ross's chair. The barrel of rum is open and Jud has decanted some into a bottle. He waves them in expansively.

PRUDIE That be Master Ross's rum.

JUD It were. Now it be Master Jud's.

PRUDIE Out, now! Or I'll gi' 'ee such a skat in the chacks!

JUD I'm away – I'm away—

He staggers to his feet and, keeping tight hold of his bottle, reels out of the library. Demelza struggles to suppress a smile.

JUD *(OS) (sings)* Blessed are the pure in 'eart

CUT TO:

12: INT. TRENWITH HOUSE, TURRET ROOM – DAY 57

Verity goes to the window to watch Francis and Elizabeth with Geoffrey Charles walking down the drive. Elizabeth and Francis don't notice her but Geoffrey Charles turns round and waves.

Verity chokes back tears. She watches as Francis, Elizabeth and Geoffrey Charles disappear from sight. Then she leaves.

CUT TO:

13: EXT. MINGOOSE COTTAGE – DAY 57

Ross rides up to the cottage and passes Keren, she smiles as he looks at her.

CUT TO:

14: INT. TRENWITH HOUSE, OAK ROOM – DAY 57

Aunt Agatha is dozing in her chair when the door opens and Verity, dressed in outdoor clothes, comes in.

She contemplates the sleeping Agatha, tenderly brushes some stray white hairs away from her forehead, then tucks a note inside Aunt Agatha's shawl. She kisses her on the cheek. Aunt Agatha rouses briefly – just in time to see Verity disappearing through the door, carrying a travelling bag.

CUT TO:

15: INT. NAMPARA HOUSE, KITCHEN – DAY 57

Demelza is giving Julia her supper. Presently she and Prudie hear the sound of Jud returning.

JUD'S VOICE *(sings)*
For a whore she be a deep ditch;
and a strange woman be a narrow pit . . .
For she lyeth in wait for a man . . .
The door bursts open and Jud appears on the threshold, roaring drunk. Demelza is amused but Prudie is disgusted.

JUD *(sings)* They that tarry too long at the wine – They eyes shall behold strange sights—

He surveys Prudie with a look of utter contempt.

JUD *(cont'd)* I know that fizzogg! 'Twould make milk cruddle!

PRUDIE Cap'n Poldark'll fetch 'ee such a colloppin'!

JUD Cap'n Poldark? An' 'oo be Cap'n Poldark to be givin' 'isself airs? When ev'ryone d' know 'e's 'ad half the maids from 'ere to Truro!

PRUDIE Keep your voice down afore the chile!

JUD The chile? This chile? What about Jinny Carter's chile?

PRUDIE What about it?

JUD Ev'ryone d' know Cap'n Ross be its father!

PRUDIE 'Tis a lie!

DEMELZA Ignore 'im!

PRUDIE 'Tis a wicked, wicked lie!

JUD No wonder 'e went to Bodmin! To see Jim Carter in the ground! *(to Demelza)* An' don' 'ee brend yer brows at me, girl. 'Ee'm naught but a trull fr' 'Luggan!

A hand comes out of nowhere and seizes Jud round the neck. Jud swivels round and comes face to face . . . with Ross. Ross's face is cold with rage. Even in his drunken haze, Jud realizes he's overstepped the mark this time. He shrivels beneath Ross's glare.

ROSS Go!

Jud is blinking at Ross in disbelief.

JUD Go? Go where?

ROSS I neither know nor care, but if you're still in this house by daybreak I will personally horsewhip you from here to Truro.

Prudie and Demelza watch open-mouthed. Neither speaks. Ross, too incensed to be reasoned with, walks out.

CUT TO:

16: INT. TRENWITH HOUSE, GREAT HALL – DAY 57

Francis comes into the Great Hall, taking off his coat, ready to tuck into the tea which is laid out. Elizabeth follows.

ELIZABETH Where's Verity?

FRANCIS Is she not in her room?

CUT TO:

17: INT. NAMPARA HOUSE, PARLOUR – DAY 57

Demelza picks at her food while Ross, still seething, wolfs his down.

DEMELZA If Jud goes, so will Prudie.

ROSS And I'm sorry for that for you'll miss her.

DEMELZA But what he said – I cannot think he meant it – an' you know how he is when the liquor's upon him—

ROSS My liquors was upon him! He's lucky it wasn't my foot! *(then)* Liquor or not, he's disrespected you – and this house – once too often. He must face the consequences.

Demelza nods, resigned. In her heart she understands Ross's fury.

CUT TO:

18: EXT. NAMPARA HOUSE – DAY 57

Jud and Prudie leave the house, weighed down by their belongings.

PRUDIE Best place I ever know'd – an' now, thanks t' thee—

JUD *(muttering)* 'Tedn't right – 'tedn't fair – 'tedn't just – 'tedn't fittin'—

PRUDIE Hould yer clack, y'black worm or I'll crown 'ee meself!

CUT TO:

19: INT. TRENWITH HOUSE, OAK ROOM – DAY 57

Francis and Elizabeth have managed to rouse the dozing Aunt Agatha.

AUNT AGATHA Little Verity? Out, I believe.

FRANCIS Did she say where?

AUNT AGATHA Not as I recall – *(then)* Left something, though—

FRANCIS *(impatient)* What?

AUNT AGATHA Sealed it was – as if I cared to know her secrets—

Aunt Agatha painstakingly rummages in her shawl and eventually retrieves the letter. Francis snatches it. He's still not cottoned on, but Elizabeth has already guessed the contents.

Elizabeth waits while Francis reads Verity's letter.

FRANCIS *(reads)* 'I have known and loved you all my life, dear Francis, so I pray you will understand the grief and loss I feel that this should be our parting . . .'

Francis is white with fury and unable to continue. He screws the letter up, throws it away and strides out of the room. After he's gone, Elizabeth retrieves the letter and reads it.

CUT TO:

20: EXT. ANDREW'S LODGING – DAY 57

Verity stands looking up at the house, Andrew beside her.

ANDREW You will lie here tonight, my dear. I've arranged to sleep aboard my ship. And tomorrow we shall be wed.

She turns to look at him – her face suffused with joy.

CUT TO:

21: INT. TRENWITH HOUSE, GREAT HALL/
CORRIDOR/PARLOUR – DAY 57

Francis, seething with anger, storms through the house, pursued by Elizabeth.

FRANCIS So this is how she cares for us! To sneak away under our very noses and marry that wife-murdering drunkard! But how was it arranged? She must have had help—

He storms into the parlour, where Mrs Tabb and the other Trenwith servants are lined up nervously.

FRANCIS Has someone been calling unbeknown to us? *(no reply)* Or been seen about the grounds? *(no reply)* Someone who knew Miss Verity and might have carried a message?

He comes face to face with Mrs Tabb. The expression on her face changes. She has remembered something.

CUT TO:

22: INT. TRENWITH HOUSE, GREAT HALL – DAY 57

Francis rampages back through the house while Elizabeth follows, trying to calm him down.

FRANCIS I knew this was Ross's doing!

ELIZABETH Why would you think that?

FRANCIS He's helped them before! I see it all now. He's encouraged Verity—

ELIZABETH We do not know this—

FRANCIS He's been acting as agent for Blamey – keeping the skunk's interest warm – and using Demelza as go-between!

ELIZABETH You're too hasty! We've no proof that Demelza's involved, let alone Ross—

FRANCIS Oh, of course you will always stand up for Ross!

ELIZABETH I stand up for no one, but it's the merest justice not to condemn people unheard.

FRANCIS There's no other way it could have been managed. She's had no post. I've seen to that. Damn Ross! Dam this family! Damn this entire pitiful excuse for an existence!

Francis storms off. A servant shows George in.

GEORGE I hope I'm not intruding? *(eyeing Elizabeth closely)* But I see that I am. Is something amiss?

Elizabeth declines to elaborate.

GEORGE *(cont'd)* Forgive me, but it maybe within my power to offer assistance.

ELIZABETH I suspect not.

GEORGE But that's precisely the reason I'm here.

CUT TO:

23: INT. MINGOOSE COTTAGE – DAY 57

Dwight is dissecting a blackened pair of lungs.
CUT TO:

24: EXT. MINGOOSE COTTAGE – DAY 57

Keren arrives and knocks on the door.
CUT TO:

25: INT. MINGOOSE COTTAGE – DAY 57

Dwight stops what he is doing and looks towards the door.
CUT TO:

26: INT. TRENWITH HOUSE, OAK ROOM – DUSK 57

Francis, his mood slightly improved by alcohol, sits drinking with George. Elizabeth sits beside Francis.

ELIZABETH So there you have our predicament.

GEORGE Extraordinary!

FRANCIS What I most despise is the deceit. And from someone I trusted.

GEORGE Your sister—

FRANCIS My cousin.

GEORGE *(surprised)* You blame Ross?

FRANCIS Entirely.

ELIZABETH *(to George, prompting)* You mentioned a reason for your visit.

FRANCIS No doubt I've omitted to pay something.

GEORGE On the contrary. *(beat)* We – our family – find ourselves indebted to you.

Francis looks at George, uncomprehending, suspecting a trick.

ELIZABETH How?

GEORGE *(to Elizabeth)* You're aware that substantial gaming losses were accrued by Francis to my cousin Matthew?

Elizabeth nods. She recalls only too well.

GEORGE *(cont'd – to Francis)* It is possible – probable – that you were a victim of Matthew's dishonesty. That being so, we wish to make amends.

FRANCIS How?

GEORGE By cancelling some of your debts to our bank.

Absolute astonishment from Francis and Elizabeth.

ELIZABETH We cannot accept charity, George.

GEORGE Charity be damned! Our family's integrity has been compromised and we wish to recover it. I insist you accept our apology. And twelve hundred pounds.

Francis and Elizabeth try – and fail – to disguise their relief and delight.

GEORGE *(cont'd – to Elizabeth)* And now we need detain you no longer.

Elizabeth gets up to leave.

ELIZABETH Do not keep Francis up too late.

GEORGE I have his best interests at heart.

He kisses her hand.

GEORGE *(cont'd)* You see? I did mend your smile after all.

A moment of complicity between them. Then Elizabeth leaves.

CUT TO:

27: INT. MINGOOSE COTTAGE – DUSK 57

Keren is arranging Dwight's remedies neatly on a shelf in his potions cupboard as Dwight continues dissecting the blackened pair of lungs.

KEREN Aniseed. Hartshorn. Senna. Aqua Mirabilis. What are they for?

Dwight looks up, distracted from his task.

KEREN *(cont'd)* I've a thirst for learning.

She smiles at him. Dwight flushes. He's at pains to keep things business-like.

DWIGHT Some are nature's remedies, others I concoct myself. All are as efficacious as any Thomas Choake prescribes, but infinitely more affordable.

KEREN You'll not make a living like that.

DWIGHT I came here to heal my patients not bankrupt them.

KEREN You've already made me whole again.

She moves closer to him, puts her hand on his shoulder. He jumps, as if stung, and moves away from her.

DWIGHT *(flustered)* This must stop, Keren. This coming here. Your husband does not like it.

KEREN Do you like it?

He turns away, washes his hands in an attempt to avoid her.

DWIGHT I've work to do. My purpose is to – to—

KEREN Kiss me?

DWIGHT No—

KEREN Just the once?

DWIGHT Oh Keren – you and I know it would not be just the once.

KEREN Would that matter?

DWIGHT What matters is where it would lead.

She kisses him lightly, teasingly.

KEREN Shall I go on? *(kisses him)* And on? *(kisses him again)* Till you tell me to stop?

She kisses him again. He doesn't tell her to stop.

CUT TO:

28: INT. WHEAL LEISURE, TUNNEL – DUSK 57

Mark is hard at work.

CUT TO:

29: INT. NAMPARA HOUSE, PARLOUR – DUSK 57

Demelza rocks Julia to sleep. Ross is distracted by paperwork. Amongst the items on the table is the list of Carnmore Copper Company shareholders.

DEMELZA 'Tisn't just Jud.

Ross looks up, startled, as if he's been locked in another world and only now remembers where he is.

DEMELZA *(cont'd)* 'Tis Carnmore d' trouble you.

ROSS There are forces – opposing us—

DEMELZA Warleggan forces? *(Ross nods)* With what aim?

ROSS To put us out of business?

DEMELZA If Tresidder won't have you, where will you go?

ROSS We'll find somewhere. The whole of Cornwall doesn't yet knuckle to George. Nor will it, if I can help it.

DEMELZA What could George do?

ROSS For now? Nothing. He's leaned on Tresidder but unless he discovers these names—

He indicates the list of Carnmore shareholders.

DEMELZA If he did?

ROSS He'd realize that – barring myself and Henshawe – all bank at Warleggan's.

Demelza takes the list of shareholders and rolls it up.

ROSS *(amused)* What are you doing?

DEMELZA Hiding it! Sssshhhh!

They both laugh. A moment of connection between them. Then the mine bell starts to ring. They look at each other. Ross jumps to his feet.

CUT TO:

30: EXT. WHEAL LEISURE – DUSK 57

The mine bell is ringing as wounded men emerge from the shaft. They are helped out by Ross and Henshawe. Now Mark Daniel emerges. His face is bloodied and his hands are bleeding.

MARK 'Twas a rock-fall – the charge was damp – we thought it dead – an' then out o' nowhere—

HENSHAWE You're badly hurt?

Mark holds up a bleeding hand.

HENSHAWE *(cont'd)* Get Dr Enys to look at it.

MARK I'd sooner bleed t' death.

Henshawe nods. He seems to understand Mark's response. Ross tears off his own neck-tie and wraps it round Mark's hand before Mark can protest.

CUT TO:

31: INT. TRENWITH HOUSE, OAK ROOM – NIGHT 57

Francis and George have now been drinking for some time. Francis, flushed with wine, freed from Elizabeth's scrutiny and relieved at having some debts cancelled, is off guard.

GEORGE It's galling for the family, but your sister will realize her mistake and soon come crying home.

FRANCIS Then Ross can take her in, since he encouraged her treachery. *(then)* Dammit, I expect more loyalty from my only cousin. What have I ever done that he should go behind my back like this?

GEORGE Well, I suppose you married the girl he loved, didn't you?

FRANCIS Oh. Yes. That. *(then)* But that's long ago. He's happily married himself now. More happily in fact than *(hurriedly correcting himself)* It's not on that score, I assure you.

CUT TO:

32: INT. MARK & KEREN'S COTTAGE – NIGHT 57

Mark creeps into the cottage. All is silent. He peers into the darkness.
CUT TO:

33: EXT. MARK & KEREN'S COTTAGE – NIGHT 57

Mark stands outside the cottage. He scans the shadows in the vain hope that Keren is somewhere nearby.

MARK *(softly)* Keren? *(louder)* Keren?

No sound. He scans the landscape. No movement. Darkness.
CUT TO:

34: INT. MINGOOSE COTTAGE – NIGHT 57

Dwight and Keren lie on the floor – Keren in post-coital bliss, Dwight already regretting it.

CUT TO:

35: INT. TRENWITH HOUSE, OAK ROOM – NIGHT 57

George leans closer to Francis.

GEORGE I sympathize. I too find Ross unfathomable. In some ways you and I are in the same boat.

CUT TO:

36: EXT. MINGOOSE COTTAGE – NIGHT 57

Keren tiptoes out of Mingoose Cottage, humming happily to herself. She begins to walk, almost skip, towards home. Unaware that Mark is hiding in the shadow of Mingoose Cottage and is watching every step she takes.

CUT TO:

37: INT. TRENWITH HOUSE, OAK ROOM – NIGHT 57

GEORGE What's perplexed me of late has been Ross's attitude towards me. When he opened his mine, the other venturers were for banking with Warleggan's – yet he fought tooth and nail to go with Pascoe's.

FRANCIS I doubt that was personal.

GEORGE Then this wildcat copper-smelting scheme – it's clearly directed against us—

FRANCIS Oh, I don't think against you precisely. Its aim is to get fairer prices for the mines.

GEORGE Oh, it's not the scheme which upsets me – for it will fail through lack of money. But it demonstrates an enmity towards me which I don't feel I deserve. Any more than you deserve his betrayal of your family . . .

Francis nods eagerly. It's good to get sympathy. And so George begins to reel him in.

CUT TO:

38: INT. MARK & KEREN'S COTTAGE – NIGHT 57

Keren, humming happily to herself, has her hand on the latch of the cottage when . . .

MARK'S VOICE Where've y'been?

The voice is coming from inside the cottage. Mark has got home before her. Now he steps out of the shadows.

KEREN Oh! Mark! You're back early. Why did you— ? *(seeing his bandaged hand)* You're hurt! What happened? Let me see—

MARK Where've y'been?

Sensing the anger in his voice, Keren is immediately on the offensive.

KEREN I couldn't sleep. I had a pain. I thought mebbe a walk would—

MARK Ye've been wi' Enys.

KEREN I've not!—

MARK Ye've been lyin' wi' Enys!

KEREN I went to see 'im – he's a doctor, isn't he? I wanted something for the pain—

MARK How long— ?

KEREN What?

MARK How long were ye there?

KEREN About an hour—

MARK I waited three.

Keren backs away from Mark, but with each denial he moves implacably towards her.

KEREN 'Twas nothing, Mark – *(then)* 'Twas on'y a kiss – *(then)* 'Twas on'y the once – *(then)* 'Twas him – he pestered me! – he wouldn't let me be—

She continues to back away. He continues to advance towards her.

KEREN *(cont'd)* 'Tis you that's to blame – *(then)* You left me alone overmuch – *(then)* You never loved me enough—

It's the final straw for Mark. With tears now pouring down his face, he grabs hold of Keren.

MARK I loved ye more'n life, I did – I loved ye, Keren—

KEREN You don't know what love is!

She launches herself at him, scratching, kicking, spitting. Her tiny frame is dwarfed by his great bulk.

KEREN *(cont'd)* You don't know what love is—

He grabs her, folding her into his chest to stop her scratching and punching him.

He's crushing her to him, tighter and tighter in a fierce embrace as her voice rises to a crescendo . . .

KEREN *(cont'd)* You don't know – you don't know – you don't know – you don't know – you don't know, Mark!

Suddenly she stops. Her body goes limp. For a moment Mark doesn't understand what's happened as they fall to the floor.

MARK Keren? *(silence)* Keren? *(silence)*

Then, as he realizes she's no longer moving, he looks down at the tiny body lying limp in his arms.

MARK Don' 'ee fool wi' me, Keren. Wake up now—

He looks more closely at her, uncomprehending.

MARK *(cont'd)* Wake up, Keren – wake up—

He strokes her face, tries to open her eyes. They're absolutely lifeless. His face crumples.

MARK *(cont'd)* No – oh no – oh no, Keren—

He rocks her in his arms.

MARK *(cont'd)* I never meant – I never meant – I never, never, never, never meant, oh, Keren—

He weeps over her lifeless body.

CUT TO:

39: INT. TRENWITH HOUSE, OAK ROOM – NIGHT 57

Francis erupts in fury at Ross's supposed betrayal.

FRANCIS Damn Ross! Damn his scheming! He's married my sister to a wife-beater and disgraced my family name! Well, if he cares so little for my interests, why should I care for his?

George's eyes flicker but he doesn't immediately reply, waiting to see if Francis will follow through. When he does not . . .

GEORGE You were saying, you thought Carnmore was well supported?

FRANCIS Mmmm. . . ?

GEORGE Surely no man of sense would invest in such a scheme?

Francis hesitates. Then . . .

FRANCIS *(laughing)* What would you call Lord Devoran? Or Sir John Trevaunance? Or Richard Tonkin – Henry Blewitt – Thomas Johnson – William Aukitt . . .

A brief smile flickers across George's face.

CUT TO:

40: EXT. NAMPARA VALLEY – DAWN 58

Establisher. The sun rises.

CUT TO:

41: EXT. MARK & KEREN'S COTTAGE – DAWN 58

Keren's tame starling is perched on the handle of Mark's mining pick-axe. As Mark stumbles from the cottage, weeping, the starling flies away.

CUT TO:

42: EXT. NAMPARA VALLEY – DAWN 58

Jud and Prudie are crouched round a pathetic fire, over which a pot hangs. Prudie is attempting to cook something. Jud wrinkles his nostril with distaste. A blanket is strung between two saplings as a makeshift shelter. Jud is muttering to himself.

JUD Wha' I sed? – 'twas nuthin' worse 'n usual—

Prudie whacks him across the head with a wooden spoon.

JUD *(cont'd)* Tis' he – gettin' soft since he did wed 'er—

Another whack from the wooden spoon.

JUD *(cont'd)* An' since the blatherin' chile come!—

Another whack.

JUD An' now 'ere be another, cakey as custard!

They see Mark Daniel stumbling past and disappearing over the horizon. Jud reaches into the cooking pot to steal some food but is rapped over the knuckles by Prudie.

CUT TO:

43: EXT. MARK & KEREN'S COTTAGE – DAY 58

Dwight rides up to the cottage and knocks at the door. There's no answer. He knocks again.

DWIGHT Mr Daniel? I regret this intrusion, but – *(hesitates, then)* I believe I've wronged you. I have no excuse – but I wish – I wish to make amends.

He knocks harder. This time the door, not being locked, swings back slightly.

DWIGHT Mr Daniel?

No answer. Dwight pushes the door open cautiously.

CUT TO:

44: EXT. MARK & KEREN'S COTTAGE – DAY 58

Seen through the window from outside: Dwight edges into the cottage. He is met by the sight of Keren's lifeless body.

DWIGHT Oh – God – no—

CUT TO:

45: INT. NAMPARA HOUSE, LIBRARY – DAY 58

Ross is digesting the news which has been brought by Zacky and Paul.

ZACKY We had it from surgeon himself.

Ross looks alarmed. He's rapidly piecing together all the parts of the jigsaw.

PAUL 'Twas mebbe an accident.

Ross and Zacky exchange a glance. It's clear they fear otherwise.

ROSS Where's Mark?

ZACKY Not seen 'im since he went home from the mine last night.

Ross nods. It's all falling horribly into place.

PAUL 'Tis never Mark's doin'. He did love 'er. *(beat)* Little as she'd deserve it.

ROSS I must speak to him, Paul. Your brother is in serious trouble . . .

Paul looks away. Ross senses Paul knows more than he's admitting.

ROSS *(cont'd)* If you know where he is—

PAUL How would I? *(then)* Surgeon d' need to watch 'is back, though. He's no more'n a boy – an' Mark could snap 'im easy as a twig.

ROSS And Keren?

A look between them. They all know Mark's strength.

ROSS *(cont'd)* We know his strength. We know he wouldn't mean to hurt her—

PAUL *(suddenly worried)* 'Ee'd niver turn 'im in?

ROSS I've known him since I was a boy. I've no wish to see him hunted down and hung from a gibbet. But if he's done this thing—

PAUL 'E'll get no justice, you know that. Just ask Jim Carter!

Ross and Zacky exchange a glance. They know Paul is right. They also know they can't condone what Mark's done.

CUT TO:

46: INT. MINGOOSE COTTAGE – DAY 58

Dwight is pacing, unable to sit still.

ROSS How did she die?

DWIGHT Broken neck.

ROSS Deliberate?

DWIGHT I could not say – beyond all doubt—

Ross frowns. This is no real help.

DWIGHT *(cont'd)* What will happen now?

ROSS If you take my advice you'll leave without delay.

Dwight looks at him, uncomprehending.

ROSS *(cont'd)* There's a warrant out for Mark's arrest.

DWIGHT Dear God—

ROSS Every villager's bound by law to help in his capture – but I don't believe a single one will do so.

DWIGHT They take his side – and rightly so.

ROSS But not against you, Dwight. *(then)* Within a week he'll be found and brought to justice. It will then be safe for you to return—

DWIGHT What d'you take me for? To skulk away to safety

while the man I wronged is hunted down like an animal? No, I'd sooner meet him face to face and take the consequence.

ROSS Which could be fatal—

DWIGHT I'll take my chance. Besides, I cannot leave these people. I've been met with nothing but kindness here – and to repay them like this? No, I thank you for your concern, but I will stay.

ROSS Then your blood be on your own head.

DWIGHT Keren's is there already.

CUT TO:

47: EXT. NAMPARA HOUSE – DAY 58

Demelza is picking flowers with Garrick beside her as Ross returns home.

DEMELZA Is it true about Keren? Folks a saying her neck was broke. *(Ross nods)* On purpose?

ROSS I doubt it. But the magistrates will think otherwise.

Demelza computes the implications of this. Then . . .

DEMELZA What of Mark?

ROSS The constables are out in force. And your admirer, Sir Hugh, has called in the soldiers—

DEMELZA How?

ROSS They're in the area, looking for smugglers. As a magistrate he has power to commandeer them.

DEMELZA And if Mark is found?

ROSS He'll hang.

MARK'S VOICE An' well deserve it.

Ross and Demelza jump. Mark, his face tear-stained and white, steps out of the trees, accompanied by Paul. Ross motions them to stay in the shadows.

CUT TO:

48: EXT. NAMPARA VALLEY, COPSE – DAY 58

Mark is staring ahead as if in a trance. His remorse has rendered him completely helpless. Paul and Ross keep glancing round to make sure no one can see them.

MARK I killed 'er – I never meant to but I did—

PAUL *(to Ross)* You know as well as I, she brought 'im to it – 'er an' Enys—

ROSS The courts will never accept that.

MARK I mun' give myself up—

PAUL No—

MARK I bain't safe. If I see Enys, I'll swing f'r him. As I'll rightly swing for her—

Something seems to shift in Ross. Suddenly he sees the futility of the kind of justice Mark would be subject to.

ROSS No, Mark. One life's already lost. What will it serve to waste another?

Mark looks at him, uncomprehending. Paul looks hopeful.

CUT TO:

49: INT. NAMPARA HOUSE, PARLOUR – DAY 58

Ross has returned and is watching Demelza make preserves.

ROSS If it's to happen, it must be tonight. And from Nampara Cove.

DEMELZA In our boat?

ROSS She's not fit for ocean going when the seas are rough but a resolute man could do worse in fair weather.

DEMELZA An' go where?

ROSS Ireland? Brittany?

Demelza digests this. Then . . .

DEMELZA And the oars?

ROSS Might find their way to the cove after dark – together with enough supplies to keep a man alive.

Demelza nods, considers, then . . .

DEMELZA 'Tisn't lawful—

ROSS No—

DEMELZA But some might say 'tis a kind of justice.

Ross nods. But it's clear that his conscience isn't entirely easy with it. Then . . .

ROSS But we must keep Mark away from Dwight. We don't want more blood on his hands.

Suddenly the sound of a horse whinnying makes them look up in alarm. Through the window they see six soldiers, five on foot, one a captain, riding, coming down the valley towards the house. For a moment Ross is caught off guard. Then a plan begins to form in his mind.

ROSS Go upstairs and change, my love – and prepare to be the lady.

Demelza hastens upstairs.

CUT TO:

50: INT. NAMPARA HOUSE, ROSS & DEMELZA'S BEDROOM – DAY 58

Demelza fumbles nervously with the fastenings on her gown. She edges to the window and looks out.

HER POV: Ross talking to the handsome, well-groomed Captain McNeil, inviting him in. The other soldiers remain outside.

CUT TO:

51: INT. NAMPARA HOUSE, PARLOUR – DAY 58

As Demelza comes in, Ross and Captain McNeil are laughing uproariously together. Ross is playing the genial host for all he's worth.

ROSS Ah, my dear, this is Captain McNeil of the Scots Greys. Captain McNeil, may I present my wife Demelza?

CAPTAIN MCNEIL The pleasure is mine, ma'am.

As he bends to kiss her hand, he gives her an appraising glance. Then . . .

CAPTAIN MCNEIL *(cont'd)* Captain Poldark and I are old comrades. We were together at James River in '81.

DEMELZA *(visibly relieved)* Oh, I see.

CAPTAIN MCNEIL I understood he was acquainted with the murderer and wondered if he could give me any pointers as to where the felon might hide.

ROSS None that spring to mind. Though I don't imagine he'll linger.

CAPTAIN MCNEIL Any suitable boats hereabouts whereby he might make his escape?

ROSS A few, I suppose. I have one myself.

CAPTAIN MCNEIL Where is it kept?

ROSS In a cave down by the shore. But it couldn't be handled by a single man. Can I persuade you to stay to supper? My wife has made kidney pudding.

CAPTAIN MCNEIL Another occasion I'd be delighted. *(then)* But if you'll oblige me by pointing out the coves hereabouts. I could search for smugglers and murderer at the same time. Two birds with one stone, ye might say.

ROSS May I offer you some brandy? I trust you'll be able to tell by the flavour whether or not duty has been paid!

Captain McNeil erupts into laughter – and Ross and Demelza eagerly join in.

CUT TO:

52: EXT. NAMPARA HOUSE – DUSK 58

Ross and Demelza stand on the doorstep watching Captain McNeil and his soldiers depart.

DEMELZA *(low)* You were so good! No one would've guessed you knew a thing.

ROSS Don't underestimate him. He's smarter than he looks.

Captain McNeil turns and waves. Demelza and Ross smile affably and go inside.

CUT TO:

53: INT. NAMPARA HOUSE, HALLWAY/ KITCHEN – DUSK 58

Ross and Demelza close the door on the departing Captain McNeil.

ROSS Now I must fetch the oars.

He goes through into the kitchen, Demelza follows. She catches sight of something on a side-table.

DEMELZA I clean forgot. This came from Trenwith.

She hands him a letter. Ross opens it, scans it briefly, then halts. It's contents seem to disturb him.

DEMELZA *(cont'd)* What does it say?

ROSS *(reads aloud)* 'As you may know, Verity left us last night for Captain Blamey. They are to be married today. Elizabeth'

DEMELZA *(feigned surprise)* So she's done it at last?

ROSS I rather feared she might.

DEMELZA Yet – why should they not be happy together? If they d' love each other—

ROSS *(distracted by the letter)* Why 'as you may know'? Why should she think I would know?

DEMELZA Perhaps the news is already about?

ROSS I must go to Trenwith. This letter is abrupt. They must be upset. *(then)* I'll call on my way back from the cove. *(then)* You'll be well enough here with Garrick to guard you?

Demelza doesn't look too reassured by the thought. Ross goes out through the back door (to the barn, to collect the oars).

CUT TO:

54: EXT. HARBOUR – DUSK 58

Establisher.

CUT TO:

55: INT. ANDREW'S LODGINGS – DUSK 58

The sunset glows across their faces as Andrew and Verity eat supper. Alone in private for the first time, they find themselves rather shy.

VERITY This is our very first meal together.

ANDREW Does it seem strange to you?

VERITY No. 'Tis only that – *(then)* In all of our lives, we have not met more than two dozen times.

Andrew takes her hand.

ANDREW Tonight we close a book on our old lives. Tomorrow we open a new one.

VERITY And write it together.

ANDREW If you should ever be unhappy, my love, I swear it will not be of my doing.

He kisses her hand tenderly. Verity is happy.

CUT TO:

56: INT. NAMPARA HOUSE, KITCHEN – DUSK 58

Demelza peers out into the gathering gloom before she closes the curtains. Garrick is snoring and looks unlikely to fulfil any guard-dog duties.

CUT TO:

57: EXT. NAMPARA COVE, CAVE – DUSK 58

Ross hides the oars and sails on a high shelf of rock inside the cave, alongside the mast.

Ross edges out of the cave, spots some soldiers some distance away. He crouches low and waits for them to move on before stealing away into the darkness.

CUT TO:

58: INT. NAMPARA HOUSE, KITCHEN – NIGHT 58

Demelza, continuing with her preserves, is horrified to hear the back door creak. Garrick lifts up his head and begins to growl. The door edges open. Demelza is rooted to the spot in fear – then almost faints with relief when the visitor is revealed to be Dwight.

DEMELZA Judas! You gave me such a fright!

DWIGHT Forgive me, I did not mean – *(then)* Ross counselled me to leave.

DEMELZA For your own safety.

DWIGHT I cannot contemplate such a thing. But I'm sick of my own company tonight. May I avail myself of Ross's?

DEMELZA He's not here.

CUT TO:

59: INT. TRENWITH HOUSE, GREAT HALL – NIGHT 58

Elizabeth is doing her household accounts when Ross is shown in.

ROSS I came as soon I could. How's Francis?

ELIZABETH He's half a mind to go after her.

ROSS Persuade him against. He's no match for Blamey.

ELIZABETH Or Verity. For I think she's now the bolder of the two.

ROSS Certainly the most reckless.

ELIZABETH She has the courage of her convictions. Which I applaud even if I seem to disapprove.

A brief moment between them. The merest hint that Elizabeth wishes she too had the courage of her convictions. Then Francis barges in.

FRANCIS Well, Ross, are you pleased with your handiwork? Clearly it was you who helped her.

Ross is looking at Francis in utter bewilderment.

ROSS I? Arrange Verity's elopement? Have you taken leave of your senses?

CUT TO:

60: INT. NAMPARA HOUSE, KITCHEN – NIGHT 58

Demelza's anxiety mounts (as she realizes what Ross is planning tonight – Mark's escape – and how it might be compromised by Dwight's arrival).

DEMELZA I – I don't think Ross would want you here—

DWIGHT Have I forfeited his good opinion? Or his trust?

DEMELZA Oh no, not that, but – he has business tonight – and mebbe visitors—

There is the sound of someone tapping on the window. Demelza almost leaps out of her skin.

DWIGHT I'll see who it is.

DEMELZA No! No, I must – 'tis mebbe the soldiers. Wait here.

CUT TO:

61: INT. NAMPARA HOUSE – NIGHT 58

Demelza opens the door to the very last people she wants to see at this moment . . . Paul and Mark. Demelza is horrified.

PAUL There be soldiers everywhere. We couldn't think where else to come.

CUT TO:

62: INT. TRENWITH HOUSE, GREAT HALL – NIGHT 58

Elizabeth is on her feet, trying to stop the inevitable escalation of the confrontation between Francis and Ross.

FRANCIS You helped them before – you allowed them to meet secretly at Nampara—

ROSS To my eternal regret! You were nearly killed! D'you imagine I want a repetition of that?

FRANCIS You cannot abide to lose face—

ELIZABETH Francis—

FRANCIS *(to Ross)* You were defeated then and this is your revenge—

ELIZABETH Francis, stop—

ROSS I think you must be drunk, Francis.

ELIZABETH I think you must leave, Ross.

CUT TO:

63: INT. NAMPARA HOUSE, HALLWAY – NIGHT 58

Demelza has reluctantly let Paul and Mark into the house. She motions them to be quiet.

DEMELZA *(low)* Ross is down at the cove. You can wait in here till he comes back an' tells you it's clear.

She opens the door to the library and is about to usher them inside when the kitchen door opens and Dwight appears on the threshold. He and Mark face each other. Mark's eyes are blazing with hatred.

CUT TO:

64: INT. TRENWITH HOUSE, GREAT HALL – NIGHT 58

Ross and Francis are still arguing.

FRANCIS Verity could not have managed it alone. It must be your doing! You and that impudent brat you married!

ELIZABETH Francis—!

FRANCIS You've been using her to carry letters between Verity and that skunk—

ROSS When I say I have not, I expect to be believed – and if you continue to doubt my word—

CUT TO:

65: INT. NAMPARA HOUSE, HALLWAY – NIGHT 58

Dwight faces Mark and Paul, whose faces are blazing with hatred. Demelza is trying desperately to mediate and keep them all apart.

DEMELZA Dwight – go back into the kitchen.

MARK 'Tes a trap – 'tes a bleddy trap—

DEMELZA How dare you say that? Mark, have you no sense? Dwight, go back into the kitchen—

MARK *(to Dwight)* You bastard—

DWIGHT *(to Mark)* You should've come for me – not broken a girl who couldn't defend herself—

MARK *(to Dwight)* I'll break 'ee soon enough—

He steps forward. Dwight steps forward. Demelza flings herself between them.

DEMELZA Stop this! Are you mad? Do you want to bring the soldiers down upon us?

CUT TO:

66: INT. TRENWITH HOUSE, GREAT HALL – NIGHT 58

Ross and Francis are squaring up to each other with Elizabeth trying to keep them apart.

ROSS I gave you credit for more intelligence!

FRANCIS I gave you credit for more loyalty! But perhaps your choice of wife has coarsened your finer instincts!

Ross leaps towards Francis to punch him. Elizabeth leaps between them.

ELIZABETH Enough! Both of you! Have you forgot you are family?

CUT TO:

67: INT. NAMPARA HOUSE, HALLWAY – NIGHT 58

Demelza has flung herself between Mark and Dwight. She pushes Mark away, though he's physically so huge he could push her aside if he wanted.

DEMELZA You would fight and kill each other in our house? Does friendship mean nothing to you?

MARK Let me finish 'un!

PAUL 'Tes finished already—

DEMELZA It isn't! Don't you see? Dr Enys can't betray you without betraying us! You can trust him!

MARK I'd as lief trust a snake.

DWIGHT What you did is on your conscience, as what I did is on mine. But three wrongs don't make a right.

Demelza continues to hold Dwight and Mark apart.

DWIGHT *(cont'd)* You have my word, I won't betray anyone.

Paul pushes Mark into the library and Dwight returns to the kitchen. Demelza remains in the hallway.

CUT TO:

68: INT. TRENWITH HOUSE, GREAT HALL – NIGHT 58

Elizabeth continues to hold Ross and Francis apart, but it's clear from the hostility on their faces that the rift between them will not easily be healed. Without another word Ross turns and walks out.

ELIZABETH Call him back, Francis. He's your cousin—

FRANCIS I have no cousin. I have no sister. I have a wife, a son – and an estate in considerably less debt today than it was yesterday. So I am content!

CUT TO:

69: INT. NAMPARA HOUSE, HALLWAY – NIGHT 58

Ross returns home to find Demelza standing guard in the hall, holding an iron poker, keeping Mark and Dwight apart in their separate rooms.

DEMELZA Ross!

ROSS What in God's name— ?

Demelza dissolves in tears of relief in Ross's arms.

CUT TO:

70: EXT. NAMPARA HOUSE – NIGHT 58

The back door opens and Ross and Dwight emerge.

ROSS Go home and sleep. And tomorrow—

DWIGHT (*firm*) Tomorrow I will tend to my patients and try – God knows how – to make amends.

Dwight disappears into the darkness. Ross goes back inside.

CUT TO:

71: INT. NAMPARA HOUSE, ROSS & DEMELZA'S BEDROOM – NIGHT 58

Demelza blows out the candle and stations herself by the darkened window.

CUT TO:

72: EXT. NAMPARA HOUSE, COURTYARD – NIGHT 58

The back door opens and three cloaked figures (Ross, Mark and Paul) sneak out.

CUT TO:

73: EXT. NAMPARA COVE – NIGHT 58

As Ross, Mark and Paul approach Nampara Cove they slow down, all senses on alert for the presence of soldiers. Ross motions them to hide behind some rocks. As they crouch there in silence, Mark seems to be in a trance. But after a moment . . .

MARK *(low)* I been 'iding down that ol' mine o' yer father's.

ROSS Wheal Grace?

MARK Wheal Grace.

PAUL Sssshhh!

MARK *(oblivious)* To keep from goin' off my 'ead, I went all over 'er.

Ross motions him to be silent, while they listen out for soldiers. Mark continues, oblivious.

MARK *(cont'd)* There's money in that mine. *(beat)* Copper. I never see'd a more keenly lode.

PAUL Where is it?

MARK On the east face. 'Twill be under water most times.

ROSS Sssssshhhh! The soldiers—

MARK I never meant to hurt 'er, Ross—

ROSS We know that, Mark—

MARK I mus' pay for what I done—

He makes to stand up and surrender. Horrified, Ross and Paul grab him and hold him down – just as a contingent of soldiers approaches. Ross and Paul drag Mark lower as the soldiers run past.

CUT TO:

74: EXT. NAMPARA COVE – NIGHT 58

As the soldiers head towards the cliffs, three shadows slink out of the shadows behind them and head towards the mouth of the cave.

As Ross and Mark head into the cave they come face to face with a soldier. He panics, fumbles with his musket. Unseen by him, Paul has slipped behind him and now knocks him unconscious – but not before the musket has gone off with a flash and a loud crack.

Paul and Ross push the boat across the sand towards the sea. They pile the sails and mast in. Suddenly there are lights, shouts and footsteps. Soldiers are running towards them. Ross and Paul push the boat out into the surf. Mark is dithering – still in two minds whether or not to turn himself in.

ROSS Get in the boat, Mark!

Mark seems rooted to the spot.

PAUL Mark! Get in th' boat!

Ross runs and grabs Mark and bundles him towards the boat.

A soldier spots them and runs towards them.

SOLDIER This way! By the surf! There's a boat!

Ross thrusts the oars at Paul, then manhandles Mark into the boat. Paul and Ross push the boat out into the waves, almost capsizing it. Behind them they hear the voices of the soldiers getting closer.

Ross and Paul are struggling to get the oars fitted into the rowlocks.

PAUL Make 'aste, make 'aste!

ROSS Take the oars, Mark! Take the oars—

A moment of connection between Mark and Ross. The whole history of their friendship in a single glance. Then finally Mark grabs the oars, fits them into the rowlocks. With superhuman effort Ross and Paul push together and launch the boat out into the waves. It catches one and is borne out away from the shore. Mark finally takes control of the oars and hauls the boat away.

Ross and Paul have sunk to their knees in the surf. The soldiers are almost upon them. Ross heaves Paul to his feet, then feels himself grabbed round the neck. Ross wheels round and knocks a soldier flat onto the sand.

Ross is running – and Paul's running. They separate and Ross hides behind some rocks until the soldiers have passed by.

CUT TO:

75: EXT. NAMPARA VALLEY – NIGHT 58

Ross lies flat on his face in the bracken, panting for breath, listening. In the distance he can hear soldiers shouting and searching. As the voices begin to recede, Ross scrambles to his feet and, keeping low, begins to run.

CUT TO:

76: INT. NAMPARA HOUSE, COURTYARD – NIGHT 58

Panting for breath, Ross reaches the back door and rushes inside.

CUT TO:

77: INT. NAMPARA HOUSE, ROSS & DEMELZA'S BEDROOM – NIGHT 58

Demelza is standing in the dark by the window keeping watch as Ross runs in, tearing off his wet outer clothes.

ROSS D'you see anything?

DEMELZA Lights in the distance. Heading this way.

ROSS Help me with my boots! Quick!

Demelza rushes from the window and crouches before Ross to help him with his boots. Then . . .

DEMELZA Ross, your hand!

She grabs his hand. The knuckles are grazed and bleeding.

ROSS It must've been when I hit the soldier – *(then)* Hide my clothes away! Hurry!

Demelza scurries round gathering up Ross's wet outer clothes while he continues to tear off the rest. Julia stirs in her crib. Suddenly there is a loud knock at the door. Demelza and Ross freeze.

ROSS *(whispers)* Gently now, love. Let them knock again before we make light.

Another knock comes. Downstairs Garrick begins to bark.

ROSS *(cont'd – whispers)* Get into bed. We mustn't wake Julia.

Demelza does as she's told. Ross has finished undressing and now pulls on a dressing-gown. He goes to light a candle. There is another, more insistent knock. Calmer now, Ross lights the candle and goes towards the window. Without urgency he opens it and leans out.

ROSS *(leaning out of the window)* Damn it, this is a fine time to call!

CUT TO:

78: INT. NAMPARA HOUSE, HALLWAY – NIGHT 58

Ross, in his dressing-gown, opens the door to Captain McNeil.

CAPTAIN MCNEIL Mark Daniel escaped.

ROSS Is that certain?

CAPTAIN MCNEIL *(nods)* And in your boat.

ROSS I see.

CAPTAIN MCNEIL Ye do not seem very distressed.

ROSS I'm becoming philosophical in my old age! Oh, not that I'm happy to lose a good boat – but sighing will not bring it back – any more than it will bring back yesterday's youth.

CAPTAIN MCNEIL Your attitude does you credit, Captain. *(then)* May I, as a man a year or so your senior, offer ye a word of advice?

ROSS By all means.

CAPTAIN MCNEIL Have a care for the law. 'Tis a cranky, twisty old thing and you may flout it half a dozen times. But let it once come to grips with ye and ye'll find it harder to be loose from than a great black squid.

Ross is silent. Captain McNeil eyes him keenly.

CAPTAIN MCNEIL *(cont'd)* I'd welcome your assurance that my advice had been heeded.

ROSS You may rest easy on that score, Captain.

CAPTAIN MCNEIL In that case, I look forward to calling upon you and your charming wife when I'm next in the county.

He offers his hand for Ross to shake. Ross takes it, inadvertently revealing his grazed knuckles.

CAPTAIN MCNEIL Have ye hurt your hand somewhere, Captain?

ROSS Ah – yes. I caught it in a rabbit trap.

They salute each other, then Captain McNeil leaves, stifling a smile. Breathing a sigh of relief, Ross closes the door.

CUT TO:

79: EXT. ANDREW'S SHIP – DAY 59

The newly-weds Andrew and Verity walk up the gang-plank and go aboard the ship, to the accompaniment of whistles, applause and toss-ing of hats from the assembled crew. Tears of happiness glisten on Verity's face.

CUT TO:

80: INT. NAMPARA HOUSE, KITCHEN – DAY 59

Demelza is bathing Ross's grazed knuckles.

ROSS First Jim, now Mark. My band of brothers is shrinking.

DEMELZA At least Mark got clean away. An' McNeil sus-pected nothing. So 'twas a good night in the end.

ROSS Not entirely. *(beat)* You forget I went to Trenwith.

DEMELZA *(eyes widening, hardly daring to ask)* Was it dreadful?

ROSS Suffice it to say Francis and I have broken. Possibly for good.

Demelza is horrified. But before she can question him further, there is a knock on the door.

Ross gets up to answer it. Demelza remains. Her expression says it all: 'What have I done'? Presently Ross returns. He looks worried.

ROSS I'm called to a meeting.

DEMELZA What manner of meeting?

ROSS An extraordinary one – to be called at such short notice – and all partners summoned.

Ross goes out. Demelza remains. Clearly troubled, she's turning something over in her mind.

CUT TO:

81: EXT. TRENWITH HOUSE – DAY 59

Demelza knocks at the door of Trenwith.

CUT TO:

82: INT. TRENWITH HOUSE, GREAT HALL – DAY 59

Francis is breakfasting alone when Mrs Tabb shows Demelza in. Though Francis doesn't look pleased to see her, he manages to restrain himself from being rude.

FRANCIS Elizabeth is not down yet.

DEMELZA 'Tis you I wished to see.

CUT TO:

83: EXT. CARNMORE SMELTING WORKS OFFICE – DAY 59

Ross arrives at the Carnmore Smelting Works and sees all the shareholders gathering: Tonkin, Blewitt, Aukitt, Johnson, Sir John Trevaunance, Lord Devoran . . . He can see from their faces that something disastrous has happened.

ROSS What is it?

Tonkin's expression says 'It's bad'. They file into the meeting together.
CUT TO:

84: EXT. TRENWITH HOUSE – DAY 59

The front door slams shut behind Demelza. She's trembling and in a state of shock and has to pause to compose herself.
CUT TO:

85: EXT. NAMPARA HOUSE – DAY 59

Establisher.
CUT TO:

86: INT. NAMPARA HOUSE, LIBRARY – DAY 59

Demelza is back when Ross returns. She's unable to keep still, as if struggling with some tempestuous emotion. At first he's too distracted to notice.

DEMELZA The meeting went well?

ROSS In a word – no.

DEMELZA Tell me?

ROSS I would rather hear your news.

DEMELZA I would rather you did not.

Ross looks at her in surprise. For the first time he realizes how fretful and distressed she looks.

ROSS What's happened?

Demelza hesitates, then . . .

DEMELZA I – I went to see Francis.

ROSS What the devil for?

CUT TO:

87: INT. TRENWITH HOUSE, GREAT HALL
(FLASHBACK) – DAY 59

Francis is not disposed to make Demelza feel at ease. Nevertheless she knows she must press on.

FRANCIS Did Ross send you?

DEMELZA Why would he?

FRANCIS Because he's too craven to face me himself?

DEMELZA I came here – of my own accord – to tell you you're mistook. *(beat)* About Ross. *(beat)* He had no hand in Verity's elopement.

FRANCIS Why would I believe you when I did not believe him?

DEMELZA Because – *(hesitates, then)* I know who did arrange it.

CUT TO:

88: INT. NAMPARA HOUSE, LIBRARY – DAY 59

Ross stares at Demelza in disbelief.

ROSS You? You've been passing letters between them these last three months? Tell me you're joking?

DEMELZA No, Ross – I only wish I were, but—

Ross looks at her in alarm. She knows she can't stop now.

DEMELZA *(cont'd)* There's more – *(hesitates, then)* 'Twas I who first sought him out. I – I wanted to see if he still had feelings for Verity – or – was as wicked as people did say—

ROSS And you were able to divine that in a single meeting?

DEMELZA Not – a single meeting—

Ross looks at her with increasing astonishment.

DEMELZA I brought 'em together again – I encouraged Verity – I wanted her to be happy—

Ross closes his eyes in dismay as the consequences of Demelza's interference begin to dawn on him.

ROSS What have you done?

Demelza looks at Ross in confusion.

DEMELZA I don't understand. All I did – was bring two people together – who loved each other and—

ROSS No, Demelza. That was not all you did.

CUT TO:

89: INT. CARNMORE SMELTING WORKS OFFICE (FLASHBACK) – DAY 59

The assembled Carnmore Copper Company shareholders sit round a table. Tension and discomfort is high. Ross watches them all intently.

BLEWITT I had yesterday a letter from Warleggan's Bank telling me they could no longer support my loan. And that I should make immediate arrangements to repay it—

TONKIN I too have had such a letter. Word for word.

Other shareholders raise their hands as if to suggest that they too have had such letters.

ROSS But that's unheard of – to suddenly withdraw credit—

TONKIN I called on George Warleggan today to ask him to reconsider. He declined.

BLEWITT And to me. And when I asked him the reason—

ROSS He suggested you look to your connection with Carnmore?

BLEWITT I regret to announce, not only do I have no more capital to contribute, I expect any day to be declared bankrupt.

Johnson nods. Blewitt too. And the other shareholders. Ross is speechless. He's beginning to realize the full extent of what's happened.

CUT TO:

90: INT. NAMPARA HOUSE, LIBRARY – DAY 59

Ross is staring at Demelza in cold fury. Demelza begins to tremble. For what seems like an eternity he doesn't speak. Then . . .

ROSS For months you have lied to me—

DEMELZA No—

ROSS Gone behind my back—

DEMELZA I thought you'd be angry—

ROSS At what? Your ignorance? Your arrogance? Your utter disregard for truth and consequence?

DEMELZA But all I've done is make two people happy – and a few others miserable—

ROSS Oh, Demelza, do not underestimate the scale of your achievement! You blithely cast a stone, but fail to see the whirlpool you whip up or the innocents you drown!

DEMELZA What d'you mean?

CUT TO:

91: INT. CARNMORE SMELTING WORKS OFFICE (FLASHBACK) – DAY 59

The mood is deathly at the shareholders' meeting as the implications of the Warleggan's letters begin to sink in.

Ross says nothing. He's too distressed.

TONKIN What now?

BLEWITT For me? Debtor's prison or the poor house?

TONKIN *(to Ross)* 'Twas a glorious scheme. And I'll never regret the impulse behind it. But it has cost us dear.

BLEWITT It has cost us everything.

TONKIN Someone has betrayed us. Someone close to us.

CUT TO:

92: INT. NAMPARA HOUSE, LIBRARY – DAY 59

Demelza is still trying to make sense of everything. But for Ross it's all falling into place.

ROSS So how did it end with Francis?

CUT TO:

93: INT. TRENWITH HOUSE, GREAT HALL (FLASHBACK) – DAY 59

Francis is stony-faced and implacable. Demelza knows she's clutching at straws but must continue.

DEMELZA What I did – perhaps it was wrong – but I did it for love of Verity—

FRANCIS Get out.

DEMELZA I came here to take the blame and so I have. Be angry with me, but not with Ross. He knew nothing about it.

FRANCIS *(struggling to remain calm)* Will you go – and never enter this house again? And the same goes for Ross. If he will marry such an ignorant trull as you then he must take the consequences.

Demelza, trembling, turns and runs out of the room.

CUT TO:

94: INT. NAMPARA HOUSE, LIBRARY – DAY 59

Demelza is open-mouthed with horror.

ROSS Good men reduced to poverty – their families – our family – everything we've built – our very lives together? Now d'you understand?

Finally the truth begins to dawn on Demelza.

DEMELZA I betrayed you. And was the cause of greater betrayal.

CUT TO:

95: INT. TRENWITH HOUSE, GREAT HALL – DAY 59
(FLASHBACK)

Francis is stony-faced and implacable.

CUT TO:

96: INT. WARLEGGAN HOUSE, LIBRARY – DAY 59

George and Cary sit at the table having a celebratory drink.
CUT TO:

97: INT. CARNMORE SMELTING WORKS OFFICE – DAY 59 (FLASHBACK)

The meeting has come to an end as some of the shareholders leave.
CUT TO:

98: INT. NAMPARA HOUSE, LIBRARY – DAY 59

Demelza is horrified.

DEMELZA I've ruined everything. *(then, with dawning horror)* And this? Have I ruined that too? Have I lost your trust? And is it forever?

Ross says nothing. Demelza begins to despair.

DEMELZA *(cont'd)* It is. I see in your eyes. Can I ever win it back?

ROSS I don't know. I'd be lying if I said I did.

Ross attempts to justify his anger.

ROSS *(cont'd)* You've married into a peculiar family. We Poldarks are hasty – and sharp tempered – strong in our likes and dislikes. Perhaps yours is the more reasonable view. If two people love each other, why not let 'em marry, and be damned to the consequences?

DEMELZA I only meant to help—

ROSS I know that. And you could not have foreseen—

It's too painful for him to elaborate further, but Demelza knows exactly what he's referring to.

DEMELZA Can you forgive me?

ROSS I will try.

DEMELZA But Francis will not.

ROSS No.

DEMELZA And you will not forgive him. And I've caused a rift between the two sides of our family.

ROSS Yes.

DEMELZA I will never be happy until it's healed.

ROSS Then I'm afraid you'll be unhappy for a very long time.

Episode 8

1: INT. KITCHEN (MONTAGE) – DAY 60

SOUND OVER: Demelza singing.

DEMELZA *(singing)*
Mem'ries like voices that call on the wind.
Medhel an gwyns, medhel an gwyns.
Whispered and tossed on the tide coming in.
Medhel, oh medhel an gwyns.
Voices like songs that are heard in the dawn,
Medhel an gwyns, medhel an gwyns.
Singing the secrets of children unborn.
Medhel, oh medhel an gwyns.
Songs like the dream that the bal-maidens spin,
Medhel an gwyns, medhel an gwyns.
Weaving the song of the cry of the tin.
Medhel, oh medhel an gwyns.
Dreams, like the castles that sleep in the sand,
Medhel an gwyns, medhel an gwyns.
Slip through the fingers or held in the hand.
Medhel, oh medhel an gwyns.
Dreams like the memories once borne on the wind.
Medhel an gwyns, medhel an gwyns.
Lovers and children and copper and tin,
Medhel, oh medhel an gwyns.
Medhel, oh medhel an gwyns.
Secrets like stories that no one has told.
Medhel an gwyns, medhel an gwyns.

Stronger than silver and brighter than gold.
Medhel, oh medhel an gwyns.

CU: hands making dough for saffron buns. Hands shaping dough. Hands taking saffron buns out of the oven. Hands putting saffron buns into a basket. Sound of Demelza singing.

CUT TO:

2: EXT. NAMPARA HOUSE – DAY 60

Singing continues . . .

Saffron buns are carried by Demelza as she heads off for Wheal Leisure. Demelza sings.

CUT TO:

3: EXT. WHEAL LEISURE – DAY 60

Singing continues . . .

The basket of saffron buns, carried by Demelza, approaches Wheal Leisure. Ross is talking to Paul and some other miners. Demelza offers the saffron buns. As Ross takes one, we sense that Ross hasn't quite forgiven her. Nevertheless he smiles his thanks and Demelza seems relieved. Ragged children who have been scavenging nearby run up to partake of the buns.

CUT TO:

4: EXT. MELLIN COTTAGES – DAY 60

Singing continues . . .

The basket of saffrons buns, carried by Demelza, approaches the cottages. Jud is lounging, stupefied from drink, outside a run-down cottage from which Prudie now emerges. Her eyes light up when she sees Demelza. Hungry ragged children come running from other cottages.

CUT TO:

5: EXT. MELLIN COTTAGES – DAY 60

Eager children share out the saffron buns. They look ragged, pale and poverty-stricken. Demelza has reserved one bun each for Jud and Prudie. Jud examines his with a sneer.

JUD Do 'ee think 'ee can buy we off wi' faggons?

PRUDIE Hush, ye black worm! As if Cap'n Ross don' already look after we by turnin' a blind eye to us livin' in 'is cottage!

JUD *(to Demelza)* Do 'e know we live 'ere?

DEMELZA Course he do!

PRUDIE An' bless 'im f'r 'it, maid! An' bless 'ee too! *(to Jud)* An' curse 'ee, y' mizzerly maazerly mongrel!

She whacks Jud across the head, threads her arm through Demelza's and walks her away.

PRUDIE *(as she leaves with Demelza)* I could leather the arse off 'im . . .

Jud is left to sprawl outside the cottage, contemplating his saffron bun. When he's sure they've gone, Jud devours it voraciously.

CUT TO:

6: INT. RED LION INN – DAY 60

Francis and George enter the inn to find Cary already there. In another corner, unnoticed at first, sits Sir John Trevaunance (as we will see, Cary's proximity to him is not coincidental).

CARY How goes your cousin's copper smelting?

FRANCIS Well, er—

CARY Difficult, I imagine? Without any actual copper?

GEORGE Impressive operation, though. The smelting works on Trevaunance land?

CARY And valuable.

Sir John's ears prick up.

GEORGE A pity it will shortly no longer be required.

Sir John strains to listen in a little closer.

FRANCIS How so?

GEORGE A smelting works requires copper, does it not? Their mines produce a fraction of what's needed. At the last four auctions they were outbid.

CARY And if they get no copper at the next auction, surely that's the death knell for Carnmore?

Francis shuffles uncomfortably in his seat. Sir John does likewise.

GEORGE Were I Sir John Trevaunance, I might regret having a brand new smelting works on my land – and my money invested – with nothing to produce.

FRANCIS *(dry)* No doubt Sir John will be hearing from you shortly.

He indicates where Sir John is sitting, pretending not to have heard.

CUT TO:

7: EXT. NAMPARA HOUSE – DAY 60

Establisher.

CUT TO:

8: INT. NAMPARA HOUSE, KITCHEN – DAY 60

Ross returns from Wheal Leisure to find Demelza has returned and is making more saffron buns with Jinny. A fire blazes warmly. Julia plays in front of it. NB Round her wrist is the embroidered ribbon (which she has worn since her christening in Episode 5). The household arrangements are basic but cheerful. Ross's slight coolness towards Demelza continues.

DEMELZA *(to Jinny)* You should go, dear. Little Kate'll be wantin' you.

ROSS How is the child, Jinny?

JINNY She'm better, Cap'n Ross, sur. Dr Enys say 'tis not the putrid throat after all.

ROSS That's a mercy.

JINNY Aye, sur, 'tes. On'y this week there's three dead of it in Sawle.

Demelza puts some saffron buns into Jinny's basket.

DEMELZA Take these. For you and Jim's mother—

JINNY I'm that glad to serve 'ee again, ma'am. I know 'ee can scarce afford me.

DEMELZA If we did what we could afford, Jinny, we'd not get out of bed!

Jinny goes out. Ross and Demelza remain. As if to avoid conversation with Demelza, Ross picks up Julia.

DEMELZA She has another tooth coming.

ROSS Soon she'll be able to bite like Garrick!

Demelza laughs. But the tension doesn't entirely disperse. And for good reason: she gingerly pushes a letter towards him.

ROSS What's this?

DEMELZA It is from Verity.

CUT TO:

9: INT. TRENWITH HOUSE, GREAT HALL – DUSK 60

Geoffrey Charles, wrapped in a blanket, is shivering on Elizabeth's knee. Elizabeth, also shivering, is wrapped in a shawl. Aunt Agatha has almost disappeared inside a cocoon of shawls from which an arthritic claw emerges to grasp a fork and spear the dinner which is laid out before her. Francis is drinking, not eating.

AUNT AGATHA When will Verity be home?

FRANCIS This is not Verity's home.

Francis pushes his food away.

FRANCIS *(cont'd)* My throat's afire. Get Mrs Tabb to fetch me a posset.

ELIZABETH She's unwell. All the servants are unwell.

AUNT AGATHA I am not unwell. Ninety-three – and the appetite of girl of twenty!

Aunt Agatha reaches across for Francis's plate and begins to tuck in heartily. Geoffrey Charles is rubbing his throat which is obviously painful.

AUNT AGATHA If Verity were here she'd prescribe honey and licorice.

FRANCIS Dr Choake prescribes leeches.

ELIZABETH I've no faith in Dr Choake.

FRANCIS Nor I. And even less in Verity.

CUT TO:

10: INT. NAMPARA HOUSE, LIBRARY – NIGHT 60

Demelza watches Ross warily as he reads Verity's letter. Will he be reminded of her part in Verity's elopement? Now he finishes it. His coolness continues.

ROSS Verity seems content.

He hands the letter back to Demelza.

ROSS *(cont'd)* So your experiment ended well.

DEMELZA And yours?

ROSS Carnmore?

Demelza nods.

ROSS *(cont'd)* Our hopes are pinned on tomorrow's auction. We have scraped together enough capital to bid high. If we get sufficient copper, we'll survive. If we had more capital we'd stand a better chance.

DEMELZA I wish to help. Let me help. *(then)* We could raise a mortgage on Nampara?

ROSS Already raised.

DEMELZA You could sell my brooch – an' my best frock—

ROSS By no means. We're not yet so desperate that I must steal the gown off your back!

DEMELZA But I would feel better – if I could somehow make amends—

Ross begins to feel he's been too harsh. He takes her hand.

ROSS You've done penance enough.

She smiles, relieved. An uneasy truce is signed.

CUT TO:

11: EXT. NAMPARA HOUSE – DAY 61

In the bleak light of a cold spring day Ross prepares his horse to leave for Truro. Demelza, with Julia in her arms, is in optimistic mood.

ROSS I will be home tomorrow. Tonight I will stay at the Red Lion.

DEMELZA 'Twill go well at the auction. You'll win your bids – get all the copper you need – and Carnmore will be safe!

ROSS That's certainly my aim.

Ross kisses her, then Julia, mounts his horse and rides off.

CUT TO:

12: EXT. NAMPARA VALLEY – DAY 61

Riding out of Nampara Valley Ross meets Dwight hurrying towards Sawle village. Dwight tries to look cheerful but he is pale and his good looks have become cadaverous.

ROSS You're wasting away!

DWIGHT I've no time for feasting!

ROSS Since Keren's death you take no care of yourself—

DWIGHT Since her husband's exile, I try to care for those he left behind. *(then)* You've had word of him?

ROSS Safe and well in France – with no plans to return. So you may cease to lash yourself into a frenzy of work—

DWIGHT May I? With this latest epidemic?

ROSS The putrid throat?

DWIGHT I'm struggling to contain it. Whole families have gone under—

ROSS If the poor were better fed and housed—

DWIGHT It's no respecter of privilege. Choake has been summoned to Trenwith.

ROSS *(suddenly alarmed)* Who has it there?

DWIGHT All of them, I believe.

ROSS Can you not call?

DWIGHT They're Choake's patients, he'd resent my interference. Besides, I lay no claim to a cure. Sometimes the weak survive and the strong go under.

Ross hesitates. What could he possibly achieve? Then concern gets the better of him. He turns his horse and gallops for Trenwith.

CUT TO:

13: EXT. TRENWITH HOUSE, DRIVE – DAY 61

Ross arrives at the gates of Trenwith, then hesitates. Given Francis's hostility, it's out of the question for him to go further. Then he sees Dr Choake coming down the drive. Choake is not pleased to see him.

DR CHOAKE Stand aside, Mr Poldark. We are on urgent business.

ROSS And I won't detain you. I came to enquire after the family. Is it the putrid throat?

DR CHOAKE Morbus strangulatorius? What fool gave you that idea?

Ross restrains himself from making a sharp retort.

DR CHOAKE *(cont'd)* We have isolated the symptoms, we have applied remedies – and they are all on the mend.

ROSS So soon?

DR CHOAKE 'Tis merely a question of competent treatment, sir.

Ross remains, staring up at the windows of Trenwith. As he turns to leave, Elizabeth comes to the window. He's already turned and doesn't see her.

CUT TO:

14: INT. TRENWITH HOUSE, TURRET ROOM – DAY 61

Elizabeth watches Ross riding away. Francis is vomiting into a bowl. Elizabeth, pale, sweating but shivering, is trying to comfort Geoffrey Charles. All of them look deathly – and not remotely 'on the mend'.

CUT TO:

15: EXT. RED LION INN – DAY 61

A bustle of activity outside the inn. Agents, mine owners, smelting company managers gather for the auction. Ross arrives and encounters Tonkin and Henshawe on his way in. They exchange looks which say 'It's make or break for us today.'

CUT TO:

16: INT. RED LION INN – DAY 61

The auction is under way. Glancing round among the usual suspects (including Sir John Trevaunance, Tonkin, Johnson, Henshawe,

Zacky, Blight), Ross is surprised to see George present. George gives Ross an affable wave. Ross forces himself to acknowledge it.

CHAIRMAN I have next to dispose of a dole of ore from United Mines. Fifty tons.

He surveys the batch of tickets. The clerk enters the bids in a ledger. Presently . . .

CHAIRMAN Sold to the South Wales Smelting Company for seven pounds sixteen shillings a ton.

Ross looks steadily at his hands. Tonkin and Sir John Trevaunance make sounds of frustration and annoyance.

CUT TO:

17: EXT. NAMPARA VALLEY – DAY 61

Demelza is giving Julia her lunch when Jinny arrives, looking anxious.

DEMELZA *(to Julia)* Do you want some bread?

JINNY Ee've heard th' news from Trenwith?

DEMELZA *(alarmed)* Tell me?

CUT TO:

18: INT. RED LION INN – DAY 61

The ticketing continues. George is watching Ross like a hawk but Ross's expression gives nothing away.

CHAIRMAN Wheal Busy. Parcel of red copper. Forty-five tons.

The tickets are opened, the bids entered. Tension mounts.

CHAIRMAN Sold to the South Wales Smelting Company for eight pounds four shillings a ton.

Ross's expression remains impassive. Johnson and Tonkin hiss their frustration. George clears his throat and stifles a smile.

CUT TO:

19: INT. NAMPARA HOUSE, KITCHEN – DAY 61

Demelza is horrified to hear Jinny's news.

DEMELZA All the servants ill? Not one fit to tend 'em?

JINNY An' Dr Choake called away to Truro an' not back till mornin'—

CUT TO:

20: INT. RED LION INN – DAY 61

Ross's expression is dark but inscrutable. Tonkin and Sir John Trevaunance are unable to suppress their frustration. George is struggling to contain his satisfaction.

CHAIRMAN Wheal Leisure. Forty tons.

A few people glance at Ross. The Chairman opens the tickets. The Clerk enters the bids in a ledger. The tension is almost palpable.

CHAIRMAN *(cont'd)* Wheal Leisure ore is sold to the South Wales Smelting Company for seven pounds nineteen shillings a ton.

Ross's expression remains impassive. George is struggling not to look smug.

CHAIRMAN *(cont'd)* And that concludes the auction for today. Thank you, gentlemen.

The auction breaks up. George strolls out, whistling. The room empties amidst murmurs of dissatisfaction. Ross, Sir John Trevaunance and Tonkin remain.

CUT TO:

21: INT. NAMPARA HOUSE, KITCHEN – DAY 61

Demelza sits, determined not to go. She sighs, then:

DEMELZA *(cont'd)* If I'm not back by nightfall, see Julia's milk be boiled and she be put to bed.

Jinny nods. Demelza kisses Julia tenderly, hands her to Jinny and goes out.

CUT TO:

22: INT. RED LION INN – DAY 61

Tonkin, Sir John Trevaunance, Johnson and Ross gather round the auction table.

TONKIN Are we all that remain?

ROSS The Warleggans have been most efficient.

The empty room tells its own story.

TONKIN I call to order this meeting of the Carnmore Copper Company.

ROSS *(impatient)* Proceed, sir.

TONKIN I have to report that today, yet again, we got no copper.

No one speaks.

TONKIN *(cont'd)* And since the prospect seems unlikely to change—

ROSS We bow to the inevitable?

They all glance at each other. No one voices an objection. Then:

TONKIN It is with extreme regret that I declare the Carnmore Copper Company dissolved.

It's a bitter blow for Ross and he struggles to contain his disappointment.

CUT TO:

23: EXT. RED LION INN – DAY 61

On his way out, Ross bumps into George, who is all charm and affability.

GEORGE Ross! You're becoming a hermit! Margaret was only saying how much she's missed you at our little gaming parties.

ROSS I've no time for cards these days.

GEORGE Cousin Matthew will be sad to hear that.

It's a deliberate provocation. Ross, not trusting himself to reply, continues down the street. George follows, continuing to accompany Ross, chatting affably to him as if they were the best of friends.

GEORGE You know Margaret's on her third lord? I don't know how, but she sucks the life out of her lovers!

ROSS Her instinct for survival is voracious.

GEORGE And you should know! *(then)* She told me she'd once had a fancy to marry you.

ROSS Not you?

GEORGE My sights are set somewhat higher.

George continues to stroll beside Ross.

GEORGE And how is your wife? She was much remarked on at the last ball. You should bring her out more.

ROSS We've no time for socializing.

GEORGE The smelting company keeps you busy?

ROSS Wheal Leisure.

GEORGE Ah, yes. One of the few mines which still offer prospects for the investor. I believe some shares are shortly coming onto the market.

ROSS And whose are they?

GEORGE I understood them to be yours.

Ross halts in amazement. Alarmed by his hostile demeanour, George backs off.

GEORGE *(cont'd)* But perhaps I was misinformed.

ROSS You were.

He walks off.

CUT TO:

24: EXT. TRENWITH HOUSE – DAY 61

The house looks dark and cold and no one answers the door when Demelza knocks. When there is no reply to her second knock, she tries the door. It's unlocked and swings back with a creak. Inside, the hall is cheerless and gloomy.

CUT TO:

25: INT. TRENWITH HOUSE, GREAT HALL – DAY 61

The shadows of the afternoon are heavy and oppressive. Demelza's breath is white in the frosty air. Absolute silence reigns.

The family portraits on the walls are dark and glowering. Demelza walks through the hall. The house is absolutely silent.

CUT TO:

26: INT. TRENWITH HOUSE, OAK ROOM – DAY 61

A weak shaft of sunlight falls on a portrait of Elizabeth. The rest of the room is in shadow. Demelza is revealed, peering round, in search of signs of life. There are none. She shudders and hurries out.

CUT TO:

27: INT. TRENWITH HOUSE, GREAT HALL – DAY 61

Coming back into the Great Hall, Demelza hears a shuffling noise and, looking up into the gloom, sees Aunt Agatha on the balcony, peering down into the Great Hall.

AUNT AGATHA Verity? Is that you?

DEMELZA No – it's Demelza—

AUNT AGATHA Ross's little bud?

DEMELZA I came to enquire—

AUNT AGATHA They're sick – every last jack of 'em – and who's to care for 'em with Verity gone? She'd no business to go – her duty's here. 'Twas a selfish, cruel thing, she did, to leave us like that—

From a room close by comes the sound of a hoarse, hacking cough. Demelza jumps up and follows the sound.

CUT TO:

28: EXT. TRURO HARBOUR – DAY 61

Ross has reached the road by the harbour. George is still in pursuit.

GEORGE It goes without saying I would offer a generous price.

Ross halts. He's had enough. Summoning up all his politeness:

ROSS I've no control over my partners. You could approach one of them.

A big moment between them. Neither will back down. Then:

GEORGE What is it that offends you, Ross? That we Warleggans have dared to drag ourselves out of poverty and aspire to gentility?

ROSS Poverty doesn't offend me, George. Nor does aspiration. But you're mistaken if you think greed and exploitation are the marks of a gentleman.

He's about to walk off. George detains him, as if out of brotherly concern.

GEORGE You know, one of these days you'll find yourself without means, without colleagues, without friends. And no one to blame but yourself.

Ross is determined not to lose his cool. He eyeballs George. Then, with supreme self-control:

ROSS Good day to you, George.

Ross walks off. Despite himself, George is impressed.

On Ross as he walks down the harbour and looks out at the ships. He then sees a brand new, impressive, brigantine – the Queen Charlotte *– being loaded with goods. Beside it, Matthew Sanson and Cary Warleggan are in conversation with its captain, Captain Bray and a young army sergeant Sergeant Tremayne (who is there with a company of soldiers).*

Ross is amazed – and outraged – to see Sanson back in town after his recent disgrace. He walks on.

CUT TO:

29: INT. TRENWITH HOUSE, ELIZABETH'S ROOM – DAY 61

A brazier of disinfectant herbs is burning smokily. Francis lies in the bed. Geoffrey Charles is in a small cot-bed, and Elizabeth, shivering but sweating, dropping with exhaustion, sits beside him. As the door opens, she barely has the strength to look up.

ELIZABETH *(in disbelief)* Demelza— ?

DEMELZA I came to see if I could help.

ELIZABETH Oh – how kind of you! I'm in despair – my poor little boy—

Demelza comes over to look at Geoffrey Charles. He is struggling for breath, every intake sounds raw and painful, his face is flushed, his eyes half-open, there are red spots on his neck and one hand keeps opening and closing as he breathes.

ELIZABETH *(cont'd)* He has these – spasms – then he vomits – and there's relief – but only for a time – then it begins again—

As Demelza looks at Elizabeth, she feels overpowering compassion.

DEMELZA You're sick yourself, Elizabeth. You did ought to be in bed.

ELIZABETH I cannot leave my boy—

DEMELZA I'll stay with him—

Elizabeth looks as if she can't believe what she's hearing.

DEMELZA *(cont'd)* I'll stay and look after you all.

ELIZABETH Oh Demelza – oh bless you—

Elizabeth bursts into tears of gratitude and relief.

CUT TO:

30: INT. WARLEGGAN HOUSE, BALLROOM – DAY 61

Loud eruptions of drunken laughter. George, Cary and Sanson are entertaining themselves – and Margaret – with thought of the collapse of Ross's venture.

SANSON *(laughing)* The man imagined he could drive up copper prices!

CARY *(laughing)* And get a 'fairer deal' for the mines!

GEORGE And so he did. Till we became wise and outbid him.

MARGARET And now?

SANSON His smelting works stand idle—

CARY Copper prices will fall again—

SANSON He'll be left with enormous debts—

GEORGE And no obvious means to discharge them.

MARGARET *(to George)* Perhaps he will throw himself upon your mercy?

GEORGE He may try!

They all guffaw with laughter.

GEORGE Excuse me . . .

George gets up to leave.

CUT TO:

31: INT. PASCOE'S BANK – NIGHT 61

Pascoe shows Ross into his office and offers him a chair.

PASCOE It must be galling.

ROSS To have nothing but debt to show for twelve months hard labour?

PASCOE Bad enough. But to see your assets now in enemy hands – *(seeing Ross look puzzled)* The smelting works? On Trevaunance land?

ROSS What d'you hear?

PASCOE That Sir John – after battling against the wind for months – is now preparing to sail with it.

ROSS By selling to the Warleggans.

PASCOE He must cover his losses.

ROSS While the rest of us go bankrupt?

Pascoe nods nervously. Ross can scarcely believe what he's hearing. Can things possibly get any worse?

CUT TO:

32: INT. TRENWITH HOUSE, ELIZABETH'S ROOM – NIGHT 61

Elizabeth is lying in the bed where Francis is sleeping fitfully. Geoffrey Charles's cot-bed is now beside the large bed. Demelza carries Geoffrey Charles and puts him into it, so he can be close to Elizabeth.

ELIZABETH If the servants had not been so ill – but Choake says half the village is down—

DEMELZA Ssssshhhh. You ought to rest.

Francis stirs in his sleep, awakens without opening his eyes.

FRANCIS *(hoarse)* Who is it?

ELIZABETH Demelza. She's come to help us.

Francis is silent a moment. Then, with supreme effort – and sincerity:

FRANCIS It is good of her to overlook past quarrels.

And Elizabeth's look of gratitude seems to echo these sentiments.

CUT TO:

33: INT. PASCOE'S BANK – NIGHT 61

The painful meeting with Pascoe continues.

ROSS So my own debts? In addition to the mortgage on Nampara?

PASCOE Around nine hundred pounds.

ROSS More than I feared.

PASCOE You have assets.

ROSS My shares in Wheal Leisure.

PASCOE I was approached only yesterday by a man named Cole—

ROSS Cole—

PASCOE With a good offer. One that would clear all your debts.

ROSS For all my shares?

PASCOE I got the impression he'd go even higher.

ROSS Oh, he would. On behalf of his master. *(beat)* George Warleggan.

PASCOE As you once remarked, 'Beggars cannot be choosers.'

ROSS This time I can. *(beat)* The Warleggans have a habit of buying up mines and closing them down just to suppress competition to their own holdings. I'll be damned if I let that happen to Wheal Leisure.

PASCOE So—

ROSS I require capital of one thousand pounds. *(beat)* Without security.

Pascoe's face expresses utter disbelief.

CUT TO:

34: INT. TRENWITH HOUSE, BEDROOM – NIGHT 61

Steam rises from a bowl of hot water. Demelza applies a hot compress to Geoffrey Charles's throat. Elizabeth moans. Demelza applies a cold compress to Elizabeth's forehead. Then she becomes aware of Francis, now awake, watching her. She mixes him a concoction of honey, licorice and blackcurrant and brings it over.

DEMELZA 'Twill ease the rawness.

He takes it from her and sips it gratefully. He glances at Geoffrey Charles, whose breathing is harsh and grating.

FRANCIS Will he die?

DEMELZA Not if I can help it.

Francis nods. He believes her. Geoffrey Charles moans deliriously. Demelza hastens to his side and applies another compress to his throat. She knows it's going to be a long night.

CUT TO:

35: EXT. TRURO HARBOUR – DAY 62

Early morning. Truro Harbour GVs.

Ross stands watching Sanson give instructions to Captain Bray for the loading of the Queen Charlotte. *As Ross watches, Sanson is joined by George and Cary. They seem in high spirits and full of optimism. Now Ross is approached by Pascoe.*

ROSS Any luck?

PASCOE Would I call it that? To saddle a man with a 12-month loan at interest of 40 per cent?

Ross gives a low whistle. It's higher than he expected.

PASCOE *(cont'd)* I urge you to reconsider. Start again, rather than plunge in so deep there might be no getting out.

ROSS I'll take my chance.

PASCOE The odds are against you.

He indicates the Warleggans below.

ROSS I know it. *(then)* And should I doubt it, the sight of Matthew Sanson parading about like a prize cockerel – permitted to trade and socialize as if his integrity were not in tatters—

PASCOE Who's to gainsay him? The Warleggans are complete masters of the district.

ROSS And this ship?

PASCOE Their latest venture.

ROSS They seem pleased with her.

PASCOE They consider her their flagship enterprise.

ROSS And themselves unassailable.

Pascoe nods.

CUT TO:

36: EXT. NAMPARA VALLEY – DUSK 62

Dusk is gathering as Ross rides home. Suddenly, up ahead, he sees a cloaked figure scurrying. He spurs on his horse to overtake. It's Demelza.

ROSS You shouldn't be out alone after dark. Poverty breeds desperate men.

He offers her his hand and pulls her up onto the horse in front of him. She huddles gratefully against his chest.

DEMELZA You have news?

ROSS It will keep.

CUT TO:

37: INT. NAMPARA HOUSE, KITCHEN – NIGHT 62

Ross and Demelza have supper. Ross has Julia on his knee.

ROSS *(cont'd)* There's sickness at Trenwith.

DEMELZA *(nods)* Geoffrey Charles had it worst – but I b'lieve the crisis is past.

ROSS That's a relief. I may never forgive Francis but I'd not wish the putrid throat on my worst enemy.

They continue to eat in silence a while, then . . .

DEMELZA Ross—

ROSS Yes?

DEMELZA I swore I would never keep secrets from you again—

ROSS And so?

DEMELZA I – went – *(beat)* To Trenwith.

ROSS But they turned you away.

DEMELZA No. *(beat)* I stayed all last night.

ROSS In God's name, why?

DEMELZA Ross, I had to. They were all so sick – an' the servants – they had no one to tend them – an' Geoffrey Charles so weak – an' twice I thought him gone – but this morning he brought round – an' Dr Choake says the worst is now over—

ROSS I cannot believe you would do such a—

DEMELZA What would you have done?

ROSS I?

DEMELZA What did you do? For Jim Carter?

It's the best thing she could have said. Ross is silent a while, then . . .

ROSS You're right. It was a kind and generous act. Perhaps in a fortnight I shall be in a mood to appreciate it.

CUT TO:

38: EXT. NAMPARA VALLEY – NIGHT 62

A thunderstorm.

CUT TO:

39: INT. NAMPARA HOUSE, ROSS & DEMELZA'S BEDROOM – NIGHT 62

Ross is sleeping fitfully. He opens his eyes suddenly. Somewhere he can hear the thin plaintive cry of a sick child. He turns to look for Demelza but she is not beside him. He sits bolt upright in bed. Demelza is walking up and down with Julia in her arms, trying to settle her. Demelza looks deathly.

ROSS You'll catch a chill. Put on your gown.

DEMELZA No, I'm hot. 'Tis she that's cold.

ROSS Bring her to bed.

Demelza brings Julia to the bed. Ross peers closely at her. Julia is awake but her face is flushed and there is a rash around her throat. Her whimpering seems to end in a sudden dry cough.

Ross takes Julia from Demelza and puts her into their bed.

DEMELZA *(cont'd)* My throat is dry. I'll get some water.

Demelza pours herself some water, drinks it, pours some more, drinks it all. Ross watches her closely. She sways slightly, puts her hand up to her head. Ross leaps out of bed, comes to look at her, eyes at her closely. She hardly dares to tell him her suspicions.

ROSS What is it?

DEMELZA My neck is swollen—

ROSS You have a rash.

Demelza looks at him in anguish. They both know the terrible truth.

CUT TO:

40: EXT. MINGOOSE COTTAGE – NIGHT 62

Ross hammers at Dwight's door. Dwight opens it, anxious at this late-night visit, takes one look at Ross's face and fears the worst.

CUT TO:

41: INT. NAMPARA HOUSE, ROSS & DEMELZA'S BEDROOM – NIGHT 62

A fire has been lit. Demelza lies in the freshly made bed. Ross is nursing Julia. Dwight is examining Demelza's throat and neck. He tries to look calm and unconcerned. He signals to Ross to follow him out. Ross hands Julia to Jinny, then follows Dwight.

CUT TO:

42: INT. NAMPARA HOUSE, PARLOUR – NIGHT 62

Dwight comes into the parlour, followed by Ross.

DWIGHT They both have it. The symptoms are unmistakable.

ROSS How bad will it be?

DWIGHT If they get through the night?

ROSS Dear God – surely— ?

DWIGHT The acute kind. There's no reliable treatment.

ROSS What can I do?

DWIGHT Pray?

CUT TO:

43: INT. NAMPARA HOUSE, ROSS & DEMELZA'S BEDROOM – NIGHT 62

Ross sits beside Demelza, holding her hand, as she moans in her sleep. Her condition has worsened.

CUT TO:

44: INT. NAMPARA HOUSE, KITCHEN – NIGHT 62

Dwight is tending to Julia, who is flushed and sweating.
CUT TO:

45: INT. NAMPARA HOUSE (NIGHTMARE MONTAGE) NIGHT 62

Demelza keeps drifting in and out of consciousness; people and sounds and images fade in and out of focus. She's not sure what is real and what is nightmare.

ON ROSS: Looking anxiously at her.

ROSS *(looking anxiously at her)* Can you hear me, my love? Can you hear me?

ON DWIGHT

DWIGHT *(peering closely at her)* Demelza? Try to drink this – just a sip—

ROSS She won't take it—

ON DWIGHT

DWIGHT The fever's worsening—

ON ROSS

ROSS But you can save her?

ON TOM CARNE

TOM CARNE *(glaring at her)* Saved? Are ye saved, daughter? Are ye saved? Are ye saved?

ON FRANCIS

FRANCIS Saved from what? An impudent trull like that?

ON DWIGHT

DWIGHT We must get her to drink something—

ON TOM CARNE

TOM CARNE Drink? Drink is the devil's work! Turn away, daughter. Coom 'ome an' live a clean an' pure life—

ON DWIGHT

DWIGHT There's little more I can do.

ON ROSS

ROSS You must fight, my love – you must fight—

ON TOM CARNE

TOM CARNE *(brandishing his fists)* Fight me, fight me? Coom on, then, coom on—

ON JINNY

JINNY Corn! We must 'ave corn! 'Ow else we meant a' feed our starvin' chillun?

ON MATTHEW SANSON

SANSON Fifteen shillings a bushel! Fifteen shillings! And not a penny less!

ON ROSS

ROSS Oh, Demelza, do not underestimate the scale of your ignorance – your arrogance – your utter disregard for truth and consequence—

ON DWIGHT

DWIGHT She's fading – she's fading – oh dear God—

ON ROSS

ROSS What can I do?

ON ELIZABETH

ELIZABETH *(smiling)* Let go, my dear. Let go. I'll take care of Ross. You know he would rather be with me . . .

CUT TO:

46: INT. NAMPARA HOUSE, ROSS & DEMELZA'S BEDROOM – NIGHT 62

Ross is holding Demelza's hand as she continues to moan and toss in her sleep. Dwight comes into the room. His face is white. Ross knows instantly that something is terribly wrong.

CUT TO:

47: INT. NAMPARA HOUSE, PARLOUR – NIGHT 62

Ross is in shock. His face is ashen. It's as if he is incapable of express-ing the depths of his grief. Dwight, by contrast, is inconsolable.

DWIGHT Forgive me – forgive me – I cannot save her.

We pull back to reveal Ross cradling the dying Julia in his arms.

ROSS I will stay with her. I would not have her be afraid.

Close in on Julia's tiny hand, the ribbon around her wrist, clutching Ross's finger.

CUT TO:

48: INT. NAMPARA HOUSE, ROSS & DEMELZA'S BEDROOM – NIGHT 62

Demelza is sleeping fitfully, from time to time moaning.

DEMELZA *(almost inaudible)* Julia . . . Julia . . .

Presently the door opens and Ross returns. As if on automatic pilot now, he resumes his place beside her, takes her hand again and con-

tinues his vigil. In his hand he holds Julia's ribbon. He is numb with grief, his face devoid of expression. As we go in closer, his face seems to harden further.

CUT TO:

49: EXT. NAMPARA COVE – DAWN 63

A day later. The bleakest of dawns. Storm clouds looming. Waves crashing violently onto rocks.

CUT TO:

50: EXT. CLIFF-TOP PATH – DAY 63

An ashen-faced Ross carries the tiny coffin of his daughter along the cliff-top towards Sawle church. Dwight walks beside him.

They walk in silence, Ross stares ahead and moves as if in a trance.

CUT TO:

51: EXT. SAWLE CHURCH – DAY 63

Ross and Dwight arrive at Sawle church. To Ross's amazement, a huge crowd awaits him: Zacky, Mrs Zacky and the rest of the Martins; Paul and Beth Daniel and all their children; Connie and her daughters; Jud and Prudie; Horace Treneglos; Sir Hugh Bodrugan; Tonkin; Blewitt; Henshawe; Mrs Henshawe; Sir John Trevaunance; Pascoe . . . scores and scores more local miners, local farmers, local fishermen . . . Ross is struggling to hold back tears now but he knows he must; if he gives way to his feelings he will fall apart. As he walks on, his exhaustion overcomes him, he stumbles. A hand comes out to steady him. He glances up – and sees it belongs to Francis. A huge moment between them. Francis looks haunted, fragile and pale – but no longer hostile. His gesture is so unexpected, Ross is unable to digest it here. As he walks on, he is lost in the crowd of mourners who close ranks and stand beside him in his grief.

CUT TO:

52: INT. WARLEGGAN HOUSE, BALLROOM – DAY 63

George is dining with Cary.

CARY Poldark will not be troubling us a while.

GEORGE Because?

CARY He'll be otherwise engaged.

GEORGE With what?

CARY His daughter's burial?

Cary continues to eat, oblivious to the fact that George looks as if he's been punched in the stomach. He's genuinely horrified to hear this news.

CUT TO:

53: INT. NAMPARA HOUSE, ROSS & DEMELZA'S BEDROOM – DAY 63

Ross, just returned from the burial, sits beside the unconscious, still feverish Demelza, holding her hand. Dwight comes in. Ross seems barely aware of him. It's as if he's still in a trance, unaware of anything and anyone around him.

DWIGHT You should try to rest.

ROSS *(as if he hasn't heard)* I should have provided for them.

DWIGHT Who?

ROSS It's the custom after a burial. This winter's been savage – and the least I could've done was fed and watered them.

DWIGHT Who would expect it? They know of Demelza's illness and—

ROSS Everything I touch is cursed.

DWIGHT You cannot believe that.

ROSS So many came.

DWIGHT Yes.

ROSS So many.

DWIGHT They care for you.

ROSS I should have provided for them.

Dwight comes over to check on Demelza.

DWIGHT There's no change. For worse or for better. You should take some air. And then sleep.

CUT TO:

54: EXT. NAMPARA COVE – DAY 63

The waves pound against the rocks.

CUT TO:

55: EXT. NAMPARA VALLEY – DAY 63

Ross sets off towards Hendrawna Beach. Everything is cold and bleak and desolate. The wind is rising and storm clouds gathering. Ross is almost dropping with exhaustion. But he refuses to go under.

Ross stands on the beach letting his face be battered by the wind. The waves are huge. He can hardly see in front of him. He is deafened by the roaring of the wind. But he will not retreat and he will not give way to his feelings. Then, as he stares out to sea, something takes him by surprise. For a moment he thinks he's imagining it.

HIS POV: In the distance, a shape looms out of the spray, tossed by waves: a ship being driven towards the rocks at the far edge of Hendrawna Beach. It's too far off for us to make out its name but Ross seems to recognize it. For a moment he is transfixed. A multitude of thoughts and feelings rush in on him. Predominant amongst them is grim satisfaction. Revenge, if not sweet, is at least balm to his pain. But then another more practical thought occurs. He turns and runs back towards Nampara.

CUT TO:

56: INT. WARLEGGAN HOUSE, LIBRARY – DAY 63

George stands at the window, looking troubled. Presently Cary hands him a glass of port.

CARY The maiden voyage of the *Queen Charlotte.*

Absentmindedly George takes it. Cary raises a glass. George's attention is elsewhere.

CARY *(cont'd)* The demise of the Carnmore Copper Company.

George is roused out of his reverie and halfheartedly raises his glass.

CARY *(cont'd)* And its chief architect.

CUT TO:

57: EXT. NAMPARA VALLEY, CORNWALL – DAY 63

Establishers.

CUT TO:

58: EXT. NAMPARA HOUSE, COURTYARD – DAY 63

As Ross hurries his horse out of the stable, Dwight comes out, takes one look at Ross's expression and looks concerned.

DWIGHT Something amiss?

ROSS Far from it.

Ross mounts his horse.

ROSS *(cont'd)* Yesterday I omitted to provide for the mourners. Today that will be remedied.

Ross gallops off.

CUT TO:

59: EXT. MELLIN COTTAGES – DAY 63

The village seems quiet. As Ross gallops up, the first person he sees is Jud, slumped outside his cottage, in a drunken stupor, snoring.

ROSS Jud! Jud, wake up!

JUD Gor damme! If a man's not king of 'is own blathering 'ouse—

ROSS There's a wreck, Jud!

JUD *(barely awake)* Where? Where's she struck?

ROSS Hendrawna Beach. Go and rouse the others. I'll to Sawle and Marazanvose.

JUD Why bring in all they?

ROSS She's a prize of a ship. Carrying food. There'll be pickings for all.

But seeing Jud appears incapable of rousing anyone, Ross rides off to warn the others. Jud settles back to sleep again.

Ross rides up to the Martin house.

ROSS *(shouting)* Zacky! Zacky! Hendrawna Beach! There's a wreck!

He shouts to the next cottage.

ROSS *(cont'd)* Paul! Go rouse the village!

People are now rushing out of their cottages, Zacky appears.

ZACKY What is she?

ROSS A brigantine. Grain aboard – pilchards – enough to fill your bellies for a month!

ZACKY How do 'ee know?

ROSS I know who owns her.

Ross smiles grimly and rides off.

CUT TO:

60: EXT. HENDRAWNA BEACH – DAY 63

Ross returns to the beach to see the boat has run aground on some distant rocks and turned over. Behind Ross the first villagers come streaming down onto the beach carrying axes, baskets, buckets, empty sacks.

Villagers (Zacky, Paul, Jud among them) line the beach, waiting by the surf for the first cargo to be washed in.

JUD How long mun we wait? Me gizzards is rumblin'.

ROSS You'll be fed soon enough.

Zacky glances at Ross. There's a savage satisfaction in his tone. The first tangles of wreckage – barrels, masts, coils of rope, sacks of corn – are now visible, bobbing away from the ship, being carried towards the shore.

ROSS Paul, Zacky – get fires going. Tell the women to form a line – keep the children clear.

With barely a moment's hesitation, Ross's instructions are acted upon. Paul and Zacky instruct Mrs Zacky and Beth Daniel and the other women, while Ross waits with the other men at the water's edge.

CUT TO:

61: INT. WARLEGGAN HOUSE, LIBRARY – DAY 63

George and Cary are going through some accounts when a servant comes in and hands Cary a note. He reads it.

CARY Hellfire and damnation!

He thrusts the note at George, who reads it.

GEORGE It cannot be!

They're both on their feet now – agitated, angry. Then . . .

CARY Hendrawna Beach? Isn't that— ?

GEORGE Poldark land.

Stung into action, George strides out of the room.

CUT TO:

62: EXT. HENDRAWNA BEACH – DAY 63

As the first barrels of cargo come bobbing towards the shallows, Nick Vigus dives in, seizes one, drags it ashore – and comes face to face with Ross. Ross takes the barrel from him – and before Nick can protest, shoulders it and carries it to where the women and children are lined up, waiting. Ross wields an axe and splits the barrel open. It contains pilchards. A cry of delight breaks out from the women.

ROSS *(to Mrs Zacky)* Feed the children first. There'll be plenty for all later.

Mrs Zacky nods. No one would dare argue with Ross today.

CUT TO:

63: INT. WARLEGGAN HOUSE, BALLROOM – DAY 63

Cary has just received an update from Hendrawna Beach.

CARY These people should hang! Give me a rope and I'll do it myself!

George seems preoccupied. Could it really be that he has some sympathy for Ross and his loss? Cary, however, is immune to such sensibilities.

CARY *(cont'd)* Captain Bray must testify—

GEORGE To what?

CARY The plunder and lawlessness! Or better still, Matthew. He can testify against Poldark—

GEORGE Always assuming he witnesses—

CARY Whether or not he witnesses! Good God, boy. You don't suggest we wait for actual evidence? *(then)* Matthew is a gentleman. He is a Warleggan – worth two of any Poldarks and his word will carry twice the weight. And I'll be damned if we don't turn this debacle to our advantage!

CUT TO:

64: EXT. HENDRAWNA BEACH – DAY 63

Kegs of rum, brandy and pilchards are washed in. On the beach fires are blazing, pilchards are cooking, children are being fed. A keg of rum is broken open and men and women rush forward with jugs and cups and drink it greedily. Ross smiles with grim satisfaction as a woman comes past, straining under a sack of flour, followed by another carrying a barrel of salt; Nick Vigus is dragging a dead pig; Paul Daniel is carrying a case of tea. Other villagers are carrying firewood, baskets of wet coal, dead chickens, more salt. Ross shoulders a barrel and brings it ashore to break it open.

CUT TO:

65: EXT. WARLEGGAN HOUSE, LIBRARY – DAY 63

George and Cary are thoughtful. Cary is thinking ahead. George, for once, is not.

CARY Do we think he'll be there?

GEORGE If the reports are true—

CARY Of his daughter?—

GEORGE He may not be in the mood for plunder.

CARY There again, he may.

GEORGE And if he is?

CARY He'll be caught in the act.

George, for once, does not seem hell-bent on pursuing Ross at all costs. At least not in view of Ross's recent loss. But Cary has no such scruples.

CUT TO:

66: EXT. HENDRAWNA BEACH – DAY 63

Ross is dragging in more cargo, helped by Zacky, Paul, Nick and various other men. Suddenly Jud comes staggering up.

JUD Cap'n Ross! Cap'n Ross! 'Ey be comin' from 'Luggan—

ROSS Who?

JUD Why, th' blathering miners! 'Ey see'd th' boat from the cliffs an' followed 'er all the way along th' coast to 'ere!

Panic and consternation begins to break out among the people on the beach.

ZACKY They'll be wantin' a piece of 'er, that's certain!

PAUL We'll giv 'em a bastin'! We bamfered 'em once, we can do it again!

ZACKY 'Tis clubbish they are tho'. 'Tis said they'll let men drown, just to 'ave the shirt off their backs.

JUD 'Tedn't right – 'tedn't fit – 'tedn't fair – 'tedn't proper. 'Tes our beach – 'tes our vittles—

Ross remembers the Illuggan miners only too well. He knows he needs to make a plan.

ROSS Clear as much cargo as we can before they arrive. Once they're here, it'll be out of our hands.

They set to with renewed vigour to clear the piles of cargo off the beach. Jud fastens upon a gilt figurehead which has been washed up and drags it away, fending off Prudie, who tries to help.

JUD *(clutching the figurehead)* Mine! Mine! She's all mine! I'll not be parted from 'er!

He runs away with the figurehead, with Prudie in pursuit.

CUT TO:

67: INT. WARLEGGAN HOUSE, HALLWAY – DAY 63

George has summoned young Sergeant Tremayne, who seems rather overawed by the splendour of the house and by the brusque authority of its owner.

GEORGE The situation is grave. I'm given to understand there's a serious risk to the passengers and crew—

SERGEANT TREMAYNE From drowning, sir— ?

GEORGE From the rabble on the beach. And since many of the passengers are gentlemen – in particular my own cousin Matthew—

Sergeant Tremayne nods politely, obviously eager to get away.

GEORGE *(cont'd)* Then there's the matter of the cargo.

SERGEANT TREMAYNE 'Tis generally accepted that what's washed ashore is property of the finder—

GEORGE It is property of the Warleggans. And anyone plundering will be guilty of theft.

He hands Sergeant Tremayne a small purse.

GEORGE *(cont'd – pleasantly)* I'm certain we understand each other.

SERGEANT TREMAYNE Indeed we do, sir.

He pockets the money, salutes and goes out.

CUT TO:

68: INT. NAMPARA HOUSE, ROSS & DEMELZA'S BEDROOM – DAY 63

Dwight and Jinny watch Demelza sleeping as the storm rages outside.

DWIGHT I had hoped – I could've sworn she'd come round by now.

JINNY Will she yet, d'ye think?

DWIGHT I wish I could know for certain. *(then)* You should go, Jinny. Help your family at Hendrawna.

JINNY But sur – who's to see to Mistress?

Suddenly there's a knock on the door. Jinny looks surprised. She's clearly not expecting anyone. She goes out to answer it. Dwight remains with Demelza, checking her pulse anxiously. It's so feeble as to be barely there. Presently Jinny returns. She looks a little startled.

JINNY I be off now, sur—

DWIGHT Who was at the door?

JINNY Someone to look after Mistress.

CUT TO:

69: EXT. HENDRAWNA BEACH – DUSK 63

The sky is darkening and the wind howling as Ross loads cargo onto a mule. Nick, Mrs Zacky, Jud and Prudie work side by side with him in silent but purposeful comradeship. Suddenly Paul runs up.

PAUL The 'Luggan miners be 'ere, Ross! Far end o' th' beach.

ROSS *(to Prudie and Mrs Zacky)* Go home – take all the women and children – see your doors be shut and bolted—

JUD Nay, I'll not budge fer no man. 'Tis our cove, 'tis our pickin's—

ROSS Leave 'em to it. They can strip the vessel if they choose. We've had the best of her.

He takes Prudie aside.

ROSS *(cont'd) (low)* Take him home – before his mouth gets him into mischief it can't talk him out of.

PRUDIE Aye, Mister Ross. Lor' bless 'ee, Mister Ross.

A moment of warmth between them. Then Prudie shoves the still mumbling Jud after the other women, who are leading mules and donkeys away. As they go Zacky comes running up.

ZACKY Survivors, Ross! Bein' washed ashore!

ROSS Where?

ZACKY Far side o' th' beach – comin' in on the tide—

JUD *(over his shoulder)* They won' last long! Not wi' 'Luggan's finest t' greet 'em!

ROSS *(to Zacky)* Get everyone off the beach now.

ZACKY What will you do?

ROSS See what I can do for the survivors.

Ross sets off across the beach as if in a trance. As he picks his way through the smoking bonfires and burning pilchard barrels, it occurs to him that this is what hell must be like. Silhouetted against the smoke and flames, nightmarish figures heave across his line of vision: drunken faces – wounded faces – two people struggling over the same bolt of cloth – two more grappling over the same coil of rope – two more with their hands round each other's throats. Manic laughter, angry curses, and, incongruously, the distant sound of a penny whistle. As he continues through this seething mass of humanity, Ross feels no disapproval, judgement or sentimentality. The world is as it is: brutal, cruel, cold and unfeeling. Or perhaps he's just numb with cold and grief. As he presses on, out of the smoke and flames come the first of the Illuggan miners – their faces brutal, drunken, demonic. They push past Ross without acknowledging him, as if he's invisible. The smoke and the flames blind him. The world seems like an inferno. All he can hear is curses, manic laughter, howls of pain. And then, as if from somewhere a long way off, the sound of a voice calling for help.

PASSENGER Help! Help!

Ross seems to snap out of his trance. He runs forward, out of the smoke. In the shallows ahead, he sees something thrashing about. Peering into the darkness he sees two Illuggan miners attacking a drowning man – one of the ship's passengers, who is struggling towards the shore. One miner is trying to hold the man under water while the other is looting the rings off his fingers. Ross rushes into the water. His rage is terrifying. He punches one man, then the other. Then he drags the passenger they've been looting back to the shore. The passenger coughs and splutters. As Ross hits him between the shoulder-blades to try and empty his lungs of water, another figure, face down, is washed up on the shore. Then another. Ross drags this third figure to safety, lays him down on the sand. Only as he turns him over does he realise it's Matthew Sanson.

ROSS Sanson!

Sanson's eyes are wide open. He's already dead. Ross kneels in the shallows, contemplating him. Face to face. The dying rays of the sun light Ross's face. Retribution is sweet. But is it? Try as he might Ross cannot feel anything other than sickened by the loss of a life. Any life. It's a turning point for him. He looks out at the setting sun. Something inside him shifts. He wants to live.

He wants to go on living, even if the pain is excruciating. He lays Sanson carefully on the beach, closes his eyes and walks away.

CUT TO:

70: INT. NAMPARA HOUSE, ROSS & DEMELZA'S BEDROOM – NIGHT 63

Demelza lies, flushed and sweating, moaning softly. A hand places a cool cloth across her forehead. We do not see who it belongs to, only that it's a woman's hand.

CUT TO:

71: EXT. HENDRAWNA BEACH – NIGHT 63

Ross walks up from the beach towards the sand dunes where a bedraggled, shivering group of men – four passengers, Captain Bray and two crewmen – is huddled. As he goes towards them, the crewmen draw knives and Captain Bray lifts his sword.

CAPTAIN BRAY Keep your distance, man! We're armed!

ROSS I was about to offer you shelter.

CAPTAIN BRAY Who are you?

ROSS My name is Poldark. I have a house nearby.

CAPTAIN BRAY Have you no control over these savages here?

ROSS None whatsoever.

CAPTAIN BRAY It's a disgrace. Two years ago I was shipwrecked off Patagonia – and treated less barbarously.

ROSS Perhaps the natives were better fed than these miners.

CAPTAIN BRAY Fed? If it were only food – but the entire cargo has been pillaged and we ourselves barely 'scaped with our lives. It's monstrous.

ROSS There is much in this world which is monstrous.

He now turns to the other passengers.

ROSS *(cont'd)* Those who prefer not to freeze to death, follow me.

The passengers eagerly get up and follow Ross. The crewmen wait to see what Captain Bray will do.

CAPTAIN BRAY How do we know it's not a trap?

ROSS You'll have to take my word for it.

CAPTAIN BRAY The word of a gentleman?

Ross permits himself a savage smile and leads the way on.

CUT TO:

72: EXT. HENDRAWNA DUNES – NIGHT 63

Distant sounds of mayhem fade as Ross leads his bedraggled party away through the dunes. Beyond the ridge, a glimpse of red, glowing ominously, comes from the beach. As they go forward, from the darkness ahead, the outline of a dozen men emerges. Ross goes forward to meet them and is surprised to see a detachment of soldiers, led by Sergeant Tremayne. Captain Bray pushes past Ross to address Sergeant Tremayne.

CAPTAIN BRAY I must get word to Mister Warleggan.

SERGEANT TREMAYNE He's already apprised, sir. 'Twas he who despatched us.

Ross barely has time to react to this news when . . .

CAPTAIN BRAY You'll set about reclaiming our goods from this rabble?

Sergeant Tremayne looks past him, down to the beach, which seems to seethe with a wild and sinister life of its own.

SERGEANT TREMAYNE Never fear, sir. We'll soon restore order.

ROSS I wouldn't count on it.

SERGEANT TREMAYNE I have my orders.

ROSS Then at least wait till daylight. These people are fighting drunk – and quarrelling among themselves. Interfere and they'll turn on you.

SERGEANT TREMAYNE But if we fired into them—

ROSS Not half of you would come out alive.

Sergeant Tremayne nods nervously. He's of a mind to take Ross's advice. Without waiting for his decision, Ross leads his party onwards.

CUT TO:

73: INT. NAMPARA HOUSE, HALLWAY – NIGHT 63

Ross leads the way inside and turns to his party.

ROSS You'll pardon me, gentlemen, but may I ask for quietness? My wife is seriously ill.

The chattering and muttering of the passengers subsides and they follow him into the house in complete silence.

CUT TO:

74: INT. NAMPARA HOUSE, PARLOUR – NIGHT 63

Ross is ushering the passengers into the parlour when Dwight's head pops up from the settee, looking sleepy and confused.

DWIGHT Ross! You're back—

ROSS These men survived the wreck. They will need your attention.

DWIGHT Forgive me, I was trying to sleep—

ROSS Then – who's with Demelza?

CUT TO:

75: INT. NAMPARA HOUSE, ROSS & DEMELZA'S BEDROOM – NIGHT 63

Ross comes into the bedroom and halts in astonishment.

HIS POV: Elizabeth is sitting beside Demelza, applying a compress to her forehead.

For a moment neither Ross nor Elizabeth speaks. It's a huge moment between them. Then . . .

ELIZABETH I was too weak to come to the funeral. But – hearing she was still in danger—

ROSS There was no need.

ELIZABETH She saved my child.

ROSS Yes.

ELIZABETH And lost yours in return.

Ross turns away so she won't see his grief well up again. But she knows only too well what he's feeling.

ELIZABETH *(cont'd)* Oh Ross – my dear, if I can do anything that would make up for—

ROSS You can.

A huge moment between them. For one brief moment, Elizabeth wonders if he will declare himself again. But then . . .

ROSS *(cont'd)* You can pray to God I do not lose the love of my life.

Elizabeth is stunned. Though she knew he had strong feelings for Demelza, the realization that her rival has so completely supplanted her in Ross's heart, is hard to accept. Yet she musters all her strength and concedes defeat.

ELIZABETH Of course.

But Ross seems barely aware of her now. He's sitting beside Demelza, holding her hand, searching her face for signs of recovery.

ROSS *(whispers)* Come back, my love. Come back. Come back—

Elizabeth rises to her feet and softly tiptoes away. At the door she pauses, as if to say goodbye to Ross – though he himself is unaware of it. His attention is glued to Demelza.

HIS POV: Demelza stirs, sighs, takes a deep breath and opens her eyes.

Behind him, unseen, Elizabeth gracefully withdraws.

DEMELZA *(barely audible)* Has she come to take you?

ROSS No, my love. She will never take me.

He takes her hand and covers it with grateful kisses. Demelza closes her eyes again and relapses into sleep.

CUT TO:

76: EXT. HENDRAWNA BEACH/SEA – DAY 64

The grey light of dawn reveals the last vestiges of the wreck – the beach strewn with human debris and a few smouldering fires. Now Ross is revealed, surveying the devastation.

HIS POV: Down at the water's edge, a man watches as a body is loaded onto a cart. The man nods to confirm the man's identity. The body is carried up the beach. The man follows. It's George.

Ross doesn't move. The body – of Matthew Sanson – is being carried right by him. Since George is following, he has no choice but to pass close to Ross. Ross's face is implacable and cold. George's, for once, betrays the emotion he's clearly feeling. He halts.

GEORGE I was sorry to hear of your loss.

Ross doesn't answer.

GEORGE *(cont'd)* The world is a darker place without her.

ROSS And a brighter one without him.

Ross turns to walk away.

GEORGE Could you have saved him?

ROSS Why would I wish to?

GEORGE Common decency?

ROSS He showed none.

GEORGE You insist we are enemies. When in fact we have much in common. And could be allies.

ROSS God forbid I should ever be so desperate.

Ross walks off. George watches him go.

GEORGE You will be.

CUT TO:

77: INT. NAMPARA HOUSE, ROSS & DEMELZA'S BEDROOM – DAY 64

Ross is stroking Demelza's face. She opens her eyes. For a moment Ross isn't sure if she's still delirious.

DEMELZA Where's Julia?

ROSS Ssssshhhh. You've slept a long while. There was a ship-wreck—

DEMELZA Where?

ROSS On Hendrawna Beach.

DEMELZA I've never seen a wreck. *(then)* Where's Julia?

Ross knows he can delay the inevitable no longer. He takes her hand and into her palm lays the ribbon from Julia's wrist. We now see it is embroidered with the name 'Julia Grace'. She stares at it – first in bewilderment, then in horror – then at Ross, seeking the dreaded con-firmation. He nods. (He moves out of her line of vision so that she can see the empty cot.) She looks at him, numb, barely comprehending.

DEMELZA But – I was not with her—

ROSS I was.

DEMELZA Could she tell she was leaving us? Was she afraid?

ROSS She was peaceful. I held her in my arms.

Demelza's face crumples.

DEMELZA Oh Ross—

She buries her head against his chest and weeps. Ross clutches her to him, strokes her head and fights to hold back his own tears.

CUT TO:

78: INT. TRENWITH HOUSE, PARLOUR – DAY 64

Francis carries the frail but recovering Geoffrey Charles into the parlour to sit by Elizabeth on a sofa by the fire. Elizabeth gently covers Geoffrey Charles with a blanket.

She and Francis glance at each other. A fragile kind of peace prevails.

CUT TO:

79: EXT. TRENWITH HOUSE, DRIVE – DAY 64

George is walking up the drive towards the house. We've never seen him quite so vulnerable before. But as he gets closer, we see the emotion begin to drain from his face and his expression begins to harden.

CUT TO:

80: INT. TRENWITH HOUSE, PARLOUR – DAY 64

Aunt Agatha appears.

AUNT AGATHA That upstart's here again.

FRANCIS I really cannot face him. Let him be told we're not recovered.

ELIZABETH I will make our excuses.

She gets up and goes out. Francis remains with Geoffrey Charles.

CUT TO:

81: INT. TRENWITH HOUSE, GREAT HALL – DAY 64

Elizabeth enters to find George has just been admitted.

GEORGE Forgive my intrusion. I was returning from the wreck. No doubt you heard – my cousin Matthew perished.

ELIZABETH I wish there was some consolation I could offer.

GEORGE There is.

He takes her hand and kisses it. Though he keeps his tone light, Elizabeth senses that something has changed.

GEORGE *(cont'd)* These are strange times, Elizabeth. We should no longer stand on ceremony.

ELIZABETH If you say so.

GEORGE Sooner or later we must all declare – for one side or another.

ELIZABETH *(trying to keep things light)* For which side do you declare?

GEORGE For no side. *(beat)* At least, for no man.

Now Elizabeth is rattled. She can no longer pretend to misunderstand George's intentions.

ELIZABETH You must not say this to me, George.

GEORGE Oh, I must. And I do. I will no longer have my feelings misunderstood. Or my intentions. *(beat)* I bid you good day, Elizabeth.

He bows and walks out. Elizabeth remains – deeply alarmed, and secretly rather flattered.

CUT TO:

82: INT. NAMPARA HOUSE, ROSS & DEMELZA'S BEDROOM – DAY 65

Demelza, still weak but feeling a little stronger, sits in a chair beside Julia's empty cot, playing with Julia's ribbon. Pale sunlight warms her. Ross comes and sits beside her. He takes her hand. Neither speaks. Eventually:

DEMELZA I wish – *(hesitates, plays with the ribbon, then)* I wish—

ROSS What do you wish?

DEMELZA That I'd had a chance to say goodbye.

CUT TO:

83: EXT. CLIFF-TOPS – DAY 65

Ross holds Demelza, wrapped in a shawl, in front of him on the horse as it picks its way along the cliff-tops.

CUT TO:

84: EXT. CLIFF-TOPS – DAY 65

Ross and Demelza stand on a cliff overlooking the sea.

DEMELZA Geoffrey Charles is well. We must take heart from that.

ROSS Can you?

DEMELZA *(nods)* And so must you. *(then)* Will you make it up with Francis?

ROSS Even though he betrayed us?

Demelza nods.

ROSS *(cont'd)* You make me ashamed. Your heart is so generous. You always see the good in things. *(then)* I will invite him to join me at Wheal Leisure. Together we shall try to resurrect the fortunes of the Poldark mines. Will that satisfy you?

Demelza smiles her agreement.

DEMELZA So there's hope. And it will not have been for nothing after all.

Now she gets something from her pocket. It's Julia's ribbon. She looks at it a long while. Then she kisses it tenderly. Then she throws it to the winds. The wind catches it, whips it up in a gust, then carries it out to sea. Ross and Demelza stand watching a long while. Then . . .

SERGEANT TREMAYNE'S VOICE Captain Poldark?

Ross and Demelza turn. Sergeant Tremayne is walking towards them. His troop of soldiers are waiting behind him.

SERGEANT TREMAYNE *(to Ross)* I have orders to take you to Truro Jail.

For a moment Ross cannot comprehend what's happening. Then:

ROSS On what charge?

SERGEANT TREMAYNE Wrecking. Inciting a riot. Murder.

Demelza looks at Ross in bewilderment and panic.

DEMELZA 'Tis a mistake! – you cannot believe it – Ross, tell him!

ROSS Who accuses me?

Sergeant Tremayne declines to reply.

ROSS *(cont'd)* Who accuses me?

Still no reply. Demelza looks at Ross, baffled. But Ross already knows the answer. He smiles, resigned.

ROSS George.

The soldiers come forward to arrest him. He and Demelza are pulled apart. No screaming, no protests. Both know it would be futile at this point.

CUT TO:

85: EXT. CLIFF-TOPS – DAY 65

A tearful Demelza watches as Ross is led away.